TARGET LOCK!

"One kilometer, Comrade Captain." Overhead, the color monitors flickered to life. The XO thumbed the joystick, pointing the forward camera toward DeepCore. Bondarchuk whistled as the brightly lit underwater structure came into focus.

"Weapons," the captain called. "Arm torpedos!"

The operator pressed the red switch on his console. A shudder ran through the ship. "One away, homing." Bondarchuk turned to the weapons operator. "Forty-five seconds to impact," the operator told him. The battle was on . . .

DEEPCORE

DEEP CORE

JAMES B. ADAIR

BERKLEY BOOKS, NEW YORK

DEEPCORE

A Berkley Book / published by arrangement with
the author

PRINTING HISTORY
Berkley edition / November 1991

ISBN: 0-425-13029-0

A BERKLEY BOOK ® TM 757,375
Berkley Books are published by The Berkley Publishing Group,
200 Madison Avenue, New York, New York 10016.
The name "BERKLEY" and the "B" logo
are trademarks belonging to Berkley Publishing Corporation.

PRINTED IN THE UNITED STATES OF AMERICA

10 9 8 7 6 5 4 3 2 1

ACKNOWLEDGMENTS

I wish to thank Tom Colgan and John Talbot at The Berkley Publishing Group for their patience and inspiration.

PROLOGUE

God, he snores like a bear, Katya thought as she pulled the thin wisp of nylon panties up over her hips and slowly tiptoed across the hotel room to the brown leather briefcase that lay on the desk. She popped the latches, holding her hands over them to smother the noise.

In the top of the briefcase were the folders, each marked with a neat colored tab that told what part of the Positrack system was described inside. She pulled out the two folders that described the computer components and the specific electronic configurations of the trackers and held her breath as she switched on the fax/phone.

Katya opened the first folder and pulled the paper clip off the thin sheaf of schematics. She switched the fax to transmit and dialed a number in nearby Maryland. In seconds, the fax machine's ready light came on. One by one, she fed the papers through the machine, instantly transmitting them to her control officer.

The number was a blind, an empty office in a warehouse owned by a holding company that had no idea there was even a phone in it. Any trace of the number would be fruitless. In a few minutes, all the documents were sent, returned to their folders, and nestled again in the briefcase.

When Katya snapped the latches closed, the sleeping scientist stirred in his sleep, snorted, and rolled over. Katya held her breath, but the man did not move again.

God bless barbiturates, she thought as she slipped back into the black strapless dress that had first caught her hapless victim's attention. Reaching behind her to zip the dress, Katya stepped into the tiny bathroom to check her hair in the mirror. She quietly shut the door, turned on the light, and winced as she looked at the tangled mop that had been her hair. For such a nerdy little guy, Dr. Bobby Talent was an animal in bed. Not good, mind you, just an animal.

She whipped her brush through the tangles and knocked her hair into something presentable, then took red lipstick and coated her lips with a thin gloss. Much better. She put the lipstick away, then had an idea and took it out again.

Writing in six-inch letters with the lipstick, Katya left a message to her target lover, something to perk up his spirits and make him feel good about the entire business.

She smiled, leaned forward, and planted a big lipstick kiss on the mirror. She slipped the purse over her shoulder, turned off the light, and slipped quietly out of the hotel room.

Half an hour later, the phone rang so loudly that Bobby Talent jumped halfway out of bed. With his heart racing and his pulse pounding in his ears, he listened to the perky wake-up voice tell him it was 7:15 and the outside temperature was 70 degrees. Talent mumbled his thanks and flopped back on the bed. It was then that he remembered her. She was gone, her side of the bed cold.

"Oh, jeez," he muttered as he rolled off the bed and slumped toward the bathroom. He had to be ready for his presentation in an hour and a half, bright-eyed and bushy-tailed for those numbskulls at the Pentagon. The bathroom light was like an atomic glare. Talent held his hand over his face as he relieved himself, his eyes adjusting to the bright light as he drained his aching bladder. A flash of color caught his eye and turned to see the writing on the mirror.

"Thanks, it was great!" the message read. It was sealed with a big red kiss at the end. Talent smiled and ran his hands through his hair. The image reflected in the mirror was not great. Still, her note made him smile and did a lot to dispel the guilty feeling inside him. Talent went over to his bag and pulled out his little autofocus camera. He had brought the camera to take snapshots of the sights, and by God, that note on the mirror was a sight indeed. Talent snapped a couple of frames from different angles, hoping the mirror would not ruin the picture.

"Eat your hearts out, swine." Talent laughed as he thought

about the team back at the lab. What a night! He felt the first stirrings of an erection as he thought about Katy. Perched on the edge of a bar stool, the snug black skirt outlining her long thighs, the deep scoop making the wide expanse of flesh above it seem even whiter against the black fabric, she had stood out in the Hyatt's hotel bar like a beacon in a fog bank. The light made her mass of honey-colored hair glow like a halo over her perfect face.

He had hardly believed it when she spoke to him. The rest of the evening was a golden blur. He couldn't remember what they had talked about, but she had been a good listener. Most women were bored to death by computer talk.

He remembered the warmth of her pale skin against him. He could feel her bloodred nails skipping across his back. Talent forced himself to think about Project Positrack, his only reason for being in Washington.

"Good morning, gentlemen," he said to the running water in the hotel tub, "I'm Dr. Robert Talent from Warp Ten Laboratory." He had rehearsed the spiel a hundred times, but that was before last night. "I'm here to discuss our progress on the Positrack Marine Tracking Inventory system, a satellite imaging system that makes the current Keyhole and Big Bird systems look like a bunch of flying Stevie Wonders."

He went through the rest of his canned speech as he lathered up in the shower. He would think about Katy on the plane home this afternoon. Reliving their night together would make the trip back to California a lot less boring.

As Talent was taking his shower, Katya was unlocking the door of her apartment in Georgetown. Inside, Colonel Constantine Petrochenko, senior intelligence analyst, electronic warfare section of the Main Intelligence Directorate of the Army and Navy (GRU), was sitting at Katya's little dining table, examining the faxes.

"Are they what you wanted?" she asked as she walked across to her bedroom.

"They are precisely what we expected," Petrochenko answered curtly. He turned to look through the barely open door, watching Katya's reflection in the sliver of mirror visible from the table. She was slipping off the evening dress and stepping out of the tiny panties, pulling on a shapeless sweatsuit over her slim white body. Petrochenko looked back to the papers as she turned.

"What is the next step?" she asked as she returned from the bedroom.

"For you, home," he answered firmly. "You have given us just what we wanted. Was the American suspicious?"

"Hardly!" she snorted. "He was like a schoolboy. The drug put him right to sleep." Not *right* to sleep, she thought, remembering the hurried and frenzied bit of sexplay that preceded his deep slumber. That was none of the colonel's business.

"Good." Petrochenko rose and shook her hand stiffly. "Your ticket will be delivered this afternoon. Until then, relax and pack your things. You have done an excellent job. I will note it in my report."

"Thank you, Comrade Colonel," she answered demurely. "I serve the Soviet Union."

Petrochenko smiled and left the apartment without so much as a backward glance. Katya watched his blue Crown Victoria pull away from the curb, then walked back through the bedroom, stripping off the sweatsuit on her way to the shower. As she waited for the water to warm up, she looked at her nude body in the mirror.

"A long way from the Miss Soviet Union pageant, eh, Katya?" she asked her reflection, "Miss Ukraine, third runner-up for Miss U.S.S.R., three years at the Leningrad Computer Institute and now a spy for the GRU. Your father would spin in his grave if he could see you."

She stepped under the hot spray and washed off the pathetic little American's sweat from her pale breasts.

1

Dr. Ringness Alton hung motionless in the clear blue water fifteen feet above the wreck site. Below him, Alan Simons was punching the description of coral-encrusted amphorae into his locater keyboard. The locater, tied into three beacons surrounding the site, would pinpoint the location of the artifacts, creating a computer picture of the wreck. The system was much easier than the old grid method, and more accurate. At the end of each day, Alton fed the information to his uplink satellite dish, which relayed the data back to the university, where his support team would log the data and send back any pertinent data from the department's files. It was like having the whole university on-site. Quite a luxury compared to the first expeditions he had gone on as an undergrad.

Alton's musings were interrupted by a faint droning sound. He craned his head around, looking for the boat whose engine was the source of the sound.

Damn local jerks, Alton swore to himself, they know that they're not allowed to approach within half a mile of the site. The dive boat was tethered directly above them and the international "diver down" flags were flying both on the boat and on floats around the perimeter of the site. He'd have these bozos' butts for this. That fat, worthless cop Calvasos would have to do something about these trespassers.

As he watched from below the intruder closed on the dive boat. It passed within a meter of the tethered dive boat, nearly snagging the safety line that ran down from the boat to the wreck site. Alton was pivoting in the water, muttering dark imprecations at the intruder when the shock of the explosion

5

boomed through the water. Sixty-five feet above him, the dive boat was surrounded by foam. The water around the boat danced as shattered bits of the deck and the equipment rained down.

When the stern and engines of the eighteen-foot outboard appeared through the foam, Alton realized the boat was sinking. As the boat sank through the foam, Alton could see the huge hole amidships. The safety line held the stricken craft as the slight current carried it away from the site. It only took a few minutes to settle onto the bottom.

Alan Simons was beside him now, his eyes huge and scared behind the corrective lenses of his mask. He had the regulator out of his mouth and was mouthing words, but Alton could not make them out. Alton reached out and grabbed the frightened student's arm and motioned for him to follow. The two scientists swam over to their sunken dive boat.

The force of the blast had completely ripped off the tiny cutty cabin and blown out all the equipment stored there. The fuel tanks were gone, their torn fuel lines still leading to the outboard engine. Black patches of flash-burned paint indicated where the fuel had exploded. The bubbles from Simons's regulator were coming in rapid pulses.

He's starting to hyperventilate, Alton thought. He reached out and tapped Simons then pointed up, gesturing for him to follow Alton to the surface. Simons shook his head no, pointing at the sunken boat. Alton nodded his head yes, made an "okay" sign with his hand, and started slowly for the surface. Simons reluctantly followed.

Just below the surface, the two divers paused. Debris from the blasted boat littered the surface. Alton tried to listen for motor sounds, but Simons's loud exhalations were the only noise he could hear. Alton motioned for Simons to follow again and slowly kicked up to the surface and stuck just his head above the water where burning bits of deck and smoldering life jackets bobbed and smoke marked the site of the dive boat's destruction. Next to him, Simons popped to the surface and loudly spat out his regulator.

"What the fuck happened?" he shouted as he floundered on the surface trying to inflate his buoyancy compensator (BC). "How did the boat blow up?"

Alton pressed the red button on his BC, bleeding air into it from his scuba tank. The inflated BC squeezed him and held him up out of the water. "It was blown up! Didn't you hear that boat?"

"I didn't hear anything but the boom!" Simons gasped. "It scared the shit out of me. Who blew it up?"

"Don't know. Whoever it was just kept going."

Alton used his hands to turn himself toward the island half a mile away. He could see the other members of the expedition pushing the zodiac boat into the water. A minute later the high-pitched whine of the inflatable's tiny engine reached him.

"Looks like the others heard the explosion," Simons said, his voice a little calmer now that help was on the way.

"They could hardly miss it. I wonder if they saw the people who did it?"

As they waited for their colleagues to pick them up, Alton thought over his options. UnderSea Corp. had offered security personnel during the planning stages of this expedition. Alton had declined, contending that the expedition was purely scientific and secretly a bit offended by the idea that his people needed watching. Those objections seemed frivolous at the moment. Someone obviously meant them harm. He would ask for help from the company in his broadcast tonight. Tomorrow he would go to the mainland and make that lazy bastard Calvasos get of his duff and find out who did this.

The message was simple and short: Site attacked, boat sunk, no injuries. No local help available, need assistance.

It was addressed to the Security Department, but as usual, it had to go through the message center to get there. Anything that went through the message center addressed to Security went over Marc LeFlore's desk. The message center was not in his bailiwick, but LeFlore had a stooge in the center, Billy Swope. LeFlore had gotten Swope his job and covered up Swope's dishonorable discharge from the Navy on drug charges.

Swope copied everything that might be of interest to LeFlore, especially the messages for the Security Dept. Security only got involved when there was trouble on a project, and LeFlore wanted advance knowledge of any trouble so he could shift the blame elsewhere or cover up any snafus of his own. Swope was diligent and efficient in this task. Marc LeFlore got a copy of every message that went to Bob Moore, head of the Security Department.

"This is all we got?" Bob Moore asked.

"Uh-huh," Swope answered, his mouth full of tuna sandwich, "that's it. You want me to ask for more?"

"Definitely," Moore answered, "ask for details. Call me back when you make contact."

"Roger that," Swope drawled as the line went dead.

Moore dropped the phone back on the cradle and sat staring out the window, watching two teenagers on the boat ramp across the river trying to launch a daysailer off a trailer.

Site attacked, boat sunk, he mused, pretty serious stuff for such a short message. Still, Alton was an academic type and academics rarely dealt well with violence in the here and now.

Moore picked up the phone and pressed four digits. On the second ring, Carla Fuentes's husky voice answered.

"Guard Station, Fuentes speaking."

"Carla, I need you to come up right now if you can," Moore said casually, "I need you to go on a trip for me."

"On the way."

I want to get ahead of the power curve on this one, Moore decided. The worst that can happen is that Carla gets a free trip to Greece.

"You got a bag packed, babe?"

"Always," the tall redhead answered brightly. "Where to?"

"Balbos, Greece," Moore said, turning the map spread on his desk so she could see it. "That archaeology bunch is having some kind of trouble. I want you to go there as a tourist and see what you can find out in the town. See if you can get a line on who's messing with them. The project director, a guy named"—Moore picked up the message and scanned it— "Alton, says the local authorities are no help. You might find out why the cops aren't cooperating."

Carla smiled, looking up through her dark lashes. She had played this role before. It usually involved dressing up like a tart and prying the information she needed out of some horny drunk. It was a role she enjoyed much more than she would admit.

"Okay, when do I leave?" she asked.

"First flight out," Moore answered. "You'll hear from us when you get there." Moore reached into his top drawer and handed her an envelope. "Here's some spending money."

She took the envelope, slid it into her uniform shirt, and started for the door. At the door she turned and asked, "What if I don't hear from you?"

"Stay until the money is gone, then come home. Same as always."

She laughed and left, closing the door behind her.

Moore sat for a moment, his chin cupped in his hand, tapping his nose with his forefinger. He'd have to notify LeFlore, of course, but he would start the ball rolling first. It was always easier to get forgiveness than permission, especially from LeFlore.

Moore punched the intercom for his secretary.

"Alice, have King and Bickerstaff called in today?"

"Not yet, they're still out at the plant on that inspection."

"When you hear from them, call me. I need to talk to them quick."

"Will do."

Now for LeFlore, Moore thought. He pulled his computer terminal around, punched up the E-mail menu, and began typing.

> From: Security
> To: Marc LeFlore
> Subject: Hiratus project security situation.

In her apartment, Carla had two large bags packed, one red for hot weather, the other blue for cold. She opened the red bag and carefully put in her red satin dress along with two more conservative dresses. She opened the top drawer of her dresser and added two double handfuls of lacy nylon, her Walkman, and a couple of Spanish novellas.

She picked up the phone to make her reservations. As usual, there was enough money in the envelope to travel fast. She'd ridden the Concorde before. By midnight, she would be in Paris. By noon the next day, she would be in business in Balbos.

"Boss, that guy could be the donor in an asshole transplant!" Elgin Bickerstaff blurted.

"You got that right," Tyrone King chimed in.

The meeting with LeFlore had been typical. The man was a petty bureaucrat of the first sort. People's lives were merely payroll vouchers and the morality was his own position in the firm.

The main topic of their hour-long meeting had not been the safety of the researchers, or the immediacy of the danger, but the transfer of the security team's pay and expenses from DeepCore's budget to the archaeology project's budget. LeFlore seemed to care less whether the scientists or Moore's team lived or died, as long as the money was straight.

"The man is so white!" Tyrone King blurted. "I mean you guys are white, but he's the whitest white man I ever saw. He looks like two handfuls of bread dough in a three-piece suit." Too white was King's favorite put-down.

"Knock it off, guys," Moore interrupted. "I personally think the man is an abortion but we're stuck with him, and that's a fact of life. We have our job, let's just do it."

At least now they could get on with the job at hand. If they could load out on the company's Gulfstream and take off by 6:00 that evening, they would be in Crete by midmorning tomorrow and over to the little island by late afternoon.

Before they left, Moore had things to take care of.

"Ty, you make sure our staff gets on the Gulfstream this afternoon," Moore said as they approached the cluster of tiny rooms that housed the Security Department. "Elgin, you coordinate with the pilot and get the trip all set up. Both of you get back to me if you have any problems. Okay?"

The two men nodded and set off on their tasks. Back in his office, Alice greeted Moore with a handful of messages as he walked through her office to his. She followed him into his office and shut the door, leaning back on it, her hands behind her.

"How long are you going to be gone?"

"Don't know until we get there. Maybe a few days, maybe longer."

She looked past Moore out the tinted window. "If it takes a while, you could leave King and Bickerstaff. And Carla."

The change in tone at the mention of Carla's name caused Moore to look up at his secretary. She clearly disliked Carla Fuentes, although Moore could not understand why. Carla treated Alice with respect and even affection, but got little of either back. Moore suspected that it had to do with Carla's red hair, impressive figure, and irrepressible personality. Alice was a decade older, looked it, and regarded a day at the mall as an adventure.

Though he hated to admit it, he was looking forward to getting out of town for a while. Things with Alice were getting a bit too serious, and Moore was more than a little nervous about it. He had known better than to get involved romantically with his own secretary, but sometimes the little head wrestled control away from the big head.

"Do you have to go?" Alice asked, a tone in her voice that Moore clearly remembered from his marriage. A tone that said "please don't." He had hated that tone then and hated it now.

"Of course I do!" he barked much more forcefully than he meant to. He dropped his voice and added. "This seems to be serious. I can't just send the others off and wait here by the phone."

"You mean you won't," she shot back with more than a trace of anger in her voice.

Moore looked at her for a long moment and said quietly, "That's right, I won't."

She spun and left the office, slamming the door behind her. Moore took a deep breath, closed his eyes, and rubbed them with his fingers as he blew out the breath. This trip would be a welcome cooling-off period.

At four o'clock King called in to report that the gear was on the plane. He was going home to pack his stuff and would meet the others back at the plane. Half an hour later Bickerstaff walked in with his bag. Everything was set to go.

After the three men left his office, Marc LeFlore sat at his desk tapping his gold Cross pen on the yellow legal pad that was the only object, aside from the phone, on his desk. LeFlore was waiting for his pulse to slow down, the usual aftermath of a meeting with those Neanderthals from Security.

Surely, he ruminated, there has to be a way to get those animals out of my department. All they do is drain money like a sponge and swagger around like cowboys. Their department is never subject to long-range planning, budgeting, or any other business norm. Worse, the Old Man always backs them up in any showdown with another department.

At least they were going to be out of pocket for a while and on someone else's tab. LeFlore hoped they would stay on the remote Aegean island for a long while, long enough to get the Positrack project on DeepCore situated and working. LeFlore could hardly remember a planning session where Bob Moore had not harped on DeepCore's security. Nearly a thousand feet below the surface of the Pacific Ocean, the only security DeepCore really needed was financial security in the form of profits.

"He wants it to be an underwater bunker," LeFlore muttered.

It was stupid, he thought as his pulse slowed to normal, to spend a bundle of DeepCore's already strained budget to house, feed, and pay a bunch of goons who didn't produce anything but bullshit.

LeFlore was suddenly seized with an idea that made him laugh out loud. Maybe not so stupid, after all! He could transfer UnderSea's entire Security Department to DeepCore! Then they'd all be a thousand feet underwater and out of his hair for good. LeFlore laughed and bounced the pen off the legal pad. It would be expensive, but he could lay off their secretary and save her salary, not to mention picking up their office space in the building. Brilliant! While Moore and his wild bunch were mucking around in the Mediterranean, he would bounce the idea off the Old Man.

Sheila, LeFlore's secretary, tapped on the door and stepped in, carrying a thick computer printout.

"My, don't you look happy," she purred.

"Maybe"—LeFlore beamed—"just maybe."

"Here's the latest DeepCore printout." She laid the thick stack of computer paper on the polished desk and turned back toward the door. LeFlore watched her walk away, her silk sheath dress moving like a snakeskin over her lithe body.

Oh, please, God, someday, he begged silently as she smiled and shut the door.

Cheered by the prospect of literally deep-sixing Moore and his crew, LeFlore dove into the long printout, whistling a little tune.

The flight was smooth. The little business jet hummed along at twenty-eight thousand feet making about 650 miles an hour. The cabin was quiet and dark. Bickerstaff was snoring quietly in his seat. King had his Walkman on and seemed to be out cold, too. Moore unbuckled his belt and stepped into the tiny cockpit.

"How's it goin', guys?"

"Smooth as a baby's butt, Bob," Alex Throckmorton, the pilot, beamed. "How're your guys doing?"

"Out cold."

"Timmy, too." Throckmorton's copilot, Tim Hawkins, was dozing in the other seat, his head against the window.

"So, Bob, why are you goin' into Crete instead of Athens?" Throckmorton asked.

"I want our arrival to be a surprise to the locals."

"Don't you get into trouble that way?"

"Not if there's no trouble."

Throckmorton twisted his head around and looked at Moore with a wry smile, then shook his head.

Moore patted the pilot on the back and went back to catch a few hours sleep. There would be plenty to do when they hit Crete. He had already talked to Rick Stanns about the flight from Crete to the small island. He had met Stanns in Vietnam when the war there was ending. Stanns had been flying for Air America. He had flown Moore's SEAL team on one of those little projects that had never officially existed. Now Stanns operated a charter service out of Larnaca, Cyprus. Officially, he flew tourists and businessmen on little day trips and inter-island hops. Moore knew that Stanns flew other people, too, some who had no passport and some who had many different passports, but that was none of his business.

Stanns's last name was short for something Greek that was much longer. He spoke Greek like a native, could understand Hebrew and a little Arabic. His little turboprop seaplane would make the short flight to Balbos with no trouble and with no radar signature.

Cosmo's bar looked like something out of a bad Zorba movie. The glaring whitewashed exterior of the building made the dark interior seem even darker. Inside, there were half a dozen worn wooden tables with one or two blocky chairs at each one.

Carla stood in the door for a moment, letting her eyes get used to the dark and letting their eyes get used to her. She peered over the top of her RayBan shades and slowly surveyed the room. There were four men in the bar, including the bartender. All of them were staring at her, their eyes scanning her from head to foot and back again, taking special note of the tight white nylon short-shorts and the cleavage that threatened to burst from the top of her navy-blue halter.

Duck, suckers, she thought as she reached up and pulled the Tootsie Pop from between her bright red lips with a wet pop and tossed it over her shoulder into the street. There was an empty table at the back of the room and that was where Carla headed, the three-inch heels of her mules giving a motion to her hips that seemed to require ball bearings.

The bartender scuttled over, wiping the tabletop as he inquired in Greek what she would have. She answered in Italian, asking for a Campari and soda. As he went back to the bar, she took a compact out of her tiny clutch purse and opened it, glancing past the little mirror at the others in the bar. They were still looking, jabbing each other in the ribs and making what Carla assumed to be the usual lurid remarks.

In a moment the bartender was back and Carla paid him with a fistful of Greek money. She sipped the red liquid and sat staring dreamily out the windows at the dark blue-green water, her long, bare legs crossed, one mule dangling from her toes as she swung her foot back and forth.

Her drink was only half gone before a silhouette filled the bright door and Stanos Popathanos walked in.

He had on his police uniform, the insignia of a lieutenant on his broad shoulders. He walked to the bar and exchanged a few words with the bartender, then casually walked over to her table.

"You are a visitor, yes?" he asked in Italian.

"Yes, I am," she answered. "Am I in trouble?"

"Not at all," Popathanos replied as he pulled a chair over from another table and sat down. "I am Lieutenant Stanos Popathanos. May I?"

"Of course," she answered, sipping the red liquid up through the thin straw as she looked out through her false lashes. "Please."

As he draped himself over the chair, Carla pulled off her sunglasses and slowly slid one earpiece down into her cleavage, letting the shades dangle from her halter. Popathanos's eyes followed the shades as they nestled between her ample breasts, then snapped back up to Carla's face. "I am Carlotta Fendi."

"What brings you to Balbos, Carlotta?" he asked, studying her face.

"The ferry boat," she answered in her best cloying tone.

Popathanos smiled. "I meant, why are you here?"

"I am on holiday. The sun and the sea are always so— stimulating."

"You are staying in the hotel?"

Carla look another sip and shifted in her chair, recrossing her legs to show a long stretch of thigh. "Yes, room fourteen."

"You should let me show you the sights," he said. "There are many exciting things to see and do here."

She arched her eyebrows and sucked the last of the Campari up out of the glass, making a soft slurping sound, then slid the straw slowly out of her mouth. "Perhaps. Now, if you will excuse me, I want to enjoy the sun." She stood and reached for her shades, pulling them out of the overstuffed halter. She walked slowly to the door, then turned and smiled. "It was nice to meet you, Lieutenant, perhaps I will see you again."

"You may be sure of it," Popathanos answered.

As Carla walked out into the bright sunshine, an earnest-looking young police sergeant pushed past her into Cosmo's, obviously looking for his lieutenant. Carla crossed the street and walked down the steps that led to the beach. Over her shoulder, she saw the two policemen emerge from the bar and start off down the sidewalk. The lieutenant was looking at her. He would definitely be back. She walked on out to the beach, wondering what the Greek word for prickteaser was.

2

Alton watched the seaplane circle the little island. It gently
settled into the low swells, finally coming to a stop at the
floating pier where the expedition's remaining boats were tied
up. Three men climbed out of the small plane as Alton walked
down to the pier. By the time he reached the three, the plane
had already turned around and was skimming the waves as it
took off, heading south.

One of the men stepped forward, his hand out.

"Dr. Alton? I'm Bob Moore, UnderSea Security Department." He shook Alton's hand and tipped his head back to
the other two. "This is Elgin Bickerstaff and Tyrone King.
They are my associates."

Alton looked the three men over. All were large, as he had
expected, but Moore and Bickerstaff were much older than he
expected. The black man, King, was truly imposing.

"I'm happy you're here, Mr. Moore," Alton said. "We have
been having quite a time."

"That's what I understand," Moore replied as they walked
up the pier toward the cluster of prefab metal buildings that
made up the research camp. "Call me Bob."

"I am surprised that you didn't come from the island," Alton
said as they approached the largest of the buildings.

"We thought it would be better if we came to the site a bit
more clandestinely," Moore said as Alton opened the screen
door and the four men walked into the staff building. The room
was Spartan. Four tables with chairs and a kitchen setup along
one wall marked the room as the dining hall. Alton indicated
a table.

"Tell me about the problems you've been having," Moore said as they arranged themselves around the table.

The sun had just gone down in flames across the little bay when the knock came at her door. She was expecting it. Carla turned her back to the balcony rail and opened the long floral robe so her hot pink culotte teddy showed through.

She had watched him come up the street. Popathanos had a little bouquet of flowers and a bottle of cheap retsina wine with him. He was dressed in a sport coat and a shiny shirt open halfway down his chest and looked like an extra in *Miami Vice*. Carla twisted her laugh into a little smile.

"Come in, Stanos."

"What's the scoop, Carla?"

"Well, I think the reason the local cops haven't been too helpful is that they are involved themselves," Carla said quickly. "I told the young lieutenant that I didn't have any time for poor policemen. He assured me that he would not be poor much longer."

"Umm. Did he give you any idea how much longer?"

"Not really," she said, remembering the long session on the small couch in her room. "I asked him where he would get that money, and he said there was gold everywhere if you knew where to look. I asked him if the Americans were looking for gold and he just smiled and said that when you work in remote places, you had to be careful. Things could happen to you and no one would ever find out what happened."

"Did he give you any trouble?"

"Not really," she snorted. "It was kinda like wrestling with an octopus, but not too bad. I think he's expecting more the next time, though." She remembered her ruined teddy and added, "The company owes me for some shredded lingerie."

"Yeah?" Moore's tone was amused but concerned. "Hopefully, there won't be any next time. For now, I want you to stay where you are."

"Don't I get in on the fun?"

"I'd rather have you there if I need support," Moore lied.

"Okay, boss."

"Thanks, Carla, good work."

"Rats!" Carla muttered to herself. "I thought I was going to get a taste of sex *and* violence."

It was more than quiet. It was silent; the sort of thunderous silence that makes your ears ring. The water was like a sheet of glass. The zodiac boat anchored over the site looked like a centerpiece on a huge onyx table. The dummy slumped in the boat looked enough like a person from a distance. If you got very close, it looked like a sweatshirt and pants stuffed with rags and cardboard. By the time anyone got that close, they would have more pressing things to think about.

King and Bickerstaff were down on the dock, already in their gear. They were leaning back on their tanks, letting the straps hold them upright, an old habit born of heavy rucksacks and parachute packs. Moore's only concern was that they might doze off, but if they didn't hit the water at the first sound of an engine, he would buzz them on their headsets. He and Alton were next to the living quarters.

"Tell me something," Alton asked, "how did you get your weapons through customs on Crete?"

"The arrow guns?" Moore smiled. "When you take them apart, they look less like a gun than anything. The only part that looks like a gun at all is the trigger group and we just mate it up with a dive light so the whole thing looks like a light with a pistol grip. The arrow tubes screw into a tripod head and pass for a camera tripod. The broadheads for the arrows all fit into a little metal box that has electric shock warning labels on it, so folks don't usually mess with it. We put the razor blades that fit into the broadheads in our shaving kits. The rest of it looks like scuba gear. We've never had a problem with clearing them."

Lost in his little lecture, Moore was the one who missed the boat. Maybe the sound carried better over the water. The splash of King and Bickerstaff hitting the water off the end of the dock was Moore's first clue that someone was coming. The ripples from their entry were nearly gone before Moore heard the faint droning.

Moore swept his 10 X 50 Steiner marine binoculars back and forth across the dark horizon until he finally picked up the little boat. The police launch was a twenty-footer, an inboard with a single prop. The boat was dark, no running lights, no strobes, nothing to give even the illusion of a normal visit.

Moore keyed the mike that hung suspended just in front of his lips. "Number One, Number Two, report."

A second later the two divers checked in, their voices slightly distorted by the underwater communication system.

"One good!"

"Two good!"

"Stand by," Moore said softly. "Bogey at 330, two klicks."

"Roger."

"Well, Professor, it's showtime!" Moore said to the nervous archaeologist. "Here they come."

"Who is it?" Alton asked softly.

"Looks like the local gendarmes."

Alton just nodded. Even in the dark, Moore could see the tension in the man's face. Alton was no wuss. Underwater archaeology was no safe desk job, but Alton wasn't used to violent confrontation.

The boat was slowing now, the phosphorescent wake thinning to a faint glow. There was a man on the bow, two more in the cockpit. The man up front was holding a short weapon of some sort. As the boat neared the zodiac, a dozen splashes sent water into the air all around the inflatable. A second later Moore and Alton could hear the soft rippling sound of the silenced submachine gun. The zodiac was gone. Ripped by a dozen slugs, it sank in seconds, taking its riddled dummy with it.

On the police launch, the two figures in the cockpit were pulling on scuba gear while the gunman on the bow dropped a small anchor into the dark water.

"Number One, Number Two, company coming times two, repeat times two," Moore whispered into his mike.

"Roger, boss," King's distorted drawl came back over the headset. "We got a full house waiting for the pair."

The two divers rolled over the side and disappeared in a welter of bubbles. Bob Moore unslung the arrow gun from his shoulder and slipped the explosive-tipped arrow down over the thrust tube. Never taking his eyes from the boat, he pulled a slender pin from the base of the arrow's cylindrical warhead to arm the combination shaped-charge/fragmentation warhead.

"Stay here," Moore whispered over his shoulder to Alton. "I'm going to get a little closer." Using the shadow of the building for cover, Moore crept toward the floating pier. The figure on the launch was peering intently over the side, ignoring the island, which he assumed to be deserted.

King and Bickerstaff were at thirty feet, waiting for the intruders. The zodiac had settled to the bottom almost directly beneath the launch. In his left hand, King held the switch that would ignite the four magnesium lights that ringed the site. The lights would only burn for ten minutes, but that would be long enough to apprehend the two divers. Above them, two big splashes announced the arrival of their uninvited guests. Bickerstaff swam off twenty feet and turned over on his back. His arrow gun was out in front of him, tracking the pair as they slowly descended. The two men had flashlights pointing straight down to light the way to the bottom. King waited until the beam of one man's light finally lit the bottom. He pressed the switch in his left hand and dropped it, swinging his arrow gun around in front of him.

The sudden glare of the four magnesium lights caught the intruders by surprise; both men exhaled huge clouds of bubbles and fought to slow their descent. King and Bickerstaff were on them in seconds, the thin shafts of blue-green light from their laser sights flickering through the water onto the men's chests.

After their initial shock the intruders became more defensive. Their heads jerked back and forth between the two men who had the drop on them. Bickerstaff, holding his gun with one hand, mimed for the pair to put their hands on their heads. One man, the taller of the two, did so immediately. The other, a slender, shorter man, began to raise his hands, then suddenly reached down for his knife, kicking powerfully for King.

King, surprised by the man's attack, fired his arrow gun. The arrow missed the attacker by inches, glancing off his tank. King barely had time to get the gun up in front of him before the man slammed into him, the knife slashing upward.

Bickerstaff, fifteen feet away, swung his gun over and as the blue-green light reflected off the man's outstretched arms, he fired. The intruder was slashing up at King's belly when the arrow struck him under the ribs, its three-razor blade broadhead slicing through a kidney and lodging in the man's liver. The man began to twist and thrash, dropping his knife as he reached back in a futile attempt to dislodge the agonizing shaft.

King was backpedaling now, reaching down on his leg for another arrow. Bickerstaff could see the blood tinging the water around the big man's waist.

The other intruder had not been idle during the attack. He was now almost to the surface, kicking hard. Bickerstaff set off after him. The man was only a few feet from the boat ladder when he clutched at the buckles holding his tank and weight belt on. The equipment fell off him and landed on Bickerstaff's upturned face. The man gained the ladder and jerked himself up out of the water. Bickerstaff was nearly to the ladder when the engine roared to life and the propellor, only a few feet away, churned the water and the boat turned in his direction. Bickerstaff porpoised as the prop whirled by a foot overhead.

On shore, Moore saw the sudden brightness below the surface. The watcher on the boat was staring down into the water now, oblivious to any movement on shore. Moore dropped into a crouch and ran down the floating pier. He was halfway down the pier when one of the divers exploded from the water onto the boat, screaming orders. The watcher jumped to the boat's console and kicked the engines to life as the diver ran to the anchor line, chopping through it with his dive knife. Dropping into a kneeling position, his arrow-gun sight weaving across the launch, Moore shouted for the two to halt and heave to.

The two men ignored him and gunned the engine. As it picked up speed, the bow swung away from the floating pier. Moore waited a split second to see which way the craft was heading, then fired. Propelled by three thousand pounds of compressed air pressure, the explosive arrow arched out, striking the police launch's stern. The black puff of the shaped charge warhead was followed by a huge orange ball of black-tinged flame that engulfed the entire cockpit as the fuel tanks detonated. Moore stood, watching the burning boat drift slowly away.

"Number One, Number Two, report," Moore barked into the headset.

"Number Two okay, boss," Bickerstaff answered. "One bogey KIA. Number One is wounded."

"How bad, Number Two?" Moore asked anxiously.

"I'm all right, boss," King's strained voice came back, "just a flesh wound."

"Get your flesh back up here, both of you. Bring your bogey."

"Number Two; aye."

Moore walked back up to Alton, who had run down to the pier after the police launch had blown up.

"Oh, my God!" Alton blurted. "Oh, God."

"You okay?" Moore asked as the frightened researcher walked past him, staring at the launch that was now sinking several hundred yards from the site.

"What? Yes, yes, I'm fine," Alton stammered. "Those men! You killed them! The police! Oh, God."

"Calm down, Professor," Moore said, patting Alton on the back. "Everybody on our side is okay. Their side is gone." Moore watched as the police launch slipped beneath the surface, extinguishing the fire that still smoldered on its bow.

Moore turned to the professor and smiled. "Looks like a boating accident to me!" Halfway between the pier and the site, King and Bickerstaff broke the surface. Bickerstaff was towing King, who was towing a lifeless form that had to be their expired bogey.

"What are we going to do now?" Alton shouted. "Those were the police! We'll all go to jail now!"

"I don't think so, Professor," Moore answered. "I don't think this even happened. I think that tomorrow morning, we will put a couple of lift bags on that new wreck and use the other zodiac to tow it as far away from here as we can."

Bickerstaff was only a few feet from the pier now, and Moore went down to help King out of the water. Alton followed. They pulled King up onto the pier as Bickerstaff pushed their gear up. The dead man floated facedown, half the length of the arrow jutting out from his back. A short nylon line ran from the arrow shaft to King's buoyancy compensator.

"How bad you hurt, Ty?" Moore asked as he unzipped the shorty wetsuit while Alton held a flashlight on the wounded diver.

"Not bad, boss," King answered, craning his head to see the wound himself. "He just cut the skin a little. Elgin interrupted him before he could get a better scald on me." The cut was about three inches long, but not deep. It had almost stopped bleeding.

Alton suddenly stuffed the flashlight into Moore's hand and ran to the side of the pier. His loud retching echoed out over the still water.

By the time they had King's wound cleaned and bandaged, the sky was turning a soft gray-pink color. Leaving Dr. Alton to watch King, Moore and Bickerstaff inflated the remaining zodiac, loaded it with the expedition's largest lift bags and the body of King's attacker, and motored out to the spot where the police launch had gone down. Both men went into the water and found the burnt-out hulk of the launch resting on its side on the bottom. There was a huge hole in the hull where the gas tanks had exploded. There was no trace of the two dead policemen, a fact that bothered Moore. It would be difficult to maintain their cover story if one of the culprits turned up alive.

Since the wreck was up on its side, it was easy to run the thin cables under the hull fore and aft. When the cables were in place, they put two of the big lift bags on each end of the cables and working on either side to keep the wreck balanced, began to fill the bags with air from their scuba tanks. It took half an hour to get the wreck up off the bottom and balance it so that it would neither sink again nor rise to the surface. When Moore was satisfied, he and Bickerstaff returned to the surface with the nylon tow rope to begin the slow pull out to sea.

The zodiac took up the slack and slowly, very slowly, the two security men moved the wreck away from the site, over the horizon. The sun was well up when Bickerstaff cut the engine and dropped back over the side to recover the cables and lift bags and to stuff the body of the dead assailant under the wreck. It was nearly noon when they returned to the little island. Alton was waiting for them on the dock.

"Good timing, I just got a radio call from the police sergeant."

"And?"

"He wanted to know if I had seen the police captain and lieutenant. Seems they took off last night in the launch and never came back."

"What did you tell him?"

"That I had not seen them, but I would keep an eye out for them."

Moore smiled and helped Bickerstaff unload the gear from the zodiac.

"How's King?" Moore asked as he and Bickerstaff shouldered the gear and the three started up the pier.

"Fine. He's sleeping."

"Good," Moore answered. "By the way, you need to get that other zodiac up off the bottom and trash it."

Alton nodded.

"So are the police on the way?"

"I don't think so," Alton answered. "The sergeant is a good man, at least compared to his superiors."

"His late superiors," Bickerstaff added.

"Indeed."

"Looks like he's in for a serious promotion here soon." Moore yawned. "I think I'm ready for some Zs."

"Myself," Bickerstaff agreed, yawning himself in response, "it's been a busy night."

Moore turned to the professor. "We'll be leaving as soon as our plane can get here, Professor. Your story is that you never saw those guys, never saw their boat, nothing. Okay?"

Alton nodded. "This did not turn out the way I expected. I had hoped there would be no . . ."

"Violence?" Moore asked. "I don't think those fellows were too interested in rational solutions. They wanted what you had, and didn't mind killing for it."

Before he called Stanns for the seaplane, Moore radioed Carla on the scrambler and told her to take off for home. She sounded very disappointed.

3

Jack Travis was only half listening to the computer tech's report. He was still trying to get used to meeting strangers in the hallways. It seemed unnatural to meet someone he didn't know in a passageway nine hundred feet below the surface of the Pacific. Even watching the big Los Angeles-class submarine dock at the end of the industrial area had not prepared him for the sudden presence of 127 strangers who were like kids in a toy store after months submerged at sea.

For some reason, the Positrack team hadn't been so unsettling. Dr. Brittan, his secretary, and the handful of technicians fit right in. The sub crews were different. Maybe it was the just the military aspect of them. Travis had never been too comfortable around military types. Janice Wellford, Brittan's secretary, said she could smell testosterone in the air when the sub docked. That could well be the explanation. The women on DeepCore were the only females these guys had seen in weeks.

Travis forced himself to listen to Will Harper, the computer man. He was explaining the computer interlock system, a concept that Travis understood well, but cared little about.

"And now, with the interlock finally operational," Harper was saying, "we can electronically control access and environment in each module and passage, from dozens of access terminals."

Travis nodded and tried to look interested.

"What the hell is he up to?" Bradley whispered.

"I don't know for sure," Hansen hissed, "but he just took a couple of pictures of the component boards and now he's pulling one of the CPUs apart."

25

"Think he's just calibrating the components?" Bradley asked.

"I don't know any calibration you can do with a camera. Come on."

The two technicians slipped around the far side of the racks, keeping the equipment between them and Watanabe. When they were directly behind him, both men peered through the stacked boxes. They watched as Watanabe pulled one of the CPUs apart and turned it upside down to expose the circuit board. He put the unit on the table and took out his little camera again, shooting photos of the motherboard from three angles. This done, he slipped the CPU back together and took his power screwdriver to the logic center. When he had the unit disassembled, he pulled the logic board out and laid it on the bench, reaching again for his camera.

When Watanabe's back was turned, Hansen slipped quietly around the rack.

"Whatta ya up to, Kinji?" Hansen barked.

The little man jumped a foot and spun around.

"You scared me!" he shrieked.

"Yeah?" Hansen asked in mock sympathy. "Sorry about that. Whatta ya doing with the logic circuits? I thought they were supposed to stay sealed."

"Well, I, uh, I needed to check something on it," Watanabe stammered.

"Really? What?" Hansen began to hammer at the little man, pushing him to see where he would go.

"Well," Watanabe lied, "I was just looking at the differences in these circuits." He reached back on the bench and picked up the board, pointing to one of the tiny gold tracks on the printed circuit board.

"Is that right?" Hansen taunted. "I don't think so, Kinji. I think Dr. Brittan should talk to you about this."

At the mention of Brittan's name, Watanabe paled a bit. "No, I do not think that will be necessary," he said quickly, perspiration beading up on his lip. "We can just . . ." Watanabe suddenly bolted from the room, still holding the circuit board.

"Come on!" Hansen yelled over his shoulder at Bradley. The two men dashed out of the room after the fleeing man.

• • •

When he heard the voice behind him, he had almost crawled out of his skin. His skin had felt like it really was moving, a hot, prickly feeling that only lasted a second. Now, with the big American technician standing practically on top of him, Watanabe felt his heart pounding. The hot, prickly feeling gave way to a cold terror. The American's sarcastic tone was making the feeling worse. Dread was replacing simple fear. He could hear himself babbling out some simpleminded excuse, his mind racing to concoct some plausible story for dismantling one of the classified components.

The possibility of Brittan's involvement turned the dread into panic. Brittan was the boss. If he got involved, it was good-bye Watanabe. Without thinking, he picked up the logic board, mouthed something about circuits, and bolted for the door. As he cleared the lab storage area, he could hear Hansen and another man, probably Bradley, behind him.

Watanabe fished in his lab-coat pocket for his only weapon, the small hyper-velocity pistol. The gun looked less like a gun than anything he had ever seen. Although it was just a single shot, it was deadly at close range. It had been developed for the Japanese Secret Service a year or so before. The Japanese had never lost one and had never shared the secrets of its development with others.

Reaching the connecting corridor, Watanabe pulled the door shut and ran down to the porthole near the far end of the corridor. He pulled the tiny hyper-velocity pistol from his pocket and pointed it at the center of the porthole. Covering his face with his other hand, Watanabe pulled the trigger. The noise from the tiny pistol was more of a loud pop, but the sliver of depleted uranium left the muzzle at over three thousand feet per second. Watanabe did not even glance at the porthole. At the far end of the corridor, Hansen and Bradley burst through the pressure door. Watanabe slipped through the door at his end and slammed it shut, spinning the lock wheel. The two technicians hit the door handle just as the locking bolts went home. Watanabe could hear the men shouting at him, the words muffled, but the intention plain. Hansen hit the door with his fist as Bradley put all his weight on the locking wheel to unlock the door. On his side, Watanabe fought hard to keep the wheel from turning. Hansen's size and strength were beginning to overcome Watanabe's when the porthole blew in behind the two men. Under the crushing pressure, the broken porthole became a cylinder of water, a jet that blew the paint off the wall and scattered the flooring grids like confetti in a tornado.

The flood control system activated instantly, a compressed air piston slamming shut the open pressure door at the far end of the corridor. Hansen and Bradley were trapped by the eighteen-inch column of water that continued to blast in from the open porthole, glancing off the far wall of the corridor in a fan of high-pressure seawater that knocked both men off their feet. Bradley managed to get to the other side of the stream. He slogged through the rising water toward the far door, but the automatic system was too fast. The door slammed shut and automatically locked just as he reached it. Bradley hammered on the door control with his fist, but the system was designed to resist pressure of all sorts. In ten seconds the entire section was sealed off and flooded.

Through the tiny door porthole, Watanabe saw a brief flash of Hansen's terrified face, then it was gone and he could see no sign of either man. He knew they were dead. No one could survive the icy water.

Alarms were booming throughout the complex now. The terminal in each building would display the break. In a minute the place would be alive with rescuers and engineers. Watanabe ran around the corner, stepped up on a conduit, and slipped the circuit board up under a ceiling tile. It would be safe there until the panic subsided. He would retrieve it then.

4

By the time Jack Travis arrived, the rescue team was already at work. They were in no hurry, because there was obviously no one alive to rescue. The team was now just trying to get the water out of the flooded corridor so they could seal the hole outside. Nancy Collins, the senior engineer, was talking on the com-line to two divers in a submersible that was just launching from the sub pool.

"Okay, let us know when you find the break, over."

"Roger, out."

"What happened, Nancy?" Travis rasped as he tried to catch his breath after the panicky sprint from the command center.

"Some sort of break," Collins answered distractedly, standing back to let the two men pulling the emergency compressor pass. "Puncture, maybe."

"Anyone hurt?"

"Hansen, Bradley, and Watanabe were in the lab," Collins replied, ticking the names off her fingers, "we don't get any answer from the lab at all."

"Jesus."

The rescue squad had the compressor hooked up now, its woven steel hose clamped into a fitting on the pressure door. The compressor came on with a deafening clatter, pumping high-pressure air back into the flooded compartment. The small porthole in the door showed a cloud of bubbles rising from the air fitting.

"When we get the cap in place, we'll be able to pump out the water instead of just blowing in air. If the other door closed, we should see some daylight in there in about half an hour,"

Collins explained. "If it didn't, it'll take a while to pump out the whole lab."

The thought of the entire lab, including the Positrack project, filled with seawater made Travis sick to his stomach. Aside from the damage to the facility, the hassle they would have with the Navy over the destroyed Positrack gear would be memorable. A scene from an old slasher film flickered through his mind, a pale specter with pins sticking out of his face saying, "Your suffering will be legendary, even in hell."

I'll probably envy that guy, Travis thought gloomily.

"Got something!" one of the rescue crew called. He stepped back from the door's porthole as Collins stepped up.

"Aw, shit," Collins moaned. "Looks like a dead one."

"Who?" Travis snapped, crowding next to Collins. "Who is it?"

"Can't tell," Collins answered, her face still pressed to the glass, "can only see an arm. Wait. Shit!" Collins turned away from the glass, her face torqued with painful recognition.

"It's Hansen," she said, "I recognize his watch." Collins held up her big Rolex Submariner. "It's just like mine."

Travis looked through the glass and caught a glimpse of the bare arm. It looked inhuman in the greenish glow cast by the emergency lights in the flooded corridor. Travis could not see the watch and didn't care to. He stepped back from the glass as the taste of bile rose in his throat and a chill ran up his spine.

"Call me when you get in there," Travis said over his shoulder, walking quickly away down the corridor. "I'll be in the command center."

"Roger that," Collins said to her boss's retreating back.

Major Alexia Drachev stepped down from the side door of the BTR-80 personnel carrier and sank up to his ankles in the thick mud.

"It is like walking in shit," he muttered as he dragged a boot out of the clinging muck and slowly made his way across the slew that passed for a road in front of the battalion's head-quarters. The mud was a worse enemy than the fanatics he was here to subdue. It clung to the tires of the personnel carriers so badly that the drivers frequently had to stop and scrape it off the tires with axes. At least the wheeled vehicles could make some headway in the stuff. The BMP tracked personnel carriers bogged down so badly that they could simply not run at all sometimes. Even the tanks had trouble. The Moslem nationalists were merely an irritation compared to the mud. At least you could shoot the heathen bastards when they got out of line. The mud was impervious.

The senior private standing guard outside the headquarters' chain-link fence snapped to attention as Drachev passed. The guard's uniform was immaculate, save for the thick coat of mud that covered his boots. Drachev absently returned the salute as he stopped to scrape the biggest clumps off his boots before entering the compound. By the time he reached the headquarters' building, the gravel walkway had cleaned most of the mud off the soles of his boots. Inside the headquarters, a young lieutenant asked for his identification, then passed him into the building.

The general's office was on the second floor, down a central corridor away from outside windows that might invite rebel rockets.

From his office here in Baku, General Yuri Gregorivich Vorshov commanded all the Special Purpose troops in the Azerbaijan Soviet Socialist Republic. Ostensibly attached to the Ministry of Interior's Internal Troops, the Special Purpose troops did not participate in the normal duties of protecting public utilities and communications, as did the Internal Troops. Drachev's Naval Spetsnaz were tasked with suppressing specific Shiite Moslem groups who were trying to form an unholy alliance with similar Shiite groups in Iran. Drachev's men intercepted defectors and infiltrators who tried to move between Iran and Azerbaijan on the waters of the Caspian Sea.

The mission was easy, indeed, too easy to suit Drachev. The Moslems infiltrators were no match for his *ikhotniki*. The only enjoyable mission had been the assault on the Iranian naval base six months ago. Even on that raid, his troops had easily bested the pathetic Iranians.

The last real challenge had been Tbilisi a year ago. Those bastards had been good and fought as hard as any Russian. He had earned his Hero of the Soviet Union during the fighting there.

As he entered the general's outer office, Lt. Tutsl, the general's aide, glanced at his watch with a piqued expression on his pasty face. Once again, Drachev was struck by how much the effeminate little aide offended him. Drachev was sure that the only way a man got a look like that on his face was by having another man's fist up his rectum the night before.

"You are late, Comrade Major!" Tutsl lisped.

"The mud shit that covers this accursed Soviet Republic delayed me, Lieutenant," Drachev answered quietly. "I hope the general has not been inconvenienced."

"As it turns out, no," Tutsl snapped. "The general has not yet come in. Please be seated, I am sure he will be here at any moment." Tutsl's simpering smile told Drachev that he could be waiting here all day.

Drachev shook the water from his coat and draped it over the desk as he slowly removed his hat and shook it dry. Tutsl hastily snatched the papers from his desk as water dripped from the coat's collar, forming a small puddle on the desk.

Drachev picked up the coat and smiled at the increasingly agitated little man.

"Sorry." He smiled, then turned and sat down on the plain wood chair that was the only other furniture in the room. Tutsl dried the puddle with a tissue, then went back to fussing over his papers.

Might as well relax, Drachev thought. Stretching his legs out in front of him, Drachev's mind wandered back to Tbilisi. That had been a real fight, not just the simple mopping up they were doing here. He smiled as he remembered.

The Moslems, a splinter group that called themselves the Warriors of God, had ripped up a motorized rifle battalion some weeks before, then vanished from sight.

Agents of Department 2 of the GRU had finally located the rebels in a warehouse in Tbilisi. Drachev's company and another commanded by Captain Vorov had been assigned to destroy the group.

The attack had started badly. Two of the vehicles had broken down and had to be repaired. The attack, scheduled for 03.00, had been delayed until 07.00, just as the sun was coming up.

Drachev's company was to assault the front of the warehouse while Vorov's company secured the rear of the warehouse and acted as a blocking force.

His company had entered the warehouse easily, too easily. There were only a few men inside, not the large armed party they were expecting. The building was nearly secure when firing erupted from behind the building. Intelligence had been wrong. The rebels were in the warehouse behind this one. They had pounced on Vorov's company from behind.

By the time Drachev and his men found the rear door of the warehouse, the fight outside was nearly over. Captain Vorov's company was hit hard. Only one platoon was still fighting, the other dead or wounded. Vorov was one of the dead.

Gathering up the remaining platoon of Vorov's company, Drachev and his company pursued the Warriors of God. The fighting leapfrogged for three blocks to an apartment building squeezed between two factories. It was there the Warriors of God made their final stand.

The building was eight stories, made of the dun-colored, chalky brick produced in the region. Each small apartment had only one window, an advantage for Drachev's men since it limited the number of firing ports for the defenders. As they approached the building, a flurry of shots erupted from the second floor.

Drachev sent one of his platoons and the remaining platoon from Vorov's company to secure the approaches to the buildings. This done, he took the other three platoons up into the factory that overlooked the apartments as the perimeter force kept the enemy occupied in the apartments.

It had been his plan to attack the building from above, starting on the top floor and working his way down. The problem had been how to get over to the building. Senior Private Orgonev had found the solution. A series of scaffolds were stacked in the factory. By roping them together, they had formed a bridge long enough to reach the apartment roof. Orgonev had been the first to try the bridge. It held, and Orgonev guarded the door as the others scampered cautiously across the rickety bridge. The last *raydoviki* or raider to cross was killed by a Moslem gunman and hung grotesquely from the makeshift bridge.

With his entire force on the roof, Drachev attacked. His men cleared the top floor like it was just an exercise. One man would kick the door. The other would bolt inside and shoot anything that moved. The door kicker would follow. They worked their way down the hall, clearing one apartment after another. Most of the top-floor apartments were empty.

His men only killed twenty or so civilians in the apartments, mostly old men and women.

Resistance had begun in earnest on the seventh floor. The rebels had dragged furniture out into the halls and formed a barricade. The narrow halls were alive with bullets. The most effective technique was to use automatic fire in the hall long enough to get an RPG-22 into the hall and fire it at the barricade. The disposable rocket would destroy the furniture and stun the defenders long enough to get a second round of hand grenades on their way. It took a brave or very foolish soul to lean out into the hallway with the RPG. Of course, the backblast from the rocket was like a hammer to the attackers as well. Drachev had used explosives and rockets in buildings before, but the narrow hallways magnified the noise and blast. Each rocket took a toll on attackers and defenders alike. Drachev lost two good men clearing the seventh floor alone.

By the time they had cleared the floor, his men were low on grenades and ammunition. As they fought their way down to the sixth floor, Drachev decided to send for resupply. In the first vacant apartment, Drachev and the radioman moved near the window. Drachev called the platoon leaders on the ground and asked them to send up all their extra grenades and whatever ammunition they could spare. He had barely finished the order when the apartment's wall blew in and three rebels, a woman and two men, burst into the room, firing wildly. The radio operator was hit half a dozen times, his body and the radio absorbing the slugs that would have killed Drachev. A bullet pierced Drachev's left wrist, knocking the radio handset from it.

Senior Private Orgonev killed the woman and one of the men with a long burst from his AK-74, but the other man shot Orgonev with a shotgun. Drachev killed the gunman with four rounds from his Makarov pistol. Orgonev was wounded but survived. His bulletproof vest had slowed the shotgun pellets. The fighting was now room to room, point-blank range. By the time he had secured the sixth floor, Drachev had lost three more *raydoviki*.

Resupplied with grenades, his men stormed the fifth floor, using the big RGD-5 grenades to open the apartment doors. The explosions were deafening, drowning out the screams of defenders skewered by wood slivers from the shattered doors. The Musselmen were fighting like devils now, keeping the Spetsnaz at bay until finally sent to their martyr's reward by two or three 5.45mm slugs or a grenade.

As his men gained the fourth floor, the civilian inhabitants of the building began to panic, trying to flee from the invaders. Several of them rushed out of the lobby, only to be cut down by the machine guns that surrounded the building. Snipers used their telescoped SVD rifles to kill others who appeared at the windows.

One man jumped from a third-floor window, rolling as he landed. Back on his feet, he stretched his arms up to a woman who leaned out of the window with a baby in her hands. A sniper's bullet hit her in the forehead just as a burst from a PK machine gun slammed him against the wall. The baby fell three floors to the concrete walkway below. It bounced nearly a meter when it hit, then rested near its father's body. The mother's limp form hung out the window, her hands dangling and bright blood dripping from the scarf around her head.

Trapped by the gunners outside and pressed from above by Drachev's force, the Moslems went wild. On the third floor, entire families rushed Drachev's men, slashing with kitchen knives and scissors. One of Drachev's sergeants died, stabbed to death by a dozen brightly dressed women who suddenly swept out into the hall and surrounded him. The sergeant's section had riddled the women, but not before they had done their grisly work.

His own men were almost out of control now, wild from killing and fear. From a blasted third-floor window, Drachev called to his two platoons outside to attack. His wound was forgotten now. It didn't hurt, nothing hurt. Time seemed to move slowly. His vision was tightly focused, like binoculars, but sharper.

As the two outside platoons cleared the ground floor, the people trapped in those apartments ran upstairs and crowded into the halls, screaming and fighting for their lives. The press of bodies pushed Drachev's men back to the end of the hallway and threatened to overwhelm them when the two downstairs platoons came up the other stairwell behind the mob and opened fire.

In the confusion that followed, the air in the second floor became thick with the sweet, acrid smell of gunsmoke, fear, and blood. Everyone was screaming; from fear, from pain, from hate. All he remembered of that fight was the roar of gunfire, the crash of exploding grenades, and the incessant screaming. A sound so loud it thundered in his ears even now.

It had taken him a few seconds to realize that the fight was over. After the din of battle, the silence in that hallway had been even louder. He suddenly remembered that he was wounded when the pain flared in his wrist.

After the fight, Drachev had spent an hour going through the apartments, looking for any holdouts, any documents, any survivors who could be interrogated. There were few of any. Two Warriors of God who had hid in a service closet jumped out and fired at a group of Soviet wounded. Senior Private Orgonev killed one, the *feld' sher* killed the other.

In one apartment he found a woman and two small children hiding in the tiny kitchen. When she saw the soldiers, the woman screamed something in Turkic and stabbed both the children with a butcher knife. She then turned on Drachev and lunged at him, screeching like an animal. Drachev shot her with his pistol, but she took the round and kept coming. Two more shots to her chest stopped her, but she refused to fall. Drachev emptied the pistol into her, driving her back a step with each shot. She finally tripped over the bodies of her children and fell with them in a pile. The three of them bled to death in front of him. The children's blood mingled with the mother's, soaking her dark red skirt.

Outside, the Soviet wounded and dead were being brought out. Drachev had lost a platoon clearing the building. Ten more were wounded. The combat had been so close that there were few wounded on either side.

Deaths among the Warriors of God and the apartment residents had been higher. His soldiers counted 446 dead Moslems, men, women, and children. No combatants had survived. The Warriors had all gone to meet their God.

It was several days later before he heard the first criticism of his attack and then just by rumor. Too violent, some said. Not good for the image of the Soviet Navy, especially in the West. The complaints baffled Drachev. The bastards had killed Vorov. So what if there had been civilian casualties? The Army had done worse in Lithuania! His own men had jokingly called Drachev the Beast of Tbilisi.

His medal had stopped all the talk. The Fleet Chief of Staff had personally awarded him his Hero of the Soviet Union. Drachev had insisted that Senior Private Orgonev be decorated as well. He was now Sergeant Orgonev, in charge of Drachev's 1st Platoon.

The destruction of the Warriors of God had been the last battle in Tbilisi. Much to his displeasure, the name had stuck. The men still called him the Beast.

"Wake up, Major," Tutsl's voice whined, breaking Drachev's reverie. "The general has returned. He will see you now."

Drachev stood, put on his coat, blew Tutsl a kiss, then knocked on the general's door and stepped inside.

General Vorshov was sitting at his desk. He stared out the window at the dark gray clouds that were again rolling in over the Caspian Sea from the southwest.

"Good weather for evasion, eh, Drachev?" the general asked, his eyes still on the storm front.

"If they're good sailors, Comrade General," Drachev answered, saluting. Vorshov stood and returned the salute, then reached over and shook Drachev's hand.

"Sit down, Major," Vorshov said, gesturing at the single hard-back chair in front of the general's Spartan desk. "I have good news for you!"

A cold spot formed in Drachev's stomach. Generals rarely delivered good news personally. Vorshov sat back down and took a long cigar from the polished mahogany box on his desk. He struck a wooden match on the underside of the desk and slowly lit the tip of the cigar, letting the young major squirm, waiting for his doom or salvation.

"You have been called to Moscow," Vorshov said between puffs.

"In what have I failed, Comrade General?" Drachev asked, trying hard to keep the dread he was feeling out of his voice. Vorshov tried to laugh in midpuff and choked, coughing and laughing at Drachev's inadvertent joke.

"On the contrary, Major," the general reassured him. "Your lack of failure has prompted this reassignment."

"May I know the nature of the assignment, Comrade General?"

"In good time, Drachev," the general answered. "In truth, I do not know the specifics of it myself. I was asked to submit the name of my best officer, and you are he."

"I serve the Soviet Union!" Drachev snapped out the ritual response.

Vorshov stood and shook Drachev's hand again. "Your orders are waiting for you outside with Lt. Tutsl," Vorshov said warmly. "Perhaps when this mission is over, I will be lucky enough to get you back." As the general spoke, the sky outside flashed with lightning and rain pelted down against the window. Vorshov looked back at Drachev. "Then again," he added, "if *you* are lucky, I will not."

Back in his quarters, Drachev pulled the sheaf of orders from beneath his jacket and opened the sealed envelope. The papers were merely travel orders for a trip to Moscow. They gave no clue as to the assignment or even the unit to which he was being posted. Such orders frequently meant danger, ordeal, and even death. Drachev frowned briefly, then smiled. What were those terrors compared to that mud outside. Drachev pulled down his bag and began to pack.

"Through the wide-open fields ride the Red Army heroes," he sang to himself as he stuffed the bag with his uniforms, "ready for the enemy, our horses are fast, our tanks are swift and mighty!" The sounds of "Meadowlands," an old army song, carried out into the hall as he packed.

On the monitor, Collins could see the little sub maneuvering up to the outside corridor wall. The pressure cap for the porthole was held by its L-shaped handle in one of the sub's four manipulator claws. As the tiny sub neared the fractured porthole, it brought the cap up and held it out in front, using its powerful light to illuminate the area while it slipped the cap down over the porthole flange like a steel diaphragm. When the cap was in place, the tons of water pressure would hold it against the outside wall. They could pump the interior dry then.

"Cap in place," a voice drawled over the radio speaker. "Can you verify placement?"

"Roger, *Hope*," Collins responded. "Cap looks good from here."

The little sub shimmied backward, the turbulence from its side thrusters obscuring the operator in his green-lit Lexan bubble.

Collins turned to watch the other engineers, who were already pumping the seawater out of the flooded tube.

"The porthole blew in and the emergency doors trapped the two men in the corridor," Collins explained to her nervous boss. "They probably died quickly. The water is real cold and the pressure was, well, you know."

Travis nodded. He knew well the effect of that much water pressure. No World War II submarine could operate at DeepCore's depth. The water pressure would implode the hull like a redneck crushing a beer can. Even DeepCore's high-tech hull was vulnerable. The complex's computers constantly monitored the pressure and the strength of the hull, reporting any change in the tension on the outer wall. On his desk was a printout of the system monitoring the corridor wall.

"Nan, look at this," Travis said, turning the long paper strip around for Collins to see. "What does this look like to you?"

Travis stepped back and leaned against the wooden credenza, one of the few pieces of wooden furniture in the entire complex.

Collins ran the paper through her fingers like a cardiologist reading an EKG. She stopped at the point where the straight lines spiked up, then straightened for a bit and then went off the graph on both sides.

"It looks like something happened here," she said, pointing to the first spike, "then the whole thing blew."

Travis nodded. "That's what it looks like to me, too, but I wanted to hear your opinion first."

"I know every bolt in this big bastard," Collins mused, looking at the multicolored schematic of the complex that dominated one wall of Travis's office. "There is no reason for a porthole to fail like that. It's damn near impossible."

"So, what happened?"

"Something broke it," Collins said softly, "or someone." She looked at Travis, whose expression was a mixture of confusion and disbelief.

"That would be pretty damn risky, wouldn't it?" he asked. "I mean, whoever did it would be in the same boat as everyone ^lse."

"Maybe," she replied, "but I do *not* believe this was an accident."

"What do you want me to do?" Travis asked immediately.

"Find out who or what did it and keep it from happening again."

"Okay"—Travis nodded in agreement—"but if you're worried, why don't we ask for a security team to come help out?"

"I think that's a good idea," Collins answered. "I think we should do it right now."

"That's right, sir," LeFlore answered. "Two dead, no one injured. Seems a porthole in one of the corridor sections blew in."

LeFlore listened, nodding his head. "Yes, sir, I'll get right on it. Yes, sir, they'll be back here tonight and I'll turn them right around and get them on their way. Yes, sir."

LeFlore dropped the phone back into its cradle. A feeling of dread was starting to well up in him, the first prickly shiver building at the base of his spine. First the ominous news from the archaeology project, then this disaster in the Pacific. It was damage-control time, and LeFlore needed an idea quick. He picked up the message from Moore that had come in over the satellite downlink. All it said was that they had cleared up the security problem there and were returning on the first available flight. That was innocent enough. There was no mention of any trouble at all, let alone any violence. What was disturbing was the little story clipped from the *New York Times*. The clipping service looked for any story that involved UnderSea Corp. The little story was from yesterday's *Times*. It told about the disappearance of two local policemen from a tiny island off the coast of Greece. The story was only one paragraph, but the note from the clipping service said that the island was the location of an UnderSea Corp. project, an underwater archaeological dig. LeFlore didn't even want to make the connection. If Moore and his gorillas had killed those two policemen, well . . . LeFlore refused to even think about the PR nightmare that would follow if UnderSea Corp. was tied to those missing cops. The deaths on DeepCore would be bad enough, but industrial accidents were no big deal. A little spin control could make the company look like grieving and compassionate family members. This Greek business could only make them look like international terrorists. When Moore and his goons got back, he would find a way to move their asses out of UnderSea.

LeFlore was suddenly seized by a vision, a mental picture so pure and elegantly simple that he jumped straight up in the air. "Yaaooow!" he whooped. "Hot damn!"

Sheila stuck her head in the door. "You okay?" she asked.

"Uh-huh!" LeFlore answered. "Sheila, make out travel vouchers for Moore and the rest of the Security Department. They need to get off to DeepCore ASAP!"

"All of them?" Sheila asked quizzically. "Even Alice?"

"No, no, not Alice"—LeFlore beamed—"she's staying here."

"Okey-doke," Sheila said as she shut the door and disappeared back into her office. LeFlore sat down, clenching both fists in a silent victory cheer. Two birds with one stone! Travis wants additional security at DeepCore, LeFlore thought, and I want Moore and his storm troopers as far away as possible. This is the perfect chance to get Moore out of sight and mind and to show how dedicated to the preservation of DeepCore I am at the same time! Travis will get his security, okay, the entire Security Department! Who said prayers were not answered?

He picked up the phone, punched the private line button, and dialed an extension.

"Planning and Maintenance," a bored voice answered.

"Let me talk to Lew Cottrell," LeFlore said brightly, "LeFlore calling."

A moment later Cottrell's thick Jersey accent boomed through the receiver, "Yeah, Cottrell."

"Lew, this is LeFlore, how ya doin'?"

"Fine, whaddaya want?"

"I need the floor plans for this floor, including the Security Department offices."

"Okay. Youse in a hurry?"

"Naw, anytime this week will be fine."

"No problem, I'll get 'em up to ya."

"Thanks, Lew, I appreciate it."

LeFlore leaned back in his chair and stretched. An accident on DeepCore. What a dream come true. He would have to notify the families of those two dead men, what were their names? He picked up the message. Hansen and Bradley. The hard part would be keeping the joy out of his voice. He pushed the intercom button.

"Sheila, would you get personnel to send up the records on Hansen and Bradley? We need to notify their next of kin."

"Already on the way up," she answered. "I knew you would need them."

"Thanks," LeFlore said as he released the button. Sheila, baby, you are what I really need, he mused. The mental picture of his secretary, naked and tied to his bedposts, nearly blotted out the vision of his all-new expanded office suites in the recently vacated Security Department. "Ooh, yeah!" he squealed.

5

The room, one of the "old rooms" of the Kremlin, was not large. It had once been part of a huge gallery that had been divided into many smaller rooms in the years just after the Revolution. The tall ceiling and the equally tall windows gave it an odd, shaftlike quality. Being in it often felt like being at the bottom of a brightly lit well. The only piece of furniture in the room was a polished black table surrounded by a dozen plush chairs, reminders of the gallery's long-lost opulence.

He was the first one present, as he had planned. Colonel Petrochenko placed his folder in front of the chair nearest the tall windows. From this position, he would see the others plainly and be able to read any inflections of expression on their faces while they would be looking at him against the glare of the windows.

This advantage was Petrochenko's fetish, the need to spy, to watch and to analyze without being observed in return. It was the very core of his interest in the American spy project called Positrack. Petrochenko stood at the window, looking at the onion domes of St. Basil's across Red Square. The ancient church was a hive of activity these days. The resurgence of religion brought about by *perestroika* had breathed new life into St. Basil's and many other churches, most of which had been reclaimed from their mundane Communist uses and restored to houses of worship.

Let them flock to their churches, Petrochenko smiled to himself, I am already in mine. The sound of the heavy door behind him broke Petrochenko's reverie.

First through the door was Major General Sergei Pavlovskiy, the GRU officer in command of the mission, followed by Lt.

Colonel Lavrov, the Spetsnaz liaison officer. Behind them came their aides and a small group of technical people who were involved in the planning phase of the operation. Petrochenko stood behind his chair and saluted the general.

"Take your seats, comrades," Pavlovskiy said bruskly. "Let us begin."

As the others sat down, Pavlovskiy turned toward Petrochenko, squinting into the bright window light. "Colonel Petrochenko, give us the background on this development."

Petrochenko had remained standing, knowing he would lead off. "We have secured information concerning an American project known as Positrack MTI. This project involves the use of spy satellites, imaging systems, and computer data bases to track and identify vessels at sea. Its deployment presents a grave risk for Soviet Naval elements around the world. It is due to become operational within the next six months, after which no Soviet vessel will be safe from detection."

The general's aide, a smarmy little bootlicker named Petrov, raised a hand. "Surely the use of computers to track shipping is not new, Comrade Colonel?" he asked. "Why is this system such a threat?"

Petrochenko smiled at the man like a patient teacher instructing unusually slow pupils. "This system not only tracks surface ships, it tracks submarines as well." Eyebrows shot up around the table. "Additionally, this system correlates all tracking information with data from its files, enabling the system to identify the ship or sub by name. It works in all weather, day and night. From it, the Soviet Navy will have no secrets."

Petrochenko nodded to one of the technicians, who stood and unzipped a black plastic folio, removing a stack of mounted illustrations. Each illustration was nearly a meter long and covered by a red-bordered sheet stamped SECRET. As the technician uncovered the first illustration, Petrochenko continued his presentation.

"The American project is known as the Positrack Marine Tracking Inventory," Petrochenko explained as the technician pointed to the different sections of the illustration. "It links spy satellites in orbit over the oceans, sound detectors on the ocean floor, and various other detection devices with a bank of computers to plot and identify every vessel on the high seas.

This information can then be downlinked to surface vessels, submarines, and aircraft."

Petrochenko glanced at the general, who was staring out the window, ignoring the visual aides. Petrochenko might have been offended by this apparent lack of interest had he not known that the general was mentally recording every word Petrochenko spoke. Others had been fooled by this technique, but Petrochenko had researched his commander as well as his assignment.

The technician put away the first panel and uncovered a second as Petrochenko went on. The panel showed an artist's impression of a huge underwater habitat. Tiny submersibles darted around the fanciful installation as larger military submarines docked at the outer rim. "The first phase of the project, the testing, has been accomplished at the Krell Institute in California. The next phase will be the installation of the system on U.S. nuclear attack submarines. This will be done at the secret American underwater research installation known as DeepCore."

"The DeepCore installation is hardly a secret, Colonel," Pavlovskiy interrupted. "It is well known in naval circles."

"Just so, Comrade Major General," Petrochenko replied. "What is secret is the military aspect of the facility that masquerades as a civilian research site."

Pavlovskiy said nothing, so Petrochenko moved onto the next panel. The illustration showed a Soviet India-class rescue submarine approaching the underwater facility, its two deep-sea rescue submersibles drifting up out of their storage wells on the sub's deck. "It is imperative that the Positrack system not be deployed. To prevent this, we propose a surgical strike on the DeepCore facility to capture the Positrack technology and destroy the installation facility."

Eyebrows shot up again around the table. An attack on an American installation was war talk. The Spetsnaz officer, Lt. Col. Lavrov, was the first to object. "Surely, Comrade Colonel, you realize that such an attack would be a serious provocation. It would be tantamount to an act of war. It would . . ."

General Pavlovskiy cut him off. "War has become a state of mind, Lavrov," Pavlovskiy boomed, "not a declared act. Our Rodina has suffered some . . . setbacks in recent years. We have lost the members of the Warsaw Pact and our ground forces have been withdrawn from Europe. One treaty after another has stripped our Strategic Rocket Forces down to a shadow of its former might. Our primary strategic power for the foreseeable future will be the Navy."

Pavlovskiy's voice had risen in both volume and tone during his patriotic speech. His normally florid face was a dark red. The veins in his neck stood out like thick subcutaneous serpents.

"We must not let that power be compromised!" Pavlovskiy hissed. "We will be at war with America as long as there is an America. Leaders on both sides may come and go, but our struggle against the *Glavny Rag*, the main enemy, will never cease!"

Pavlovskiy's diatribe put an end to Lavrov's protest. The young officer sat back in his chair and studied the illustration. He knew now that he was here to learn the Spetsnaz's involvement in the operation, not to discuss its merit. Petrochenko continued with his briefing.

"A VSN (force of special designation) consisting of two teams of Naval Spetsnaz will attack the military compound and secure it. When it is secured, they will acquire the Positrack equipment and move it into one of the submersibles. When this has been accomplished, the VSN will destroy the facility and return to the submarine for extraction."

Easy to say, Lavrov mused as Petrochenko detailed the phases of the attack, too bad you won't be there to see that it all goes well. Petrochenko was detailing the sterile equipment that the raiders would carry so as not to identify them as Soviets. What a joke, Lavrov thought, as if anyone else would have the resources to pull off such an attack.

During Petrochenko's explanation of the mission, General Pavlovskiy's color had returned to normal. He had returned to staring out the window. As Petrochenko asked for questions, Pavlovskiy turned back to the group.

"Colonel Lavrov," Pavlovskiy said, staring at the young man, "how do you intend to prevent the sort of international incident of which you are so afraid?"

Lavrov knew he was on the spot. Despite the *perestroika* that had swept his country, the Soviet military was still as traditional as ever. An old saying went, "Initiative is punishable." Its corollary was, "Dissent is suicidal."

"Comrade Major General, I did not mean to imply that the mission was not in the best interests of the Rodina, nor that it cannot be accomplished," Lavrov began. "The remote location of the installation and its depth under the surface will help in our *maskarovka*." Lavrov looked quickly around the table. "Under three hundred meters of water, much can be concealed. The sea will provide much of the destructive force needed to destroy the facility. The possibility of survivors is practically zero in such an environment. My men will reduce that possibility to absolute zero."

General Pavlovskiy did not respond but nodded. Lavrov sat sweating as a thick pall of silence fell over the small room. Pavlovskiy finally broke the aching silence. "Comradés, Colonel Petrochenko will brief each of you individually about your part of the mission. Colonel Lavrov, you will be responsible for forming the special designation force to execute the mission." Lavrov did a fair job of concealing his relief at his apparent redemption. "In forty-eight hours," Pavlovskiy continued, "I want all of you back here to elaborate on your progress." Around the table, a chorus of "Just so!" and "Exactly so!" replied.

As Pavlovskiy stood, the others leaped to their feet. The general and his aide swept out of the room and the meeting broke up. As Lavrov gathered his few notes, Petrochenko spoke. "I want you to compile a roster of suitable *raydoviki*, Colonel. Please have it on my desk in an hour."

"Just so, Comrade Colonel," Lavrov snapped. "It will be done!"

As he left the room, the tall GRU colonel was still standing silhouetted against the tall windows. Lavrov did not allow himself to smile until he was far down the hall.

"You will have your list in an hour, Comrade Petrochenko," Lavrov chuckled, "I have had it for two days now, ever since I got wind of this little party."

Elena Terescova, Petrochenko's trusted secretary, was an excellent source of information. She was also an excellent source of something else. Her tip about the underwater mission had been timely indeed. Lavrov had already requested the reassignment of the entire raiding force. Major Drachev, the man who would lead the raiders, was already on his way to Moscow.

Back in his tiny office, Lavrov began to outline the equipment, training, and support his force would need. Unlike other underwater missions, this one would require no scuba gear or midget submarines. The pressure at three hundred meters was too great for prolonged direct exposure. His teams would rely on the deep rescue submersibles to get into and out of the target. The problem with the submersibles was that they could not carry many men. It was difficult to put more than ten armed men in even the larger of the two submersibles. The assault phase of this mission would have to be carried out by a maximum of eighteen men.

6

"Sharks and little fishes!" Dallas Knickerbocker exclaimed as he lowered his frame into the tiny bubbling tub. After six weeks inside the U.S.S. *Houston*, a whole tub of hot water was a real luxury. Even though DeepCore was really just a stationary submarine, it was well equipped and offered far more in the way of creature comforts than even the largest attack sub. The whirlpool attachment in the tub was a special treat.

Knickerbocker slid down until the frothing water was just beneath his chin. He was almost asleep when the Klaxon horn scared the living hell out of him. By the time he was out of the tub and into a set of coveralls, a recorded message was playing, telling the inhabitants of DeepCore to stay where they were and close all watertight doors as a precaution.

Fuck that, Knickerbocker thought as he bounded out into the hall and raced toward the underwater dock where the *Houston* was tied up. Their "shore" quarters were in the industrial module where the *Houston* was docked. There would be no sealed passages to keep them away from the boat.

Terry Hamilton, the executive officer, was at the sub dock when Knickerbocker arrived, checking in the crew as they quickly reboarded the sub.

"What's up, Terry?" Knickerbocker asked as he stopped and bent over to catch his breath.

"Not sure, sir," Hamilton replied, "a leak or a break somewhere, I think. They called for a damage repair team in one of the corridors."

"Are we ready to cast off if anything goes wrong here?"

"Affirmative, Skipper. We are at General Quarters. We can be away in less than a minute. So far, everything seems copacetic here."

"I hope so. I thought this layover would be a rest but now I'm . . ."

"*Houston*," the intercom speaker crackled, "come in, *Houston*."

The captain stepped over to the intercom and pressed the talk button. "Knickerbocker here, go ahead."

"Oh, Captain, I'm glad you're there," Travis answered. "I was afraid that you might have gotten caught out of the area."

"I'm right here, Dr. Travis, what's going on?"

"We had a break in one of the lab corridor portholes. It flooded the corridor, but I don't know if the lab is flooded, too. The rest of the facility is okay."

Knickerbocker cut his eyes over to his exec, who was whistling softly through his teeth. If the lab was flooded, *Houston* was stuck here half-finished for a while.

"Do you need any help, Doctor?" Knickerbocker asked.

"I think we have it under control, Captain," Travis answered.

"Okay, we'll be here if you need us. How long will this delay the installation of our equipment?"

"That'll depend on the lab," Travis answered. "If it's not flooded, we should be back on track tomorrow. I'm afraid that two of the technicians, Hansen and Bradley, are dead though. Until we get replacements for them, the installation will take more time."

Knickerbocker cut his eyes over to Hamilton. "Roger that. Thanks Dr. Travis. Sorry about your two men. Knickerbocker out."

Knickerbocker released the talk button and stood looking at his executive officer. "Looks like we're here for a longer stay anyway. Terry."

"Aa-firmative," Hamilton agreed, nodding his head. "Shall I stay at General Quarters?"

"No, stand down. Looks like we're just at business-slower-than-usual for a while."

"Relax, Herk," Janice Wellford pleaded as she stepped out of the bathroom and wrapped the terry-cloth robe around her small body. "The lab is okay! You heard Travis. He'll have it pumped out tomorrow and we can get back in. Everything is either in waterproof containers or up off the floor."

"I know, I know," Brittan sighed, "it just scared the hell out of me when they said it was flooded. Bad enough to lose Hansen and Bradley, but to lose the whole project!"

Janice stood and looked at Brittan. Slumped on the edge of her narrow bed in his boxer shorts and undershirt, Brittan looked older than his forty-eight years. She knew that the two men meant less to Brittan than the project. He had begun the project five years before and nursed it through the research and development, corporate infighting, marketing and sales, and now was finally bringing the project to completion. The two technicians were only acquaintances, Positrack was his baby. It meant more to him than anything or anyone else, herself included.

She sat next to him on the bunk and put her arm around his shoulders. "I know, honey," she reassured him, "but there's nothing we can do until they pump out the corridor, so you might as well relax."

Brittan looked up and grinned sheepishly. "Yeah, I know." He tried to stand up. "But I need to check—"

Janice pulled him back down onto the bunk, slipped her hands under his thin undershirt, and began to rub his shoulders. "You don't need to do anything right now."

He strained against her hands for a second, then gave in. She kneaded the soft skin on his back, working her way down his spine, massaging in long strokes until she reached the waistband of his shorts. Brittan made a sound deep in his throat and turned toward her.

"Umm, nice," he said, reaching up for the lapels of her robe. He pulled her close and buried his face in the hollow of her throat, nuzzling and kissing her soft damp skin. She raised her chin and ran her fingers through his thinning hair.

Brittan nuzzled down farther into her robe, using his chin to separate the terry cloth, his arms circling her. He slid his face between her small breasts and licked the skin over her breastbone.

"Herk—" she protested, trying to pull back. He held her close and slid his mouth over her breast, his mouth searching. "Herk, this isn't—"

His tongue found her nipple and encircled it, pulling it into his mouth. "Ohh!" she moaned, her head falling backward, the fingers of both her hands clutching his head.

They lay back on the narrow bed, their legs dangling off the edge. Brittan pulled the belt to her robe loose and ran his hand down her thigh, pulling her leg up and over him as he slid his face up to hers and kissed her.

"Heerrkk," she protested again. He covered her lips with his and used his tongue to stifle any further protests. Janice pushed at him for a second, then went limp, her hands slipping around him, her tongue parrying Brittan's. They pulled themselves up onto her bed, never breaking the kiss. Janice suddenly pulled her head aside, gasping softly for breath. Brittan took this opportunity to slide his face down, kissing his way toward her breasts. He teased them both, sucking greedily on each one while tugging and twisting the other. She began to breathe faster, her arms circling his neck.

She arched her back as Brittan continued his downward exploration, licking and nibbling his way to her navel. She squealed and writhed, the tickling in her belly a preview of coming attractions.

Brittan shifted his weight off the bed, easing down onto his knees beside the bed. His tongue slid down her belly to the damp tangle of dark curls below. She was still, her thin body almost rigid as she waited for his tongue find its mark. Brittan pushed her legs open. Janice began twisting her body, pushing it up at him.

"Oh, yeah," she moaned, "oh, Herk!"

Brittan laughed to himself that such a quiet woman could make so much noise when she came. He was certain that the woman who lived on the other side of the metal wall and shared the bathroom with Janice heard them.

So what, he thought as Janice began to wind down, let her eat her heart out!

Janice was limp now, shuddering and stretching as she tried to catch her breath.

"Oh, Herk," she whispered, "that was so good!" Brittan kissed her lightly and pushed her farther back on the narrow bed. He pulled off his shorts and slid up over her. She reached down and held him, guiding him into her. She was still very wet and he slid easily up inside her.

"Oh, Herk," she moaned. "Oh, yes."

She wrapped her legs around him and held him down on her as he began to pound on her in earnest.

"Oh, Herk," she gasped, "you're so big in me!" The tone of her voice changed. "You're also breaking my legs! Wait. Owww!" She dropped her legs down and stretched them out underneath him.

"Here," she whispered as she put her thighs together under him and ran her hands down his back.

Brittan held himself up on his elbows and began to thrust as fast as he could. His breath came in gasps, the sweat pouring out of him as he strained toward his own climax.

Finally his breath caught in his throat and he strained hard against her.

"Oh, God," he sighed, collapsing against her. "Yeah!"

"Oww! Honey," she whispered, "lean up a little. You're smushing me!"

"Sorry, sweetie." Brittan propped himself up on one elbow and slid off her. A minute later, he was asleep.

His breathing was slowing to something like normal now. Even in the dim light, she could see his florid face. Every time they made love, she was terrified that he would have a heart attack or a stroke. He got so excited so quickly and she knew that men usually had heart attacks with their mistresses, not their wives. That idea depressed her. She could just picture the phone call.

"Hello, Mrs. Brittan? Sorry to call you like this, but I just screwed your husband to death!" Charming.

She lay there next to him, her wet crotch beginning to itch a little, trying to remember how she got herself into this mess. When Brittan began to snore, she slid down to the end of the bunk and stepped into the tiny bathroom.

The reflection in the mirror was a sad little woman none too happy to have just made love.

Brittan woke later to find her turned away from him, facing the wall as she always did. He tried to slip his arm around her and underneath her breasts, but her crossed arms blocked him. Even in her sleep, she was almost rigid. He could not understand how someone could sleep wrapped up so tight.

I wonder if she ever really relaxes, Brittan thought as he tried to roll over on his back in the narrow bed. He put his hand behind his head and sighed. It wasn't that sex with Janice wasn't good. It was in a limited sort of way. She seemed to enjoy it, but only to a point. She could turn loose long enough to orgasm, but then she slammed the lid back on quick. She really enjoyed it when he went down on her, but he had known better than to suggest that she do it to him. They had already had that conversation.

It wasn't that she didn't seem willing, but he sometimes came away from their lovemaking feeling like Lester the Molester. It was really frustrating.

Still, he reminded himself, it's better than what you get at home, Ace. At least Jan is a little bit interested. He sighed again.

How the hell do I get myself into these things?

7

Moore stormed past Sheila into LeFlore's office, ignoring her protests.

"Are you just bull goose loony," Moore shouted, "or is this some kind of sick corporate joke?"

LeFlore waved Sheila away and motioned toward a chair. "Sit down, Bob," he crooned. Moore looked like a volcano about to erupt. LeFlore had been expecting this reaction. "What's on your mind?"

"What's on my mind?" Moore blurted. "Are you out of yours?" He waved the memo at LeFlore. "This says that the entire Security Department has been transferred to DeepCore!"

"That's right, Bob," LeFlore cooed, "it is."

"You want to maybe tell me what this is all about?" Moore demanded, pacing back and forth in front of LeFlore's desk.

"The Old Man is worried about DeepCore," LeFlore explained. "He wants to protect our investment there."

Moore stopped and leaned down over the back of one of the two chairs in front of LeFlore's desk. "I know that, what I don't understand is you. You've always fought tooth and nail against sending security to DeepCore."

"He's the boss," LeFlore answered, looking out the windows. "I do what he tells me." LeFlore looked back at Moore. "He was very insistent! I sent Jackson out there immediately while we were waiting for you to come home."

You mean you were very insistent, Moore thought. He forced himself back under control and fixed LeFlore with what he hoped was a withering stare.

"What the hell do you intend to do about the security of the rest of UnderSea Corp. while we're gone?" Moore asked.

LeFlore sat down behind his desk and tented his fingers in front of him. "We will still have the guard force, Bob."

"Right," Moore snorted, "and who is going to deal with little problems like the one in Greece?"

"I'd like to talk to you sometime about that business in Greece," LeFlore replied, flashing a Cheshire cat smile. "I received some disturbing rumors the other day."

This is pointless, Moore reminded himself.

"I want to talk to Mr. McLaughlin, Marc," Moore snapped, "as soon as possible."

"And so you shall, Bob," LeFlore promised. "As soon as he gets back from his vacation in Australia."

"When is he due back?" Moore asked, afraid of the answer.

"In a month," LeFlore lied, beaming.

We're fucked, Moore realized, the little bastard ambushed us.

The flight to Manila had, surprisingly, been less boring than usual. Boredom, even to the point of brain damage, would have been heaven by comparison. The cab ride to the Intercontinental Hotel was the finishing touch. The driver had cursed and shouted in Spanish the entire trip, barely missing every solid object, stationary or moving, between the airport and the hotel.

In the hotel, Jackson dumped his bags, slipped into his swimsuit, and headed for the hotel's elaborate hot tub to bubble the kinks out of his back. An hour later, his fingertips all pruned by the hot water, Jackson sat cross-legged on the king-size bed and spread out the DeepCore data package around him. He had planned to study the information on the long flight, but the younger members of the obnoxious American family had scotched those plans.

The two parents and five children were a veritable flying Joad family. It was bad enough to get your dinner knocked into your lap, much less on your work. It was also difficult to read with the back of your seat constantly being kicked. After an eternity, the flight attendant had taken pity on him and slipped him up to a vacant seat in first class. He had slept the rest of the trip.

Now he could review what he already knew. DeepCore

was an undersea habitat, the largest continuously manned underwater facility in the world. Located on an underwater mountaintop, nine hundred feet below the surface, it was home to dozens of scientists, engineers, biologists, and others from all over the world.

Although it belonged to UnderSea Corp., DeepCore was also subsidized by the U.S. government, which used it as a research facility and occasionally as an R and R site for visiting nuclear subs. The subs prowled the Pacific Ocean on two-month tours. DeepCore was the only American facility that they could visit without surfacing. That secrecy made it perfect for secret modifications and weapons tests.

Besides the main DeepCore complex, there were small satellite stations on other underwater atolls. The smaller stations were mostly research labs, hydroponic gardens, or desalination plants.

DeepCore was run by Dr. Travis, a maverick scientist who had sold UnderSea Corp. on the DeepCore project four years ago. All Jackson knew about the man was that Marc LeFlore despised him, and that was a good enough recommendation.

After half an hour, the pages began to blur. For a few moments, Jackson toyed with the idea of visiting the Ermita, the old red-light district next to the hotel. His last visit here with Bob Moore had included visits to both the Blue Hawaii and the Firehouse, two bars that offered a wide assortment of earthly entertainment. Moore had proposed that they quit their jobs and buy the Firehouse. Jackson had talked him out of that idea, although now, he couldn't remember why.

"That was then and this is now, Bucko," Jackson said to himself. "For less than twenty U.S. dollars, you can have the companion of your choice for the evening! What's it going to be?"

He was halfway into his clothes when he remembered the long flights tomorrow and the certain panic and confusion at DeepCore. He would be on the company jet headed for Guam tomorrow morning at 8:00 A.M. On Guam, he would board the company's V-22 Osprey and fly out to the floating dock above DeepCore. The tiltrotor Osprey was the only plane capable of landing on and taking off from the floating platform tethered above the underwater complex. Once down in DeepCore, he would undoubtedly go to work at once. The prospects for sleep in the next few days were slight.

With a heartfelt sigh, Jackson dropped his clothes into a pile at the foot of the bed and crawled under the crisp hotel sheets.

This burst of responsibility is a mistake, he thought as he switched off the lamp, and I will surely regret it.

"Don't yell at me!" Moore shouted, then fought to keep his voice quieter. "I didn't ask for this." Alice wailed and ran into the next room.

"Oh, God," Moore moaned, "I hate this." Domestic scenes like this one were the one thing he couldn't handle. They never went anywhere and both participants came away feeling like shit. His head felt like someone was driving a nail right between his eyes. Reluctantly, he followed Alice into his cramped living room. She was standing by the sliding glass door, staring out at his pitiful patio furniture, her shoulders shaking as she sobbed.

"Alice, honey," he pleaded, "cut me some slack here. My options, at least for now, are slim and none." She looked back over her shoulder, the tears on her face leaving twin tracks of mascara down her pale cheeks. He walked up and put his hands on her shoulders. "Maybe when the big boss gets back, I can change his mind. Until then I'm screwed."

"And I'm not screwed," Alice whined. "What am I supposed to do while you're a thousand feet underwater with that slut Carla!" She twisted away and turned her back on him again.

Moore rolled his eyes back into his head. Now it felt like a railroad spike was being driven into his forehead.

"Carla's not a slut and this isn't getting us anywhere. Sweetheart," he sighed, "I either have to go or quit. It's just that simple."

"Then why don't you quit?" she asked softly.

"Right. And join the army of unemployed security guards. No thanks, babe. I get a few bucks from Uncle Sam every month but not enough to keep me in this lavish style." He swept his arms out to show off his small apartment.

"Admit it," she keened, "you don't care about me at all!"

"That's not true," he answered, trying uselessly to placate

her. "I do care about you." He suddenly loathed himself for being such a wuss. Even though they worked on him like a charm, guilt trips pissed him off.

"If you cared about me, you'd. . . ."

"I'll tell you something," Moore barked at her, "the more you whine at me about this, the harder it is to care about you! Just back off, okay?"

A fresh flood of tears poured down her face and her expression screwed up into a tight, pitiful look, then flashed into anger. She stormed for the door, grabbing her purse as she went. His front door slammed hard.

Moore looked up at the ceiling, then closed his eyes and rubbed his temples. "What did I do in some previous life that I have to suffer like this in this one?" he asked himself. He walked over to the bar and poured himself a small snifter of B & B.

Fuck it, he thought, I'm not moving out of here. Won't be no rent on DeepCore and no place to spend much money. I'll just keep this place and have 'em take the rent out of my account every month. He tossed back the B & B in a gulp, savoring the bite of it in his mouth and the warmth that spread through him.

8

Senior Sergeant Oleg Kron eased his hands down his thighs, kneading the stiff muscles with his fingertips. The temperature was down to 48 degrees in the cramped minisub. As long as the patrol boat was overhead, he could not operate the heater or any other equipment. Silence was his only defense. When the Norwegians left him alone, he would turn on the heater and try again to gain the safety of the open sea.

At least the fjord was an excellent place to hide. The irregular rocky bottom and temperature boundary layers made it hard to pinpoint his small submarine with sonar. Not that the Norwegians weren't trying. Their sonars had boomed over him twice in the last two hours. They had not gotten a good fix on him though. If they had, the sonar boom would have been followed by depth charges or a torpedo. The Norwegians had little sense of humor these days.

His hydrophones still heard only the one vessel. That was a good sign, too. When a patrol boat got a good fix on an underwater intruder, a crowd always gathered on the surface. Poor old Gashkin had not come back from just such a gathering. His thoughts wandered to the nights he and Gashkin had spent drinking and chasing the girls in half a dozen countries. Their last trip to Vietnam had been the best. They spent the days surveying the bottom of Da Nang harbor and the nights sampling exotic pastimes. The women had been so lithe and inventive compared to Russian girls. Thinking about it now warmed him. After a boring winter in Estonia, Vietnam had been a warm, sensual vacation.

Another boom rattled the minisub, breaking into his thoughts. Two minutes later another swept over him. They were ranging on him!

He shot a tiny bit of air into the ballast tanks to pick him up off the bottom. As the tracks broke loose from the rocky bottom, a series of small splashes sounded in his earphones. Hedgehog!

The hedgehog was an antisubmarine weapon developed by the Americans. It was a cluster of rocket tubes that fired a group of small armor-piercing depth bombs at an area where an intruder was thought to be submerged. Each small charge could penetrate the pressure hull of a large submarine. It would demolish a small sub such as his. The cluster of rockets could cover an area many meters wide, depending on the range and the wind conditions.

The Norwegians used a weapon of their own design, but the name hedgehog had stuck to all weapons of the type.

When he heard the splashes, Kron threw the throttle forward. No need to worry about silence for a few seconds, the sonar operators on the boat would have their headsets off so the blasts from the small bombs did not ruin their hearing. For those few seconds, he could get up to speed and race away from the pattern. The first bomb went off on the rocky bottom twenty meters behind his sub. The blast sent spikes of noise through his ears. He had forgotten to turn off his own headphones. A pained cry ripped loose from his throat as he clawed the headphone off and rubbed his ears with his palms. The blast had been close. Now the other bombs in the cluster went off one by one behind him, each a bit farther off. They had missed him. If he could put enough distance between them, he might escape.

He was almost to the entrance to the fjord when another sonar boom swept over. Kron cut the engine and let the sub sink to the bottom again. He was in an underwater ravine, the walls of which swept up at a steep angle. In such terrain, it was hard to find anything, much less a small, silent sub. The Norwegian wasn't giving up, though. He swept back and forth overhead, guarding the entrance to the fjord like a hockey goalie defending the net.

Kron was straining for any sound in his headphones when he heard the loud splash. It was far away, but Kron could tell that it was a torpedo. The screws were turning, a high-pitched whine in the phones. Its search sonar was active, too, looking for a target. Convinced that there was a target below, the patrol boat skipper had fired a homing torpedo, hoping it could locate the sub underwater better than he could from above.

It was a good plan. The torpedo's sonar would search for any metal contact while the torpedo's on-board computer ran it in a spiral search pattern. If it found a target, it would switch to attack mode and bore straight in at top speed. Kron listened as the search sonar swept to and fro, looking for him. The torpedo had been running for several minutes when the sonar pitch changed from search to attack. It had locked onto him and was on the way.

Kron threw the throttle forward and sped toward the rock overhang at the end of the ravine. He had noted the overhang on a previous mission. If he could reach it, the torpedo might lose him. If he did not reach it, the torpedo would rip his sub apart like a ax hitting a tin of canned meat.

The visibility at that depth was gloomy, but Kron could see the overhang. He pointed the nose of the sub down and raced along the bottom. Once under the rocks, he shut down again.

The whine of the torpedo screw was louder now. It continued to increase in pitch as it came closer, finally growing so loud that Kron jerked off his headphones to protect his ears from the coming blast.

The explosion of the two-hundred kilo warhead shook the bottom of the fjord, slamming Kron against the side wall of the tiny control sphere, bruising his shoulder and the side of his head. The sub shook for a second, then jolted as rocks from the overhang fell on it.

Kron held on tight as the sub slid sideways a few meters, then stopped. He tried the propellor. Nothing. The falling rocks must have jammed it. That was no real problem, though, unless the marine avalanche had pinned his sub to the bottom.

He engaged the track drive and carefully moved the throttle forward. The sub moved a bit, jerked as a rock slid off its tail, then crept forward slowly. Kron shut off the drive and sat quietly. He could still make it out by using the caterpillar tracks on the minisub to crawl along the ocean floor to the mother sub. All he had to do was wait out this Norwegian rock-head.

Two hours later Kron's CO_2 was building up in his sub. The temperature had dropped to 45 degrees. The Norwegian's sonar was sweeping behind him now, getting farther and farther away. Finally, it stopped all together. A large, high-speed propellor noise followed. The patrol boat was giving up.

Kron looked at his watch. He had been in the sub for seventeen hours now. When he could barely hear the patrol boat's props, he engaged the caterpillar tracks and slowly crawled free of the overhang. Rocks clanged off the cruciform tail surfaces as the little craft pulled free of the avalanche debris.

Three hours later Kron's mother sub, the *Riga*, materialized out of the dark in front and off to the right. It was nestled in a shallow rock canyon, a larger version of his hiding place in the fjord. The *Riga* was a Kilo-class sub especially equipped with racks on the back to accommodate the little minisub. A diesel-powered sub, the *Riga* was very quiet, but could not run submerged indefinitely, like the nuclear boats. It could lie stationary on the bottom for quite a while, though.

Kron carefully blew air into his tanks to lift him off the bottom, letting his forward momentum carry him onto the flat rear deck of the submarine. Docking was easy with the propellor; it was a real feat with the tracks. Kron had done it once before to see if it could be done. It could, although he had been reprimanded for trying it. Now the same trick would save his life and the damaged minisub.

When he was in place over the access hatch, he shut down the motor and dropped the locking flange into place, locking the small sub to the larger one. He barely got his hatch open before the sub's hatch opened and fresh air whooshed up into the minisub. Compared to the stale smell of sweat and ozone in his vessel, the fresh-scrubbed air from the mother sub smelled like perfume to Kron.

"We thought you had been taken for a moment," Captain Bogat, the *Riga*'s captain, said casually. "Congratulations on your escape."

"I serve the Soviet Union," Kron answered automatically. "They were never sure where I was. They fished, but they caught nothing."

Bogat smiled thinly. His patronizing manner annoyed Kron, but submarine commanders cared little about the opinions of Naval Spetsnaz sergeants.

"Go below and warm up," the captain ordered, "you look a bit chilled."

"Just so, Comrade Captain," Kron answered, heading for the ladder, "just so."

The executive officer, Rost, gave him a small wink as he passed. Kron liked Rost. He was a real sailor, not an icy martinet like the captain. The rest of the bridge crew was silent. On Bogat's bridge, you didn't speak unless ordered to.

In the tiny galley on the deck below, the crew was waiting. They whispered a cheer for Kron and crowded around to pat his back and congratulate him. The cook had a glass of brandy warming over a candle. He offered it to Kron, who greedily tossed it back. The fiery liquor took his breath away, the warmth flowing down through his cold body like a liquid orgasm. He shook as the welcome fire consumed his insides.

A few minutes later, as Kron was changing out of his insulated suit into his uniform coveralls, Rost appeared and sat on the narrow bunk.

"And how did it go," he asked brightly, "did you get in?"

"Yes, Comrade Commander," Kron answered, smiling. "The entrance is easily navigated and the instruments are all in place. They should be transmitting in a few hours."

"You did well, Sergeant Kron," the exec said, rising from the bunk and starting out into the corridor. "The captain is pleased."

Kron only smiled in reply, and the exec disappeared.

How happy I am to hear that, Kron mused, I would hate to have displeased the captain by dying in some frozen Norwegian fjord!

The *Riga* lifted off the bottom and slipped away while Kron was sleeping. Nine hours later he was in the tiny galley having some strong tea and a big breakfast when Rost walked in.

"Sergeant Kron," the executive officer said, "when you finish your breakfast, report to the captain."

"I am finished now, comrade," Kron mumbled, his mouth full. "I will report at once!" He hastily washed down the food with a sip of tea and followed the executive officer, wiping his mouth on his hand.

The captain was waiting in the small communications room.

"Sgt. Kron," the captain said, "you must be a very important naval infantryman."

"In no way, Comrade Captain," Kron replied, wary of such praise.

"On the contrary," the captain corrected him. "These orders are for you." He handed Kron a printout from the communications printer. "This says that we are to rendezvous with a fleet helicopter that will carry you away from us."

Kron quickly scanned the sheet of paper. There was no indication of the reason for this extraordinary business.

"I serve the Soviet Union, Comrade Captain!" Kron snapped as he came to attention.

"So do we all, Sergeant," the captain replied as he left Kron and Rost in the tiny room. "So do we all."

9

"Okay, here's the key," Carla said, stripping the silver key off her ring and handing it to her sister. She fixed Marie with a hard stare. "Do not give a copy of it to Carl," she said, pointing a finger at her sister for emphasis, "under any circumstances."

Marie nodded, biting her lip. Although she was two years younger than Carla, Marie looked a decade older. Two kids and an alcoholic husband had taken a terrible toll on Marie's five-foot frame. Her skin was pale and anemic-looking. The only color came from the big bruises that ringed her left arm and peeked up out of the top of her T-shirt.

The two kids were in a foster home, pulled out by a worried social worker. Marie's husband Carl, a welder, had been served with a restraining order to keep him away from Marie, but he had been known to overlook legal orders before.

Marie had met Carl just out of high school. They met in a honky-tonk and Marie had fallen for him in a hurry. They were married while Marie was still in her teens. For the first few years of their marriage, Carl had been a good provider and husband. He was bright and fun to be around. They had their two boys right away.

During the oil boom of the early eighties, Carl had made good money welding oil-field pipe, but after the boom turned to bust, money had gotten tight. Locked into welding by a lack of education and stuck with a wife and two kids to support, Carl had become bitter.

Bitterness had turned to violence and Marie began to turn up with odd bruises that she blamed on accidents, but fooled no one. Now Marie was locked into a cycle of violence, apology, and despair.

When Carla had gotten her transfer order from UnderSea, she had offered her place to Marie. Now, on the verge of leaving, Carla was suddenly worried about her little sis.

"I don't want Carl in here at all," Carla reiterated. "Understand?"

Marie nodded meekly again.

"When is that social worker coming back?" Carla asked.

"A week from next Thursday," Marie whispered.

Carla stood looking at her sister. It was hard to believe that this frail, battered little waif was the same sister who had played softball and volleyball in school. She looked like something from the *Grapes of Wrath* now. "When are you going to get to see the boys?"

"Day after tomorrow," Marie answered, looking off to one side.

Carla glanced at her watch. It was twenty minutes after three. Carl got off his job at 3:00.

"I'll be right back, honey," Carla reassured Marie. "You just make yourself at home for a few minutes."

It took half an hour to drive to Marie's trailer house. Carl's pickup was not there.

Probably stopped off for a six-pack, Carla thought as she parked her Camaro in the visitor's slot and walked back to wait for Carl.

She didn't wait long before Carl's rusty old Chevy pickup rattled up to the trailer.

Carl got out, carrying the inevitable six-pack, and started for the door. He was nearly there before he noticed Carla on the tiny porch.

"Well, if it isn't my namesake," he crooned as he stepped up onto the porch, fishing his keys from his pocket. "What brings you here, hot stuff?" His eyes scanned Carla up and down as they always did. He had hit on her and she had turned him down so often that it was almost a ritual. "Come by for a shot of good lovin'?" he began as he turned the key in the lock.

"No, just a shot," Carla answered, slamming her fist into his kidney. He fell against the door, then whirled around, the beer falling from his arms.

"What the hell is . . ."

Carla kneed him in the groin with all her might, catching his head with both her hands as he doubled over in pain. She slammed his head against the trailer door. It held. She grabbed his long hair, pulled back into a greasy ponytail that stuck out under his gimme hat, and jerked up hard. As his face came up, Carla punched him with a hard right cross that would have spun him around if she hadn't held him by the hair. He swung a wild punch at her body but she jerked on his hair, pulling him off balance.

"You bitch," he hissed, reaching up for her hands, "I'm gonna . . ."

Carla twisted her body, stepping around Carl, still holding the ponytail. She bent forward quickly, twisting her shoulder, and threw Carl off her hip down the stairs. He hit hard on his back and she heard the air whoosh out of him.

"Now that I've got your attention, asshole," Carla barked, "I want you to stay away from Marie while I'm gone! You understand?"

Carl was struggling to his feet, gasping for breath. He tried to stand up straight, but the pain in his testicles prevented it.

"You goddamn meddling bitch," he gasped, jabbing at her with his finger, "I'll hurt you for this!"

Carla stepped forward and caught his finger. She snapped it back, dislocating it. Carl choked on the pain and grabbed the grotesquely bent finger with his left hand.

"You won't do shit to me or to my sister, either," Carla hissed. "If I hear that you even got in the same zip code with her, I'll come back here and do the same thing to every bone in your body."

She walked past Carl, who sat down on his porch, still clutching his broken finger. As she pulled out of the parking lot, she could see him in her rearview mirror, sitting on the porch, pouring the contents of a cold long neck over his twisted finger.

10

The woman across the aisle convulsed in a fit of dramatic coughing as the stream of smoke from his cigar drifted over her.

Drachev smiled and looked out the window of the Aeroflot Tu-122 airliner at the sea of clouds below them. The late-afternoon sun was glancing across the clouds, giving them a bright golden color. The sight never failed to move him. Beneath the golden fleece of clouds off to the right, the Ural Mountains stood guarding the entrance to Siberia.

The woman coughed again, trying to get Drachev's attention, but too timid or too smug to simply ask him to put out the cigar.

She can ask all she wants, he thought. In their infinite socialist wisdom, Aeroflot, the Soviet airline, had designated the left half of the plane nonsmoking, the right half smoking. Naturally, smoke drifted all over the cabin. Drachev shot a glance at the cougher. She was obviously the wife of one of the *nomenklatura*, the elite who ran the Soviet Union. Her sable hat, imported shoes, and white porcelain skin all said money.

Probably went home to lord it over her poor relations, Drachev presumed. Snooty bitch, let her cough. They would be in Leningrad in a few hours, she could stand it until then.

The orders were a stroke of luck. He did not have to report to Moscow for two days. The airline had been most accommodating. Commercial flights from Tbilisi were always full. Short notice tickets were impossible to find. Perhaps his reputation had preceded him. At any rate, he had a chance to go home for a day. It had been four years since he had seen

Novgorod and his family. His father had died while he was in the Far East. His mother wrote from time to time, but less frequently now. It would be good to see her and his brother Anatoly.

"Laaarrryyy," Rhonda whined again, "please!"

Ramos stopped scrubbing for a second and sat down on the floor next to the tub.

"Forget it, Rhonda," he barked, gesturing with the sponge at her, "I am not going to quit over this!"

She went back into her pout and began to suck on a knuckle. That particular trait, knuckle sucking, irritated him more than any of her other little-girl mannerisms. Those same mannerisms had once been erotic to him, now they were just boring.

"Can I live here while you're gone?" she asked softly.

A vision of his immaculate condo after a few months of her occupation flashed through his mind. Rhonda had no concept of clean. Her apartment had been a pit. The first time she took him there, Ramos wanted to put a bio-hazard sticker on the door. When she moved in with him, he managed to keep the condo as spotless as ever. The only times it had been otherwise had been his occasional overnight trips. Inevitably, she had trashed his place. She was great in bed but she didn't know a dustpan from a diaphragm.

Ramos rinsed the tub and pulled the toilet bowl brush out of its plastic holder. He poured some Ajax into the bowl and began to scrub.

"Let's eat out tonight," she suggested, "I'm tired of watching you clean."

"I'll compromise with you," he answered, his voice echoing in the porcelain bowl, "call for some Chinese takeout."

After they finished the Hunan beef and ate their fill of fried rice, Ramos rinsed the dishes and placed them in the dishwasher.

"Larry, what am I gonna do while you're gone?" she asked as he turned on the noisy machine.

"I don't know, Rhonda," he answered over the pulsating noise, "come on in here."

Back in the living room, she perched on the couch. Her eyes were glowing like a doe caught in headlights.

"Rhonda," Ramos went on, "you have a job. You can move in with Linda again. She wants you to move back." Linda was another hairdresser at the salon where Rhonda worked. Every time they saw her, she complained that she needed Rhonda back to help pay the rent.

"I don't want to move in with Linda," Rhonda pouted, "I want to live with you!"

"You can't go with me to the bottom of the ocean!" Ramos snapped. "And don't tell me again to find another job. I like the one I have."

"You just want to break up with me!" she wailed. Huge tears carried a river of mascara chinward.

This is not getting me anywhere, Ramos thought. It's time to get to the hard part.

"That's right," he said flatly. "I think that would be the best thing for both of us."

She screwed up her face into something truly pitiful and began to sob. Ramos went back into the kitchen and pulled a pair of Diet Cokes out of the fridge. He pulled the tab and handed her one. "Here."

She took the can and looked up at him with wet eyes that could melt the heart of a storm trooper. "Larry, please . . ."

"Rhonda, you only have your clothes here," he pointed out. "It's not like it'll be a big chore to move!" Another cascade of tears eyelined their way down her face. They repeated this sequence of talk/tears for another half an hour before she abruptly stood up, wiped her face with the back of her hand, and disappeared into the bathroom. Ten minutes later she appeared again, her face newly made up, her hair perfect.

"I'm going out. I may be back later." With that, she picked up her purse and flounced out the door into the humid night.

Ramos took a deep breath and blew it all out. He waited a minute to see if she would be back, then walked back into the kitchen and poured an inch of Crown Royal into his Coke can.

Not too bad, he thought as the bourbon burned its way down his throat, could have been a lot worse. He'd move her out tomorrow, then he could let the folks that were going to rent his place while he was gone move in over the weekend. That would work.

In the front seat of her Pinto, Rhonda checked her makeup in the rearview as the motor roughly warmed up.

What a bastard, she thought, I can't believe he's throwing me out so he can rent the place while he plays frogman. I really wanted to live there. She twisted the mirror back up and eased the old car into reverse.

Oh, well, she mused, easy come, easy go. It was still early, she could still get over to the Avalon and see what was going on there. What the hell, he wasn't the only fish in the sea, even if he was the cleanest.

Their complex near the Industrial Amalgamation factory in Novgorod looked like four huge dominoes set on their long sides. Two apartment buildings faced each other across a narrow park. The other two were set at 45-degree angles to the parallel buildings, giving the complex the look of a giant Y. The buildings were all the same, built from some state architect's standardized apartment plan. Although the buildings were only a few years old, the concrete had already started to deteriorate. His brother's apartment was in the right-hand branch of the Y.

When she opened the door, his mother looked at him for several seconds before she recognized him. Then her eyes flew open and she reached out, pulling him into the room and hugging him to her. She felt thin and bony as he hugged her, much thinner than the last time he had seen her. Her face was pale and pinched, anemic-looking.

"Look, it is Misha!" she called into the tiny kitchen. "Anatoly, come see your brother!"

Anatoly slowly walked in from the kitchen, wiping his hands on a small cloth. His expression was not one of welcome, more of curiosity. He nodded at Drachev.

"Come sit!" his mother insisted, pulling him to the threadbare couch. "Dinner is almost ready!"

Drachev sat on the couch, sinking deep into its tired springs. His brother perched on the arm of the upholstered chair.

"What brings you home?" his brother asked flatly.

"Orders to Moscow," Drachev answered, wondering at the faintly hostile tone of his brother's voice.

"A bit out of your way, isn't it? Weren't you down in the south somewhere?"

"Yes," Drachev answered warily, "I have an extra day. I wanted to come home—to see Mother."

"How convenient."

The tense conversation was broken up by the arrival of dinner. The fare was simple, cabbage soup and hard black bread. The portions were small. When he complimented her on the soup, his mother stared down at her bowl. "I'm sorry there is not more."

After the meal, Drachev offered his brother a cigar. Anatoly ran the long smoke beneath his nose.

"Cuban?" he asked. Drachev nodded. "Naturally," his brother observed as he leaned forward and lit the tip of the cigar from the match Drachev offered.

"So, Anatoly," Drachev began, hoping to change the mood of the conversation, "how goes it with you?"

His brother blew a cloud of tobacco smoke above his head and stared up at the ceiling through it, dropping his eyes down to Drachev after a long moment.

"Not good, Misha. *Perestroika* is killing us." At Drachev's quizzical look, Anatoly laughed. "You in the military don't know how it is. Everything is still provided for you. For us, *perestroika* is a nightmare."

"In what way?" Drachev asked.

"We are promised everything, but get nothing," his brother began. "To compete with the West, the factories are letting people go. Without a job, they are lost. There is nothing in the store to buy, not even food. When there is something, it is gone in a minute."

"I thought your plant was doing a lot for its employees," Drachev said. "You told me last time that the factory was providing medical care and housing."

"Yes," Anatoly answered, looking out the window at the gathering gloom. "The factory does take care of its own. Groceries and a sports club, too." His brother snapped his eyes back to Drachev. "But what does that matter when there is nothing to buy and the fear of unemployment hangs over you?"

Drachev was silent. His brother clearly had something to say. He would let him.

"It is the bureaucrats!" Anatoly exploded. "We are smothered in bureaucrats!" His brother stood and paced behind the chair. "Do you know, Misha, that there are four million bureaucrats whose only job is to tell the farmers what to do and how to do it?" Drachev shook his head. "The Americans feed all their own people and sell us wheat besides with only two million farmers," Anatoly continued. "We have over twenty million farmers in the Soviet Union and still we do not have enough food to eat!" His brother's shoulders suddenly slumped.

"What is there to do?" Drachev asked, uncomfortable with this conversation.

"Revolution!" his brother snarled. "The privileged class and the bureaucrats must be eliminated!"

"How?"

"Killed!" Anatoly snapped, his eyes glowing. "Killed in another revolution! Only then can the workers of this country prosper. That is what communism is all about!"

"Anatoly," Drachev said quietly, "this talk is reactionary. Perhaps even traitorous. Please do not continue it." Drachev sensed a trap here. His brother could just be one of the new breed of Russian nationalists or he could be one of the old breed of KGB informers. Either way, this conversation could be dangerous.

His brother was just staring at him. Finally, Anatoly shrugged and sat down. "I should have known that you would not understand," he said wearily. "You are part of the system. Why would you want to change it?"

The rest of the evening was spent in family chatter with his mother. She made no reference to Anatoly's speech and Drachev did not mention it, either.

Later, as he lay on the couch waiting for sleep, Drachev was almost sorry he had come.

In the morning his brother was up and out of the apartment early, muttering only the quickest of good-byes to Drachev. His mother had fixed him a small breakfast of tea and black bread with a tiny dollop of strawberry jam. Drachev realized that the jam was a special treat for her returning son.

As he hugged her before he left for the station to catch the bus to the airport, Drachev slipped all but a few rubles of his travel money into her apron pocket. By the time she discovered it that afternoon, he was already on the plane for Moscow.

"Come on, Bick!" King said. "We're movin'. We gotta clean all this crap outta here!"

"Fuck 'em," Bickerstaff answered, carting his last load of boxes toward the door. "The place was a rathole when we moved in."

"True, but I want that deposit back," King answered, "I don't plan to repaint, but there is dust here from when we moved in."

Bickerstaff stopped in the door. "I got an idea," he answered, "I'll be right back."

King was filling a plastic trash bag with old newspapers when Bickerstaff returned, lugging a large machine over his shoulder. The roar of the gasoline engine startled King.

"What the hell, Bick!" King shouted over the roar. Bickerstaff turned around, hefting the power blower up on his shoulder. "I borrowed it from a Mexican guy in the parking lot!" he yelled over the noise. "It'll have this place cleaned out in a minute!"

With that, Bickerstaff walked into his bedroom and turned on the air blast. Dust, bits of paper, paint flecks, beer cans, a pizza box, and other flotsam flew from the room, filling the living room with a thick cloud of swirling debris.

"Jesus!" King shouted, covering his nose with his T-shirt. He headed for the front door. Outside, he hung over the rail and took a deep breath. Below in the courtyard, the manager stepped out of his office and looked up at the cloud of dust that poured from the apartment door. King flashed the man his best "No problem, we know what we're doing" smile. The manager scowled and turned on his heel back into the office.

They'll be ice skating in hell before we see that deposit, King thought as a cloud of dust devils broke from their lair under the couch and whipped out the front door.

Behind them came Bickerstaff, wearing his scuba mask to keep the dust out of his eyes. Bits of paper and dust balls clung to his hair and covered his body. The thick lenses of his mask magnified his bloodshot eyes. He looked like the monster in some cheap sci-fi movie—*The Beast from the Planet No-Bucks*. King dissolved in laughter, holding the rail as he howled at his deranged roomie.

11

Drachev stepped into the small office, came to attention, and saluted.

"Major Drachev reporting as ordered, Comrade Colonel," he said, snapping the words out. Across the desk, Lt. Col. Arel Lavrov returned the salute and gestured toward the single hard-back chair.

"Sit down, Major."

Drachev placed his orders on the edge of Lavrov's desk and perched on the edge of the chair. Lavrov took a pair of reading glasses from his desk, put them on, then opened the orders packet and idly scanned the contents.

"Do you know why you are here, Comrade Major?" Lavrov asked, never looking up from the orders.

"In no way, Comrade Colonel," Drachev snapped. When you were unsure of the purpose of such a meeting, it was better to play the role of a perfect Soviet soldier.

Lavrov looked up. "You know nothing of the reason for these orders?"

"Nothing, Comrade Colonel!" Drachev insisted. "I—I hope it is not in relation to the action in Tbilisi."

Lavrov looked up over the rims of his reading glasses, a thin smile playing at the corners of his mouth for a second. He dropped Drachev's orders on the desk. "Excellent"—he smiled—"this mission is of the most delicate nature, and I assure you it has nothing to do with Tbilisi."

Seeing Drachev's flicker of relief, Lavrov added, "Although your actions at Tbilisi had a part in your selection. We need an officer who can adapt to a changing situation and take whatever steps are necessary to complete the mission."

Lavrov unlocked his desk drawer and took out a thick folder. He pulled off the rubber band that held the folder shut and turned it so Drachev could see the contents. "How much do you know about the American underwater complex known as DeepCore?"

Drachev looked at the artist's rendering of DeepCore. "I know only that it is located three hundred meters underwater in international waters on the edge of the Challenger Deep, Comrade Colonel," Drachev answered. "I have heard that the American CIA operates the facility."

Lavrov chuckled. "It is too bad that they do not, Major. If they did, we would know everything that went on there from the meetings of their congressional intelligence over-watch committee. The committee is very helpful in telling us what the CIA is up to. Unfortunately, DeepCore is operated by a private American corporation." Lavrov picked up DeepCore's specification sheet. "It is probably a front company for the CIA or the National Security Council, but it enables the Americans to hide the true nature of the place from their congressional watchdogs."

When Drachev did not answer, Lavrov went on. "We have learned that the American Navy is set to deploy a new marine tracking system, and that they will be installing it at the DeepCore facility."

When a grin flickered across Drachev's face, Lavrov stopped. "There is something amusing?"

"No, Comrade Colonel," Drachev snapped, wiping all emotion from his face. "I was only reminded of a barracks joke about the American Marine Corps."

"Really?" Lavrov said. "Tell me."

Drachev looked pained to have been thought frivolous. "They say the easiest Marine tracking system is the trail of empty beer cans leading to Camp Lejuene," he blurted.

Lavrov laughed and looked out the dingy window at the Kremlin wall. "That is the old Marine tracking system, this is something a bit more sophisticated."

Drachev relaxed a bit, but kept his face blank.

"This system will continuously track everything in the Soviet Navy and identify it by name," Lavrov explained. "It will be installed on every American submarine and surface ship."

Drachev was not able to conceal a look of surprise and concern. "If they are able to do that, they would be able to neutralize the entire Soviet Navy!"

"Just so, Major," Lavrov agreed. "Your mission will be twofold in nature. You are ordered to enter the DeepCore facility, obtain the necessary components of the tracking system, remove them from the facility, and destroy the facility itself."

Drachev fought hard to keep the shock from showing. "Comrade Colonel, such an operation would seem to be an act of war."

"Correctly done," Lavrov answered, "it will seem to be a catastrophic accident. See that it is correctly done."

"Exactly so, Comrade Colonel!" Drachev snapped back.

"You will be briefed further this afternoon by technical experts about the electronic components we wish to obtain," Lavrov continued. "Afterward, you will travel to one of our bases, where you and your men will rehearse your operation. Do you have any questions?"

Drachev blinked, reluctant to ask what might seem like an obvious question. "Comrade Colonel, would it not be easier to obtain this device in the usual way?"

"You mean by buying it from some greedy American traitor?"

Drachev nodded.

"Yes, it would be easier, but in this case we want more than to simply obtain the technology. We want to stop the American program to give us time to defeat or at least to duplicate the device. The destruction of the installation facility will give us that time."

"The components are made there?" Drachev asked.

"Not made there, but assembled there," Lavrov explained. "The entire project team is there for the initial submarine fitting and testing. If they can be eliminated, it will take months or even years to replace them."

Drachev nodded. The weight of responsibility began to settle on him like a yoke. Failure on such a mission would mean death, or worse. Declining to accept the mission would have the same effect.

Lavrov looked at his watch. "Come, we will have something to eat, then I will escort you over to see the electronics experts."

He stood and reached for the hat hanging from a hook by the door. "Comrade Major, you have been given a difficult and dangerous assignment. Nothing less than the future of the Soviet Navy rests on its outcome."

"I understand, Comrade Colonel," Drachev answered gravely. Somehow the thought of food was not appealing.

"Hello, Bobby, how do you feel?" Brittan called as Talent climbed down the wet ladder into the decompression module.

Talent looked over and frowned. "I feel like shit, Herk," he replied as he stepped off the ladder and wiped his hands on his coveralls. "Thanks for asking. Hi, Janice." He stepped over to his colleagues and shook Brittan's hand

Janice Wellford stepped up and hugged Talent. "Welcome to Davy Jones's Locker."

"No shit," Talent agreed. Behind him, his bag fell from the hatch to the floor with a wet plop. The hatch clanged shut as Talent walked back over to fetch the bag.

"We have to walk from here to the main complex," Brittan explained. "All the modules that have access to the sea are out on corridors. Safer that way, I'm told."

As they walked over to the big pressure door, Talent stared at a row of what appeared to be space suits hanging in a fenced-off area.

"What are those weird things?" he asked.

"They call them deepsuits," Janice answered. "You breathe oxygenated liquid in them so you can work really deep."

"Breathe liquid?" he asked incredulously.

She nodded. "Not this boy!" Talent assured her.

"No, not us," she went on, "our life here is pretty boring compared to that."

"Come on, Jan," Brittan said as he pulled open the heavy pressure door, "it's not as bad as all that!"

"Whatever you say, Herk," she answered, rolling her eyes at Talent.

On the walk back to DeepCore, Talent could feel the tension between them. Wellford was much friendlier than usual, which meant that she was friendly at all, and Brittan seemed jealous. The idea of working for weeks with these two made his heart sink.

"Breathing liquid, eh," Talent said, changing the subject to everyone's relief, "sounds impossible to me."

"They do it all the time here," Brittan jumped in. "They can work on the outside easier and not have to worry about the depth or the bottom time."

"I thought they used ROVs to do that," Talent observed.

"A remote vehicle can't tie a knot in a line or run a bead with a welder," Brittan answered.

"Will miracles never cease?" Talent asked.

"I hope not"—Janice laughed—"I rely on 'em!"

12

The visit home had been depressing. Drachev was struck by
the change in Soviet life. All *perestroika* had done was make
the people more discontent and even poorer. Drachev shook
his head, remembering how much better it had been before
Gorbachev had embarked on his ill-advised social scheme. Not
since the days of Stalin had such economic disaster befallen
Russia.

As the plane swooped low over the coast of Sakhalin island,
Drachev marveled at the harsh beauty of the place. The location of the training bases was not on his orders, but Drachev
assumed it would be near one of the Soviet Navy's many secret
facilities on the island.

It was raining when the plane landed in Yuzhno Sakhalinsk.
An unmarked car with a pretty female driver was waiting
for him. Her accent was hard to place, but her skin was
fair.

The rain made the drive to Kohlmsk a long, tedious affair.
Twice they stopped because she could not see the road at all.
Her name was Irina and she was Ukrainian. She had been
here for four months. She had seen the training area, a huge
warehouse complex on the end of a large dock, but knew
nothing of its contents. She was pleasant and Drachev was
a bit disappointed when they turned off the road and stopped
in front of the chain-link gates of the Soviet Navy Sea Life
Research Station. She dropped him off at the headquarters
building, opening his door and snapping a brisk salute as
he got out of the car. He winked at her as he returned the
salute. Her slight smile and direct gaze sent a message that
had nothing to do with military courtesy.

• • •

"Okay, honey," Carla said, "you got everything you need?"

Marie nodded. She was still a little scared. Carla's violent encounter with Carl had terrified her, but nothing had come of it. Carl's one phone call had been amazingly polite.

"All right," Carla sighed. "One more thing." She took Marie by the hand and led her into the bedroom, closing the door behind them. Carla stepped over to the closet and ran her hand along the highest shelf. She turned to Marie and handled her a snub-nosed .38 revolver. Marie handled the small handgun like it was a snake.

"If worse comes to worse," Carla told her, "use this. All you have to do is point it and pull the trigger. Don't use it unless you really have to. I want you to have it, though, just in case."

"I couldn't shoot him," Marie sighed, "I just couldn't do it."

"Maybe so, but keep it anyway," Carla answered as she took the gun and replaced it on the high shelf. Outside, a car horn sounded twice.

"That's the van," Carla said, hugging her sister and kissing her forehead, "I gotta go." Carla went back into the living room and hefted up the two big zippered bags next to the door.

"Bye bye," Carla called as she opened the door and stepped outside.

"Be careful!" Marie called as Carla disappeared down the steps to the parking lot.

"I will!" came the reply from below. Marie stood in the apartment door and watched until the van carrying her only real protector pulled out of the parking lot.

"Attention!" Kron barked. The twenty-five men leaped to their feet and stood like statues as the officer walked to the front of the room and turned to look at them. He wasn't the most imposing officer they had ever seen, but his reputation was larger than the man himself. Every one of the Naval Spetsnaz soldiers knew of Drachev, the Beast of Tbilisi. He was looking them over, measuring them. They stared straight ahead, reluctant to call attention to themselves. Finally, he told them to take their seats.

"You men have been selected from all the units of the Soviet Naval Infantry," Drachev began. "You have been selected for a mission as important as any that Soviet soldiers or sailors have ever done."

He paused a moment, then went on. "This mission is an attack on a facility that endangers the entire Soviet Navy." He looked at each man's face. "It is a dangerous mission requiring timing, courage, and determination. You men possess those qualities. That is why you are here." Drachev sat on the edge of the small desk at the front of the room. "I cannot tell you the exact target for reasons of security, but I can tell you this. We have been selected to stop the most perfidious threat yet devised by the *Glavny Rag*."

The mention of the main enemy, the United States, got their attention.

"We will train at this facility until such time as we are ready," Drachev continued. "Then we will strike. None of us will be permitted out of this facility until we leave on the mission."

The men were clearly impressed, even if they were still in the dark about the nature of the mission. Drachev stood and turned to Sgt. Kron.

"Take command of this sub-unit, Sergeant," Drachev instructed. "Get them settled and ready to commence training tomorrow morning."

"It is done, Comrade Major!" Kron answered.

After the major left, one of the privates, Filipov, came over to Kron and asked, "What is the target, Sergeant? Do you know?"

"No, I do not," Kron replied truthfully. "But I know one thing." He hooked a finger at the door. "They would not have sent the Beast if it were not real trouble."

13

Beneath them, the flat, sun-washed valley flared toward the ocean, a green and brown quilt stitched with black asphalt roads and gray concrete highways. Farther north, the horizon was obscured by the dark haze of Los Angeles's perpetual smog. San Diego flashed beneath them and less than an hour later, Bob Moore and his crew were in another UnderSea van, headed for the lab and training facility on the coast south of San Diego.

"Tell me again about this liquid breathing stuff," Ty King asked. "I don't think I understand all I know about it."

"You know as much as I do," Moore answered. "The old man himself personally asked that we get qualified on it."

There were looks of apprehension all around. The van driver, Andy Potter, laughed.

"It sounds a lot worse than it is," Potter reassured them. "It takes a little getting used to, but after a few minutes, you can't even tell the difference."

"Yeah, I think drowning would take some getting used to," Bickerstaff responded.

"You don't really feel like you're drowning," Potter went on. "The liquid's warm and it carries even more oxygen than the air."

"Uh-huh!" King injected. Five sets of eyes rolled nervously.

After a quick California lunch of fruit and cheese, the security team went to work. Al Mixon, head of the fluorocarbon division, began the orientation next to the big indoor pool.

"Let me give you a quick history of the process," Mixon began. "The initial work was done in the early sixties at Duke University. Dr. Johannes Kylstra discovered that mice could breathe oxygenated fluids. In 1976, Dr. Kylstra worked out the problem of absorbing CO_2 buildup. In 1990, we finally got federal approval for the Liquidair suit."

Mixon held up one of the thick nylon suits and the bulky helmet that went with it. "With this system, a diver can operate down to three thousand feet." Mixon let this figure sink in. Three thousand feet was ten times deeper than any scuba diver could work. "The pressure is not so much a problem," Mixon continued, "since the body is also filled with liquid that is not compressible."

Larry Ramos held up his hand. "Did you, like, test this on prisoners, or what?" he asked.

Mixon laughed. "No, actually, we tested it on Navy divers," Mixon answered.

Ramos was still shaking his head. "I mean, what does it feel like to inhale that liquid? Don't you feel like you're drowning?"

Mixon shook his head. "There is a bit of anxiety at first. Some people shake a bit, but after a few breaths, it evens right out." As usual, Mixon was staring at a group of skeptics.

"Why don't we give you a quick demo, so you'll see what we're talking about?"

"We'd like that," Bob Moore answered quickly.

Mixon motioned toward the door and their driver, Andy Potter, emerged wearing one of the suits, carrying the helmet in one hand. A plastic bucket swung from his other hand. On his back was a small, squarish backpack with two hoses that ran up over his shoulders. The suit looked like a cross between a diver's dry suit and an astronaut's space suit. The helmet was nearly spherical. The faceplate was smooth and allowed 180-degree vision.

"You've all met Andy," Mixon said, helping the diver get the helmet over his head and locking it into position. "The helmet is Lexan and graphite composite material to make it as light as possible." He pulled at Potter's sleeve. "The suit is made of Kevlar fabric so it's almost impossible to tear it. The suit has a heater in it, 'cause the water temperature below five hundred feet gets really cold." As the locking latch snapped shut, Mixon looked up and smiled. "Now we'll show you how easy this really is."

Mixon turned a valve on the side of the helmet and a pale

pink liquid began to flow into the helmet. From inside, Potter grinned and winked.

"The fluid is continuously pumped through the helmet so that oxygenated fluid replaces depleted fluid and the waste CO_2 is pumped off."

The fluid had risen to Potter's nose. As it covered his nostrils, a stream of bubbles broke the surface in a thin pink foam.

"Andy is exhaling all the air from his lungs in preparation for filling them with fluorocarbon," Mixon said as the fluid rose above Potter's eyes and filled the helmet's facemask. Inside, Potter grinned again and inhaled deeply through his nose. A slight shudder ran the length of his body, then stopped. Inside the helmet, Potter made a hideous face, then grinned again and gave them a thumbs-up signal. He brought up his left sleeve and showed them a small, thin keyboard about the size of those found on palm-top computers.

"Since there is no air to flow over his vocal cords," Mixon went on, pointing to a computer screen off to one side, "he communicates by means of the keyboard to a display. He can, of course, hear just fine, but he also has a heads-up display in his helmet so he can communicate with other liquid-breathing divers."

Potter punched the keys with his right hand, typing out a message. On the computer screen, green letters appeared. "Seeing the world through rose-colored glasses," his message read.

Potter was now striking a series of bodybuilder poses for their amusement and to show that he was not too traumatized by breathing liquid instead of air.

"The only really hard part is getting out of the rig," Mixon said. He turned to Potter and pantomimed pulling off the helmet. Potter nodded and knelt down on both knees, placing the bucket in front of him.

"This is the ugly part," Mixon said, standing behind Potter. "Always make sure you're behind someone when you take the helmet off." He shut off the valves on the sides of the helmet and disconnected both hoses.

"Why behind them?" Ramos asked.

"You'll see."

Mixon patted Potter on the shoulder. Potter gave a thumbs-up and pulled the locking latch open himself. Mixon turned the helmet, breaking the seal. The pink fluid began to leak out around the rim. In one quick motion, Mixon pulled the helmet up and off Potter's head. A cascade of pink fluid poured out of the suit.

Potter pitched forward onto his hands. Pink fluid erupted from his nose and mouth, flowing toward the watching group. As they sidestepped the pink tide, Potter vomited loudly into the plastic bucket. His inhaled breath sounded like the death rattle of some prehistoric beast. He threw up another pink-tinged mouthful into the bucket, then sat back on his knees, sucking in chestfuls of air.

The security team was exchanging dubious glances when Potter sighed and said, "Hi, there!"

"How do you feel?" Carla asked, leaning forward.

"Like I just had my lungs washed!" Potter answered brightly.

"I know I always like that!" Carla smiled back at him.

"Oh, man," Ramos groaned from the rear of the group.

"Hey, Ramos," Bickerstaff teased, "you could use some of that stuff right now. The pink would balance out your green face."

Ramos's face wasn't really green, but it was pale. He had been spooked by the demo.

"Okay," Mixon began again, "who's going to be first to try it?"

Every face turned toward Moore, who frowned. "Looks like I'm elected."

"Me, too," Carla said quickly, "I want to see what this feels like."

Twenty minutes later Moore and Fuentes were suited up in the stiff nylon suits walking uncertainly out onto the grate next to the pool.

"Me, first," Carla called.

Mixon took her helmet. "All right," he instructed her, "when the liquid gets up to your nose, start blowing out all your breath. When you can't blowout anymore and you have to take a breath, inhale deeply through your mouth, not your nose. That will fill your lungs faster."

"Okay," Carla answered, the first hint of nervousness in her **voice.**

"Here," Mixon said, pointing to the grate, "sit down here."

Carla sat cross-legged on the steel grate. Mixon stepped in front of her and bent down with the helmet. "Ready?"

Carla nodded and Mixon slipped the helmet over her head, seated it on the ring around her neck, and twisted it into place. Through the mask, they could see Carla's face. She was nervous now, her eyes darting from side to side. Mixon connected the two hoses and knelt down in front of her. Andy Potter stepped up behind her and knelt down as well.

"Here we go," Mixon said as he turned the valve on her helmet. Pink fluid flowed up around Carla's face. At the touch of the warm fluid, her eyes got very big. Mixon gave her a thumbs-up. She returned it as the fluid came up over her lips.

"Start blowing out your air now, Carla," Mixon told her, "and don't take a breath."

She nodded, the fluid lapping up over her nose. A thick foam of bubbles erupted from her nose, the bubbles carried away by the rising pink flood in her helmet. When her mask was completely filled, Mixon spoke to her again.

"Come on, now breathe real deep through your mouth," he soothed.

Carla looked scared for just a moment, then that look of determination that the others had seen so often came over her and she tipped her head back, sucking the warm pink liquid into her lungs as hard as she could.

Her reaction was vastly different from Potter's. He had merely shuddered when the fluid filled his lungs. Carla convulsed. Potter took her shoulders from behind and held her tight. Mixon got right up to her mask and spoke firmly to her.

"It's all right, Carla," he said, holding her face in front of him, "It's natural the first time. Take another deep breath, come on."

She clutched at Potter's arm and coughed in her mask, sending a few more bubbles up toward the exhaust tube. Gradually, her shaking stopped and finally she looked up at the others, a little smile playing at the corners of her mouth.

"You okay, babe?" Moore asked when she looked over at him.

She nodded and tried to speak, then remembered she

couldn't. She put the keyboard up in front of her, typing out a message.

Moore looked over at the computer screen.

"What a rush!" it said. Everybody laughed. If she could make a joke, she must be all right.

Moore was next. He shook, too, when the fluid went down his trachea, but he settled down quickly. He and Carla began exchanging messages over their keyboards as the others eavesdropped via the computer. After twenty minutes both Moore and Carla looked quite calm.

Then the helmets came off. Carla had typed out, "After you." Moore responded with, "Ladies first."

Carla knelt down, bucket in front of her. Mixon and Potter took off the helmet. Fluorocarbon, vomit, and snot went into the bucket and splashed out again. Carla was seized by racking coughs that took a minute to subside. When she settled down, she looked like hell.

"Oh, fuck!" she gasped at last, then looked a bit sheepish. "Pardon my French."

Mixon laughed. "That's okay, when Andy came out the first time, he said some awful things about my mother."

Carla smiled a little, then crawled on hands and knees over to the pool and washed her face with a handful of the heavily chlorinated water.

Moore was next and fared only a little better. After the two had recovered a bit, the others got their turn. Of the rest, only Ramos had a bad time. He was the only nonveteran among the men, and his underwater experience was purely sport diving. He took longer to calm down going in and suffered more coming out.

After they were all cleaned up and dressed again, Mixon walked them out. "So, what do you think?" he asked as they walked to the door.

"We'll be back tomorrow," Moore answered. "Can you let us have Andy again?"

"No problem," Mixon said, nodding, "Take it easy, tonight. Alcohol and fluorocarbon don't mix too well."

"We'll be good," Moore assured him as they filed out and walked to the van parked at the curb.

When they were in the van, Ramos leaned up to speak to Moore.

"Are you serious, boss?" he asked, "Are we going to do that again tomorrow?"

"That's right, Larry," Moore replied. "We're going to learn how to get into the things ourselves and out of them, too."

"Do you mind if I ask why?" Ramos persisted. "I mean, we are all qualified divers anyway. Why do we need all this fancy stuff?"

Moore turned and squinted into the sun. "Because we are going to a place that's a helluva lot different than any of us are used to. I really doubt that the folks there will be too happy to see us in the first place and I don't want us to look like a bunch of boobs." He leaned back again in his chair. "Plus, if there really is some problem down there, I want us to be able to handle it. Don't think for a second that this isn't a test. Marc LeFlore would love to make us look like jerks, I don't intend to give him any ammunition to use on us."

Ramos didn't answer, but sat back heavily on the bench seat.

"Hey, Ramos," Bickerstaff crooned, "relax. It'll be better next time. Maybe you won't puke in the pool tomorrow!"

The others laughed, but Ramos was not amused.

14

"Now!"

Valerian pulled the heavy hatch up and leaned back, holding it open. The fifteen other black-clad men poured through the hatch into the space below. As each man hit the steel floor, he rolled away and came up on his feet running for the corridor hatch. A muffled two-round burst echoed back into the tiny sub.

Drachev dropped through the hatch, following his troops. Behind him, Valerian dropped onto the floor, the rear guard. His men were already sprinting down the corridors, heading for the lab area where the Positrack equipment was tested and stored. Along the way, dummies simulated the DeepCore crew. The soldiers fired at each dummy, using the same low-velocity ceramic ammunition they would use on the assault. Their German MP-5K machine pistols were small and easily handled even with one hand. The silencer screwed onto the barrel reduced the muzzle blast to a soft pop.

The 9mm ceramic bullets broke up on impact with hard surfaces, decreasing the chances of ricochets and the greater risk of hull punctures. The ceramic slugs also broke up on contact with bones and were nearly impossible to detect on X rays, making them unusually lethal as well.

As each man reached his assigned destination, he reported in via the small radio he carried. When the last man called in, Drachev inspected the mock-up.

Every dummy had two or three holes in it, usually in the head or chest. The men were skillful shots and the silenced MP-5s made it even easier to place the bullets in vital organs. There seemed to be no damage to the structure.

It had taken less than five minutes to shoot all the dummies and clear the entire mock-up. Drachev recalled all his raiders to the area beneath the hatch.

"Four minutes, forty-five seconds," he said to the assembled group. "Pathetic!" Their faces fell. This had been their best time in eight rehearsals.

Drachev glared at them, watching them squirm. He was actually pleased with this rehearsal, but they would never know it.

"A group of Young Pioneers could do better!" he bawled at them. "Arthritic grandmothers could do better!" Drachev looked up at the ceiling and sighed. "One more time!"

There was no grumbling or complaining as the men climbed back into the sub. Although he could see the strain and fatigue on their faces, his men would never let their commander hear them bitch. Drachev stifled a smile as he climbed back up into his position. These were damn good men!

"I thought you were sick," Carla asked as Ramos sat next to her on the vacant bar stool.

"I got better," he answered, flashing his best smile. He ordered a Cuervo shooter.

"The man said no alcohol tonight, remember?" Carla said, scanning Ramos with a quick look. As usual, he was perfect. Tan shoes peeked out from under white pleated pants. A polo shirt under a tan blazer rounded out the ensemble. She couldn't place the shirt's color, off-mauve was close. His hair was the standard blond helmet, moussed and blown to perfection.

"So, got any plans tonight?" he was asking.

"Huh uh," she replied, "Why?"

"Well, I thought you and me might have a drink here, then go see the sights, maybe dance a little somewhere."

She stirred her drink with one very red fingernail. Ramos was like a broken record.

"I don't think so, Larry," she demurred, "I'm pretty tired."

"Come on, Carla," he schmoosed, "loosen up! We'll have a few laughs, no big deal!"

No big deal until we get back and the dancing turns horizontal, she thought, and I have to pry your hands off me. She and Ramos had had one date a year ago. She told her friends it had been disgusting. He told his friends he had scored with her.

He had asked for another date at least twice a month since.

"Larry," she began, "we've had this conversation before. I don't think it would be a good idea for us to date, okay? Especially since we're going to be shut up in DeepCore together for a while."

"An even better reason for us to get acquainted!" he interrupted. "Come on! What have you got to lose?"

"My disease-free status?" she quipped.

"That wasn't nice, Carla," he whined. "You know I don't have anything."

Yeah, right, she thought. Carla had heard the stories about Ramos's girlfriend. The guys called her "Ever-ready."

"Whatever," she sighed. She slid off the bar stool and put a dollar under the coaster for her Pepsi. "Thanks for the offer, Larry, but I'll pass. See you tomorrow."

"Okay, but you don't know what you're missing!" he said as she started for the door.

That's true, she thought. Thank God.

She hadn't taken ten steps before Ramos's eyes were searching the dark bar, hunting more pliable prey. As Carla walked passed the brightly lit jukebox, she ran her eyes down the list of tunes. There it was. She dropped a quarter into the slot and pressed G12. She was walking out the door as the strains of Warren Zevon's "Werewolves of London" boomed out over the bar's sound system.

"Message, Captain," the young signal ensign said, offering the clipboard holding the recently received signal. Pavel Bondarchuk glanced up at the eager young officer whose face always looked like a recruiting poster for the submarine service. As the captain took the clipboard, the ensign stepped back, waiting for a reply.

A secret cover was on top of the message. Bondarchuk stepped to the far end of the control room, just behind the helmsman's station, as secluded a place as could be found without retiring to his cabin.

The message was simple. Change course to arrive at a set of coordinates by a specified date and time. Further orders to follow. Bondarchuk initialed the signal and returned it to the ensign.

"Signal acknowledgment to Pacific Fleet, Ensign."

"It is done, Comrade Captain!" the ensign gushed, then disappeared down the ladder.

Bondarchuk stepped over to the chart table and pulled out two large charts. He plotted the new course himself, checking the satellite navigation readout for their current position and running a line to their destination. The spot was east of Iwo Jima island, almost due south of their present location.

"Helmsman, set course 179 degrees, Bondarchuk instructed his crew, "ahead full speed. Mr. Koslov, I will see you in my cabin."

As the crew went about their tasks, Bondarchuk and his executive officer, Yuri Koslov, made their way down the ladder to the deck below. They stepped down the narrow passageway and into Bondarchuk's small cabin.

"Close the door," Bondarchuk instructed as he slid behind the small desk.

"Koslov, I have sealed orders to open at this time," the captain began. "I need you present to confirm them."

Koslov nodded, watching as the captain spun the combination lock on the small safe under his desk. He opened the door, took out a thick envelope, and shut the door again.

Bondarchuk read the instructions on the envelope aloud.

" 'The enclosed orders are to be opened following reception of a course change on or about the twelfth day of this patrol.' " He looked up a Koslov. "Today is the twelfth day, correct?"

"Just so, Comrade Captain," Koslov answered.

Bondarchuk went on. " 'On opening these orders, you will initiate them immediately and deviate in no way from them.' " Bondarchuk slipped his thin letter opener, a miniature Soviet Navy sword, under the flap and slit open the envelope.

On top was a secret warning label of the highest level. Bondarchuk read the first page and turned to the second. He read halfway down the page and stopped, looking up at the curious exec.

"Assemble the officers in the wardroom, Lieutenant," Bondarchuk ordered. "This will require the attention of all."

Koslov stepped to the intercom and pressed the button to speak throughout the boat. Never taking his eyes off the captain, he called all officers to the wardroom.

Ten minutes later all eyes were on Bondarchuk as he read the orders.

" 'The submarine *Odessa* will proceed to Operational Area 127, where it will rendezvous with an aircraft of the Soviet Air Transport Service, which will drop a contingent of Naval Special Designation troops. *Odessa* will provide navigational assistance for the aircraft, but will remain submerged at all times during the rendezvous.' "

The officers exchanged curious glances as the captain continued.

" 'These Special Designation troops will enter *Odessa* while submerged and deliver further orders. Encryption instructions for the delivered orders will follow by radio transmission.' "

"Comrade Captain, what do they mean that the encryption orders will follow?" the signal officer, a senior lieutenant, asked.

"It means, comrade, that the troops delivering the orders will not have the means to decode them," Bondarchuk said, looking up, "you think the process unusual?"

"Yes, Comrade Captain, I do," the lieutenant answered nervously.

"So do I, Lieutenant," Bondarchuk observed, "so do I."

Commander Gonsharov, the deck and submersibles officer, broke in. "Comrade Captain, this insertion is to take place at what time?"

"There is no time specified," the captain responded, looking again at the orders. He looked up at the deck officer. "I would assume that the operation would take place at night."

"Comrade Captain," the deck officer went on, "I have done such operations before, but never submerged and never at night."

Bondarchuk smiled. "That is a claim you will not be able to make much longer, comrade." The deck officer did not look reassured.

"It is apparent that this is not a training exercise," the captain said, looking each officer in the eye. "Although it will be difficult and possibly even dangerous, I doubt seriously that the orders that follow will be less so. We have a good crew and a good boat, comrades. We will perform this mission."

If there was any doubt in any of the officers' minds, it did not show on their faces.

The remainder of the hour-long meeting was devoted to the process of meeting, signaling, and coordinating a parachute drop with an aircraft and with the process of getting the *desantniki* aboard once they were in the water.

"Hey, Ramos, you did good today!" Bickerstaff called out as he slid open the sliding-glass door and stepped out onto the pool deck. King followed. Both men walked to the edge of the pool, dropped their towels, and dove into the deep end of the pool next to the No Diving sign. King broke the water first.

"Man, this pool's warm as bathwater!"

Bickerstaff swam underwater to the shallow end of the pool. He emerged next to the edge and spit a stream of water at the others sitting at a table under an umbrella.

"Eat shit and die, Elgin," Ramos shot back. "You didn't look so hot yourself today."

"True, true," Bickerstaff bantered, "but I'm an old man who's lived a wicked life. I'm frail."

"Yeah!" Carla laughed. "Like a pit bull with PMS!"

"Hey, Carla," King said, plopping his elbows up on the pool side, "know what to do if a pit bull is humping your leg?"

"No, Ty, what?"

"Fake an orgasm, quick!"

"You mean like this?" Carla said. She leaned her head back and began to moan. "Ohh. Ohhhh. OOOOhhhh!"

Each moan was longer and louder than its predecessor. Carla leaned back in her chair and shifted into high gear.

"Oh yeah, oh yeah, ohh, OOOOOHHHHH! Oh! OH GOD! OH GOD YES! YES! YES! Oh, oh, oh."

By now, everyone else at the pool was staring at the tall redhead who seemed to be coming her brains out in a lawn chair next to the bar. Carla simply shook her red mane, took a deep breath, and sighed. A moment later the bartender appeared with a refill on her daiquiri.

"Thought you might be thirsty," he said, smiling. "It's on the house." Carla gave him a big smile and he went away chuckling.

"Yeah, just like that," King said in answer to her question. Everybody laughed.

"So what are we doing next week, again?"

"Goin' over the DeepCore site plans and learning all we can about that Positrack thing."

15

"It will be in place by then?" Colonel Petrochenko's voice betrayed no emotion, but Lavrov could feel the tension over the phone.

"Yes, Comrade Colonel, it left a week ago," Lavrov replied. "It will be on station ten hours before the drop."

"See that it is, Colonel," Petrochenko went on, "I do not relish the thought of dropping a team of Naval Spetsnaz into the middle of the Pacific Ocean with no one there to meet them." Petrochenko added, "They are experienced combat swimmers, but that would be too much to ask even of them!"

"Just so, Comrade Colonel," Lavrov answered. He gave the general a polite laugh.

"Notify me when the rendezvous had been made," Petrochenko concluded the conversation.

"I will, Comrade Colonel," Lavrov assured him.

As he hung up the phone, Lavrov went over the long list of unforeseen events that could prevent or complicate the mission. It was a long list: mechanical failure, human error, bad weather, stupidity, jealousy, misunderstanding, and pigheadedness. That was just the list for possible problems on his side. It did not include the thousands of possible actions by the Americans or the simple laws of chance.

Best not to dwell on the possible, he remembered, but to concentrate on the desirable.

Lavrov picked up the phone again and called the communications center for a status report on the submarine. The duty officer reported that the signal had been received and acknowledged.

So far, so good, he mused as he went back to his list. He would check with the training base next.

"Ready to disconnect!" Drachev said into the tiny mike that hovered just in front of his lips. He felt his pilot nod and heard Kron's voice crackle "Ready!" over the interphone.

"Disconnect!" Drachev barked. There was a slight rocking motion to the side, then the small sub rose a few meters up out of the storage well on the mother sub's back, pivoted to the right, and sped off toward its destination.

Behind them, Kron's minisub with Popov at the controls was repeating the maneuver, heading off to the left of the mother sub toward its simulated target. The two subs remained silent as they approached their targets. Kron was the first to speak.

"In place," he said only once.

"Execute," came Drachev's order. Drachev knew that Popov was placing his limpet mines now and would finish in less than five minutes. By then, Drachev and his raiders would be at the airlock on top of the mock-up. Today, for the first time, they would run through the complete attack, ending up back on the mock mother sub when they were finished.

The airlock loomed up before them. His pilot skewed the craft around and hovered over the locking ring. When he was in place, he threw the thrusters up and slammed the small submerible onto the airlock.

Valerian had the hatch open and the raiders were in the mock-up and on their way in seconds. Drachev was next to last into the mock-up behind his group. Valerian followed, pulling the airlock hatch shut behind him. The two men started off after the section headed for the Positrack facility. From somewhere deep in the elaborate mock-up, two sharp explosions echoed.

The mock-up itself was a series of simple rooms in a waterproof concrete building. No effort had been made to simulate the actual configuration of the target. The mock-up was intended solely to give the *raydoviki* an idea of the size of the target and the direction in which they would have to go to reach their targets. As he walked through the wooden rooms, he noticed that the concrete structure outside was not as watertight as it could be. Huge puddles in the floors and large damp areas on the walls spoke of the need for repair.

In moments, all his raiders reported that they had secured their objectives. All communication had been silenced, the laboratory area was secure, as was the submarine dock.

As Drachev entered the laboratory, he noted the "dead" dummies. Each had been shot twice in the head and chest. The lab mock-up was undamaged. The raiders were busily stuffing the electronic gear into rucksacks. Valerian shucked off his empty pack and joined the looters. In minutes, the packs were full, the raiders had shouldered them and were waiting for the order to return to the minisub.

"Go," Drachev said. As his men quickly filed out, Drachev scanned the room for unrecovered electronics parts. He found a box of circuit boards perched on top of a metal shelf. He took the parts, intending to use them in his critique.

Back at the airlock, his men were climbing back into the minisub. Sgt. Kron's raiders were now acting as rear guard for the attackers.

"Any problems?" Drachev asked the burly sergeant as he walked up.

"None, Comrade Major!"

Drachev nodded and motioned for Valerian to open the air-lock hatch. Popov's minisub was still tethered to the airlock. Its seal was a bit off and when the airlock hatch was opened, a stream of cold water showered Drachev and his raiders. They climbed up into the sub through the icy spray.

Drachev pulled the airlock hatch shut as he clambered into the sub. Valerian secured the sub's hatch. When the second minisub had picked up its raiders and pulled away from DeepCore, they would leave the airlock open to flood the facility.

As they slipped away from the mock-up, Drachev put on the interphone headset and leaned up over Popov, pouring the cold water caught in his jacket pocket over the man's head. The pilot stiffened, but said nothing.

"Do not be in so great a hurry that you miss your mark, Popov," Drachev hissed into the mike. "At three hundred meters, that leak could cut a man in half."

Popov nodded. "I understand, Comrade Major."

Drachev sat down on the thin bench and unzipped his com-bat smock. He dried his face on his shirt. The interphone crackled with Kron's voice. The second sub was away.

Not bad, he complimented himself, in fact, very smooth. If the real mission went as smooth, it would a stunning success.

Too bad they never go as smooth as the rehearsals, he lamented.

"Man, I don't know about you, but my head is spinnin'," King moaned as he flopped down on the hotel couch.

"Mine's just overdosed," Bickerstaff said, pulling a beer from the tiny refrigerator. "I never wanted to know so much about any place before. Did you understand all that computer stuff this afternoon?" He tossed King a cold long neck.

"Some," King answered, twisting the cap off and taking a long swig. "Without being there, it don't help much to get a lecture about it, though."

The briefing on the electronic environmental control of DeepCore had been filled with electronics jargon and computer buzzwords. Bickerstaff had nearly fallen asleep half a dozen times.

"What are we doin' tomorrow?" King asked between swigs.

Bickerstaff picked up his class schedule. " 'The Effects of High-Pressure Nervous Syndrome on DeepCore Personnel,' " he read.

"All day?"

"Nope, just the morning."

"What's High-Pressure Nervous Syndrome?"

Bickerstaff thought for a moment. "I think it's like when your boss is an asshole, your wife's on the rag, your girlfriend's two weeks late, and the IRS wants to look at your tax returns for the last five years."

"Works for me," King agreed. "How 'bout another brew?"

"Gentlemen, and lady," the speaker began, nodding at Carla, "I am Dr. Geoffrey Burns and I am here to explain to you the nature of High-Pressure Nervous Syndrome and to relate those effects to living and working in a deep-sea environment such as the DeepCore facility."

Bickerstaff looked over at King and crossed his eyes, then rolled them back into his head. King stifled a laugh and tried to concentrate on the speaker. The man looked like a college professor. Tweed jacket with elbow patches, madras sport shirt, chinos and Top-Siders made up his ensemble. The unlit pipe he sucked on and the slightly superior attitude said researcher and college professor.

"High-Pressure Nervous Syndrome or HPNS is a rare and little understood medical phenomenon associated with deep diving," he began. "It affects about one person in twenty and strikes unpredictably."

He placed a complicated chart on the desktop easel.

"The primary effects of the syndrome are trembling, slurred speech, feelings of fear and paranoia."

"Sounds like you every Saturday night," King quipped at Bickerstaff. Burns waited for the chuckling to settle.

"The extreme form of the syndrome includes nausea, convulsions, and hallucinations."

"Sounds like my divorce hearing," Bickerstaff said solemnly.

Even Burns laughed at that. For the next fifty minutes, he explained the function of pressure on neurons and the use of anesthetics to ward off the syndrome. After class, Burns managed to speak to Carla alone.

"You seem a bit out of place in this group."

"I beg your pardon?" Carla snapped.

"I just mean that you don't seem to be the usual security-type person," Burns stammered, trying to get his foot out of his mouth.

"What type might that be?" Carla asked sweetly, enjoying the man's discomfort. For all his academic assurance, he was a bit tongue-tied with her.

"Him," Burns answered, gesturing at Bickerstaff.

She laughed. "Don't underestimate Elgin," she warned, "sometimes he can surprise you."

"No doubt," Burns answered, searching for a way to change the subject before he dug himself in deeper. "How did you get into this business?"

Outside, their van pulled up at the curb.

"Why don't you buy me drink tonight and I'll tell you the story of my life," she said, fixing him with a steady stare.

"That sounds great," Burns answered, a bit startled by her directness.

"Fine, then. We're at the Executive Suites," she smiled. "About eight?"

"I'll be there."

She shook his hand, letting hers stay in his a beat longer than necessary, then joined the others as they walked out to the waiting van.

16

He was standing in the lobby when she stepped out of the elevator. His nervous smile reminded Carla of a prom date she had once.

"Hello," he said, "shall we get a drink here or . . ."

"Let's go somewhere else," she interrupted, "I'm getting tired of this place."

"Surely," he answered as she took his arm and steered him toward the door.

When they were in his car and on the road, he turned to her. "Would you like to go somewhere quiet or loud?"

"Actually, I'd rather not go to a bar at all," she replied, "I'm bored with bars. Why don't we just go to your place." Her direct gaze seemed to unsettle him a bit, but he recovered fast.

"Fine"—he nodded—"I'm afraid I only have Scotch to drink. No, wait, I have some champagne, too."

"Champagne would be lovely," she purred, sliding over in the seat to slide her arm through his.

Twenty minutes later they were settled on the love seat in his small apartment.

"So, how did you get into this business, Carla," Burns asked as he unwrapped the foil and pulled the wire cage off the champagne.

"Well," she said, "I started out in the Navy Reserve while I was working on a criminal justice degree. After I graduated, I went to work for a police department for a while." Carla watched the cork warily as Burns pushed on it with his thumbs. "I met Bob Moore when he came to train my reserve unit." The cork seemed to be stuck. "I had some trouble on the force and left police work. Mr. Moore hired me and here I am."

"I see," Burns said as he tried twisting the cork.

No, you don't see anything, Carla thought, but that's all you need to know.

"The other guys are all ex-military, mostly Navy SEALs," she went on. "Except Ramos. He's our token civilian."

About that time, the cork exploded and a thick column of champagne started up out of the bottle. Carla grabbed the top of the bottle and shoved it in her mouth, sucking back the foaming champagne.

"Adroitly done," Burns laughed.

"Practice," she replied, wiping her mouth with her hand as he poured the champagne into a pair of thin glasses.

"Cheers!" he said, holding his glass up by the long stem. The glasses made a musical sound as they touched.

By the end of the bottle, she knew his history, which was mostly books and classes. He knew little more about her, but that was better anyway.

"Is it warm in here?" she asked, shedding her thin jacket. Under the jacket, the silk camisole clung to her. His eyes widened as they roamed over her lush figure and the clothes that covered her left little to the imagination.

Burns began to squirm and quickly agreed. "Here," he said, jumping up and turning to adjust his pants, "let me turn on the fan."

He reached up to pull the chain on the ceiling fan and she smiled at the newly erected tentpole in his pleated chino slacks.

Burns shed his jacket, tossing it toward the plush wingchair next to the love seat. The jacket missed and landed in a heap on the floor, but Burns ignored it. His eyes were riveted on the swell of cleavage that peeked up over the lace top of her camisole.

"Want the rest of this champagne?" he asked, tipping the bottle up to drain the last bit of bubbly.

"Save it, we'll use it later," she cooed. She took the bottle from his hand and set it on the coffee table.

She reached up and ran her palm across the bulge in his slacks. "There is something I'd like, though," she purred. She felt his knees go weak for a second, but he recovered quickly.

"Would you like to go back to my bedroom?" he inquired hoarsely.

"Why?" she answered. "Isn't this couch Scotch-Guarded?"

He laughed at that and she cut short the laugh by pulling down the zipper of his slacks. She slipped her hand inside his slacks and grasped him.

Burns was weaving a bit, trying to keep his balance as she massaged him roughly for a moment. She looked up at him through her long dark lashes and smiled. "Umm!" she observed. "Nice."

"Well," he stammered, "I . . ."

She cut short his remarks by sliding her lips down him. He gasped and, for a second, Carla wondered if he was going to faint or just fall over on her. She reached up to steady him with one hand, using the other to push him farther into her mouth.

Animal noises issued from him as she demonstrated a talent with which he was not familiar.

"Please," he begged, collapsing onto the small sofa, "I can't stand up anymore!"

"Not all of you feels that way," she observed, tugging at him with her hand. "Here," she said quickly, "let's get this out of the way."

She jerked his belt buckle loose and swept the slacks off in a single motion that surprised him with its economy.

"That's better!" she said, sliding off the couch onto the cheap oriental rug. She pushed his knees apart and slid between them, the silk camisole teasing the soft skin of his inner thighs. He stiffened all over in response to the oral assault.

Carla kept up this routine until she felt his orgasm building, then abruptly pulled him from her mouth and stood up, taking his face in her hands and engaging in a brief mouth to mouth tonsillectomy.

"My turn," she whispered. Carla pulled the skirt button loose letting the straight black skirt fall to the floor. She kicked it off to one side and stood in front of him with her feet apart.

"Nice panties," he observed, his eyes glued to the tiny wisp of red nylon emblazoned with the legend "You can't be first, but you can be next!."

"Let's go for the big money," she recommended, pushing him back onto the couch.

She settled down onto his lap and began to rotate her hips, grinding into him, wrenching a series of inarticulate moans from his throat.

"You're still all dressed up," she said. "Put your hands up!"

"Yes, Officer." He complied, leaning forward. Carla pulled the button-down shirt off over his head and tossed it across the room.

"Better." She crossed her arms and pulled the camisole off, her abundant breasts swaying inches from his face. Burns took the opportunity to pull one of Carla's dark nipples into his mouth, sucking noisily on it as he roughly fumbled for her other breast.

Carla began a back and forth rocking motion, thrusting powerfully against him, driving him deeper into her.

Burns had his head wedged between her breasts, gasping for breath and making a variety of animal sounds.

"Carla," he gasped, "here." He pulled her up and off him, turning her shoulders away from him as he pushed her over onto her knees beside him on the sofa. She quickly figured out where they were going and held onto the arm of the sofa.

"Good idea!" she agreed.

Burns put his knees between hers and slid back inside her.

"Yes!" she encouraged. "That's it."

Burns, aflame, buried himself in her. Holding her by her hips, he began to slam against her firm buttocks, their bodies slapping together like some kind of sexual applause.

Burns's breath grew ragged as hammered against Carla. He began to gasp. "Oh, oh, oh, Carla," he moaned.

Burns stiffened and slammed into her, holding her against him as he exploded. She cried out and reached back between her legs, fondling him as they came together.

Afterward, Burns released her hips and fell back on the loveseat.

"That was like getting struck by lightning!" he gasped.

She turned around on her knees and looked at him quizzically.

"It didn't last long," he explained, "but it sure made my hair stand up on end!"

She smiled, fluffing her red tresses with both hands. "Honey, that was just the first."

"The first what?" he inquired.

"The first of many," she answered, laughing. His eyes were filled with a mixture of fear and anticipation. Carla closed them with her lips and slid down the damp brocade to demonstrate her ability to bring back the dead.

"Don't hurt me," was all he had to say.

Captain Cyrus Zagalsky opened the mission profile packet and scanned it. A long flight followed by an airborne drop of twenty *desantniki*. He jotted down the drop coordinates and pulled up his map sheets. Ten minutes later he looked up at Col. Shargunov, the aircraft commander.

"Comrade Colonel, I believe there has been some mistake on these flight orders," he began. "The coordinates for this parachute drop are over the ocean. There is no land anywhere near these coordinates."

Shargunov tugged at his ear and looked at the poster on the wall. The poster condemned the use of alcohol by flight crews.

"Captain, have you ever been given incorrect flight information before?" he asked Zagalsky. His commander's tone told the navigator that he had made a mistake somehow.

"No, Comrade Colonel," Zagalsky replied.

"Is the location inconsistent with the rest of the flight profile?" Shargunov went on, studying the poster.

"No, Comrade Colonel, it is on the flight path."

"Then it would seem logical that the location for the drop is correct?"

"Exactly so, Comrade Colonel!" Zagalsky snapped, hoping to get back into good grace somehow.

Shargunov turned his gaze on the nervous navigator. "This is no ordinary training flight, Captain Zagalsky. I have not told the rest of the crew this yet, but I will tell you now."

Zagalsky assumed a position of attention, his eyes on the aircraft commander.

"This flight is not classified," Shargunov began. "In fact, it will never happen, officially. There will be nothing to classify. Do you understand?"

"Perfectly!" Zagalsky answered.

"Good," Shargunov said calmly, "continue with your work."

"It is done, Comrade Colonel," Zagalsky snapped. He returned to his planning table. Longitude east 145 and latitude north 24 degrees put the drop about the Tropic of Cancer, 750 kilometers east of Iwo Jima island. From there, they would fly to Vietnam to land and refuel. A grueling and most unusual trip.

What in the name of God are we dropping twenty men in the ocean for? he wondered. It was not that unusual for a tanker plane to drop small units of paratroopers. Most Soviet aircraft were multipurpose. They had dropped troops before on exercises, but never in the ocean.

He recalled his commander's stern tone. None of my business, he thought as he finished the necessary calculations for the flight.

17

"So, what do you think," Travis asked.

"It's unbelievable," Jackson answered as they returned to the control room. "I knew it was a big operation, but I didn't realize how complex it was."

Travis smiled. He liked giving the nickel tour of his baby. The looks of awe and wonder on the face of his few visitors were like a tonic to him.

"Let me see if I understand something," Jackson said, walking over to the central board. "You monitor everything from here, but you control the various functions of the place from different areas?"

"Not exactly," Travis answered. "We monitor everything from here, but we can control a lot of the functions from anywhere in the complex." Travis sat at a computer console and typed in his code.

"Watch." As Jackson kibitzed over his shoulder, Travis brought up the lighting control system on his screen. "Look out there at the sub dock," he told Jackson, pointing out the large front porthole.

Travis ran the cursor down the computer screen to the line that referenced the outside lighting. He double clicked on the outside lights and clicked once again in the "on" box. Outside, the sub dock blazed, lit by banks of sealed xenon floodlights. "We can access the entire system, electrical, environmental, the airlocks, everything from any remote terminal."

"Doesn't that make the system really vulnerable?" Jackson asked as Travis clicked again on the screen and the industrial area was plunged back into darkness.

"It could," Travis answered as he backed out of the system.

"But not everyone has code authorization. Most people can only access the areas in which they work. It's kinda like the code cards some companies use to open doors. If you aren't cleared for a particular area, your card won't open the door."

"Right"—Jackson nodded—"we use that system ourselves in the corporate headquarters."

"I expect that your next question is whether you will have access to the entire system."

Jackson smiled and nodded.

Travis swiveled the chair around to face Jackson. "I'll admit that I was reluctant to give you that authorization," Travis said. "But you are cleared all the way up and the Old Man himself told me to give you carte blanche on security here."

Jackson nodded. He hadn't known that the CEO had gotten involved.

"We might as well do that right now," Travis added. He turned to the screen and called up a menu. He entered Jackson's name and clearance. "Okay, you pick a password," he said, standing so Jackson could sit at the machine, "as many letters as you like."

Jackson sat at the machine and thought for a second. He settled on the name of a character he had created in a fantasy adventure computer game. He had run that character, a mythic warrior, through all four versions of the game, wasting all his free time for months.

Jackson smiled at the memory of that game. It had been an elaborate quest fantasy that required you to think and fight and map and generally taxed your brain every step of the way. He had loved it.

Jackson tapped the keyboard to insert his character's name Orcslayer. The computer asked him to verify the name. He hit return. Orcslayer had complete access to DeepCore's mainframe from any remote terminal, even from the outlying modules.

"Ready?" Travis asked. Jackson nodded and stood up from the terminal. Travis leaned over the chairback and exited from the system.

"It's about lunchtime," Travis said. "Why don't we get a bite to eat and then I'll introduce you to the lab people."

"Great," Jackson answered, "I'd especially like to talk to

the engineers who repaired the damage after the accident."

Travis looked up over his glasses, then took them off and put them in his coat pocket. "Certainly."

Kinji Watanabe's heart jumped as the door to the computer room opened. Hidden behind the tall console, he quickly dropped the tiny camera into his coveralls and pulled the screwdriver out of his pocket. As Tom Jackson and Dr. Travis walked around the console, Watanabe was busily twisting a screw back into the panel.

"Hey, Kinji," Travis called, "how's it goin'?"

"Very good!" Watanabe answered brightly. "I'm finished with the circuit checks. We should be able to power up again in a few hours."

"Excellent!" Travis answered. "Kinji, this is Mr. Jackson, from UnderSea Security. He's going to be with us for a while."

Watanabe nodded and bowed a few inches. Jackson stuck out his hand. "Call me Tom."

After a bit more chitchat the two men went on through the room into the control bay. Watanabe exhaled deeply. His heart was still racing. Thank heaven the Americans were so ingenuous. They suspected nothing until it fell on them.

Kinji's mentor, Kirby Kurosawa, always referred to the Americans' lack of guile as a Pearl Harbor mentality. It was an allusion that Watanabe found unsettling.

He had gotten a few good shots of the circuit board before Travis and Jackson had interrupted. He would get one or two more after they left.

That little Nip looked funny to me, Tom Jackson thought as he and Travis walked down to engineering, his hand was sweating. Watanabe had impeccable credentials, but so what? Jackson made a mental note to drop in on the oriental gentleman after he met with the engineering people.

The senior engineer turned out to be a pert, energetic woman named Nancy Collins. She explained what they had seen at the accident site and how they had patched the hole.

He asked to see the corridor itself.

"We sent the pieces of the broken porthole back to the manufacturer," she told him as they walked down two flights of stairs and through the maze of hallways to reach the lab corridor.

"The whole place is modular," she explained, "from the central core, you could add dozens of external facilities."

"Like the lab?" he asked.

"And like the industrial area, too," she answered.

In the damaged corridor, the effects of the water were still apparent. The porthole was black, covered on the outside by the steel cap. There was new paint on the opposite wall where the water had blasted it off.

"The emergency system is automatic," she said, pointing out the sensors and the power system on the door. "If something fails in here and the pressure changes either way, the doors automatically seal to keep the water in here."

"It worked when the porthole went?"

"Like a charm, unfortunately," she answered. Jackson gave her a quizzical look. "The two men were trapped in here because they couldn't get to either door before it closed."

They were both silent for a moment. "Tough way to die," she said, breaking the silence.

"Not any good ones," he said quietly as they walked back to her office in engineering.

"Did you get a tour of the place yet?" she asked.

"Just a quick flyby," he answered.

"If you want to see the good stuff," she told him, "give me a call. I'll show you the reactor and the sub bay. All the fun toys."

"I'll do that," Jackson answered. "How 'bout tomorrow?"

"Fine. Call me, my extension is 234."

"See you then." As Jackson walked off down the hall, she called to him.

"You might want to talk to the tech that worked with those two guys."

Jackson stopped and turned.

"He's Japanese," she added, "I think his name is What-a-nobber or something like that."

"Thanks, I will," he answered. She waved and disappeared into the bowels of the engineering section.

Jackson laughed. What-a-nobber, indeed.

As he walked away, he was struck again by the intricacy of the place. Pipes, ducts, wiring conduits, and hydraulic lines twisted and writhed along the ceiling and down the walls. It felt like a big snake pit, or maybe more like the insides of a car engine.

In reality, it was just a huge, stationary submarine whose shape could be rearranged to adapt it to any underwater endeavor. Jackson was fascinated that it could be controlled from any computer terminal. Running this huge place from a keyboard must have a godlike feeling to it.

He chuckled, visualizing Nancy Collins as a god figure. She was more practical than spiritual. That was probably good. Spiritual gods could be capricious.

18

"Bridge, Sonar," the intercom squawked, "contact has changed course, bearing 175."

Dale Hawkins, captain of the ballistic missile sub *Cleveland*, looked quickly at the chart. The Soviet sub was turning away.

"Stay with him, Sonar," Hawkins said.

"Aye, sir."

The Russian had been headed right at them. Hawkins had let the big Ohio-class sub settle just above the bottom, its reactor all but turned off, the boat silent as the Russian bore in on them. Now he was veering off. Had he heard something after all?

Twenty-five minutes later, the sonar chief was back with a report. "Sir, that Russian is acting squirrelier than a road chicken!"

Hawkins grinned at Walt Fletcher, the exec. "Well, Chief, I don't know much about the behavior of road chickens, why don't you tell me what he's doing?"

"Well, sir, he ran on that course for a while, then he stopped and went up to periscope depth," the sonarman drawled, his Texas accent more pronounced as he got excited. "We figured he needed some air, since he's a diesel boat. Anyway, he fired off a lot of radio traffic, UHF stuff. He got back some, too. Now he's just hanging there, nose into the current, maintaining his position."

"Thank you, Chief, that is unusual behavior," Hawkins answered the sonarman, who looked disappointed that his report had garnered so little reaction. "Keep an ear on him."

"Aye, sir."

"What do you think, Walt?" Hawkins asked his exec.

"I think he's up to something else and doesn't know we're here," Fletcher answered, holding his palms up.

"Let's sneak up on him a little and see what he does."

"Helm, get a bearing from sonar and put us on that Red's tail," Hawkins instructed the helmsman. He turned to Fletcher. "Squirrely as a road chicken, eh?" Fletcher grinned.

"Position check," Bondarchuk snapped again. It was the fifth time in the last fifteen minutes he had asked.

"Unchanged, Comrade Captain," the helmsman reported.

Bondarchuk sighed. This was nonsense! Ocean air drops! Secret orders! What crap!

"Contact! An aircraft, Comrade Captain, inbound," the radar operator called, "thirty kilometers."

"Signal the aircraft," Bondarchuk told the radioman, who switched on the tone signal that would guide the aircraft to *Odessa*'s underwater hiding place.

In the aircraft, the flight crew were pushing up the plane's side doors. When the doors were locked open and the blast deflectors locked in place, the flight crew stepped aside and let the two jumpmasters take over. The big refueling plane slowed, the noise of the jet engines dropping over the whistling of the wind through the open doors.

"Prepare!" Kron and Yevtushenko shouted at their brood. The men stood and hooked their static lines over the taut steel cable that ran from the back end of the big fuel tank to the tail of the IL-76. The tension in the big plane was like an electric charge in the air.

After the long flight, they were ready to jump. The tanker had only a few seats. Some of them had been sitting on their equipment in the rear of the plane. Others had nestled in the maze of pumps and hoses that led back to the refueling boom.

An hour ago they had readied their equipment bundles and slithered into their orange wetsuits. Now the cramps and stiffness of the long flight were forgotten as adrenaline shot through their systems.

The jumpers looked like religious zealots, their eyes focused on something outside the plane. The chants of the jumpmasters and the parachute ritual only emphasized their primitive spirituality.

When everyone was ready, the two jumpmasters moved the first jumper into place behind the door bundle. In the right door, Major Drachev looked calm. He was staring straight ahead, waiting for the jump signal. In the other door, Valerian looked tense, glancing down at the dark ocean that rippled below.

Kron was trying hard not to think about the ocean himself. Jumping at night over the water was risky enough in training. There were no boats below, except, hopefully, the submarine. His gloomy thoughts were interrupted by the green light that flashed on and off just beside his head. He shoved the bundle out the door and jumped back.

"Go! Go! Go!" Kron shouted at the major. Drachev disappeared out the door. The others were moving now, rushing to get out the door with the others, hoping not to get separated.

In a few seconds the last man flashed by him and Kron pivoted, reaching out for the cold metal skin of the aircraft, hurling himself into the black void.

After the noise and tension in the plane, the sudden silence was startling. His parachute blossomed perfectly and Kron was jerked upright. The noise of the plane was already disappearing. To his left, Kron could see the other jumpers. They were already turning their steerable chutes toward the flashing lights of the door bundles, clustering together in the dark sky. Kron pulled the plastic knob on the left steering line and turned his chute toward the others. In two minutes they would be in the water. Kron prayed that the Soviet Navy was there, too.

In the *Odessa*, the radio reported, "Jumpers away."

"Surface," Bondarchuk ordered. "Sail only awash. Deck party, report."

The orders said remain submerged, but he was damned if he was going to make those men find him underwater in the dark.

"Sail awash, Comrade Captain!" The three-man deck party was standing by the ladder.

"Open the hatch," Bondarchuk said. "Helm, keep your depth steady."

"It is done, Comrade Captain!"

A splash of water and a blast of cool air rushed in as the hatch opened. Bondarchuk was first up the ladder into the small open bridge.

19

"Sir, you're not going to believe this!" Fletcher said, stepping back from the periscope so Hawkins could step up to the eyepiece. "Do we have tape rolling?"

Hawkins focused the night-vision periscope. "What the hell . . ." he whispered as he focused on the image of parachutes in the night sky. He glanced over at Fletcher, then went back to the scope.

"Seventeen, eighteen at least. Now what do you suspect eighteen Soviet parachutists are doing out here in the middle of the night?"

"Beats the hell out of me," Fletcher shrugged. The figures were splashing down in the water now. In only a few seconds, all the men were in the water. The dark shape of the submarine's long sail was just visible above the water.

"Well, I've been to a picnic, a rodeo, and a world's fair and this is the damnedest thing I've ever seen," Hawkins said, his face pressed to the scope. "I've seen Ivan run some strange training exercises before, but this is in a class by itself." As Hawkins watched, the long sail slipped below the surface.

"Bridge, Sonar. Contact moving at high speed, coming to course 180."

"I guess we need to send this one, Walt," Hawkins said as he flipped up the periscope handles. "Write it up and encrypt it. We'll let the spooky boys figure out what it means."

Drachev saluted, slinging a stream of seawater against the wall. "Comrade Captain, I am Major Alexia Drachev. I have orders for you."

"Welcome aboard, Major," Bondarchuk replied, returning the salute and shaking Drachev's wet hand. Drachev reached inside his wetsuit and removed the sealed black plastic envelope. He handed it to the captain, who turned to a lieutenant, probably the political officer, and handed him the envelope. "Decode these." The lieutenant disappeared. "Major, get yourself some dry clothes and report to my quarters as soon as is convenient."

"Just so, Comrade Captain." Drachev saluted again as the captain walked off.

Half an hour later Drachev knocked on the captain's door and stepped in.

"Please, sit down, Major," Bondarchuk said, "would you like some tea?"

"Do you have any coffee?" Drachev asked. Bondarchuk waved to the cook, who nodded and disappeared. "Congratulations on your operation tonight," Bondarchuk began, "I will admit I was concerned about recovering all of you."

"As was I, Captain," Drachev admitted. The cook returned with a small pot of coffee and a cup. The coffee smell filled the small cabin as Drachev poured a cup. He took a sip. The hot brew pushed the cold out of his chilled body. "This is excellent coffee, Captain. Where is it from?"

"Mocha from Yemen," Bondarchuk replied.

He pressed the button on his interphone. "Executive officer and Lt. Dubovik to the captain's quarters." They were joined in a minute by the Yuri Koslov and Lt. Dubovik, the political officer.

"You have the orders decoded, Lieutenant?"

"Just so, Comrade Captain," the political officer snapped. He handed the captain a large envelope marked SECRET.

"Attention to orders," the captain said as he opened the envelope. He read the orders aloud. " '*Odessa* is to convey Major Drachev to the destination indicated. Once there, it will support his operation in obtaining data and material from the facility known as DeepCore. If necessary, *Odessa* will neutralize any hostile targets.' " Bondarchuk's eyebrows went up. " 'Details of the operation follow.' "

Bondarchuk scanned down the page. "Well, comrades. This is a very warlike mission for a peaceful rescue vessel."

"Indeed," agreed Koslov.

"Major, are you permitted to share with us the nature of this material we are seeking?"

"Unfortunately no, Comrade Captain," Drachev answered. "That information is classified."

Bondarchuk nodded. "Well, then. Major, you and your people will want to rest. When you wish to begin briefing my crew on their part of this operation, please do so." Drachev stood, saluted, and left the room.

The three submarine officers stared at each other for a moment. *"Yob tvoyov mats!"* Lt. Dubovik swore. The captain laughed. "Indeed, Lieutenant, fuck all our mothers!"

"My, don't we look perky this morning!" Ramos crooned as Carla climbed into the front seat of the van. She smiled at him and stretched. "Eat your heart out, Larry!"

"I don't think that's what he wants to eat out, Carla," Bickerstaff called from the rear of the van.

Carla gaily shot them all the finger. "You are all disgusting slimeballs," she said as she reclined the bucket seat and slept all the way to the airport.

"What do you think, Sgt. Kron?" Drachev asked, "Will they be ready by the time we reach DeepCore?"

Kron nodded. "Oh, yes. They are ready now, Comrade Major."

After five hours sleep, the men were running minisub drills with the *Odessa's* crew, practicing everything but actual separation from the mother sub. Drachev and Kron had gone to the submarine's small galley to give the raiders more room to work with their gear.

"This is my first experience with one of these submarines," Drachev said casually. "I suppose you have spent a great deal of time in them."

Kron grunted. "A great deal of time, Comrade Major. Too much time."

Drachev arched his eyebrows. Kron was usually not so glib.

Kron saw his look and continued. "These rescue boats are not spacious. Spending days or weeks in one submerged is no holiday."

Drachev nodded in agreement. Compared to the *Odessa*, even the mock-up of DeepCore seemed huge. It seemed that there was no room to do anything. Kron was still talking.

"After a week, the walls seem to close in," he said, looking uncomfortable. "After two weeks, no mission is too dangerous if it allows one to get off the submarine. After three weeks, it feels like a metal coffin."

"Thankfully, we will not be on this vessel that long," Drachev said. "We should be in place in three days."

20

The plane touched down like a feather. For some reason, it always surprised Moore that a big plane like a 747 could land so easily. The flight attendant's soft voice welcomed them to Guam.

In the baggage claim area, a short heavy-set man in bermuda shorts and a knit shirt held a sign that read DeepCore.

"You Mr. Moore?" the man asked as Moore and the others walked up. "I'm Howard Beecher from the UnderSea office here. I have a van waiting."

As they loaded the van with their gear, Beecher gave them their itinerary. "You'll be flying out tomorrow morning on the tiltrotor. Your heavy stuff has already been shipped out. It'll be waiting for you in the compression module on DeepCore."

Beecher ferried them to their hotel and dropped them off out front. "Listen, there isn't too much to do on Guam," he said as they filed out of the van. "But if you want a guide, just holler. Here's my number." He handed Carla his card.

"Thanks," Moore replied. "But I think we'll just bag it tonight." He didn't mention that they had partied hard on Maui the night before. The flight across the Pacific had been long and tomorrow would be a busy day. Tonight they would sleep.

"Ever flown in one of these before?" the copilot asked.

Moore shook his head. "First time!"

The copilot smiled. "They're different. I think you'll like it!"

The V-22 tiltrotor had taken off normally. The twin turbo-props with their huge propellors had whisked them easily into the sky. The landing would be a lot different. The plane would tilt its engines up and land on the support ship like a helicopter. The V-22 was perfect for this job. In rough weather, it could hover over the support ship and drop supplies onto the pitching deck like a helicopter. It could whisk twenty passengers to and from Guam like a passenger plane.

His crew was still sleepy. They all woke up when the plane slowed and the rotors turned skyward. Below the Pacific, DeepCore's support ship gleamed white against the glassy blue ocean.

The V-22 slowed to a crawl above the big cross that marked the landing platform. The sea was calm, so there was no trouble setting the plane down. The moment its wheels touched, two crewmen from the support ship ran out and hooked tie-down straps to the fuselage, then waited until the rear ramp came down to come in and pick up the baggage. Moore and his people followed the men down the ladder into the ship.

"I'm Lars Schroeder," the man introduced himself as they stepped into the ship's galley. "That other fellow is Juan." Juan set the bags down and waved. Schroeder walked to the far wall and switched on the video monitor above a small intercom console. Next to the monitor, a small video camera stared out.

On the monitor screen, Dr. Travis greeted them. "Hello, Mr. Moore. I'm happy to see you," Travis began. "I have a friend of yours here with me." Travis disappeared and Tom Jackson's face appeared on the screen.

"Hi, boss!" Jackson said, "Good to see ya!"

"Hi, yourself," Moore answered. "How's it going?"

"No prob so far," Jackson replied. "All the gear's here in the cargo dock. See you soon."

Travis's face appeared again. "*Faith* will be up to get you soon. We'll come see you when you're down."

"Roger that," Moore answered. The screen went dark.

"Faith'll be up soon?" King asked. "Who's Faith?"

The crewman grinned. "Our three subs are named *Faith, Hope*, and *Charity*," he explained. "They're really just big ROVs, remote-operated vehicles. We can bring one up from DeepCore or they can bring it down from here. 'Course, you can drive 'em yourself, too."

"Dumb names for subs," Bickerstaff grumbled.

"Beats Larry, Curly, and Moe," Schroeder replied. "Come on, we'll take you on down to the sub tub. You'll be stuck in *Faith* for eight hours getting pressurized."

"Eight hours?" Ramos moaned.

"Yep," Schroeder answered. "Takes that long to build up the pressure without getting any HPNS. It'll take you two weeks to decompress when you leave."

"Why isn't the Navy here instead of us?" Ramos asked as they settled into the small sub to wait out the compression phase before the trip down to DeepCore.

"Low profile," Moore answered. "Navy types start hanging around, everybody gets curious. Besides, nothing's happened to the Navy's stuff yet."

"That ain't the real reason and you know it," Bickerstaff interrupted. "That asshole LeFlore is the only reason we're here."

"He loves us!" King declared.

Lars Schroeder's voice came over the speaker. "Starting compression now. Watch your ears."

Faith's passengers all pinched their noses and blew, popping their ears to equalize the pressure. The pressure gauge slowly crept up as the hours crept by. Most of the security team sacked out, waking at intervals to pop their ears. Only Ramos stayed awake, looking at the gauge and reading a cheap adventure novel.

21

"One kilometer, Comrade Captain."

Bondarchuk thumbed the interphone switch. "One kilometer out, Major. Get ready."

Drachev's voice crackled over the speaker. "Ready."

"Five hundred meters."

"Dead slow," Drachev instructed the helmsman.

"Answering dead slow," the man replied. The *Odessa* gradually slowed as it approached the drop-off point. The drop-off was a notch in the rock wall half a kilometer from DeepCore. It would allow the minisubs to disengage from the *Odessa* and start their attack undetected. It also gave the *Odessa* an excellent firing position for the support ship tethered above.

"One hundred meters."

"Stand by, Major," Bondarchuk told Drachev. "Weapons control, ready tubes one and two."

"On site, Captain."

"Cameras on," Bondarchuk said. Overhead, the color monitors flickered to life. The executive officer thumbed the joystick, pointing the forward camera toward DeepCore. Someone whistled as the brightly lit underwater structure came into focus.

Koslov ran the lens to maximum telephoto and scanned it slowly across DeepCore. At one end, the dark shape of an American attack submarine was clearly visible. Involuntary groans escaped from several sailors in the control room.

"Major Drachev!" Bondarchuk called on the interphone. "Execute! Execute!" The aft camera showed the shadowy forms of the two minisubs lift out of their storage wells. One shape disappeared off to starboard, the other to port.

"Submersibles away," Koslov observed.

Bondarchuk turned to the seaman at the small weapons control panel. "Ready torpedoes for firing," he ordered. "Open outer doors." He turned back to the helmsman. "Twenty degrees up angle on the bow."

"Twenty degrees up angle," the helmsman answered. He pulled back on the aircraft-style yoke. The *Odessa*'s nose began to climb. Bondarchuk and the rest of the crew held on to whatever they could to keep their balance. "Twenty degrees up, Comrade Captain," the helmsman confirmed.

Koslov was twisting the forward camera's joystick, bringing the target back onto the screen. He ran the telephoto lens out to find the minisubs. They were halfway to the target, hugging the bottom.

"Weapons," the captain called. "Arm torpedoes."

The weapons operator flipped his switches and a second later a soft tone sounded from his board. "Torpedoes armed, target acquired."

One minisub was almost to the parked American submarine. The seconds passed like hours as the minisub, dwarfed by its target, moved into position. A bright blue-green light signaled that it was placing its charges on the American's hull.

The second sub was nearing the emergency airlock atop one of the structure's rounded modules. When the bright light shined from it, Bondarchuk turned to the weapons operator. "Fire one!" The operator pressed the red switch on his console. A tremor shook the *Odessa*. "One away, homing."

"Fire two and reload both tubes!" Another shudder ran through the sub. "Two away, homing. Reloading tubes one and two."

The *Odessa* only carried two torpedo tubes. Since it was supposed to be a rescue ship, it claimed to be unarmed, but no Soviet warship had ever been constructed without weapons of some sort.

Odessa's torpedoes were small 400mm antisubmarine torpedoes. They lacked the range and power of the 533mm standard torpedoes, but they were more than adequate for this job. *Odessa* carried six of them.

"Torpedoes one and two running normal, homing on target," the weapons operator informed the captain. "Forty-five seconds to impact."

In less than a minute, we'll be in this, win or lose, Bondarchuk thought, it had better be win.

"How much longer?" Ramos whined. The isolation was beginning to tell on him. They had been in *Faith* for six and a half hours now, acclimating to the pressure before making the descent to DeepCore.

"What difference does it make, Ramos," King asked, "we're here for the duration. Besides, the rest of the place isn't going to be much bigger than this." That idea had obviously not occurred to Ramos. He suddenly looked even more nervous.

"Here, Larry, take these," Carla said, offering him two small capsules, "they'll help you relax."

"What are they?" Ramos asked nervously.

"Benadryl," she replied.

"Oughtta be Midol," Bickerstaff drawled, "or Thorazine."

"Everybody relax," Moore said, sitting up and stretching. "We're almost ready here. Then we can go back to work."

"I'm ready," Bickerstaff observed. The small submersible was a bit cramped for five, especially for both genders. They had brought books to read and talking with the others actually helped pass the time. At least it had until Ramos had gotten nervous.

"Say, boss, do people bring their families with them here?" King asked. "I mean, are there kids here, too?"

"I don't think so, Ty," Moore replied, "husband and wife teams, but no kids."

"At least you got lucky there, boss," Bickerstaff commented. "All of us are single."

"Yeah, single again," Carla laughed. "That's what we can do, we can talk about our divorces!"

"Oh, please," Ramos moaned.

"Sorry, Larry," she crooned, "I forgot that you're a virgin."

Ramos said nothing and stood staring out the round porthole on the floor of the sub.

"Now, Carla," Bickerstaff chided, "Larry could've married anyone he pleased!"

"Yeah," King finished the joke, "he just didn't please anyone!"

"Lighten up, guys," Moore said hopefully.

"Elgin, what happened to your marriage?" Carla asked, determined to pursue their marital histories.

"Well, I don't really know for sure," the big man answered, slowly cleaning one fingernail with another. "Veronica was a great one for drama. Nothing just happened, you know, it had to be an event. You couldn't just come home and put your feet up, you had to burst through the door, sweep her off her feet, and put your tongue down her throat. If you didn't, she thought you didn't care about her anymore." He looked up at the others. "It was like living on a roller coaster." He smiled and looked away. "She sure was a pistol in bed, though."

"Did you leave her?" Carla asked.

"Nope, she left me after a year," he answered. "Said we didn't have anything in common."

"Isn't she the one who fed you creamed chipped beef on Pop Tarts?" Moore asked.

"Uh-huh."

"Bleackk!" Ramos observed from the porthole.

"How 'bout you, Carla?" King asked. "What was your hubby like?"

"He was just your ordinary brain-dead party pig . . ." she began.

"Hey, hey, guys!" Ramos interrupted. "Look at this! Something's happening!"

The others crowded around the porthole. Outside, two thin bubble trails streaked toward the surface.

Two massive booms thundered from above. The entire ship seemed to rise out of the water, pulling the tiny sub with it.

"Holy Mother of God!" Moore shouted. He lunged for the D-shaped disconnect handle that held the sub to the crane hook. The others were tossed around like dolls.

"Hang on!" Moore screamed.

"To what?" Ramos yelled.

Moore pulled the handle with all his might. *Faith* broke loose and fell away from the stricken ship. The alarm and light stopped when the umbilical broke away.

Moore scrambled forward into the tiny cockpit, flipping the banks of switches that lined both sides. He grabbed the twin joysticks and slammed them forward. The electric motors whined to life, pushing the small sub forward and down. As the sub picked up speed, he jerked the controls to the left, slewing the craft to the side. Behind them, the support ship was breaking up. As they sped out from under the big twin-hulled ship, it rolled over. An antenna whipped the water twenty yards away, leaving a welter of bubbles. The tiny sub rocked wildly in the turbulence.

"What the hell is goin' on?" Bickerstaff yelled.

"I think our ship just got torpedoed!" Moore shouted.

22

Clyde Terrell licked his lips. He was just getting to the juicy part of the thin sci-fi paperback, the part where the American agent seduced the wily KGB operative and stole the plans to the Russian secret mission to arm their moon colony. The weightless sex scene got four stars from the Houston's official sex book reviewer, Alex Robinson. Robinson knew every trash paperback and stroke book by heart. He was the ultimate authority on the printed fuck.

This book, *Shuttle Puppy,* was a crew favorite. Half the pages had come loose and the book was held together with a rubber band, but even that did not diminish its prurient appeal. In this passage the wily American CIA agent had the tough Russian up against the weightless toilet.

"I need some proof of your capabilities," Anita whispered as she ran her hands down his smooth chest.

"Perhaps you would like to check my credentials?" Stovic answered huskily, unzipping his coveralls down to his bulging crotch.

She was quick to grasp the concept.

The loud clang that rang through the hull next to Terrell's bunk scared him so badly that he rolled out of the bunk and was standing on the deck before he really realized what had happened.

"Mother of screaming God!" he yelled as Dalton, another torpedoman, looked around the end of the bunks.

"What was that?" Dalton yelled, his voice drowned out by a loud metallic scraping from outside the pressure hull.

"I don't know, but I thought it was coming in here after me!" Terrell answered. The scraping started up again, quieter this time. A pair of solid clanks followed.

"I don't know what they're doin' out there," Terrell called over his shoulder as he stepped across the narrow aisle to the intercom box on the bulkhead, "but they're gonna tear the skin!"

He thumbed the talk button. "Bridge, this is the torpedo room. Some silly bastard is bashing the hull!"

"Roger, Torpedo," Leon Mulkey's voice came back over the intercom. "We hear it. Checking on it now."

"They're gonna rip the skin off us if they're not careful," Terrell added.

"Roger, we'll tell them."

"Fucking stupid civilians!" Terrell muttered as he located the paperback and climbed back into his bunk. Some of the pages had fallen out and Terrell took a minute to replace them. This done, he turned back to the sex scene and began to read.

The possibilities were endless. She spun herself upside down into 69 position, her head over his throbbing love engine. He grasped her long legs and . . .

Terrell did not even hear the sound of the explosion. The two shaped charge blasts cut through the hull like an acetylene torch. One of the white-hot plasma jets burned straight through Terrell's head, searing it off his body. The flashes of fire were followed instantly by high-speed jets of water that shot across the bunk.

It took Dalton a second to realize what was happening. The blast had stunned him, the noise stabbing his ears like twin icepicks. The spray of ice-cold water snapped him out of his paralysis. He spun up off the bench and wheeled around into the open space that led to the watertight door at the end of the torpedo room. The twin torrents of water filled the air in the room with streams of salt water that caromed off the stored torpedoes and splattered against the bulkhead. Dalton was nearly to the door when the force of the water jets rolled a Mark 48 torpedo off its rack onto him.

The thirty-four-hundred-pound torpedo slammed down onto his right calf and ankle, smashing them and pitching him against the other Mark 48s stored on the starboard side. The torpedo hit the deck and bounced as Dalton fell. It came to rest on his left foot, pinning it to the deck and wrenching his ankle.

Dalton hurt too much to scream, besides, there wasn't anyone to hear it. The door was only four feet away. If he could get through it, he would be safe. He clawed at the torpedo rack, trying to pull himself along the deck. The water was already a foot deep and rising quickly. Dalton pulled hard, the pain from his trapped right foot shooting up through his leg like a hot steel wire. His foot was caught in the torpedo's shrouded prop.

Dalton grabbed with both hands on the rack and pulled with all his might. The pain was awful, but the torpedo moved, helped along a bit by the flood of seawater. He gathered his strength again and heaved.

This time, his foot slid free of the propellor shroud and he lunged through the water toward the door. The numbing cold of the rising seawater was working with his own rising panic to blot out the pain in his shattered feet. He pulled himself to the edge of the torpedo rack and threw himself toward the door.

Water was already washing over the threshold into the companionway beyond. Dalton missed the door and had to thrash his way over to it. The water was well up over the edge of the door now. Someone was shouting, but Dalton ignored them. When he got through the door, he would worry about answering.

The cold was sapping his strength, making his muscles slow to respond. He could not feel his legs at all now. They didn't hurt, they felt as if they weren't even there.

Dalton was halfway through the door when the sub shifted. The weight of the water pouring in through the blast holes had shifted its balance. The shift slammed Dalton against the edge of the pressure door opening, stunning him. He reached up to pull himself farther through the door as the water surged up over him, filling his mouth and nose. He flailed and struggled to get a handhold as he felt the cold water take him. He could hear screaming from the crew quarters.

The lights went out and the last thing Dalton saw was the red glow of the emergency lights shimmering through the rushing water. Above him, the intercom squawked. The sound was drowned out by the icy flood that drowned him as well.

Water poured into the passageway toward the center of the stricken sub. A watertight pressure door slammed somewhere and high-pressure air shrieked into the blasted torpedo room, but Dalton could not hear any of it.

The minisub settled over the orange and white hatch.

"Stand by!" Drachev yelled. The tiny sub was filled with the smell of adrenaline-charged sweat. Drachev had that familiar metallic taste in his mouth, the taste of battle. He felt like he was vibrating. From far away, a dull boom rang through the sub, followed by the clang of the locking ring.

"Now!"

Valerian heaved on the sub's hatch. It swung up easily. Beneath it was the orange and white airlock hatch. Valerian spun the locking wheel and the hatch dropped open. Drachev's raiders spilled through the hatch, rolled to their feet, and bounded off on their assigned paths. Before he even got through the hatch, Drachev heard the muffled report of a MP-5. The killing had started.

"What the hell do you mean they're not yours?" Hamilton yelled. "Whose the hell are they then? What?" Hamilton slammed down the phone and slapped the intercom with his hand. "General quarters! General quarters! Secure all watertight doors! I repeat, secure all doors!" Two sharp explosions echoed through the *Houston*'s cylindrical body, shaking it. Hamilton held down the intercom button again. "Damage Control, report! What have we got, Chief?" Hamilton shouted. Phil Howser, chief of the boat, the senior enlisted man aboard, came back on the speaker.

"Holes, sir!" Howser answered. "We got holes in both ends! Somebody blew our shit away! Weapons and engineering don't even answer."

"Keep pumping air into those spaces. Evacuate everybody but damage control."

"Aye, sir."

"Chief," Hamilton asked, afraid of the answer, "how many casualties?"

"Five confirmed dead, sir, about twenty-five injured," Howser reported. "We don't know for sure about the crew quarters and weapons control."

At least we're tied to the dock, Hamilton reassured himself, we can't sink. We can just fill up with water, and then maybe drag the whole dock down with us. I guess we can sink after all, he realized.

The floats that held the sub up into the dock were primarily designed to keep the sub in position in the watertight dock. The sub's own ballast tanks kept it afloat.

Hamilton turned as O'Brien, an auxiliaryman, clambered down the ladder.

"Sir, all hell's breaking loose up there!"

"What?"

"Well, I heard someone say that there was a break-in on one of the escape hatches over by the sub pool. Then somebody else heard shots."

"Shots? Like gunfire?"

"Yes, sir. Gunshots."

"Secure that hatch," Hamilton held the button down. "Reactor Room, report."

"Reactor, Robinson here," the speaker crackled. "No damage. Doors to engineering are closed, repeat closed."

"Hang in there, Robinson, good work. Be ready to shut down if we have to, but, for now, maintain power on the reactor. We'll need the power to pump us out."

"Aye, sir."

If we can pump us out, Hamilton thought. The sub shifted again. Hamilton grabbed at the plot desk to keep his balance.

"Cox, what's our angle?"

"Six degrees down, sir," the seaman answered, his voice trembling with fear and excitement.

"What are we goin' to do?" King yelled.

"I don't know, Ty," Moore yelled back. "The ship's gone. Our only home now is DeepCore. Have we got any weapons with us?"

"Nothing!" King answered.

"No," Bickerstaff corrected King, "we got one arrow gun, the one we didn't get packed. I brought it as baggage!"

"Get it assembled!" Moore yelled as the lights of DeepCore shone up through the gloom. "I got ta feeling we're gonna need it! Anything else?"

"Pocketknife," Ramos answered.

"Me, too," Bickerstaff chimed in.

Carla was frantically digging through the jumble of luggage at the far end of the little sub. "I've got this!" she cried as she found her duffel bag and plunged her hand down in it. She pulled out a small automatic pistol. "It's a 9mm." She handed the gun to King and dug back into her bag, pulling out a nylon shoulder holster that held two magazines of ammunition. "Here, there's twenty-four rounds all together."

The sub suddenly slewed to one side, slamming Carla against the metal wall. A thick, snakelike form writhed across the front of the sub.

"Shit!" Moore barked, jerking the controls back toward him, reversing the sub's thrusters. The sub pitched nose down as the heavy umbilical line to DeepCore slid off them and twisted toward the bottom, still tied to the sinking support ship.

"Oh, man!" Ramos gasped. "Oh, man!"

"Get a grip, Larry," Bickerstaff urged. "This shit's just getting started."

"Any sign of the folks who shot us?" King asked, crowding up behind Moore to peer out the front bubble.

"Not yet," Moore answered. "Haven't had a chance to look, really." He shot a nervous grin over his shoulder at King. King scrambled back to the big round hatch in the floor of the sub. He peered down through the small vision port in the hatch, looking for anything.

"Got something!" he called.

"What?" Moore called.

"Off to port," King called, "straight down."

"Hang on!" Moore called, standing the little sub on its nose. Below them, dozens of lights twinkled like a distant galaxy.

"That's it, folks," Moore cried, "DeepCore." He jammed the joysticks forward. *Faith*'s motors whined as she headed for home.

"*UnderSea Pacific*, do you read, over?" Jack Travis turned up the volume on the phone line until the static rasped. He keyed the mike again. "*UnderSea Pacific*, this is DeepCore, over." The static snarl was the only answer.

"What the hell's going on?" he asked.

Malcom, on the hydrophones, suddenly shouted, "Oh, Christ!" He looked up, his eyes wide as saucers. "It's breaking up!"

"Put it on speaker!" Travis snapped. Malcom flipped the speaker switch and a loud snapping, gurgling sound filled the room. The muffled sound of metal groaning, tearing, and breaking was accompanied by a hissing, bubbling noise.

"She's sinking!" Malcom blurted as the death rattle of the *UnderSea Pacific* rasped from the speaker.

"Dr. Travis," Poppy Pearson, DeepCore's sonar operator, interrupted, "there's something on sonar. Two somethings."

Travis tore himself away from the speaker and stared at the circular sonar screen. Two tiny blips were hovering near DeepCore, one moving away from the sub dock, heading for the emergency escape module where the other was docking.

"Have we got an external camera there?" Travis asked. Poppy rolled her chair over to the next console and flipped a switch. One of the six small monitors above them flipped to a view of the airlock hatch. A small cigar-shaped sub was setting down on the airlock. Red and orange vertical stripes on the sub's white sides gave the little intruder a festive look.

"What the hell?" Travis said. "Malcom, sound the collision alarm!" He turned and thumbed the intercom to all decks. "Attention in DeepCore, close all watertight doors and lock them! We are being boarded! Repeat, we are being boarded! This is no drill!"

The little sub was parked on DeepCore. Travis picked up the phone and dialed Jackson's extension.

"Jackson here, what's going on?" Tom answered.

"Someone's parked on the escape module!" Travis yelled, his voice trembling. "I don't know who they are!"

Jackson glanced at the camera sheet and punched up the camera in the escape module. As the screen flickered to life, a man in dark coveralls dropped in front of the lens, rolled to one side, and came up on his feet clutching a tiny weapon. Jackson recognized it as a German MP-5K.

Other men were falling through the hatch now, rolling away and disappearing.

"Travis," Jackson barked into the phone, "they're Russians! Send a Mayday! Repeat, send a Mayday." There was no answer from control.

Jackson slammed the door of his small office and sat at the terminal, scanning the bank of monitors. The Russians were streaming down the corridors that led to control, the labs, and the industrial area.

Jackson pulled up the menu for DeepCore's electrical system. He shut the emergency doors ahead of the invaders to keep them out of the corridors that led to the heart of DeepCore. Five seconds later the lab doors read closed and locked. Red malfunction lights showed on the control and industrial area systems. The doors there were already blocked or damaged.

"Damn!" Jackson muttered as he struggled to put together a plan. He brought up the main menu for the computer and asked for the access menu. The computer asked for his password again. He keyed it in. The access menu appeared. Jackson took a deep breath and locked out all access not preceded by his own password.

24

Corporal Anatoly Ghiurov was first through the escape hatch
with Plaski and Bukavich on his heels. The ladder leading
down from the hatch ended in a large, circular decompression chamber. The chamber was actually a small room, large
enough to accommodate two dozen people. The door at the far
end of the chamber had been left open and Ghiurov rushed
through it, his weapon at the ready.

It looked like they had invaded an undersea hydroelec-
tric project. The boarding party was jogging between what
appeared to be enormous water pipes that ran along the walls
through wide I-beam supports.

The first resistance the party encountered came at the entrance
to the generator room. One of DeepCore's crew had hidden in
the valve area near the juncture of the escape hatch and the
corridor leading to the command center.

Ghiurov rounded the corner and was blown sideways,
screaming in agony as the crewman stepped out and hosed
his body with a long burst of superheated steam. When a burst
from the MP-5Ks ripped overhead, the crewman dropped his
hose and ran out of the compartment. He was closing the compartment door as three rounds from a MP-5K pinged off it.

One of Ghiurov's uncooked comrades leaped past his body
and crammed a long steel pipe into the opening before the
hatch closed. Using the pipe as a lever, Plaski pried while
Bukavich pounded sharply on a protruding hatch pin with the
butt of his automatic. The crewman on the inside let go of the
hatch wheel, giving Plaski time to lever the door open.

As the crewman started to run toward the command center,
Plaski leaped through the open hatch and hurled the pipe with

all his might. The pipe impaled the running crewman, who dropped to the floor, writhing.

By that time, Sgt. Kron had arrived to take charge. Grabbing Bukavich by the arm, he yelled, "Remember your orders, damn it. Come on." Kron headed through the hatch to find Bukavich finishing off the hapless crewman by smashing his head with the pipe.

"Good work, Plaski, I see that you have avenged Corporal Ghiurov." Kron led the assault team to the command center and stopped for a moment outside to take stock. He could see through a window into the center and could not detect any human movement. He took his weapon and smashed the glass. He could still hear no sounds of movement inside. Kron motioned for Arbatov to come forward. He indicated the small window he had broken out.

"I am going to try to force the door. When I do, you go through here." Arbatov began clearing the remaining glass from the window with his knife blade. Kron was already fingering the door lock. Stepping back he looked over at Arbatov and shouted, "Now."

Lunging forward with his shoulder, he hit the door and burst through into the command center. It was unoccupied and he looked up to the sound of screams as Arbatov was stuck halfway through the small window, where he was being cut with a small piece of remaining glass. Kron stretched his boot up and kicked Arbatov back out of the window. "Idiot!" he shot at the embarrassed private.

Kron then turned to examine the control room. There were several consoles around him and he looked for the communications equipment. He found the intercom and turned it to broadcast.

"Attention, crew of the DeepCore," Kron said in English, "you will follow the orders I give to you. As soon as I finish transmitting, we will begin flooding all compartments except the crew quarters. All personnel will have five minutes to return to the crew quarters. Do not delay and do not resist. That is all."

Kron turned to Plaski and Bukavich who had joined him in the command center. "You will give them four minutes and then begin searching for anyone lagging behind. If you find anyone, kill them."

• • •

Drachev found the lab team wrestling with a closed emergency door. Sergeant Shelkaitis was prying off the cover of the electrical box next to the locked steel door.

"What is the problem, Sergeant?" Drachev asked.

"It shut as we were clearing the room," Shelkaitis answered, "Korotich tried to jam it with his weapon, but it was sheared in half." Drachev looked over at the nervous private, who held up the rear half of a gun.

"Can you open it?" Drachev asked as Shelkaitis strained at the electrical box. The cover bolts groaned, then broke, hurling Shelkaitis against the far wall. The little sergeant jumped to his feet and stepped back up to the junction box.

"We will soon know, Comrade Major," he answered, pulling from his pocket a one-meter length of thick braided cable tipped with two insulated alligator clips. He clipped one end onto the ground wire and touched the other clip to the row of hot terminals. There was no response, not even a spark.

"The panel is dead, Comrade Major," Shelkaitis said, turning to Drachev. "Someone has cut the power to the door controls."

"Keep trying to get it open manually," Drachev ordered. "Use explosives, if necessary."

Each team had four linear-shaped charges designed to cut a half-meter slice through steel up to four centimeters thick. The charges were the last resort in breaching obstacles. Drachev did not like the idea of using explosives in a pressurized environment. The sudden spike in pressure could cause the structure to fail, killing everyone.

Kulakov, the section's strong man, stepped up and jammed his pry bar into the door's recessed jamb. He put all his weight on it and the door seemed to move a centimeter. When he relaxed, it snapped shut again.

"Keep trying," Drachev said as he stepped away and took out the schematic plan he carried in his leg pocket.

This delay is irritating, Drachev thought as he searched the plan for another route into the lab complex, we are wasting time.

"Shelkaitis," Drachev called, waving the sergeant over, "take Korotich and try to get into the lab from here." Drachev pointed to a connecting door that appeared to enter the lab complex from another direction. "If you gain access to the lab, send Korotich to open the door while you secure the items we require."

"It is done, Comrade Major," Shelkaitis answered, eager to be out from under the major's scrutiny. With Korotich in tow, he disappeared back down the corridor.

25

At least I saved the lab for a while, Jackson thought as he watched the frustrated Russians on his monitor. The Russians were in such a hurry, they hadn't yet noticed the small CCD cameras that watched DeepCore's corridors and work areas. As he watched, two of the Russians spoke to a third man, then ran back down the corridor. Jackson studied the man's face, wishing for a zoom lens on the tiny camera.

Must be one of the wheels, Jackson thought. He switched the next monitor to follow the split-off pair. They were searching for the back door to the lab, looking for a narrow service corridor that housed water and heating pipes. Jackson called up a display of the passage on his computer.

It ran to the lab through a series of small watertight rooms. The display showed the contents of each room. One had an air hatch, designed to accommodate the addition of another module to the structure. Through the room, additional fixtures could be connected from outside into the service compartment. There was no camera in the service passage, but a line of tiny green pixels showed the doors along the corridor to be shut. As he watched, one of the pixels turned red. The Russians were in the passage. One by one, the dots turned red as the two Russians made their way toward the lab. When they neared the airlock room, Jackson called up the emergency control panel, closed the watertight door on the far side of the airlock room, and waited for one more dot to turn red.

"Are we close?" Korotich asked as they pulled open yet another narrow service door.

"We should be very close, now," Shelkaitis answered, following Korotich through the door into the next tiny room. Korotich tried the handle on the far door. "It seems to be locked," he called to Shelkaitis.

"Try it again," Shelkaitis answered, "I cannot see in this light." He stepped back through the door and held his schematic up under the dim service light. The hiss of a hydraulic cylinder caught his attention. The door was nearly shut. Shelkaitis jumped to hold it open, but it closed and locked. A deep ringing thump sounded beyond the door, followed by Korotich's cry of surprise.

Shelkaitis wiped the round view window and peered through. Korotich was holding his head with both hands, his face knotted up in pain. He fell to the floor, disappearing from view. Shelkaitis stepped upon the door's locking lug to see down into the room. Korotich was lying on the floor, curled up in a ball, twitching. A thin mist swirled around him. Shelkaitis twisted the door handle. It swung down, but he was not able to pull the door open. Shelkaitis strained against the handle, then stopped when he realized that the door was locked by the pressure in his room. Korotich was suffering from a sudden decompression in the room. The gases dissolved in his blood were bubbling out of solution now, causing excruciating pain.

If he broke the seal somehow, he would suffer the same fate as Korotich. Shelkaitis peered back into the room. Korotich was writhing from side to side from the pain in his joints. Moving as quickly as he could through the dim passage, Shelkaitis retreated to the safety of the main corridor.

One down, Jackson thought, as he watched the single Soviet soldier emerge from the service passage and run off down the corridor. Now at least he had a weapon, DeepCore itself. He put the camera system back on scan to find out where the Russians were. It wouldn't take them forever to find the cameras, he wanted to get in a few licks before then.

The crew back in the lab corridor was still fighting the locked pressure door. Jackson looked for some dirty trick to play on them, but there was nothing on the board.

Wait, there is something, he thought, remembering his guided tour. The memory of that tour made him think of Nancy Collins. He punched up the engineering camera. There was no one in sight. He was reaching for the switch when he saw the slight movement. Inside the engineering office, a figure moved. It wasn't possible to tell much about the person from the silhouette on the wall.

Probably a Russian left to guard the place, Jackson thought, no sign of Nancy.

One of the scanning monitors flipped by the entrance to the crew quarters. There were no cameras inside. The crew refused to have any camera monitoring the comings and goings from their rooms.

At the entrance, Jackson could see a group of DeepCore crew, about half a dozen, being herded inside by three Soviets with guns. He pulled down the schematics for the crew quarters and looked for options to help the folks trapped there.

"Boarders?" Knickerbocker yelled over the clanging of the collision bell. "Did he say boarders?"

"That's what he said!" Alan Darcey, the *Houston*'s nuclear officer, answered.

"Holy shit!" Knickerbocker yelled, hooking his thumb over his shoulder. "Come on, we gotta get back!" They made their way back through the maze of steam pipes that ran the generators on DeepCore. Knickerbocker and Darcey had been down in engineering to look at DeepCore's reactor controls. The DeepCore reactor had been built for installation on the scrapped Sea Wolf attack subs. When the Congress had canceled that program, UnderSea bought the reactor for ten cents on the dollar.

Installed in a separate module half a kilometer away from the main complex, the reactor was controlled by robots manipulated from the engineering complex. The two Navy officers had been swapping reactor lore with the DeepCore engineers when the alarm had gone off.

As they neared the engineering office, popping noises erupted up ahead. Darcey jerked his captain between two huge pipes, hiding them as a pair of dark-clad men with guns ran past.

Although Knickerbocker was eager to get back to the *Houston*, Darcey held him, waiting for the intruders to finish their sweep. The two men finally returned, pushing four DeepCore engineers ahead of them. There had been six men in DeepCore's reactor control room. The invaders had obviously killed two. Darcey signaled for them to go back to the reactor control room and Knickerbocker nodded. The two men made their way back through the maze.

There was no sign of anyone in the reactor control room. Darcey and Knickerbocker slipped through the door. Inside, two of the engineers, Wallace and Simpson, lay shot. Wallace was dead, a hole in his forehead and a mat of blood in his crew-cut hair. Simpson was sitting up against the central console, shot through the chest. He was awake but losing blood.

"What happened?" Knickerbocker hissed. "Who are they?"

"I don't know"—Simpson coughed—"they had accents." Darcey was looking at Simpson's wounds. He turned to Knickerbocker and shook his head slightly. Simpson was dying.

"Reactor?" Darcey asked the wounded man.

"On automatic," Simpson answered. "It'll run by itself for eight hours."

"Come on, Darcey," Knickerbocker snapped, "let's get back up there and see what these mothers are up to now."

26

"There's two of 'em!" Moore shouted as the second submersible swam up in front of *Faith*. "Hang on!"

Moore jerked up on the joystick, pulling up the nose of the sub as he cut the power. *Faith* continued down under its own inertia, the intruder disappearing underneath it.

Faith slammed into the intruder with a loud clang and a kidney-busting jolt. The impact threw King onto the floor and all the baggage landed on him. A chorus of screams and cries erupted from the back.

Moore jerked his head around, looking for damage. "You okay back there?" he yelled. "What've we got?"

"Water coming in around a gauge," Bickerstaff answered, wrapping his jacket around the leak. "Nothing besides that."

"Whew!" Moore sighed. He applied power again, half expecting the controls to be dead. *Faith* came back to life and sped off. Moore ran for a hundred meters, then spun *Faith* around to look back at DeepCore.

The intruder submersible was slowly sinking, a stream of bubbles rising from the flattened hatch cover on top.

"Aw right!" Ramos cheered. "You got him, boss!"

Moore didn't answer. He was searching for another spot on DeepCore to set their sub down. The wild ride had disoriented him.

"Where the hell's the decompression module?" Moore asked. Carla moved forward and stuck her head over Moore's shoulder.

She pointed down and to the left. "There."

"Thanks, babe," Moore answered, slewing *Faith* around and streaking for the outlying module. Three minutes later *Faith* settled over the docking hatch. Moore eased the sub down over the hatch, with Bickerstaff guiding him.

"Easy down," Bickerstaff said. "Easy. Now!"

Moore cut the power and let Faith settle onto the hatch. The little sub suddenly tipped to the side and slid away from the hatch.

"Shit," Moore snapped, revving the engines and pulling away from the hatch, "what happened?"

Bickerstaff leaned close. "Guess we damaged the skirt when you clobbered that little sub."

"Great!" Moore groaned, slumping back in his seat. "Now what?" He turned around to the rest of his crew in the back. Carla was sitting by King, holding a cloth over his forehead. "What's the matter with him?"

"Hit his head on the seat," Carla answered. "Cut's not bad, but it rung his bell pretty good."

"I'm okay," King said, reaching up for the rag.

"So, anybody got a suggestion?" Moore asked.

"If we can't dock on a hatch, how're we going to get out of here?" Ramos asked. "There's no ship up there to go back to."

"Sub pool," Carla said, "that's how the work parties go out from DeepCore. They just surface in the sub pool."

"I imagine that there are some unpleasant visitors in the sub pool right now," Bickerstaff warned.

"Maybe," Moore agreed, "but I don't really know how else to get in there."

"We're pressured up, boss," Bickerstaff said. "We could send in a scout to check out the sub pool."

"That water is like ice," Ramos reminded Bickerstaff, "plus, we got no gear, remember?"

Bickerstaff gave Ramos his best condescending smile. "You got me, scuba breath. What else do you need?"

"Yeah, right," Ramos snorted.

"What you got in mind, big guy?" Moore asked.

"How about I slip out of here and come up under the sub pool for a little recon?" Bickerstaff offered.

"Pretty risky," Moore answered. "Anybody else got a suggestion?"

The others shook their heads. Moore turned to Bickerstaff. "Looks like you're on."

Bickerstaff nodded and began to dig through the pile of baggage for the arrow-gun case.

• • •

"Herk, what the hell's goin' on here?" Bobby Talent yelled, following Brittan into the connecting corridor. "What did he mean boarded?"

Brittan reached the corridor just in time to see the emergency doors shutting. At the far end of the corridor, a group of men were running toward the closing door. One of them shoved something through the door, trying to keep it open. The hydraulically powered door snapped the doorstop in half and slammed shut. Brittan ran up to the small window as the near side door closed.

He peered through the small window. "Somebody just tried to get through the other corridor door," he told Talent, who was now coming up behind him. The broken piece of whatever that had been jammed in the door was lying a few feet inside the corridor on the floor grate. It took Brittan a few seconds to recognize it as the barrel from a weapon.

"Oh, shit! Come on. Get out of here!" Brittan urged his confused colleague. He turned Talent around bodily and pushed him back into the lab module.

Once inside, Brittan shut the watertight door and spun the ring. Behind them, Janice Wellford was standing nervously in the door to the assembly room.

"Jan!" Brittan yelled over his shoulder at her. "Bring me that metal stool!" She stood rooted to the spot, unable to move at all. Brittan glanced back and stopped. He looked at her, then over to Talent. "Bobby, get me that metal stool from the next room, please."

Talent nodded and stepped past Janice. Brittan walked over and took her hands. "Come on, honey. I need you. You have to get with it."

"Herk, what's happening?" she asked. He could feel her hands trembling.

"I don't know, Jan," he answered, rubbing the backs of her hands with his thumbs, "I think we've been invaded. There are some guys trying to get through the emergency doors right now. We need to lock this door if we can." He looked up as Talent came back with the chair. "We need to lock every door in the lab," he said to both of them.

Brittan took the chair from Talent and jammed it down into the door's lock ring. He tied it in place with the bungee cord they usually used to hold the door open.

"Dr. Brittan, what is happening?" Kinji Watanabe asked as he walked up behind the others. Janice jumped a foot, gasping.

"Damn it, Kinji," she screamed, "you scared me to death!"

Her outburst scared the Japanese technician, too. Watanabe cringed and stepped back, his hands outstretched in front of him. Janice stood shaking, her hands crossed over her heaving chest.

"Looks like we're under siege, Kinji," Brittan answered. "Some guys are trying to get in through the emergency doors."

"Who could attack us so far underwater?" Watanabe asked incredulously.

"Lots of folks," Talent answered, "Russians, Arabs, Chinese." He looked hard at the little tech. "Japanese."

A strange look flickered across Watanabe's face.

"Come on, guys," Brittan interrupted, "it doesn't matter who they are, they don't mean us any good. Let's get to work locking this lab up tight."

The four scientists fled to the the rearmost area of the lab complex, closing and locking each watertight door behind them. The complex, basically a huge cylinder, had four main compartments, each with a watertight door that sealed it from the other compartments. That put at least five locked doors between them and their attackers.

Knickerbocker peeked around the base of the big cooling jacket. There was no sign of life in the engineering office, but he could not believe they hadn't left anyone to guard the place. A movement in the office startled him. He pulled his head back, then peeked around the plastic insulation again.

The guard appeared to be alone. He was looking at the readouts in the office. Knickerbocker slid back around out of sight.

"I only see one man," he whispered to Darcey. "What do you think?"

"I think we're in big trouble!" Darcey hissed. "What do you want to do?"

Knickerbocker put his head back on the cooling jacket. He thought for a minute, then looked up at the valve above them on the cooling jacket. "I've got an idea," he whispered, sliding slowly up onto his knees. "I'm going to slip around the office under the window. When I signal, open up this valve. When he comes out, I'll jump him."

Darcey glanced toward the office. "I got a better idea," he countered. "You turn the valve and I'll jump him. I'd sooner have a live captain than a dead hero."

Knickerbocker looked at the floor for a second, then back at Darcey. Much as it irritated him, the man was right. Darcey was younger and quicker, if not as strong. "Okay," Knickerbocker agreed, "but you be careful!"

"I'm the nuclear officer"—Darcey grinned—"I'm *always* careful!"

Darcey kicked off his shoes and slithered through the maze of pipes toward the office. He lay still for several long minutes while the guard stared out the window in their direction. Finally, the man turned his attention to the far console and Darcey scuttled across the thirty-foot open space to the wall panel below the office window. He pulled himself up into a crouch, hugging the wall as hard as he could, then nodded to Knickerbocker, who slipped the wrench handle over the valve hub and pulled it as hard as he could.

Steam blasted from the jacket, hissing and roaring. The startled guard burst from the door, headed toward the cooling jacket. Darcey tripped the guard and jumped on him, locking the small weapon in a death grip.

The guard was good, too. He flipped Darcey up and over him. Darcey hit hard, but held on to the weapon for dear life. The guard tried to roll away, but Darcey went with him. In a lightning move, the Russian was up on one knee: Darcey felt the gun being torn from his grip. "No!" Darcey screamed as his right hand was wrenched from the gun barrel.

The guard's head jerked back and the Russian fell on Darcey, bashing Darcey's head with his own. Darcey jerked his head off to one side and found himself face-to-face with Dallas Knickerbocker.

"Shh!" Knickerbocker hissed, bringing his forefinger up to his lips, the bloody wrench handle still in his grip. Darcey pulled himself out from under the guard as Knickerbocker stepped quietly over to the pressure door and spun the locking ring, wedging the wrench handle into the ring to jam it.

"So far, so good!" Knickerbocker said as he came back over to help Darcey drag the unconscious guard back into the office.

"What do we do with this guy?" Darcey asked when they were safely hidden in the office.

"Go find some big cable ties," Knickerbocker answered. "We'll hog-tie him." Darcey nodded and took off for the maintenance room. Knickerbocker scanned the control board. All the gauges seemed to be in the green. Darcey was back in a minute with a handful of thick black plastic cable ties and a roll of wide tape.

"Watch him," Darcey cautioned. He flipped the Russian over on his stomach and jerked both hands back behind him. He crossed the man's wrists and slipped the thick tie around them, slipping the end of the tie through the one-way catch and pulling the band tight. He used another tie to secure the man's wrists to his pistol belt, then repeated the process with his ankles. When he jerked on the man's feet, the Russian moaned.

"Thanks for reminding me," Darcey told the stunned Russian. He tore a strip of duct tape off the roll and pressed it over the man's mouth. This done, Darcey rolled the Russian over to the small desk and stuffed him up under it.

Knickerbocker stood near the console, cradling the gun as he watched Darcey manhandle the helpless Russian.

"What do we do now?" Darcey asked as he stood up.

"See what shape our ship is in!" Knickerbocker exclaimed. He picked up the phone and read the intercom directory under it. "I hope to God there's someone still there to answer!" Darcey prayed as Knickerbocker dialed the sub's intercom number.

27

Incredibly, the phone rang. "I hope to God this is the skipper," Hamilton said as he picked up the receiver. "Hamilton."

"Terry, what's your status there?" Knickerbocker blurted.

"Bad, Skipper," Hamilton replied, nodding at the chief. "We took a couple of hits fore and aft. Weapons control and crew quarters are flooded and there's water in the machinery room. I've blown everything, but the only thing holding us up is the sub dock and it's jammed."

"God Almighty!" Kinckerbocker swore. "What about the crew?"

"Don't know, sir," Hamilton went on. "We lost a bunch here when we were hit. I don't know about the ones off the ship."

"Listen, Terry," Knickerbocker interrupted, "if you have anybody to spare, break out the M16s and get them out to defend the sub itself. There're Russians here!"

"Are you kidding, sir?" Hamilton stammered. "Russians?"

"I killed one myself, Commander," Knickerbocker snapped. "Don't let them take the boat. We're on our way back."

"Aye, aye, sir. Be careful!"

"Knickerbocker out."

"Chief, get into the arms locker," Hamilton said. "Prepare to repel boarders."

"How do you do that, sir," the chief replied, "I been thirteen years in submarines and that's never been a problem."

"I know, Chief. Just do it, okay?"

As Howser went aft to get the weapons and find some defenders, the deck shifted up slightly. The air was forcing some of the water out of weapons control.

"Please, God," Hamilton prayed, "let it keep on working!"

The arms locker was aft of the sonar control center. Howser took two rifles and two combat harnesses full of loaded magazines out of the locker and slung them over his shoulder, then took a 9mm pistol for himself and stuffed two extra magazines in his pants pocket. He reached in for two grenades, thought better of it, and picked up two tear-gas grenades instead. He shut the door, leaving it unlocked, and went below in search of riflemen.

On the deck below, pandemonium reigned. The small sick-bay was flooded and injured seamen were being treated on the galley tables. Most had cuts or fractures suffered when the explosives ripped through their compartments. Those uninjured were working frantically to pump air into the flooded spaces. Howser was sickened by the blood, but relieved that so many were still alive.

"Okay, who's only hurt a little bit?" he called out. The terrified sailors looked at Howser like he was an alien, their eyes locking on the weapons slung over his shoulder. When no one replied, Howser looked through the crowd and found two volunteers.

"Davis, Monihan, come on," Howser barked, "you get to be marines for a while."

"Against what?" Monihan, one of the cooks, asked.

"Whatever gets close to your ship," Howser snapped. "Now cut the guff and get your ass in gear!" He turned and went back up to the deck above. The two scared sailors followed Howser up the steps.

Hamilton met them in the control center. "Gentlemen, I don't know what's going on for sure, but this sub's under attack and I need firepower out there."

Davis and Monihan slipped into the nylon harnesses and pulled out loaded thirty-round magazines. Davis got his rifle loaded easily, but had to help the fumbling Monihan.

"Ready?" Howser asked as he stepped up on the ladder. He cracked the outside hatch. Howser clambered up the ladder with his reluctant riflemen right behind.

As Sergei Chulaki rounded the corner, two American sailors were just coming through the watertight door that led to the submarine dock. Chulaki fired low and to the left side of the nearest American, walking the rapid burst up across the man's belly and chest. He let off the trigger for a split second as he jerked the muzzle toward the second man, who was too stunned to react. Chulaki's next burst caught the second man in the neck and face, ripping his features apart. Both Americans sprawled at his feet and Chulaki jumped over their dying bodies as he sprinted for the American submarine dock. He bounded through the watertight door and found the door controls. He pulled the control box door open, threw the switches to manual, then fired a close range burst into the box. Sparks flew and smoke trailed up from the blasted controls. He was turning back toward the objective when his vision erupted in a red flash and the lights suddenly went out.

In the corridor, Yevgeny Prischepa saw the American hit Chulaki with a metal bar. As Chulaki fell, Prischepa fired a high burst at the American, trying to miss his falling comrade. The American took a round in his shoulder. Another grazed his head as he flinched backward. As Prischepa fired again, the muzzle of Chulaki's weapon poked around the door. Prischepa did not see the weapon until it fired. Four ceramic slugs slammed into his chest, knocking the breath from him. He tried to raise his weapon, stumbled, then watched in amazement as the steel floor rose up and knocked the life out of him.

Two more of the bastards were rounding the corner when Murphy fired again. He missed but they ducked back around the corner, giving Murphy time to reach out and grab the dead bastard in the corridor and drag him close enough to get his weapon from him. Allen was leaning against the wall, holding his head. Blood streamed from the crease that ran across his forehead. Allen's left shoulder was bleeding, too, the blood staining the khaki sleeve and running down his arm to drip off his elbow.

They had been lucky. The second gunman could have killed them both. It was just beginner's luck that they had gotten him first. The one Allen had hit with the cheater pipe was still out, maybe dead.

"Come on!" Murphy shouted over his shoulder. "We need help up here!" He and Allen had been nearest the watertight door when the alarm had sounded. Behind him, the other four sailors cautiously approached the door. John Banner slipped up behind him and took the weapon Murphy shoved in his hands.

"There's some more around that corner," Murphy said, "They're . . ."

A burst of fire from the corner splanged off the wall and the door, interrupting Murphy's briefing. Murphy returned the burst as Banner dropped to one knee and fired wildly down the corridor.

"Easy!" Murphy yelled. "Don't shoot it all up at once!"

Another burst erupted from the corner, followed by a grenade that bounced up in the corridor and went off with a roar, a bright flash, and a shower of hot sparks that sprayed the Americans with burning bits of metal. Murphy saw two of the attackers rounding the corner. He kicked Banner back and swung the door with all his might. As it closed, the barrel of a weapon stuck through, firing a long burst as it kept the door from closing.

"Push!" Murphy screamed at the other Americans as he slipped his own weapon through the crack in the door and emptied it at the attackers. He pulled on the door, saw the weapon's barrel fall out, then slammed the door as Banner spun the locking ring. Murphy jammed the lock with the pipe Allen had used for a club.

"Get Allen," Murphy yelled, "fall back to the sub."

The ragtag defenders of the industrial area had won the first skirmish.

The return fire had surprised them, especially coming from one of their own MP-5Ks. They had expected to gain the submarine without any resistance. Filipov and Ostrovsky had put cover fire around the corner while Potyomkin threw a stun grenade. When the grenade went off, the three jumped around the corner to overwhelm the defenders. The watertight door was closing as they reached it.

Filipov jammed his weapon into the door, keeping it open, while Ostrovsky pulled the pin on another stun grenade to slip through the door. He was reaching up with it when the barrel of a MP-5 slipped through the door and fired. The burst ripped up Filipov's arm and hit Ostrovsky in the face. Filipov's weapon fell out of the door and the steel door slammed shut.

Ostrovsky's grenade fell from his hand. Potyomkin screamed, "Grenade!" and threw himself backward to the floor, covering his face with his hands as the grenade went off with a thunderclap and showered them with burning sparks.

Back on their feet and brushing off the sparks, they heard the door's locking lugs slide into place. Potyomkin banged on it in frustration. Two dead, one wounded, and one captured. It was not a good start.

28

The scene in the dining hall and lounge was not pretty. The intruders had most of the DeepCore crew prisoners. Three of the black-clad men were guarding them. On their knees with their hands behind their heads, the helpless crew were perfect hostages.

Jackson switched the dining-hall camera to monitor two while monitor one still scanned the other cameras throughout the complex. The flickering shots showed only empty corridors and rooms, except for the occasional body sprawled on the floor where he or she was shot down in cold blood.

Jackson was watching the dining hall when a quick glimpse of a person flipped by on the scan. He quickly stopped the scan and ran it backward, looking for the still free crewman. Nancy Collins was in one of the machinery rooms, pressed up against the door, listening.

Jackson looked up the room's intercom number and pressed the buttons. "Nancy," he whispered into the speaker, "is that you?"

Hearing a voice call her name, she jumped a foot, her mouth open in a silent scream.

"Nancy!" Jackson repeated. "It's Tom Jackson from Security. Be quiet, you'll give yourself away."

She darted to the intercom panel and pressed the button.

"Tom," she gasped, "what's happening? Did something hit us?"

"Yeah," he replied, "the Russians hit us. They're still aboard, too. Stay where you are for now. Are you all right?"

"Fine," she answered, "scared, but fine."

"I wish you were here to help me," Jackson sighed, "I don't know the place well enough to jerk these bastards around very much. I need a guide."

"Are you in your office?" she asked.

"If you can call it an office," he laughed. He called it a broom closet, but it was the only room available that had access to all the computer and video feeds. The phone box and radio transmitters were located there, too. It was tight, but it was the nerve center of the installation.

"I'm right above you, I think," she said, "no, wait, I'm down the corridor a bit."

"Are you close to the lab corridor or the industrial area?"

"No, not at all," she said. "Why?"

"Why don't you see if you can get out of there and come here?"

"How?"

"Wait a minute." Jackson switched the camera to the corridor outside her room. There was no one in sight. He switched to all the rooms and corridors in the area that had cameras. Nothing.

"Nancy, I don't see any baddies around you," he explained. "Why don't you make a run for it here?"

"No"—she shook her head—"I can't. I'm scared."

"You can do it," he reassured her. "If anyone knows this place, it's you."

"I can't," she stressed, "the stairs are too far away from here. I'll get caught!"

"Is there any way other than the stairs?" he asked. "Think."

She rubbed her forehead and bit a knuckle. "Wait," she said, "there should be a ventilation duct down the hall. If I could get into it, I could get down to your floor."

"Great!" Jackson answered. "I'll check it out and give you a go."

"No, Tom, I couldn't open the grating on your floor," she said, "besides, I'm still too scared."

Jackson sighed. He really wanted her with him, but if she panicked in the hall, she could wind up dead. "I'll open the grate for you," he offered. "As soon as I see you go into the shaft, I'll wait for you at the grate."

She stood for a moment, her head back against the wall. "Nancy," he said softly, "if they find you in there, they'll shoot you for sure."

She turned to the speaker and snapped, "Okay, I'll do it, but you be there for me! I'm no gymnast, I can't wait in that shaft forever!"

"I'll be there!" he promised. "Hang on, I'll check the halls."

He flipped through the corridors, looking for any sign of Soviet traffic. The complex seemed deserted, except for the dining hall. Two more guards had joined the others. One of them had his right arm in a sling and was holding his weapon in his left hand.

Good, Jackson thought, someone else got in some licks!

There was no picture from the industrial area. In front of the lab corridor, there was a small crowd of Russians working on the door.

When he was satisfied that there were no Russians nearby, he called her back. "Looks good, Nancy, anytime you're ready!"

She took several deep breaths, her eyes wide with fear. "Okay," she said, crossing herself, "I'm going now."

She reached for the door handle as he switched to the hall camera. Jackson watched as she ran down to the metal wall grate and pulled it open. She turned around and backed into the shaft. In a second she reached out, pulled the grate back shut, and disappeared.

Jackson switched to the camera just outside his door. Nothing. He stood and reached for the doorknob. As his hands closed around the knob, the dark form of one, then another Russian appeared on his monitor. The two men were trying the knobs on the doors. When they found one open, they went inside and searched the room.

You pond-scum bastards, he hissed under his breath. She was bound to be in the shaft on his floor now, or nearly there.

She had learned to do this in a course on rock climbing but she had never envisioned doing it in a ventilator shaft eighteen inches deep. The smooth sheet aluminum was not really designed to support any weight, and although she was light, she could feel the metal bending as she pressed with her hands and feet on one wall and her back on the other. If she stayed in one spot very long, she would push the rectangular shaft into a circle. If she weren't so scared, she would be claustrophobic by now.

A noise from the corridor below caught her attention. Jackson was there! She breathed a quick sigh of relief as she slithered slowly down toward the grate four feet below her.

Someone spoke. The voice was not Jackson's. The language was not English. A door shut. She froze motionless in the shaft as the blood froze inside her. Russians! She closed her eyes and cursed Tom Jackson to heaven for talking her into this suicide.

They were wasting no time in searching the place, darting from one room to another. One emerged from a room three doors down with a handful of cassettes, stuffing them into his coverall pockets. It suddenly dawned on Jackson that the men would be right outside his door in a minute. He reached over and pushed the button lock on the knob. The lock's soft click sounded like thunder in his ears. He watched as the men entered another room, then turned the deadbolt lock as quietly as he could. It sounded like a shovel being scraped along the bottom of a cement-filled wheelbarrow. If they can't hear that, he thought, they're deaf as posts.

The two men reappeared and walked past the ventilator shaft. One of them stopped and said something to the other. They stood still for a moment, their heads tilted up. Listening.

"Be quiet, Nancy, for God's sake," Jackson whispered.

When the two shadows went by outside the grill, she had just about peed herself. She was afraid to breathe and afraid not to. She pressed her palms and her feet against the metal shaft, locking herself in it.

The palms of her hands were wet with sweat and one of them slipped a little. She crammed it against the wall tight. The metal gave under the push and popped. It sounded louder than church bells to her and for a second her heart almost stopped, then raced as she waited for a bullet from below. And waited. And waited.

The men stood listening for what seemed like an eon, then started back down the hall. The knob on his door rattled, breaking Jackson's concentration on the monitor. He held his breath as he waited. The two men disappeared off the monitor screen. There were two more rooms in this hall. Jackson pressed his ear to the door and listened. There were no real sounds to identify. He listened for a minute, then slid back the deadbolt and carefully opened the door, releasing the knob lock. The hall was empty.

Jackson ran down the corridor to the grate and pulled out the locking pin. "Nancy," he called softly, "come on, it's safe!"

She came clattering down the shaft and he caught her before she could fall the rest of the way to the bottom of the shaft. She pitched out of the grate into a heap on the floor, rolled, and was on her feet in one awkward, faltering move. He got her by the hand and pulled her into the small security room. When he had the door locked again, he turned to her.

"Boy, am I glad . . ."

She slapped him so hard his glasses flew off his face and skittered across the monitor console.

"You silly son of a bitch!" she hissed. "You nearly got me killed! Come on down, you said. It's all clear, you said! I nearly got a machine-gun enema in there!" She collapsed into the folding chair against the wall.

Jackson retrieved his glasses and sat down on the floor against the door. "Sorry," he apologized, "they showed up after you'd already started down."

She was sobbing quietly, her head down in both hands, her breath rasping. She put her head between her knees for a second and he wondered it she was going to throw up, but after a minute she sat back up and wiped off her face.

"They were searching the rooms," he explained lamely. "They'll get to the room you were in eventually."

She nodded. "I know, it just scared the shit out of me."

"Me, too," he agreed, looking sheepish. She gave him a little smile, then looked around the room.

29

They had run the pressure up a bit more before they cracked the bottom hatch. Some water had surged up over the flange, but drained right back out as King gave the pressure handle another shove. Like DeepCore's sub pool, the air pressure kept the water out.

Bickerstaff had pulled a light jacket on over his knit shirt to keep the cold away. He took the arrow gun from Ramos and checked the thick CO_2 cylinder again. Ramos handed him two more arrows, which he stuck through his belt.

"Ready?" Moore asked the big man.

"No, but so what?" Bickerstaff snorted. "Where's that mask?" Carla handed him the diving mask they had found under one of the seats. It was too small for Bickerstaff's big face, but it would do. Bickerstaff spit in the mask and rubbed the inside of it with his fingers until the lenses squeaked. He rinsed it in the water and put it on.

"Here goes nothing," he said as he took several deep breaths and slipped down out of the hatch into the icy water.

Moore had maneuvered *Faith* as near as he could without risking discovery. That still left a swim of about sixty feet through water that was just above freezing.

Bickerstaff frog-kicked through the water, holding the arrow gun in his right hand. The little mask felt glued to his face, but that was a minor irritation. The bright green glow of the sub pool appeared ahead and Bickerstaff kicked for the edge, gliding up under the sub parked nearest to him.

The underside of the sub was two long cylinders that ran the length of it, probably battery packs. Bickerstaff felt around the edge of the cylinder nearest to him till his fingers came up out of the water. He slowly eased up to the surface until his nose and mouth were out of the water. He fought the urge to gasp and instead let the air out slowly, sucking in a deep breath the same way as he searched the sub pool for intruders.

A radio squawked. Bickerstaff eased himself out from the side of the sub, just his eyes above the surface. On the other side of the sub, a voice spoke into the radio. Bickerstaff dropped silently back under the water and came up quietly on the other side. The guard was still speaking into his radio. Bickerstaff watched the man, the arrow gun just below the surface. Finally, the guard answered one more time and clipped the radio onto his belt. As he clipped the small radio in place, Bickerstaff brought the arrow gun up out of the water and pulled the trigger. The hollow aluminum arrow streaked off the gun tube with a soft pop and buried itself in the guard's spine right between his shoulder blades. The man gasped, choked out a cry, then fell to his knees and onto his face on the steel deck. Bickerstaff reloaded the arrow gun and dog-paddled over to his victim.

The man was struggling to reach his radio, but the arrow had cut his spine and now he was flopping like a fish out of water, scratching at his belt to find the radio to warn his comrades.

Bickerstaff hauled himself out of the water and slid over next to the wounded Russian.

"Nyet, nyet," he cooed in the man's ear, "you don't want to do that." He took the radio, turned it off, and slid it across the deck out of harm's way.

"Come on in," he whispered to the helpless man, "the water's great."

Bickerstaff slipped back into the icy water and pulled the paralyzed Russian in with him. The man's eyes were pleading, a babble of Russian tumbling from his lips. He tried to scream, but Bickerstaff grabbed his throat and pushed his head under the water.

"Sorry," Bickerstaff whispered as he held the man underwater by his neck. He held the man as he searched the sub pool for any sign of other guards. The guard's struggling had just about ceased when Bickerstaff decided there were no others.

He slipped back into the water beside his still victim and stuffed the man up under the sub, whose name Bickerstaff had noticed was *Charity*.

He swam back to *Faith*.

Inside the sub, Carla was waiting with a foil space blanket to wrap around him.

"All clear, boss, I think we can just waltz in there if we do it now." Moore slipped back into the driver's seat and plunged down under the edge of DeepCore. He centered the little sub under the bright square of light and eased *Faith* to the surface.

King had the hatch open and was out in a second, armed with Carla's pistol. Carla followed with the arrow gun. Ramos and Bickerstaff came up behind her and Moore was the last one out of *Faith*. He shut the hatch and jumped over to the deck where the others were crouched.

"Ramos," Bickerstaff whispered, "there's a gun over there by that sub. Why don't you get it?"

Ramos nodded and slipped around the edge of the pool where the dead Russian's weapon lay. He was back in a minute.

"So," Bickerstaff asked, shivering, "what now?"

"I'm thinkin'," Moore answered, "and I'm open for suggestions."

"Comrade Major," Kron said, "the guard in the sub pool does not answer his radio."

Drachev turned to the sergeant, a look of irritation on his face. "See to it!" Drachev snapped. "Do not interrupt me!"

Kron motioned to Filipov. "Go to the sub pool and relieve Ustinov. Send him back here."

"It is done," Filipov answered, slinging his weapon over his left shoulder. His wounded right arm was tucked into his coveralls, the arm tied to his chest with the long tails of the dressings wrapped around his wounds.

Drachev was questioning one of the captives, a sallow little man who knelt before the major, his hands bound behind him with wire.

"No, please," the man pleaded, "I don't know anything about that lab. I just run the desalinization plant! I can't even go there. It's off-limits to most of us."

Drachev grabbed the man's thinning hair with his left hand and pulled his face up, pinching his puffy face with his right hand, leaning down to stare into the man's terrified eyes.

"Who does go there?" he hissed. "Tell me which ones!" Drachev twisted the man's head around toward the other frightened prisoners. The little man searched the room for someone who might take his place. None of the Positrack people seemed to be in the room. Travis was not here, either.

"I—I don't see any of them!" he stammered. "I don't know . . ."

Drachev looked down at the man with disgust. "Perhaps I am speaking to the wrong person," he said. The little man looked relieved.

"Yes, I mean, no," the man begged, "I mean, I am the wrong person to ask!"

Drachev looked down, twisting the man's head up to him. "And who should I ask?"

"I don't know!" the captive whined. "I don't know anything."

Drachev looked at the pathetic man for a long minute. "Perhaps you can still be useful," he said softly. The man's expression was pitiful. Drachev stood up and kicked the prisoner in the stomach. The man's gut felt like a marshmallow as the boot sunk in deep.

Still holding the man's hair, Drachev flipped up the flap on his holster and pulled out the silenced Makarov pistol. He jerked the captive forward by his hair, bowing his neck. The man was gasping for air, unable to resist at all. Drachev placed the muzzle of the thick silencer against the base of the man's skull and pulled the trigger.

Drachev's gun popped and his victim's head jerked forward as blood and bone chips gushed out of his open mouth. Drachev let the corpse fall. The dying man crumpled forward, kneeling on his knees and forehead. He stayed in that position for a moment before toppling over to the side.

The crowd of captives was wailing and screaming now. The execution had achieved the desired effect. The next subject would be much more cooperative. Drachev selected a tall blond woman who was doubled over, sobbing. He stepped through the crowd and took a big handful of her long blond hair.

"Come." As he began to drag her by the hair, she fell over on her back and began to scream in terror. He had to use both hands to drag her over next to the still-bleeding body. He turned to the other captives who were wide-eyed with fear.

"I want information about the Positrack laboratory," he explained. "I will get that information if each one of you has to die for me to get it."

Drachev knelt down by the blonde. Her eyes were shut tight and she was whispering something as rapidly as she could speak. Drachev leaned close to hear over the wailing of the crowd.

"Our Father, who art in heaven," she prayed, "hallowed be thy name . . ."

Drachev tapped her on her pert nose with his pistol. Her pale blue eyes snapped open wide, staring cross-eyed at the pistol.

"Talk to me, now," he cautioned her, "or you may get to speak to your God in person in a few moments!" The prayer caught in her throat.

30

Filipov stopped at the hall junction, unsure which way to go to find the sub pool. His group had not practiced for that area of DeepCore and he had to strain to remember which hallway to take. The sign in the hallway was no help. The pool was down one floor anyway. Down the hall to the right were stairs leading down. Filipov took them hoping to find a better clue on the next floor.

Sure enough, an elaborate map board showed him not only where he was, but his destination as well. He walked down the hall leading to the sub pool, adjusting his bandages as he went. His arm was still mostly numb, but it ached. If it got any worse, he would ask for a painkiller.

"We need to find Tom," Moore said, "if he's still alive."

"I'll bet he's still kickin'," Bickerstaff remarked. "He's too smart to get caught that easy."

"I hope you're right," Moore went on. "He would at least be able to tell us where things are around here."

"We need to figure out where the bad guys are, first," King observed.

"Does anyone remember where the security office is?" Carla asked. The others shook their heads. "Well, I guess we get to play dungeons and dragons until we figure out what's where."

"Sounds like a great way to get killed to me," Ramos snapped. "What we need to do . . ." The sound of metal hitting metal rang from across the pool. The five newcomers dropped to the floor, scurrying behind whatever cover they could find. Bickerstaff took the arrow gun from Carla, gave her the dead guard's weapon, and slid back into the icy water. She looked confused, but slipped behind a packing case.

A black-clad figure stepped through the far door and called out to his missing comrade. His right arm was bare except for the bandages wrapped around it. Blood trails snaked down to his elbow. When he got no reply, the man hefted his weapon in his left hand and slipped behind a steel pillar. His face reappeared at the base of the pillar, searching the room. He called out again to his comrade. His eyes slowly swept the room until he saw the radio lying where Bickerstaff had tossed it. As he began to move carefully toward the radio, Bickerstaff slipped below the surface and swam toward the other side of the pool.

The man made his way around the room, then stepped quickly over to the radio. He bent down to pick it up, his eyes scanning back and forth for any sign of trouble. Bickerstaff was coming up under *Charity* when the black-clad man saw a shadow glide under the parked sub. He pocketed the radio and fired a quick burst into the water above Bickerstaff's head, then ran for the exit.

The slugs ripped into the water next to Bickerstaff, leaving long trails of bubbles behind. Bickerstaff fired at the shape moving beyond the surface. The arrow broke the surface and arced into the ceiling, clattering through the pipes that ran there.

The man fired another burst as he neared the door, the ceramic slugs spouting geysers in front of *Charity*.

King, hiding behind some cylinders, came around and popped off two 9mm slugs at the fleeing gunman. The shots roared like cannon fire, but missed the man by inches, ricocheting off the steel walls with loud buzzing whines.

The man whirled as he neared the door and fired a final burst, emptying the magazine. He vanished through the door unscathed.

"Well, they know we're here now," Moore sighed as the man disappeared.

"At least they don't know who we are or how many there are of us," King observed.

Moore nodded. "Right."

Bickerstaff pulled himself out of the pool and jogged around the edge, dripping water as he ran.

Moore stopped him and took the arrow gun and his last two arrows. "Get back in there and change into something dry," he ordered, pointing to *Faith*. "You'll freeze."

Bickerstaff nodded and jumped aboard the sumbersible. He disappeared into the hatch. Outside, King covered the door.

"What are these things?" Carla asked, looking at the gun Bickerstaff had handed her.

"MP-5Ks," Moore answered, "German submachine guns." He looked up as Bickerstaff reemerged from the sub, clad in dark sweatpants and a black cloth jacket.

"Look, Elgin," Moore said, holding up the weapon.

"MP-5," Bickerstaff said. "Wonder who these boys are?"

"Spetsnaz," King suggested. "Probably combat swimmers. They're the only ones got little subs like that."

"Do what?" Ramos asked. "They're who?"

"Russian commandos, Larry," Carla explained, not trying to hide the irritation in her voice. "Didn't you read those antiterrorist bulletins we got last year?"

"Hey, I read them but I didn't memorize them!" he responded.

"Maybe if you'd read those things, you'd know what . . ."

"Later, guys," Moore interrupted, "we need to get out of here."

"Any more magazines for this?" Moore asked Bickerstaff.

"Yeah, wait." Bickerstaff ran around the pool to *Charity* and took a boat hook from its rack on the wall. He ran he pole up under *Charity* and pulled the dead Russian up to the edge of the pool. He stripped the two extra magazines from the man's pouches and left him floating.

"Weird bullets, Bob," he observed as he handed them to Moore. Moore didn't even look at the ceramic slugs as he slipped a magazine up into the small black machine gun.

"Excuse me," Carla interrupted, "anyone want to show how the thing works?"

"Jeez, Carla, sorry," Bickerstaff apologized, realizing he had handed her a weapon she had never even seen before. He began to show her how to shoot the tiny machine gun.

"Here," she said, handing it back to him, "you take it. You know how to run it. Ty, gimme back my pistol!" King handed over the 9mm and Bickerstaff gave King the arrow gun.

"Are you about finished?" Moore asked, looking exasperated. "Let's get the hell out of here!"

With Bickerstaff leading, the DeepCore security team made its way to the door.

"Two teams," Moore instructed, peering around the door. "Me and King on one, the rest on two. You cover us, we cover you." He looked at King and nodded. The two men jumped through the door and sprinted down the hall as Bickerstaff covered the hall with his gun. When they reached the first intersection, King went one way around the corner and Moore the other. Both sprang back into the hall and trained their guns down the hall. Moore looked back at Bickerstaff and jerked his head.

"Come on," Bickerstaff told the others as he jumped through the door and sprinted down to where Moore and King covered the intersection.

The hall sign said You Are Here. They were all studying the map when Tom Jackson spoke to them.

"Holy Christ!" Jackson said, pointing to the monitor. He froze the picture on that camera and stared at it. On the screen, a group of men and a woman were clustered at a hall intersection, staring off-screen.

"It's my guys!" Jackson beamed. "They made it!"

"Who?" Nancy asked, leaning over him to look at the new strangers.

"Security!" he gushed. "That's my boss, Bob Moore. I thought they bought it when the support ship went down!" Jackson looked up the intercom code in the book and thumbed the switch.

"Hi, boss, man," he said gaily, "welcome to DeepCore!"

"AAHH!" Ramos yelled when the voice crackled from the speaker grill. King clamped a hand over his mouth as Moore pushed the button to talk.

"Keep it down, Tom," he hissed, "we're not alone down here!"

"Sorry, boss," Jackson replied softly.

"Where are you?" Moore asked. "Where are we?"

"I'm in my office, you're right outside the sub pool, and we're both in deep do-do," Jackson replied. "The bad guys are in the crew quarters, outside the Positrack lab, and somewhere in the submarine dock."

"How many?" Moore asked.

"About a dozen, now," Jackson answered, "we managed to kill a few of 'em."

"Excellent," Moore complimented him. "Help us do the rest of them."

"Roger that!" Jackson agreed. "Stay put, I'll get right back to you."

31

LeFlore watched the monsoon rain beat against the wall of plate glass. Through the downpour, he could see the blurred red twinkling of hundreds of taillights on the freeway.

Wonderful, he complained, ten minutes till five and it's pouring outside. The drive home would take forever, the chances of a fender bender enhanced by the slick pavement and impaired vision of the other commuters. The thought of a dent on his Beemer made him sick.

What the hell, he mused, there's a great titty bar two blocks away. I'll hole up there and watch the show until either the rain or the other drivers go away.

He heard the phone in Shiela's office and glanced out the corner of his eye as she answered it. She stiffened, her eyes growing wide as she looked in at him. LeFlore turned to see what was so important.

"It's McLaughlin!" she blurted. "For you!"

LeFlore stepped over to his phone. "Yes, sir," he snapped, "what can I do for you?"

"Marc," McLaughlin said, "come up here for a minute, will you? There are some men here who need to speak to us."

"On the way, sir," LeFlore replied, dropping the receiver back into its cradle. The Old Man had spoken with the soft, casual voice he used when he was about to destroy careers, companies, and sometimes entire industries. Whoever was up there, it would be a bad meeting.

"I'm going upstairs for a minute, Sheila," LeFlore said as he passed her desk. She was gathering up her purse, ready to leave. "Will you hang around here for a while," he asked, "I may need you."

She stared at him for a few seconds, weighing the plans she

173

had for the evening against making a few brownie points.

"Okay," she replied, "how long?"

"Not too long," he answered on his way out the door, "I hope."

Sheila put away her purse, turned up the radio on her file cabinet, and pulled out the paperback she had started at lunch. The rain had screwed up her plans anyway, she might as well do him a favor. She would ask him for a day off at the end of the month. She wanted to see her mother in Dallas. An extra day would be nice.

Another scenario occurred to her, making her laugh. LeFlore might not be here at the end of the month! He may want me to help him pack his stuff this afternoon, she chuckled. If he does, he's out of luck!

McLaughlin's secretary, Paula, was still at her desk when LeFlore got to the forty-second floor. That was a bad sign. Paula was legendary for her prompt departure every day at five.

"Go right on in, Marc," she said as he walked across the thick mauve carpet. He stepped up to the twin carved doors and knocked softly, then opened the door.

"Come on in, Marc," McLaughlin called from the far end of the room. McLaughlin's office was the size of a basketball court. Two walls were glass, giving the boss an incredible view of the city. Today, a wall of gray hid the view like thick curtains.

LeFlore walked past the polished rosewood desk, on which there was only a telephone. McLaughlin was sitting with two men in the gray leather pit group at the far end of the room.

As he approached, the two men stood and turned toward him. They were both tall, solid guys with short-cropped hair and the sort of inexpensive suits that said Government Men.

"Marc, this is Mr. Bennett and Mr. McBride," McLaughlin said, introducing the pair.

LeFlore shook their hands, unsure which was which.

"Mr. LeFlore, you are responsible for operations on the facility known as DeepCore?" Bennett/McBride began.

"In part," LeFlore answered warily, "there are several different support entities." The men nodded.

"But you are responsible for its security, are you not?" McBride/Bennett asked.

"Well, yes," LeFlore replied, suddenly nervous. "Why, has something happened?"

"We don't know, Marc," McLaughlin explained. "We thought you might tell us."

"Not to my knowledge, sir," LeFlore snapped. "We haven't received any message to that effect! Not since that accident a few weeks ago!"

"The porthole failure?" Bennett/McBride asked.

"Yes. There's been no problem since. What makes you think there's a problem?"

"We have a system called TACAMO that maintains contact with subs at sea," McBride/Bennett explained, "TACAMO has not been able to make contact with the *Houston*, which is docked at DeepCore for modifications."

LeFlore felt a cold spot develop in his guts. This could only get worse, much worse, especially for him. Time for damage control.

"I would be notified of any emergency transmissions from DeepCore," LeFlore began. "There hasn't been any such transmission, to my knowledge."

"Why don't you get on the horn right now, Marc," McLaughlin suggested. "And see what you can find out. Use the phone on my desk."

As he walked back to the Old Man's desk, LeFlore's career flashed before his eyes.

The rose-wood desk looked as big as an aircraft carrier as he picked up the phone and dialed the communications room. LeFlore almost perched on the edge of the desk, but thought better of it and stood looking at his own reflection in the mirrorlike desktop as the number rang.

"Communications," the voice on the phone answered, "Willet."

"Willy?" LeFlore asked. "This is Marc LeFlore. Have you heard from DeepCore today?"

"I just came on," Willet replied. "Let me look at the log."

The seconds dragged like days as LeFlore listened to Willet shuffle through the day's communications. By the time he came back on the line, sweat was starting down LeFlore's spine.

"No, not since this morning early," Willet said. "Just a routine commo check. Why?"

"Could you try to make contact with them, Willy," LeFlore asked, ignoring the man's question, "I'll hold."

"You mean right now?" Willet asked.

"Yes, I mean right now!" LeFlore barked, trying to keep the urgency out of his voice. "It's important that we talk to them."

LeFlore looked down at the desktop while he waited. His own scared face looked back up at him. LeFlore forced his face into a mask of calm.

"Nothing, Mr. LeFlore," Willet reported after a minute. "They don't answer."

"What do you mean they don't answer?" LeFlore hissed.

"I mean either they aren't receiving," the radioman explained, "or they can't transmit."

"I understand that!" LeFlore snapped. "Don't they have backup equipment?"

"Lots of it," Willet answered. The man's calm was starting to infuriate LeFlore. "They have nearly as much stuff there as we do here."

LeFlore fought hard to keep from shouting. "Can you think of some reason why they wouldn't be in touch?"

"Nope, no reason at all. We're transmitting, they're not."

"Hold the phone a moment, Willet," LeFlore said as calmly as he could, "Mr. McLaughlin will want to hear this."

"Sir," LeFlore called to McLaughlin, his throat tight. "Communications says that we are not in contact with DeepCore and they cannot explain why."

One of the government men stood and excused himself. He walked out of the room, taking a large cellular phone out of his briefcase as he went.

32

"If this is a rescue mission," Mike Bowman, the copilot, asked, "what are the torpedoes for?"

"Luck?" Rodney Pierce, the pilot, suggested. "Listen, if I hadn't convinced them we need more fuel than weapons, we'd have four of 'em!"

"Tango Delta Three Two," the voice from the control tower told them, "you are cleared for takeoff."

"Roger, Control," Pierce answered, "we thank you."

The SV-22 rolled forward a few yards, then lifted up off the runway, its huge props flailing the air. Over the end of the runway, Pierce began to rotate them down for horizontal flight.

When they were in level flight, headed south toward DeepCore, their civilian passenger came forward. Bowman looked around as Howard Beecher stuck his head through the bulkhead door.

"Good morning!" Bowman said over the noise of the engines.

Beecher nodded, staring at the cluttered cabin. "This is a lot different from our Osprey," Beecher observed. "You can hardly walk in here!"

Bowman nodded. Although basically the same airframe, the Navy plane was vastly different inside. UnderSea's V-22 was a cargo and people hauler. The cargo hook in its belly was its only heavy equipment. It was light and agile, the perfect hauler.

The Navy's SV-22 was a sub killer. Armed with sonobuoys, a dunking sonar, and four M50 antisubmarine torpedoes, it was the nemesis of Soviet sub captains. Its aerial refueling probe allowed it to stay aloft for long periods, refueled by flying tankers.

"I didn't think the Navy was going to let me come along," Beecher went on, "I'm glad they changed their minds." Bowman nodded again. He was not too glad to have a civilian aboard.

Their briefing had indicated that a U.S. nuclear sub was out of contact at the underwater facility. At best, it would be an embarrassing technical foul-up. The worst-case scenario was the loss of the sub itself. In either case, having a civilian along to go back and blab was undesirable.

"Better go back and have a seat," Bowman suggested. "We still have a long way to go."

"Let me know when we are about a hundred miles out, okay?" Beecher asked.

"Will do," Bowman lied. Beecher made his way back through the welter of sonar sets, sonobuoy reloads, radio equipment, and torpedo controls.

Will (Boomer) Parker, the sonar operator, looked up from his paperback as Beecher passed. "Might as well take it easy," Parker said, "can't do nothing till we get there."

The other two crewmen—Salvador, the engineer, and Michaels, the sonobuoy operator—were laughing at a joke. Beecher buckled himself into the nylon fold-down seat. Parker leaned over and tapped Beecher's knee.

"Don't worry, Mr. Beecher," the petty officer reassured him. "These things are usually just communications foul-ups!" Beecher nodded.

"I hope to God you're right!" Beecher replied. The sonarman went back to his book. Beecher looked out the small window at the darkening sky. The sun was just down. A bright line of orange sky under the clouds lit the interior of the plane with a pleasant glow. Beecher watched until the glow faded and the dark Pacific night swallowed them.

Topside, the sub dock seemed okay. Howser and his two nervous riflemen surveyed the dock from the side door of the *Houston*'s sail.

The dock was designed to flex with the movement of the submarine tethered there. The *Houston*'s violent motion had torqued the sub bay a little, but there was no major leakage, just some fine sprays that misted around the *Houston*'s hull and from a few spots on the dock walls. The electricity was still on and the dock, half as long as a football field and attached to DeepCore by a large, watertight ball joint, was nearly level.

Howser slipped down the curved side of the *Houston* and motioned the two sailors to follow.

"Spread out," he warned them, "keep some distance and watch where you're going!"

They had only gone a few meters into the bay when a gang of men raced around the corner, sprinting for the *Houston*. Davis jerked his gun up and fired. The shot ricocheted off the far wall and whined around the sub dock like a lethal bank shot.

"Hold your fire!" Howser screamed. "They're your ship-mates, Dumbass!"

The six sprinters slid to a stop, breathlessly pointing back toward the watertight door where they had stymied the invaders.

"Back there!" Murphy pointed. "We locked 'em out! They shot Allen!" The wounded technician was on his feet, but his eyes rolled and his head seemed to be on gimbals.

"Banner, get Allen on board!" Howser ordered. "Then take everything out of the arms locker and bring it all up on deck." Howser motioned to Murphy, pointing at Davis and Monihan. "Murphy, take these two and set up some kind of cover by the door. Use whatever's there, but make it as solid as you can!"

As the three set off to fortify the dock, Howser went back into the *Houston* to tell the exec what they were up against.

In the control room, Hamilton was still struggling to keep the sub afloat.

"If you don't have good news, Chief, I don't want to hear it."

"Good news and bad news, sir," Howser answered. "The good news is that some of our guys whipped ass on some Russians at the door. The bad news is that the Russians will probably be back."

Hamilton stopped for a second and looked at Howser, then took him by the arm.

"Chief, I'm going to put these guys on you. Hold them off, okay?" The exec ran his hand up his forehead. "Shit, Chief, half the crew's dead below decks, the rest of 'em are hurt or scared to death. The dock's the only thing holding the boat up. I don't know . . . ."

"Right, sir," Howser answered. "If it gets any worse, I'm not reenlisting!"

Hamilton looked up at the petty officer and smiled. "Me, either. In the meantime, let's try to keep this tub together."

Banner stepped into the control center, laden with rifles and ammunition.

"Come on, me hearty!" Howser exhorted the heavily armed machinist mate. "It's time to do Fellatio at the Bridge!"

Hamilton laughed. "I think that's Horatio at the Bridge, Chief!"

"Whatever!" Howser answered as he followed Banner up the ladder to defend his ship from the barbarians.

"Comrade Major, the section at the submarine dock has come under fire. We have had some killed and the Americans have secured the dock area." He waited for a torrent of abuse from his commander.

"And the American crew?" Drachev asked.

"We caught many of them in the corridors and killed them on the initial assault," Kron answered. "The others have taken refuge in the submarine dock. Undoubtedly, many others were killed in the submarine." Drachev rubbed the back of his neck, looking up at the maze of pipes that ran above them.

"The Navy crew has weapons," he observed. "We cannot let them get out of the submarine dock to attack us from behind. Leave a guard on the laboratory entrance and two on the prisoners. Bring the others to the submarine dock. We will reduce their numbers first, then enter the laboratory complex."

"Exactly so, Comrade Major," Kron snapped, relieved at the major's calm reaction.

"Who the hell are these people, Chief?" Banner asked as they waited behind their makeshift barricade for the next assault.

"Beats me!" Howser answered. "Russians, maybe. All I know is that they're bad motherfuckers."

That was a stupid thing to say, Howser realized. The last thing these scared bubbleheads need to hear is how tough the other side is. He tried to bolster them a bit.

"They aren't armed worth a shit, though," he said loud enough for everyone to hear. "Those little popguns are no match for M16s."

Maybe a little humor to loosen things up, Howser thought.

"Hey, you guys hear about the priest who was going around the parrish visiting everybody?" One or two heads turned toward him for a second. Howser was known for his jokes. "Well, the priest knocked at one house, not knowing it had become a whorehouse. Two little babes answered the door and the priest asked, 'Is the man of the house here?' The girls giggled and said, 'There is no man here, Padre, Mother Green runs this house.' So the priest says, 'Is Mother Green here?' The girls said no and asked if they could help him and the priest said, 'I just want to invite you all to come to church on Sunday.' The girls said thanks for the invitation and that they would be sure to tell Mother Green."

Even those sailors who weren't looking at him were listening now. Howser pressed on.

"So the next Sunday, the priest was up at the front of the church with the other priest and the door opened and this knockout dame in a tight miniskirt and a low-cut blouse pranced down the aisle, sat down on the first row, and crossed her legs real wide. The priest leaned over to his friend and asked. 'Is that Mother Green?' The other priest looked at her and said, 'No, I think it's just the way the light's hitting it!' "

The punchline was drowned out by the concussion of the blast that blew the watertight door off its hinges. The door spun and slid across the floor, winding up a few feet from the barricade. Half the sailors ducked when the door blew, the other half opened up with their weapons. A barrage of rifle fire roared out, whining and splanging off the steel walls of the corridor. None of the sailors saw the stun grenades bounce in.

The grenades went off in front of the barricade, showering the defenders with hot sparks and deafening them with rapid concussions. Howser's men were stunned. In the second after the grenades went off, four of the attackers slipped through the smoking doorway and fanned out along the sides of the huge room.

"Watch 'em!" Howser yelled. "Don't let 'em flank us!" He jerked Banner and Davis away from their cover and turned them toward the dark forms that were slipping around the crates and shipping containers.

Howser's men were the best in the business, but their business was chasing submarines, not urban combat. One by one, the sailors fell, riddled by the invaders' ceramic bullets. Banner and Davis were shot in the back by an attacker that Murphy missed.

When Monihan fell bleeding up against him, stitched by half a dozen slugs, Howser knew it was time to fall back. He pulled the two tear gas grenades from his pockets and tossed them out in front of the barricade. In seconds, the big room began to fill with the dense vapor.

"Murphy!" Howser screamed over the roar of Murphy's rifle. "Come on! We're leaving! Help me with Monihan!"

Murphy fired a long last burst, slung his rifle over his back, and grabbed Monihan's waist, slinging the wounded man up over his shoulder in a fireman's carry. Howser opened fire on the attackers, firing short bursts to cover Murphy as he ran toward the sub with Monihan.

Murphy took cover behind some metal drums stacked near the sub's sail. Dumping Monihan behind the barrels, Murphy changed magazines and began firing to cover Howser's retreat.

Howser, his eyes stinging from the gas, fired a final burst and ran for the relative safety of the barrels. He was almost there when two slugs ripped into his right leg below the knee. Howser yelled, fell, rolled, and came up limping but still running. Murphy emptied his magazine at the hidden attackers as Howser dove past him and scrambled behind the drums.

A hail of tiny ceramic slugs rained against the barrels and glanced off the side of the *Houston*. The attackers worked their way down the room, one group keeping the defenders occupied while the other moved closer.

"Get some help up here, Chief!" Murphy screamed as another fusillade slammed the barrels. "Get everybody up here!" He pumped another magazine of 5.56mm rounds at the attackers as Howser dumped his remaining ammunition and dove for the door under the diving planes on the sub's tall sail. As he pulled open the steel door, a ceramic bullet ripped through his left shoulder.

Howser spun through the door, pulling it shut and leaving Murphy to defend the sub alone. Howser fell down the ladder into the control room, landing on the deck in a bloody pile.

"Get up there!" he screamed at the startled crewmen. "They're all over us! Get everybody up there!"

The crew, already working furiously to keep the *Houston* afloat, stood in stunned amazement as the chief struggled to his feet and staggered toward the arms locker.

"Come ON!" Howser bawled again. "He's up there alone!"

Hamilton turned to the seaman nearest Howser. "Help the chief!" he ordered. He turned to the intercom and broadcast throughout the ship. "All hands on deck to repel boarders! This is no drill!"

Two handfuls of terrified sailors showed up. The others were locked in battle with the sea. Hamilton's heart sank when he looked at them. They were technicians, mechanics, computer operators. In the open sea, they were the pros, hunter/killers to be reckoned with. In a firefight with rifles, they were out of their league.

Hastily armed with a rifle and a few magazines, the sailors scrambled up the ladder to relieve Murphy. Howser tried to follow them, but didn't have the strength to climb the ladder. He fell to the deck again, cursing.

"Pharmacist's mate to the bridge," Hamilton barked into the intercom, then stepped over to help the floundering Howser.

"Come on, Chief," Hamilton said, helping Howser to his feet. "You've done enough!"

"Gotta go back!" Howser gasped. "Monihan's hurt! Murphy needs help!" The chief's eyes rolled back in his head and he slumped to the floor. "Gotta go back!" he gasped. The pharmacist's mate's face swam into his vision as Howser passed out.

33

It had taken several minutes to place the charges on the elliptical door frame. The door had several locking lugs and each one had to be cut to get the door open. Finally, Potyomkin turned and nodded at Kron.

Kron relayed the message. "Ready, Comrade Major."

The assault team took their places on either side of the door, leaving as much distance between themselves and the charges as the space would allow. Drachev took cover behind an I-beam wall support and nodded to Kron, who was holding the waterproof fuse lighter.

Kron pulled the metal ring, firing the lighter. The short fuse burned for ten seconds, giving Kron enough time to seek cover.

Wired together with detonating cord, the charges all went off at once. Each linear-shaped charge created a wedge of fire that burned through the steel locking lugs like a hot knife through butter. The door blew into the big submarine dock.

Drachev had his hands over his ears, but the blast pounded his eardrums. By the time he recovered and wheeled around the I-beam, his troops had thrown stun grenades into the room. Two more blasts buffeted his ears. Before the echoes of the blasts had faded, his men were darting through the burnt door, firing short bursts at the defenders to keep them off balance. The entire eight-man force was inside in seconds.

The Americans were firing back in typical American fashion, firing a large amount of ammunition, but hitting very little. His men began to work their way around the Americans' poorly chosen position. His men, armed with small short-range weapons, began to pick off the American sailors who were fighting back with assault rifles.

Sgt. Kron was directing the fight, moving the men in a pincer around the Americans. Drachev left the fighting to Kron and began to study the American nuclear sub still tied to the dock. It appeared to be intact, which surprised Drachev. He had expected the American sub to be destroyed by the limpet mines, possibly even to sink. The sub was tilted, but still very much afloat.

The contradictory desires of sinking the huge sub or capturing it intact flashed through his mind for a second. He discarded the latter idea. He was here to sink this American, not capture it.

A change in the shooting focused his attention back on the fight. The three remaining Americans were withdrawing. They made the cover of some drums near the sub and continued to resist. Kron would make short work of them. Then he would have to decide what to do about the others. He watched Kron move his men into position for a final assault on the Americans.

As his shipmates welled up out of the *Houston*, Murphy yelled at them. "Spread out, spread out!" he shouted. "Both sides!"

The sailors ran both ways along the submarine, firing bursts of automatic fire to keep the attackers' heads down. In a few seconds, M16s were raking the submarine dock area.

Murphy yelled at his reinforcements, pointing out the locations of the enemy. The tide of battle changed, but only for a moment.

The Soviets were stalled for a moment by the fresh reinforcements, but quickly changed tactics. Two fire teams of Soviets, now equipped with captured M16s, pinned down the sub's defenders with constant semiauto fire while the rest of the assault force moved carefully toward the stern of the sub. Taking advantage of the crates and waterproof containers for cover, the Spetsnaz slowly flanked the Americans.

"Listen!" Darcey held Knickerbocker back with his arm. Around the corner, the sounds of gunfire echoed.

"God damn it!" Knickerbocker spat. "The bastards are after my ship! Come on!"

He raced around the corner before Darcey could stop him.

"Damn, Skipper," Darcey muttered under his breath as he followed his commander. The captain was running now, hurrying to get back to his stricken ship. The sounds of combat were closer, ripping bursts of automatic weapons fire. Darcey broke into a sprint to catch up.

"Skipper!" Darcey called to Knickerbocker as the captain neared the short corridor that led to the industrial area. "For God's sake, stop!"

Knickerbocker looked back, puzzled. "Come on, Darcey," he exhorted the panting nuclear officer. "They're killing our shipmates!"

"They'll kill us," Darcey gasped, "if we just go running in there!" The sound of firing erupted again. Knickerbocker looked toward the sound.

"We can't just stand here! Come on."

Hugging the wall, the two officers moved slowly toward the battle. At the corner, Darcey held the captain back and dropped to the floor. He inched up to the corner and glanced quickly around the corner.

He jumped to his feet and motioned to Knickerbocker. "It's clear, come on." The two men turned the corner and slid down the wall toward the watertight door that led into the industrial area.

Darcey stopped the captain again while he looked at the burned oval door frame. Ragged black gashes in the metal marked the positions of the blasted locking lugs.

Darcey felt a sudden chill. The noise was louder now, echoing in the big sub bay. He could feel the captain's nervous energy washing over him from behind. Knickerbocker was wild to get into the fight. The frustration of not being there to defend his own ship was killing him.

"Darcey," Knickerbocker hissed, "let's slip through the door and make our way around to the motel." The personnel rooms in the industrial area were called Motel 6. Darcey nodded and pressed himself against the burned bulkhead as Knickerbocker crouched off to one side and looked through the door, searching for the enemy. The little gun following his eyes as he sought a target.

The sound of the firing was booming in the big sub dock. A light fixture in the corridor sparked and fell, hit by a wild burst. They flattened themselves against the steel walls as a ricochet whined past. Darcey looked scared. Knickerbocker gestured to the right. Darcey nodded. The motel would at least give them some cover. Here against the corridor's steel walls, they were too vulnerable.

The sound of running feet behind them changed their plan. Both men spun toward the noise. A wounded invader came around the corner, saw the two Americans, and dived back from whence he had come. Knickerbocker snapped off a burst at the man. It hit the wall, but missed the fleeing target.

"Come on!" Knickerbocker yelled, stealth forgotten. "We gotta . . ."

Darcey saw the movement out of the corner of his eye. The figure slipped up behind Knickerbocker and swung before Darcey could even speak. Hit from behind, Knickerbocker staggered forward. The little gun fell from his hands as he dropped to one knee.

Darcey dived for the gun and rolled, bringing the weapon up to fire at his captain's attacker. The man dropped down behind Knickerbocker, holding the captain as a shield. Knickerbocker, stunned by the blow from behind, struggled to get free. Darcey stood to get a shot over the captain's head. Knickerbocker elbowed the man and threw him sprawling off to the side. "Shoot!" Knickerbocker shouted.

Darcey lined up on the man, who rolled quickly to one side. Darcey's burst missed, ringing off the metal floor plates just next to his writhing target. The second burst would get him.

Darcey never got off the second burst. Ten ceramic slugs ripped through his chest, tearing his heart and most of his lungs apart.

"Alan!" Knickerbocker tried to stand, to catch his friend as he fell bleeding to the floor. He pulled Darcey to him and cradled the man's head in his lap. Darcey was still conscious. He looked up at his skipper.

"I'm always careful," he murmured, then passed out and died in Knickerbocker's arms. Knickerbocker sat holding Darcey, more stunned by the death of his friend than by the physical blow. A dark shadow stepped in front of him. Knickerbocker looked up at the man who had struck him from behind. The man wasn't that big, but he exuded danger.

"Hello, Captain," the man said in English. "I'm so happy to meet you!"

"I'm fucked!" Knickerbocker replied. The stranger smiled and nodded. Behind him, Knickerbocker could hear the wounded man walk up. Forgotten for a second, he had come back and killed Darcey. Knickerbocker reached down and closed Alan Darcey's eyes, then looked back up at his captors.

The firing was close now. The major and the assault party were close by. He had gotten lost again in the maze of corridors. The sound of firing had given him his bearings.

Filipov's arm was beginning to hurt. It had been numb for a while but it was throbbing now. The jostling and exertion were bringing back the circulation. A trickle of blood ran out from under his bandages. After he reported the new threat to the major, he would tighten the bandages.

He was already around the corner when he realized the stupidity of such recklessness. He had not checked first for the enemy and of course, there they were. He dived for the safety of the corridor as the two Americans turned. Shots glanced off the wall in front of him, but he dove for the cover of the corner, sprawling on his face. Coming up to one knee, Filipov spun around. The Americans were certain to pursue. Maybe he could get them if he could get off two quick bursts.

The sound of scuffling caught his attention. He peeked quickly around the corner. The bigger American was on the floor. The other dove for their only weapon. As he struggled to his feet, the big American threw off his attacker and Filipov recognized Drachev. The other American was firing. Filipov lunged around the corner and brought up his machine gun, aiming quickly with his left eye. He fired the remaining rounds in the magazine and was relieved to see the American twitch and fall to the floor. The major jumped to his feet and covered the two Americans with his pistol. Drachev was speaking to the big American, an officer who held his head comrade on his lap.

Filipov smiled. He had saved his commander and helped capture an American officer. Surely this would mean a decoration. "Comrade Major!" Filipov blurted, suddenly remembering the enemy force in the sub pool. "There are security troops on board!" Dark lacy curtains began to form around the edges of his vision. Filipov staggered.

"On your belly!" Drachev shouted at his prisoner. The American slid out from under his dead companion lay facedown on the floor. "Hands behind your head!" The American complied.

"Where?" Drachev demanded, catching Filipov by his coveralls and easing him down the wall until he sat on the floor. "How many?"

"In the sub pool!" Filipov said. "I do not know how many, but several. They fired an arrow at me, and a rifle."

"An arrow?" Drachev echoed.

"From underwater!"

Drachev shook Filipov to wake him up. "Take this prisoner to the escape hold! If he tries to run, shoot his legs. If he tries again, kill him!"

"Just so, Comrade Major!" Filipov replied, shaking his head to clear away the black lace. Drachev ran for the sub dock.

34

"Well, Lavrov," Petrochenko asked eagerly, "what do you have to report?"

Lavrov took a breath, then answered as calmly as possible. "We have had no transmissions as yet, Comrade Colonel." The silence on the line begged more information. "It is still early. They may not have left the area yet."

The silence hung on the phone like funeral drapes. Finally Petrochenko spoke. "Perhaps you are right. Please inform me the moment you receive any communication."

"Of course, Comrade Colonel," Lavrov replied. The phone went dead.

This is the part I hate, Lavrov thought, I would rather be there fighting than here waiting.

He called the communications center again, excoriating the radio operators. They assured him they would wait for any message.

"Are you monitoring all bands?" Lavrov questioned the radio supervisor. "They could be damaged and not able to use the satellite antenna."

The supervisor assured him they were monitoring all possible bands and pleaded with him to be patient. Lavrov hung up wondering if the man knew how impossible that was.

"Bob, you there?" Jackson's voice whispered from the intercom.

"Speak, Lips," Moore murmured into the microphone grill. "What's up?"

"Looks like the baddies are jumping on the sub crew over

in the industrial area," Jackson reported. "They left a couple of guys to guard the DeepCore people in the dining hall."

"Thanks, Tom," Moore whispered. "We'll see if we can get to them while the others are busy with the Navy. Can you give us any diversion?"

"Can do," Jackson answered. "I'll wait until you get in place and give me a nod. Call in when you're close to the dining hall."

"Will do, Tom. We're moving. Moore out."

Moore turned to the others. "Hear that?" They all nodded yes. "If we can get the DeepCore people loose, we can beat these bastards. Let's do it!"

"Okay, they're on their way," Jackson sighed. "Maybe we got a chance now."

"Against a bunch of Russian commandos with automatic weapons?" Collins asked. She looked skeptical.

"Don't sell these guys short," Jackson cautioned. "They're no virgins. Elgin Bickerstaff has already killed more Russians than are in here."

She looked at him sideways. "Oh?"

Jackson nodded. "Bickerstaff was on a SEAL team that specialized in taking out air defense command posts in North Vietnam during the war. Those posts were always manned by Russian advisors to the North Vietnamese. Elgin killed five of 'em in one raid alone."

"By his own account?" she asked skeptically.

"By Bob Moore's count," Jackson answered. "Moore was his C.O."

She's getting depressed after coming down from her adrenaline high, Jackson thought. I probably am, too. He reached between the TV monitors and took out his ancient battered thermos.

"Here," he said, pouring her a cup of the now-tepid brew, "we both need a pick-me-up." She took a sip and made a face.

"What is this stuff?" she asked.

"Chicory coffee from Louisiana," he told her. "I brought it from home. Think of it as medicine." She drank the cup in a long gulp, grimacing horribly.

"What can we do to divert the Russians long enough for my

guys to knock them off?" Jackson asked as he took back the cup and refilled it for himself.

"I don't know," she answered. "This isn't my line of work."

"It's not mine, either," he told her, reaching out for her hand, "but it's about the only chance we've got. Come on, help me!"

Bickerstaff stood next to the corner, looked back at Carla, nodded, and jumped around the corner. His feet were hardly on the ground before he fired a muffled burst.

"Shit!" he swore.

Carla, her pistol up next to her face, watched as he jerked up the barrel of his gun and started down the hall. She dropped to one knee, swinging her gun around the corner to cover his progress.

A few feet in front of her, two people, a man and a woman, lay sprawled on the floor. They were both dead. The man's head had three new holes in it from Elgin's gun. At the next corridor intersection, Bickerstaff had taken cover in the hollow of a wide I-beam. She rose quickly to her feet and ran down to join him. The others would follow behind her.

She slipped up behind Bickerstaff, taking cover behind his large bulk.

"Why'd you shoot that guy back there?" she whispered.

"It looked like he was bent over her," Bickerstaff hissed over his shoulder. "I thought he was a bad guy."

"Wonder who they were?" Bickerstaff shook his head in reply.

After what seemed to be an endless maze of corridors and intersections, Moore called a halt beside the metal speaker grill.

"Elgin," he said to the point man, "go down one more intersection. King, you go back one. I don't want any surprises."

The two men nodded and moved out.

Moore pressed Jackson's intercom code.

"Tom," he said softly, "we're right around the corner from the dining hall."

"Roger, boss," Jackson answered. "We've got an idea. You'll know when it happens, just be as close as you can."

"Roger Willco, Tom. Just give us a couple of minutes."

"Will do."

Moore motioned for King to return and moved his brood down to where Bickerstaff crouched, watching the next stretch of corridor.

"It's right around there," Bickerstaff whispered, "I can hear 'em talking."

The faint sound of laughter echoed around the corner. "We wait for Jackson's diversion, then hit 'em. Okay?"

Moore looked at each face. King and Bickerstaff looked like a couple of Dobermans eyeing a pork chop. Carla's face was moist with nervous sweat, but she seemed more excited than scared. Ramos was the one who worried Moore. His eyes were darting back and forth and he was trembling a bit.

Probably since he's only got a pocket knife, Moore noted.

"Ramos," Moore hissed, motioning him closer, "you and I will go in last. We'll let the gunslingers go first."

Ramos nodded vigorously, obviously happy with the plan.

"Bick, you go in first," Moore ordered. "Carla, give King your gun for this one. Ty, you follow Bickerstaff. The rest of us will come in after you. Don't try for any prisoners, okay?"

King soundlessly snapped his fingers, frowning in mock disappointment. He handed Carla the arrow gun and took her pistol. He checked the chamber for a live round. They waited nervously for Tom Jackson to distract the opposition.

35

"Ready?" Jackson asked.

"Anytime."

"I hope to hell my Russian isn't as rusty as I think," he said. "I'd hate to order a cold beer by mistake." She grinned as he punched in the dining-hall code on the intercom and turned the volume up slowly on the speaker and microphone. They could hear voices speaking softly in Russian, as well as some sobbing and moaning from the hostages.

Jackson looked over at Nancy and nodded. She keyed in the command that turned on the red emergency lights, flashing them on and off as fast as she could. Jackson leaned close to the mike and shouted in Russian.

"Put down your weapons! Do not resist! Put down your weapons!"

The flashing red light was visible even from where they crouched against the wall. When Jackson's voice boomed out over the intercom, Moore hissed, "Go!" The five moved out at a dead run toward the dining hall.

Bickerstaff got to the door just as a burst of gunfire rippled inside the dining hall. The guards were firing at the voice. He plunged through the doorway without breaking stride, darting off to one side. King paused for half a heartbeat at the door, then whipped around the opening off to the other side. They fired together, the loud booms of Carla's 9mm drowning out the staccato stammering of Bickerstaff's silenced weapon. Carla knelt at the door, the arrow gun searching for a target.

"Clear!" King called from inside. "Me, too," Bickerstaff called. Moore and Ramos stepped into the room as Carla slowly rose and stepped in, the arrow gun pointed at the floor.

Inside, the two Soviet guards were down. One was sprawled on his face on a table off to the left, hit by King's pistol shots. The other was on the floor, rolled into an aborted fetal position by the stream of slugs from Bickerstaff's machine pistol. As Moore and the others entered the room, King and Bickerstaff crouched at the door, watching the corridor outside for any counterattack.

A voice boomed in the room. "Bob? You there?" Moore walked back to the intercom panel through the mob of hostages who were only now beginning to look up after flattening themselves on the floor. They were whimpering and coughing, scared out of their wits. Ramos followed in Moore's wake.

Moore spoke into the mike. "Turn down the volume, Tom. We're okay. hostages appear okay."

"Anybody hurt?" Jackson asked, unable to see Moore on the camera.

"Couple of dead Russians." Moore looked around at the hostages who were hugging each other and gushing thanks for their rescue. It was hard to hear over the rising din. "Where is Dr. Travis, Tom?" Moore shouted over the noise.

Two of the women hostages yelled as the storage bench they were sitting on moved. As they jumped up, the seat, which doubled as the lid to the storage locker beneath, snapped open and Dr. Jack Travis climbed stiffly out.

"Looking for me?" he asked nervously.

"Speak of the devil," Moore laughed. Travis suddenly bent over and blurted, "Excuse me!" He ran for a door across the dining hall and disappeared inside. Moore looked at the nearest hostage and pointed after the fleeing administrator.

"What's that?" he asked.

"Bathroom," the man answered, breaking into a nervous laugh.

It hurt to breathe and he was afraid to move. Valerian felt like he had been hit from behind with a shovel. Around him, the prisoners were on their feet, laughing and crying. He could hear two men talking at the far end of the room. Forcing himself to remain still, he opened one eye and looked around. Two strangers were standing by a metal box at the far end of the dining hall.

An intercom! They had been fooled by a voice on a speaker!

Sergei had fired at the voice. He remembered that much. Valerian looked around, but Sergei was not in sight. Dead, he realized, like me.

The two men were still talking on the intercom. One, a large man, seemed to be doing most of the talking. The leader.

It was hard to feel anything, so Valerian looked to his right. The weapon was on the table, still in his hand. Good. He looked back at the pair. Maybe ten meters away.

If I can move, he thought, one long burst will do.

He took a deep breath that hurt like hell, and pulled the gun up in front of him to kill the men who had killed him and Sergei. Behind him, someone was screaming.

Carla was right behind the Russian when he came back to life.

"Gun!" she screamed, bringing the arrow gun up in front of her. She fired without aiming, staring at the target the way she had been taught in combat shooting school. The arrow flew out the end of her gun as the Russian fired.

The arrow's impact knocked the Russian's aim up, the last few rounds snapping and whining into the dining hall's false ceiling. Two ceiling tiles came clattering down. It was all over in two seconds.

The arrow was sticking up at an angle, buried in the dead man's head. Carla walked over to make sure he was really dead this time. The arrow had hit him at the base of the skull, slamming his head down on the table. There was no exit wound, but nearly a foot of the shaft was buried in the man's head. Carla suddenly felt sick to her stomach and rushed for the metal sink across the room. As she ran by, she could see Ramos on the floor. Bob Moore kneeling over him.

"Oh!" she moaned as the bile rose in her throat and she heaved everything into the sink.

"Dr. Travis!" Moore shouted. The man was so shaken, he seemed not to hear. "Do you have any medical personnel?" Travis's eyes focused on him.

"What?" he stammered. "Yes, yes, we have a nurse!" Travis turned to the others. "Colin, where's Patty?"

The other hostages looked stricken. One of the men, a big strapping fellow, stepped forward. "She's over there with Milton from the desal plant," Colin said, pointing to the front of the room. "The bastards killed them both." He fixed a hateful stare on Travis. "They wanted the people in charge."

Travis looked sick. Moore was less interested in placing blame than in getting treatment for his wounded man. "Anyone else?" he barked. Travis shook his head.

"Is he okay?" Carla asked as she knelt by Ramos.

"I'm okay," Ramos answered, "I'm just . . . OOWW!"

"Take it easy, Larry," Moore cautioned. "You're hit. Just lie there for a second."

Moore looked Ramos over for wounds. There was a jagged blood-soaked hole in his left sleeve and another two high on his back above the shoulder blade. Moore pulled Ramos's shirt up over the two wounds.

"Having any trouble breathing?" Moore asked, watching for signs of bubbling from either of the small holes.

"No, don't think so," Ramos replied. His breathing was rapid and shallow, but more from fear than the wounds. There were no bubbles, just dark red blood that oozed up and ran down the side of Ramos's muscular back.

"That's good," Moore answered. He slid his hand down under Ramos's chest, feeling for blood on his front. There wasn't any.

"Larry, my boy," Moore assured Ramos, "you are a lucky guy, even if it doesn't feel that way now." He looked up at Carla. "Get me something to use as bandages."

Carla jumped up and darted to the counter. There were bins of silverware, condiments, and napkins. She took an entire dispenser of napkins back with her.

Moore pulled all the napkins out and covered each bleeding wound with them. He tore up Ramos's shirt, over loud protest to the contrary, and used it to tie the makeshift dressings in place.

"This'll hold 'em in place until we can get you to the dispensary," he told the wounded man. Ramos sat up, grimacing and moaning. "This shirt cost forty-five dollars, boss," Ramos whined, picking at the ripped fabric.

"We'll give you a voucher," Moore promised. Carla helped Ramos up into a chair.

"I'm sorry, Larry," she apologized. "I shot as fast as I could!"

Ramos looked at her, then looked over at the spiked Russian. It took him a second to realize that she had saved his life. "No sweat, Carla," he answered. "He would have blown my head off."

Moore walked over and picked up both the dead Russians' guns. "Larry, I want you to stay here with the crew." He turned to Colin and motioned him over. "Colin, can you handle a gun?"

"Too right I can!" Colin answered. Moore hadn't noticed his Australian accent before.

"I need you to help defend the crew," Moore said. "Is there a better place to defend than this?"

"Damn right. The crew quarters has only one entrance and there's an escape hatch at the far end."

"Great, move everybody there as fast as you can," Moore said. He handed Colin one of the captured weapons. He looked at the two dead crewmen who were now partly covered with white tablecloths. "We're going after those bastards." He turned to Ramos. "Hang in there, Larry. We'll be right back."

"You'd better," Ramos replied deadpan, "I want to talk workmen's comp."

Moore stepped to the intercom and called Jackson, "Give me directions, Tom. We're coming where you are."

36

"Sgt. Kron," Drachev snapped as he slid next to the big aluminum container Kron was using as cover, "we must secure this area immediately. The Americans have security forces on board."

Kron looked at his commanding officer and smiled. "We will have them very soon, Comrade Major. These sailors are no match for our *raydoviki*." The Americans were slowly being driven back toward their submarine. One by one, the Spetsnaz had killed them. Now there were only a handful of Americans left.

Drachev watched as three stun grenades arced up over the last American strongpoint. They exploded in the air, showering the hidden defenders with hot metal sparks. The boom was still echoing when four *raydoviki* rushed the position, firing short bursts as they burst around the Americans' flank. Wild gunfire erupted from the position. Drachev watched as four Americans bolted for the safety of the submarine's sail. Two died before they could reach the sub and another was wounded as he plunged through the steel door.

Kron signaled to the two men near him. They ran across the remaining open space and jumped to the curved side of the submarine, scrambling up on top of the long cylindrical hull. Another raider followed the fleeing Americans, jumped in front of the sail, and tossed a stun grenade into the open bridge atop the sail. A Roman candle of sparks burst up from inside the sail.

Deprived of targets, the raiders crouched nervously on the huge submarine, unsure what to do next.

"Leave those three here to guard the submarine," Drachev barked. "Bring the rest. We need to get into the laboratory quickly."

Kron gave the orders and the remaining *raydoviki* set off after the secrets of Positrack.

Jackson was laughing with Moore about Dr. Travis's escape. The man the Soviets wanted was right under their noses all along.

Nancy saw the Soviets on the monitor first. "Tom," she called, switching the cameras to follow the knot of Soviets running through the corridors. She pointed to the monitor as he looked over. "They're back." She punched up the lab corridor camera. "They're headed back to the lab."

As they watched, the Soviets again approached the water-tight door. This time, they took a different approach to getting in. One of the invaders pointed up to the bundle of pipes that ran through the bulkhead into the corridor. The other man nodded and spoke to the others. In moments, they had out a metallic-looking bar and had what appeared to be a fuse attached to it. One of the men stepped up on another's shoulders and slid the bar behind the pipe bundle, wiring it into place. When he was finished, he pulled the igniter ring, jumped down, and joined the others farther down the corridor.

"Jesus Christ!" Nancy yelled, jumping to her feet. "If that's a cutter charge, they'll cut right through the skin!" Her eyes and mouth were wide with fear as she watched the bar explode. A black cloud of smoke filled the corridor as the charge went off.

"No, no, no," she prayed, waiting to see the fan of water that would signal a break in the outer wall of DeepCore. The spray did not come.

"I can't believe it didn't cut through the skin!" she marveled.

"They turned it away from the wall so the blast would go into the center of the corridor instead of out through the wall," Jackson speculated. "Pretty smart."

"Smart, hell," she cursed. "Motherfuckers!"

In the smoky corridor, the Soviets were back at work on the door. This time, when they pried it back, it slid open. One of the pipes in the bundle had held the wiring for the automatic door. With the power cut, the door could be manhandled open. The Soviets were quickly through the corridor, where they prepared to use the same trick on the watertight door that led to the lab complex itself.

"They'll be in there in nothing flat," she observed, "God save those people."

The second blast shook the lab and echoed through the steel walls and doors.

Janice Wellford was gasping in fear, making little animal sounds. Her face was rigid and her thin frame shook all over. When the intercom came to life, she screamed.

"Positrack lab, this is DeepCore Security," the voice asked, "anyone home?"

Brittan stepped over to the panel, moving Janice out of the way.

"Brittan here, who is this?"

"Tom Jackson, Dr. Brittan," Jackson answered. "What's your situation?"

"We're locked in here," Brittan answered. "Help us!"

"We're on the way, Doc. Hold the fort as long as you can."

"What choice do we have?"

Jackson looked over at Nancy Collins. She raised her eyebrows and shrugged. Jackson did not reply. He had no advice to offer.

"Excellent," Drachev congratulated Kron, "now the next one."

In minutes, another linear shape charge was in place at the far end of the corridor leading to the lab. The blast severed the cable, but a thin stream of water spewed in behind the blast from a weld that cracked under the force of the explosion. Drachev's men ignored the icy spray as they pried open the door leading to their primary objective. Once inside, they were stymied again by a watertight door that was locked. These were smaller versions of the door that led to the industrial area. Each locking lug had to be cut separately.

"It will take a few minutes to rig this charge, Comrade Major," Kron apologized. Drachev stood looking at his schematic drawing.

"Have the men construct a series of these charges," Drachev ordered. "There are several of these doors in this lab. We may have to cut through all of them."

"It is done, Comrade Major."

If we have enough explosives, we may finish this yet, Drachev speculated, and if the security force gives us enough time.

He had positioned four men back down the corridor. They could keep a large force at bay long enough to gain access to the labs and load up the Positrack equipment. The submarine captain was already waiting at the escape hatch. They would return to the *Odessa* through the emergency hatch as planned. His plan was behind schedule, but it was proceeding. The cost had been higher than he had expected.

Five minutes later the first charge was finished and on the door. Drachev and the others retreated behind cover as Kron pulled the fuse and ran back to join them.

The door blew in with a tremendous boom. Even with their mouths open and their hands over their ears, the concussion stunned them. In a moment, though, they were into the first room, searching for the electronic objets d'art that were the cause of all this suffering and death.

There were several packing crates unopened. Drachev stood watching as two privates twisted the catches and popped one of the containers, open. Inside were circuit boards, each board nestled in a foam-lined slot.

"Move these to the escape hatch and return," he commanded the two privates. He would loot each room as they gained access, that would speed the process and get him and his troops out as fast as possible.

The next room yielded another load of electronics treasures. Drachev sent this load of parts back as well, leaving only himself, Sgt. Kron, and Filipov to apply the charges to the final door.

"We have taken a large amount of equipment, Comrade Major," Sgt. Kron observed. "Should we not depart now with what we have rather than risk losing it while we attempt to obtain more?"

Drachev nearly said yes, but remembered Lavrov's words. The future security of the Soviet Navy was his responsibility. "We will take whatever is in this room," he replied, "and depart only then."

Kron did not answer, but went on placing the charges over each locking lug. The chain of charges did not reach completely around the door.

"We did not have enough charges to ring this door completely, Comrade Major," Kron explained. "The top two lugs will not be cut, but the door should still come open."

"Do it," Drachev answered.

Once more they sought cover and set off the explosives. This time, a long muffled scream followed the concussion. The door was still in place when the smoke cleared.

Filipov was running for the door, his weapon up. Drachev screamed at him. "No shooting! Take them alive!" Filipov looked back over his shoulder as he kicked the door and jumped back. The door fell into the next room with a clang. Filipov was first through the door, with Kron right on his heels.

Inside the final room, three men and a woman were cowering behind overturned worktables.

"Hands up!" Kron shouted in English. "Stand up, move away from the tables!" The four captives instantly complied, huddling together in the middle of the room. Filipov stood guard as Kron began to fill the remaining empty rucksack with printed circuit boards that read Logic Board in white letters on their green surfaces.

"Your names!" Drachev shouted at the captives.

37

They got lost looking for Jackson's office. He finally found them on one of the cameras and turned them around. They were wasting time, but now was not the time to be hasty. They had knocked off two guards, but the Soviet main force would be another story.

Finally, they rounded a corner and found Tom Jackson standing in his open doorway.

"Jesus, I'm glad to see you!" Jackson said as the four new-comers crowded into his tiny room. "This is Nancy Collins, senior engineer on DeepCore."

"You people are sure fucking up my backyard," Collins said in reply to their greetings.

"That's what happens, ma'am," King answered. "Let one Russian move into your neighborhood and it's ruined!"

She just stared at the big black man, unsure how to reply.

"Where are they, Tom?" Moore was asking. Jackson pointed to monitor one, locked on the camera in the first room of the lab. The room was almost empty.

"They had to cut through every door in the lab," he explained. "Dr. Brittan and his people, Jan Wellford, Bobby Talent, and a guy named What-a-nobber are in there." He cut a look over at Nancy. "Anyway, they're carting stuff out of there as fast as they can and taking it back to the emergency airlock."

"Anywhere we can jump 'em?" Moore asked.

"Not really," Jackson answered, "they sealed the passage-way doors leading to the escape airlock."

"How'd they do that?" Bickerstaff asked.

"Put the controls on manual, then shot the control boxes

when the door closed," Nancy Collins answered. "Have to cut the power to the doors to get them open."

"Can you do that?" Moore asked.

"Maybe, I never tried."

"Any other way to get there?"

"You could do it outside, but it would be hard."

"How hard?" Moore asked, eager for some way to take the fight back to the invaders.

"If you came up through the bottom hatch of the emergency airlock," she began.

"They'd blow your ass off," Bickerstaff finished the sentence for her.

"Anyway," she went on, "it's too far to swim."

"Is there any gear around here we could use?" Moore asked.

"All the scuba gear is kept in the sub pool area. If you could get there, you could use it. Otherwise, the only other thing would be a deepsuit from the decompression module."

Moore stood watching the monitors. His mind flickered through one scenario after another, searching for a way to stop the invaders. As he struggled with a plan, the camera caught sight of a group leaving the lab complex. Moore's heart sank. The four civilians, their hands tied behind them, were being herded along by three Soviets.

"Ain't that the one we ran into in the sub pool?" Bickerstaff asked, leaning up to get a better look at the wounded soldier who was using his pistol to push the one woman in the group.

"That's him, Bro," King observed, "shoulda shot him when we had the chance."

"Tried to," Bickerstaff remembered.

"Where are they going?" Moore asked. "The escape hatch?"

"Yeah, looks like it," Jackson answered.

"Come on, guys," Moore snapped. "Tom, I'm going to need some help with this one, buddy."

What a prize, Drachev thought as Kron and Filipov herded the captives ahead of them. Not only do I have the Positrack system, but I have its inventor as well. *Ochen Horosho*! And to top it off, the captain of a Los Angeles-class submarine! The cost has been high, but the rewards will be great!

As they neared the command center, Filipov dropped back to speak to him.

"Comrade Major," the private began nervously, "I am afraid . . . I am concerned about the security force I encountered in the sub pool."

"In what way, *raydoviki*?" Drachev asked.

"Only that we have not seen them since," Filipov answered. "They could be planning an ambush."

"Your concern is well taken, Filipov," Drachev answered. "We will act on it."

"They're headed for the command center!" Nancy shouted.

Moore glanced at the schematic board. "Can we intercept them?"

She thought for a second, running the layout of the complex through her mind. "No."

"Damn it!" Moore cursed.

"Sgt. Kron," Drachev ordered as they entered the command center, "get all the wounded aboard. If there is any room left, take one of our guests."

"It is done," Kron answered. He motioned Filipov toward the escape hatch as Drachev scanned the many readouts, gauges, and keyboards in the command center.

"Perhaps we will give our other friends on board something more urgent to worry over than us," Drachev said in English. He sat down at a console and began flipping switches with a familiarity that stunned his captives. "Air and light are two attention-getters," Drachev observed. He flipped the master switches on DeepCore's main electrical panel.

The fluorescent lights went dark. Half a second later the red emergency lights came on, giving the command center an eerie science-fiction look. Drachev switched on the small incandescent lights over the console and searched for the environmental controls. Unable to find them, he turned to Brittan.

"Where are the oxygen and pressure controls?"

Brittan slumped impassively against the door. He seemed to be in a state of shock. Watching strangers load up his life into backpacks and cart it out had unnerved him. Drachev asked again. Brittan glared at him and spat, "I don't know!"

Drachev pulled his pistol and stepped over to Janice Wellford. He grabbed her by her hair and jerked her out in front of Brittan.

"Where are the pressure and air controls?" he asked once more, jamming the barrel of the silenced pistol against her face. She gasped as the knurled edge of the silencer abraded her cheekbone.

"The computer!" Brittan blurted. "The computer controls all that."

"Then you will show me!" Drachev snapped, forcing the gun barrel up into her eye. She squirmed and twisted, making little sounds in her throat.

"I'll try!" Brittan said. Drachev motioned to the guard, who stepped over and untwisted the wire from Brittan's wrist. Brittan sat at the terminal and brought up the main menu. He punched up some commands. The message bar flashed. UNAUTHORIZED ENTRY.

Brittan typed more commands. The message bar read PLEASE ENTER ACCESS CODE. Brittan typed in his code. The message bar read ACCESS DENIED, UNAUTHORIZED CODE.

"I can't get into the system," Brittan complained. Drachev dragged Janice over next to Brittan.

"Perhaps if I blow her brains all over you," he sneered, "you will be able to remember better!"

Brittan looked up, his eyes pleading. "No!" he stammered. "I don't know the code!"

"Then I will shoot each of your friends until you make it up!" Drachev assured him.

The oriental captive stepped forward. "Excuse me, sir," the little man began, "I know the access code to the system." The other Positrack team members looked at the small Japanese. "I broke into the system," he went on, "I am a computer hacker. I can bypass the code. If you spare me, I will be happy to do so for you."

Drachev smiled and looked down at Brittan. "You see, I knew that your memories would improve." He struck Brittan a backhand blow with the pistol, knocking him out of the chair.

Still holding Janice's hair, Drachev motioned Watanabe over. After removing the wire from his hands, he pushed the little man down into the chair.

"Flood the submarine pool and the dock where the American submarine is tied up," he commanded. "Then we will attempt to find the security force." He threw Janice back toward the others as one of the Russians rewired Brittan's hands behind his back.

Watanabe nodded and entered the command code he had extracted from the computer.

"They're flooding the place," Nancy Collins shouted as the red warning signals flashed on the computer screen. Low-pressure warnings were flashing in the sub pool and the industrial area.

"How could they do that?" Jackson asked as she sat down at the console and attempted to reverse the commands.

"Somebody's gone around the code," she answered distractedly.

"Can we override them?" Jackson queried. She looked up at him.

"Maybe, but we'll have to pump out the water." The monitor display showed water bubbling up in the sub pool. DeepCore's subs, *Faith, Hope,* and *Charity* were already banging on the ceiling of the sub pool room.

The cameras in the industrial area were dark.

"Looks like we need to go to work," Moore observed. He motioned to the others from security. "Leave us go amongst them, brethren." With that cryptic remark, Moore walked out of Jackson's little office with Carla, King, and Bickerstaff in tow.

"Whoever is doing this is not one of us," Nancy remarked. "He knows how to do some things, but not the real tricks. I can lock him out." She tapped the keys, waited for a prompt, then typed another quick phrase.

"Got him!" she snapped. She looked up at Jackson with the first happy expression he had seen on her face. "I locked out any commands not preceded by my own code!"

"You'd better tell me what your code is," Jackson suggested. "In case I have to . . ." He started to say "take over," but managed to change it to "give you a hand."

She looked at the screen and muttered something he could not hear.

"What?" he asked.

"I said, Babydoll," she barked. "That's my code word."

"Babydoll," Jackson repeated. "Really?"

She shot him a look that terminated the conversation, then

went back to countermanding the invader's orders.

Jackson forced the smile off his face. Babydoll, indeed.

"I do not understand!" Watanabe whined. "Someone has locked me out! I can't get the computer to respond!"

Drachev looked at the pathetic little technician. He was tempted to shoot him on the spot, but he might yet have valuable knowledge. He jerked the Japanese out of the chair and thrust him toward another Russian who caught Watanabe and bound his hands again.

"You did well enough!" Drachev said. "We will finish the job in the old-fashioned way." By blowing the place to pieces, he thought, completing the death sentence.

"Recall the sub-unit from the American submarine and move the prisoners to the escape hatch!" Drachev ordered. "We will wait there for Sgt. Kron's return." The escape hatch had only one entrance. It would be easy to defend against the security force if they ever reappeared.

38

"Bob," Jackson's voice hissed from the metal grill, "you got company coming."

"How many?" Moore asked. They were still some way from the command center.

"Three," Jackson replied, "from the *Houston*."

"Roger!" Moore answered. He turned to the others. "Okay, let's do this the easy way," Moore snapped. He took Carla by the arm. "Stay here behind the I-beam. Keep as flat up against it as you can. Shoot when I do. Understand?"

"Right."

Carla flattened herself back up into the I-beam's wide channel, her pistol held next to her face. The burnt powder smell tickled her nose and she moved the muzzle away from her face a bit. This was no time to sneeze. She peeked across the hall at Bob Moore.

He was contorted behind the opposite beam, scrunched into a space much narrower than his body. He grinned and winked.

When she heard the sounds of boots in the corridor, she leaned back, took a deep breath, and let half of it out. She held her breath as the running men grew closer.

When the first man flashed past, she could hardly keep still. She wanted to shoot, but there were two more to account for. A second later, they flashed by.

Moore stepped forward with the machine pistol and fired. For a split second, Carla was frozen, watching the little machine gun spit bullets, the brass cases streaming up from the breech like a golden cascade.

Moore fired when the two men were nearly lined up, making it easier to engage them both at once. Hit from behind, the man closest to Moore lay facedown, sprawled where the burst from Moore's gun had ripped through him. Down the hall, the other man crumpled, hit by Moore's second burst that walked up across his chest and face.

Carla brought her pistol down and stared at the man closest to her. He was turning now, swinging his weapon around. She stared at his chest and fired three rounds. She could feel the pistol jump in her hand, but the noise was muted, somehow irrelevant. The man jerked to the left, hit by at least one of her shots. He made a horrible face, but continued to turn, the muzzle of his gun lining up on Bob Moore. She fired four more rounds as fast as she could squeeze the trigger. The man seemed to jump backward. He fired his weapon, the ceramic bullets splanging off the ceiling in glittering showers of ceramic shards.

The fight, if it could be called that, had taken maybe three seconds. Three dead men in three seconds. Carla felt numb, like she should feel something more after killing a man in cold blood. There was nothing to feel. Jackson's voice startled her.

"Nice work!" he complimented them.

"Watch 'em, Carla," Moore snapped, stepping over to the intercom. "Any more out there?" he asked their unseen genie.

"Can't see any," Jackson replied, "I'll holler if I do."

"We're joining the others," Moore said. He stepped over to each man and fired a single shot into his head, a coup de gracè. She winced at each shot. Shooting them down as they ran had seemed easy, even surreal. Shooting them again seemed ugly.

Moore stripped the men's equipment pouches for magazines and picked up their weapons. "Here," he said, handing her one of the little guns. She tucked it under her arm and let the hammer down on her pistol. Pocketing the pistol, she took the two magazines Moore held up for her.

"Let's go," he snapped. She followed him down the hall, turning nervously to look at the three sprawled attackers.

"Boss, this sounds like suicide to me," Bickerstaff said.

"I know, you already said that," Moore quipped. "I'm still open to suggestions." There were only blank looks from the others. They were skeptical about his using the deepsuit to get into the escape hatch, but had no better ideas of their own.

"Even if you can get into the hatch well," Bickerstaff went on, playing devil's advocate, "they'll hear you open the hatch and blow your head off!"

"Like an Eskimo shooting a seal, huh?" Moore answered.

"Exactly!"

"Well, Bick," Moore answered, "that's your job. Give them something else to think about." He stood up and hooked a thumb over his shoulder. "Ty, you and Carla keep 'em busy," he ordered. "I'll send Bick back as soon as I get into the deepsuit rig."

Carla spoke up. "Why don't you wait until they get the sub pool pumped out?"

"It'll take hours for them to pump out the place," Moore explained, "and I can't swim that far without air of some sort."

As Moore and Bickerstaff ran off toward the decompression module, Carla turned to Ty King. "Is this going to work?"

He smiled at her. "Maybe."

When they got to the decompression module, Moore and Bickerstaff went straight for the deepsuits.

"Do you remember how to put this thing on?" Bickerstaff asked warily as they pulled one of the Liquidair suits from the rack, checked the gas cylinders, and filled it with fresh fluorocarbon from the bottles stored overhead.

"We'll find out in a second," Moore replied, slipping quickly into the Kevlar dive suit and mounting the front console on it. Bickerstaff helped him with the helmet and the two men walked over to the egress hatch at the far end of the module. Moore sat cross-legged on the metal floor. Bickerstaff knelt behind him.

"Okay, here goes nothing," Moore said, opening the valves that fed the liquid fluorocarbon into the helmet. Bickerstaff put his arms around Moore's chest and waited. The pink fluid rushed into the helmet and soon covered Moore's face. He exhaled, a cloud of large bubbles foaming to the top of the faceplate, then inhaled the liquid deeply into his lungs.

Bickerstaff held him as Moore convulsed. In a moment, the shaking stopped and Bickerstaff looked around at Moore's face.

"You okay?" Bickerstaff asked. Moore made a face and pointed to his ears. Bickerstaff realized that he could not hear or talk to reply. There was no computer link in the decompression module. Bickerstaff gave Moore a thumbs-up sign, raising his eyebrows to show it was a question.

Moore returned the gesture, then added a waggle of his hand to show it was mostly okay. Moore struggled to his feet and stepped over to the hatch, pulling the metal grid up to expose the hatch. Bickerstaff checked the magazine on the MP-5, then slipped the little gun over Moore's shoulder, securing it with a Velcro tie-down on the suit. Moore pantomimed opening the hatch and Bickerstaff did just that, then picked up the arrow gun, checked the cylinder and the remaining arrow, and passed it to Moore. They stood looking at each other for a second.

"Get 'em," Bickerstaff said, exaggerating the words so Moore could read his lips. He jammed his forefinger into his other fist to reinforce the message. Moore nodded and smiled. He held up his middle finger and pointed to himself, a gesture Bickerstaff recognized as "Fuck me!"

With that, Moore stepped off into the hatch and disappeared from sight. Bickerstaff shouldered his weapon and started back for the main complex, then stopped and went back into the decompression module.

"I think we ought to wait for Elgin!" Carla whispered.

"And if he don't come back?" King asked rhetorically. "Listen, Carla, you remember all those cop classes you took on urban combat shooting?"

"Uh-huh," she nodded.

"Forget them," he cautioned her. "There're no good guys but you and me. Anything that moves is bad by definition." King stuffed two full magazines into his pockets and shoved two more into the side pocket of Carla's jumpsuit. "If it moves, shoot it!" he stressed. "If it moves again, shoot it a lot." He turned to look at her. "Uncle Bob needs some time to make his move. We have to give it to him. If we fuck up, he's dead meat."

A horrified look flickered across her face.

"But don't let me put any pressure on you," he quipped.

"Fuck you, Tyrone!" she hissed.

"That's my girl!" he chuckled.

King held his finger to his lips. He eased one eye past the corner and took a quick peek down the hallway. "I'll go first," he whispered back to her. "Then you come when I tell you."

"Ty, let's wait for Elgin!" He ignored her and suddenly dashed around the corner and across the hallway. She lunged into the space he had left and whipped the barrel of her MP-5 around the corner to cover him.

There was no gunfire in the corridor. King flattened himself against the wall behind one of the wide I-beam ribs and peeked around it. After a few seconds he motioned to her.

She felt a huge knot in her stomach and her hands suddenly felt clammy on the plastic grips of the submachine gun. Carla took a deep breath, focused on where she was going, and jumped up.

She was across the corridor before she knew it, slamming her back into the wall behind King. There was no firing. As she caught her breath, she saw the body across the corridor. The man was in bib overalls and a plaid shirt, one of the DeepCore crew. He had a length of pipe clear through him and lay staring at her quizzically.

His expression seemed to say, "Are you going to join me?" Her stomach flip-flopped and she looked away from the dead man, trying to focus on her job.

"Your turn," King whispered, pointing down the corridor. Carla saw a good position behind a large circular pipe that ran from floor to ceiling next to the wall about ten meters down the corridor.

"Ready?" King whispered.

"Yeah!" she breathed next to his ear.

"Do it!"

She sprang up again and dashed for the pipe. Soft popping noises seemed to come from everywhere and tiny ceramic bullets shattered and buzzed around her like a swarm of killer bees. She dropped and rolled against the wall, struggling to get her weapon up and return the fire. Behind her, King was firing short bursts down the hall.

Carla shoved her gun around the side of the pipe and fired a short burst so she could sneak a look down the corridor. In that fraction of a second, she saw a dark form lying facedown in the corridor on her side and another dark shape firing from the other side. Bullets whined off the pipe next to her head, showering tiny ceramic shards down the corridor.

She twisted around the other way, facing the wall. There was a two-inch gap between the pipe and the wall. Carla shoved the barrel of her gun into the gap and fired, estimating the angle to hit the gunman down the hall. More shots splattered against the pipe. She looked through the slit down the wall. Another dark shape appeared above the fallen one, dragging his comrade out of the line of fire.

Carla fired two shots at him, then ducked back as a burst from down the corridor whined off the wall next to her, showering her with ceramic bits that stuck in the fabric of her jumpsuit. Both sides traded bursts, ducking and firing blind.

We're stuck here, Carla thought as she dropped an empty magazine from her weapon and slipped a full one into the MP-5. Mexican standoff.

39

Salvador tilted his head, listening. He leaned over and tapped Beecher. Beecher, almost asleep, jumped at the touch, blinking. Salvador pointed forward. "Pilot wants to talk to you!" he called.

Beecher made his way forward through the mass of equipment. In the cockpit, the red instrument lights lit the two flyers with an eerie glow.

"Mr. Beecher," the pilot asked, "can you confirm these coordinates for your facility?" He pointed toward the navigational display where DeepCore's location was punched up.

"That's it," Beecher replied. "Why?"

"Because your ship should have come up on our radar by now and there's no sign of it." The copilot, Bowman, pointed to the square search radar display. The green screen was blank, the line sweeping back and forth like an electronic metronome. "We haven't been able to raise her on the radio, either."

Beecher felt a knot tighten in his guts. If the support ship went down, DeepCore would still survive. Unless the ship sank on DeepCore itself. Beecher clenched his fists, fighting to keep the image of the *UnderSea Pacific* smashing down onto the DeepCore complex out of his mind.

"How long until we're over the location?" Beecher asked.

"Twenty minutes, maybe," the pilot answered. Beecher nodded. Twenty minutes suddenly seemed like an eternity. He checked his watch, then returned to his seat in the back. The copilot was talking on the radio to his base, updating them.

"Good news?" Parker asked as Beecher passed.

Beecher shook his head. "Bad news!" he said, slumping into the seat. "The worst."

Parker made a face and keyed his intercom. He nodded, answered quickly, switched on his sonar sets, and began to check them. Next to him, Michaels turned on his equipment and went aft to prepare his sonobuoys for deployment. Beecher's heart sank. All this fancy hardware would only measure the extent of the disaster.

The cold penetrated his suit immediately and Moore realized that no one had shown them how to turn on the suit heater. He was searching the console for some control switch when the suit began to heat on its own. Moore was headed for the escape hatch, bounding over the rocky bottom like a moon astronaut. He had no weights to hold him down, but the Liquidair suit held no air to make him buoyant. Taking long, bounding strides over the rocks, it only took ten minutes to reach the hatch.

Moore reached up and gently tried the hatch ring. It moved easily. He looked at his watch. In four minutes, Tom Jackson would start the show. Moore let himself sink to the bottom and stood there, looking up at the hatch and glancing at his watch.

This was the bad part, the waiting time, the time you had to think about what you were doing. At least this would only be a few minutes, not like so many missions during the war when they'd waited hours or days. It was so odd, being back in action with Bickerstaff and King. Odder still that they were fighting the same people after so long.

The exertion and the suit heater had warmed him. Now Moore felt the tickling of sweat as it made its way down his spine. He took a deep breath, feeling the warm liquid flow down his throat into his lungs.

When you're doing something, you don't notice that sensation, he thought, but when you're still, it feels weird as hell.

Moore closed his eyes and mentally ran over the plan again. Tom Jackson would sound the collision alarm as loud as it would go and turn off the lights for ten seconds. He would also jump up the pressure in the escape hatch to make everyone's ears hurt, then drop it to pop them real loud. During this distraction, Moore would open the hatch, climb up into the well, put an arrow into any guard he encountered, then throw off the grid and climb up into the room. King, Bickerstaff, and

Carla would keep the invaders busy. If Moore could surprise them, the invaders would be caught in a cross fire. It was a big "if," but not impossible. Keeping the hostages out of the way would be the other major problem.

Moore looked again at his watch. One minute. He bent his knees and jumped up to catch the hatch ring and missed. He sank back to the bottom and jumped again, his hand coming up within a foot of the ring, missing again. As he sank again to the bottom, he looked at his watch. Thirty seconds.

Moore bent his knees and waited for them to touch the rock bottom. As soon as they touched, he lunged up, putting everything he had into the leap, his arm stretched above him, hand reaching for the metal wheel. His fingertips slipped up through the spokes of the hatch ring and Moore clawed with them for a handhold. He found it and pulled himself up. He held the hatch with one hand and looked again at his watch. Ten seconds. Moore hung from the hatch ring, waiting for the excitement to begin. Even in the heated suit, he felt cold.

"Ten seconds," Jackson said. "Ready?"

Nancy Collins had her hand on the collision alarm. "Your friends are nuts!" she observed. On the monitor above Jackson's head, Carla Fuentes and Ty King were still trading shots with two of the invaders, keeping each other occupied.

"Probably," Jackson replied. "Five, four, three, two, one."

On zero, Collins hit the collision alarm. The loud shriek went off in every compartment of DeepCore, the signal to shut every watertight door and prepare for impact. Flashing red lights went on in every room and corridor.

Jackson keyed the environmental controls for the escape hatch, put a burst of high-pressure air into the area, then shut off the lights.

"Go get 'em, Bob," Jackson said, watching the monitor. The screen was dark, lit only by the flashing emergency light that provided snapshots of the action in the corridor.

Well, if they act like they are going to torture me, Bobby Talent thought, I'll spill my guts. No way I'm going to suffer for Warp Ten Labs or these DeepCore jerks. Anyway, I hear they treat scientists pretty well there. Maybe I can cut a deal.

Leaning against the wall and staring at the floor grate as he mused on his future, Talent nearly jumped out of his skin when the alarm sounded. The lights went out, replaced by the flashing red emergency lights. The guard turned to the doorway, his gun in front of him.

Talent thought for a second that he was seeing things. Under the grate, a figure moved. As Talent watched, a helmeted head appeared, followed by the tip of an arrow that stuck up through the grate, reflecting the flashing red light off its sharp edges.

Movement behind him diverted Talent's attention. The guard had seen the figure, too, and was turning to shoot.

Whoever the helmeted newcomer was, he wasn't one of them, and that was enough for Talent. As the guard raised his gun to fire, Talent lashed out with his foot for the man's gun. The Russian was quicker, though, and jerked back. Talent felt his foot glance off the gun.

He pulled his leg back, trying desperately to get his balance for another kick. He almost succeeded. The guard took a step back, then stepped into a half turn that brought the gun's muzzle around toward him. Talent was bringing his foot up for another kick when the stream of ceramic slugs caught him in the chest, slamming him against the metal wall. He hit his head, the pain from that impact worse than the ache in his chest. He fell, sliding down the wall. It seemed that the red lights were dimming. His head felt heavy, too heavy to move. At his feet, the Russian guard was kneeling, holding a long thin tube up to his chest. The Russian looked up and fell over backward as the red lights went black.

When the watch's second hand passed 12, Moore spun the ring and let the hatch swing down. He pulled himself up into the opening and looked up. The grid was in place, but no one was on it. Moore pulled himself up into the hatch well, braced himself with his legs, and eased his faceplate out of the water.

The hatch seemed empty, but then a figure moved into view. Moore stuck the razor-tipped arrow up through the grid and watched the man, waiting to see if he was friend or foe.

The dark shape of an MP-5 answered the question. The man saw Moore beneath the grid and turned, the muzzle of his gun dropping.

From the side, a foot lashed out at the guard. The guard, stepped back, then turned and fired at the unseen kicker. Moore aimed the arrow at the guard's center of mass and shot. The arrow disappeared off the end of his gun and reappeared in the man's chest.

Moore dropped the arrow gun and pushed up on the grid. It tipped up and Moore slipped it off to one side as quietly as he could, pulling himself up into the escape hatch as the spent arrow gun fell out of the well and sank to the bottom. Off to his right, a man in a white lab coat, his hands tied behind him, lay slumped against the wall. Dark red splotches stained the white coat. The guard was on his knees, both hands clutching the arrow that protruded from his sternum.

As Moore clambered up onto the floor, the guard's head tipped backward, the rest of his body following. He lay sprawled on his back next to the dead hostage, the arrow twitching as the man's heart gushed the last of his blood out into his chest. Moore was reaching around for his submachine gun when another invader stepped into the room from the corridor.

He hadn't heard the shots in the escape hatch. They had been masked by the flurry of gunfire in the corridor. The scuffling sound caught his attention. Drachev stepped back into the hatch to check on Arbatov. He didn't want any of his precious hostages killed because one of his troops overreacted.

The first thing Drachev saw when he stepped into the hatch was the man in the cosmonaut suit. The sight was so out of place that it took him half a second to respond, but when he saw an MP-5 strapped to the spaceman, Drachev reacted.

After I kill him, Drachev thought as he brought his gun up, I want to find out what he is. Just as his finger tightened on the trigger, a wall fell on him.

Lost in worry about the *Houston*, Knickerbocker struggled to his feet when the alarm sounded. He looked up as the new Positrack man, Talent, tried to kick the Russian guard. The Russian shot Talent with a burst that hit him square in the chest and slammed him against the wall.

An arrow streaked from the floor grate and hit the guard in the chest. Clutching the shaft, the Russian dropped to his knees and fell backward as Knickerbocker stood there, his mouth open in astonishment.

The floor grate slid open and a figure out of a space movie emerged from the dark water under the grate. In the red glow of the flashing emergency lights, the newcomer looked like an alien invader in his white suit and gleaming white helmet.

The figure was struggling to its feet when the leader of the Russians walked into the escape hatch. The alien was reaching for a gun, but the Russian already had his.

Before he had time to think about it, Knickerbocker was moving. Back a hundred years ago, when Knickerbocker had been a defensive lineman on the Naval Academy team, his nickname had been Knickerblocker. Using a skill he thought long forgotten, Knickerblocker hit the Russian with a body slam that carried them both up against the wall next to the two dead men.

A burst from the Russian's gun went wide, pinging off the metal walls. Knickerbocker planted his feet, leaned back from the waist and hit the Russian with the only weapon he had, his head. The Russian's head bounced off the wall. Knickerbocker ignored the pain in his own head and twisted, reaching around with his bound hands for the Russian's weapon. He managed to get hold of the weapon's nylon sling and held it in a death grip. The Russian jerked his arms up, grabbed his own wrist, and hit Knickerbocker's face with an elbow that felt like a battering ram.

The room spun as Knickerbocker reeled across the room, still clutching the Russian's gun sling, the small gun swinging out in an arc as Knickerbocker fell against the other prisoners. The three of them landed in a heap with Knickerbocker on the bottom, the gun trapped beneath him. As he tried to shake off the cobwebs and get back to his feet, Knickerbocker could hear the scuffling and the Russian's muttered curses.

Pain shot through Drachev's head as the huge American sub-mariner slammed him with his head. His weapon was pinned between them. Fighting to keep his wits, Drachev twisted his arms around and hit the American with all his might, using his elbow to hammer the man's face just above his nose. The American went reeling, but snatched the small gun off

he fell. The wet cosmonaut was fumbling for
_ied to his suit.

_ crossed the room in two steps. The spaceman was
_g up the weapon to fire. Drachev snap-kicked the gun
a _ fired. The bullet was a hot stab in his lower leg. The
weapon somersaulted over the man's shoulder and splashed
into the hatch well.

Drachev, his foot still in the air, aimed another kick at
the now unarmed intruder. The man was quick, though, and
grabbed Drachev's foot, twisting it to the outside and throwing
Drachev backward. He stumbled and fell, the spaceman rising
to his feet in front of him.

Arbatov's weapon was lying next to him a meter away.
Drachev rolled toward it, his hand seeking the pistol grip.
He nearly had it when a hammerlike fist slammed down on
his wrist and the hard metal case on the front of the spaceman's suit knocked the wind from Drachev's lungs as the man
crashed down on him.

Fearing another head butt, Drachev thrashed, trying to throw
off the attacker, but the man was heavy as stone. The equipment
packs added to his weight and to the pressure on Drachev's ribs.
Mustering all his strength, Drachev fought to escape the pain in
his chest and the blows from the man's gloved hands.

The man brought up his knee to keep Drachev from rolling
away. Strapped to the man's calf was an orange-handled dive
knife in a plastic sheath. Drachev pulled one hand free and
tugged on the knife. It stubbornly clung to its sheath until
Drachev's finger happened onto the button that released it.
Holding the knife blade down, Drachev pushed away to give
him room to stab this bizarre stranger. As the blade plunged
down, Drachev noticed the dull, flat chisel point on the blade.
It was not a knife, but a tool with a knife handle. The flat point
struck the man's chest.

If it had a point, Drachev thought, it would be in his
heart now!

He struck again at the suit with no greater success. The
stranger's face, bathed in some liquid inside his helmet, gri-
maced in pain. At least I'm hurting the bastard, Drachev
thought as the man tried to grab the flashing blade.

Drachev hooked his leg behind him and levered himself up,
rolling over on top of the man. He brought the serrated edge

of the blade up and began to saw into the hose that ran from the chest-mounted console to the helmet. The cloth covering resisted the blade.

What is this stuff? Drachev wondered as the seemingly invulnerable attacker landed a solid right cross on Drachev's head. Drachev rolled to the side and came up in a crouch, his left ear ringing from the blow. The man in the suit was up on one knee, trying to rise. Drachev planted a roundhouse kick to the man's side, rolling him. The invader used the roll to get to his feet.

Drachev took a running step and jumped into the air, lashing out with his foot at the man's head. The stranger tried to duck, but the kick caught his shoulder and sent him sprawling on his back. Drachev was on him in a second. Using both hands, he brought the chisel point of the blade down on the helmet's clear faceplate as hard as he could. A silvery chip flew from the surface, leaving a deep gouge in the plate above the man's left eye. If the fabric could not be cut, the faceplate could. Drachev began to pound on it. On the fourth blow, the plate cracked and the pale fluid in the mask began to pour out. Drachev kept up the pounding.

Janice kicked with her feet, thrashing and floundering to get off Herk's back and see what was going on. She had nearly peed herself when the alarm went off. Now, the noise had stopped, but the red emergency lights were still flashing.

She managed to roll off Brittan and push herself back up against the wall. She pulled her legs up and rolled to the side, bringing her up into a tight sitting position, leaning back against the wall to hold herself up.

Next to her, the Navy officer was yelling at Herk to get off him and Herk was floundering around trying to do just that.

The Russian and the stranger were still fighting and the Russian seemed to be winning.

She had been too scared to speak since the invaders had cut through the door into the lab and taken them prisoner. Since the business in the command center, she had been too scared to even think, huddling against Herk. As the knife fell again on the man's face and fluid poured down the side of the helmet, Janice found her voice.

She threw back her head and screamed, "NO" as hard as she could, screaming it over and over, stretching out the word as long as she had breath.

40

The screaming broke the stalemate. King was the first to move, yelling, "Cover me!" as he dashed toward another support pillar. He had gone only a few steps before he fell, clutching his leg and rolling toward the wall.

Carla fired a burst down the hall. The weapon stopped after a few shots, empty. She threw it down, pulled out her pistol, and jumped out to help King. She was barely on her feet when she stepped on two of the dozens of brass shell cases scattered all over the corridor and fell headlong onto the floor. For a second panic seized her, pinning her to the floor.

King, sitting against the wall, leaned out and fired a wild spray down the corridor to keep their opponents behind cover while she got her footing again. Carla was firing, trying to get to her feet when a roar from behind caught their attention.

Elgin Bickerstaff looked and sounded like a locomotive coming down the corridor. He leaped over Carla, shot one of the enemy in passing, and jumped in the face of another at the end of the corridor. As he passed, one of the enemy fired a long burst at Bickerstaff. King watched the slugs hit Bickerstaff's side and back. Preoccupied with the wild man in their midst, the enemy forgot about King and Carla. They promptly emptied their ammunition into him.

Moore could hear someone screaming in the room, but it was impossible to tell who was screaming or from what direction. It didn't matter, Moore had enough to deal with. The Russian had stabbed him twice with the dull tip of the dive tool. His ribs hurt like hell. One was probably broken. The flat blade had not penetrated the Kevlar suit, but the blow had been punishing enough.

Now the Red was pounding on the faceplate with the knife, chipping away at the curved polymer surface. He was pinned on his back, the thick backpack holding him awkwardly up off the floor. Moore's right hand was pinned under him by the Russian's leg and foot. Moore swung his left as hard as he could, but the man seemed oblivious to the blows.

He heard the faceplate crack and saw the starfish pattern of the crack splash across the clear surface. On the next blow, pink fluid splashed onto the surface of the plate. The liquid fluorocarbon was leaking.

Now he was in trouble. When all the breathing fluid ran out of the helmet, he would start to choke. When that happened, he would be meat on the table for this Russian bastard.

Bickerstaff was nearly to the corridor that led to the escape hatch when he heard the loud pistol shots followed by a coughing sound that could only be MP-5s firing together. He skidded to a stop just short of the corner and flattened himself against the wall to check the magazine in his weapon. It was nearly full, maybe twenty-five rounds.

As he slipped it back into the magazine well and tapped the bottom to seat it, a woman screamed. Bickerstaff looked quickly around the corner. There was Carla, stretched out on the floor, firing her pistol while King scrambled up against the wall. King's leg was bloody.

There were two dead men in the hall. One had a length of pipe stuck through him and the other looked like a pizza. At the far end of the corridor, two figures darted in and out of the short corridor that led to the escape hatch, firing short bursts and ducking Carla's jacketed hollow points that whined off the metal walls, striking sparks as they ricocheted around. Those bastards were killing his friends!

The flashing red emergency lights became a deep red glow. Bickerstaff's vision narrowed down to a bright circle, a telescope through which he could see very clearly. Carla and King blurred out. Inside him, a slow explosion started, an explosion he could not control. His teeth locked together. The muscles in his jaw bulged like the veins in his neck. Elgin's face screwed up into a tight knot that broke with his scream of rage.

He was around the corner and past Carla and King before they could even react to the scream behind them. Bickerstaff jumped over Carla like a low hurdle and went straight down the corridor at the hidden enemy.

The bright circle fell on one of the enemy crouching behind a support beam, changing magazines in his weapon. Bickerstaff's gun, now an extension of his vision, coughed three times very slowly. The startled enemy's throat opened up in a slow-motion tracheotomy. His lip split as he swallowed one of the bullets and his large blue frightened eye imploded, then sprayed out clear jelly.

The door to the escape hatch was only a few steps away. Another scream echoed from inside. As he neared it, another figure emerged. Bickerstaff was knocked to his left by a force he couldn't see and didn't much care about. The enemy in front of him was slowly bringing up an MP-5.

Bickerstaff stepped into a slow kick that arced out so slowly and gracefully that it felt like a ballet move. His foot hit the side of the weapon, turning the muzzle away from him as the enemy fired. Bickerstaff centered the bright circle on the man's face and eased the muzzle up until it hovered just in front of his face. The enemy was screaming now, the sound dull and far away. The screaming offended him. He thrust his weapon toward the open mouth and fired half a dozen shots into the man's offensive mouth. The gun was firing so slowly now that Bickerstaff almost became bored waiting for the final rounds to amble out of the muzzle. He watched the bright shell cases leap from the ejection port and disappear off to the right, glittering as they left the bright circle.

The enemy disappeared and Bickerstaff was in the escape hatch. The screaming was still ringing in his ears. Off to the left, an enemy was straddling Bob Moore, stabbing him in the face with an orange-handled knife.

Bastard! Bickerstaff thought as he stepped up behind the man and took his MP-5 in both hands.

The last blow had split the faceplate. The pink fluid was gushing out now. The knife point fell again and this time

Moore felt the sharp edge of a piece of the broken faceplate dig into his face. He turned his face to the side, seeking to escape the next blow. The flat knife point hit the metal rim of the faceplate and slid off, digging into the soft skin behind his left eye. Moore thrashed, twisting his head to the other side.

When he turned his head to the side, the fluorocarbon ran from his nose and mouth. The air that replaced it brought the first tickle into his throat. He would have to get the rest of the fluid out of his lungs soon, and that would make him gag. He tried to hold his breath, to hold the pink liquid in his lungs.

The next blow hit the rim on the right side, digging the thin chrome strip from its plastic trough and pulling it away from the helmet. Moore tried again to grab the blade and missed again as his attacker jerked the blade up above his head for what Moore feared would be the final blow.

Moore reached up to try to deflect the blow and managed to take the stab on his arm, which slammed down across his eyes. When he jerked his arm away, there was Elgin Bickerstaff standing behind the man, a look on his face that Moore had seen only twice in twenty years. His attacker was smiling. He spoke, holding the knife in front of Moore's face. Moore couldn't understand the words, but the tone was familiar.

The man didn't get a chance to finish his speech. Bickerstaff dropped his weapon over the man's head and jerked it back against the man's neck, pulling him up and off Bob Moore in one powerful stroke. The sound of bones breaking was clear, even over the screams that just now began to register in Moore's ears.

Bickerstaff was holding the limp form up against him, whispering in the dead man's ear. Moore tired to speak and choked. Bickerstaff dropped the corpse and knelt down beside him, reaching under his back and turning him over onto his side. The pink fluid gushed from his lungs onto the wet floor. Bickerstaff had his fist under Moore's diaphragm, forcing the fluid out with a makeshift Heimlich maneuver.

Moore pushed hard twice, forcing out the liquid, then took a deep, ragged, wet breath. He looked up at Bickerstaff, who

knelt beside him with a smile so peaceful and content it scared
Moore to look at him.

"Thanks, Elgin," Moore began. He tried to finish the sentence, but choked, gagged, and vomited all over the floor,
lying in a pink pool of fluid as his hulking friend knelt plac-
idly next to him, patting Moore on the back above his bulky
breathing equipment.

"No problem, boss," Bickerstaff answered. "Killing Russians is my hobby."

Carla jumped into the hatch, her pistol up in front of her.
Moore looked up and waved. Carla's face was a mask of
amazement. She pocketed her pistol and immediately went to
the hostages, untwisting the wire that bound their hands. The
woman hostage was sobbing. As soon as Carla had his hands
free, the older man took the sobbing woman in his arms, trying
to comfort her.

Last to be freed was the Navy officer. As soon as the wire
was off him, he leaped to his feet and streaked for the corridor.

Knickerbocker nearly ran over King as the wounded security
man limped around the corner.

"Where are you goin', sir?" King called as the man pin-
wheeled around him and ran off down the corridor.

"My ship!" he called back over his shoulder.

Carla was unwiring the last hostage when King entered the
escape hatch. "Elgin!" King yelled. "Are you okay?"

Bickerstaff looked up with a beatific smile. "Of course," he
answered. "Why?"

"Maybe 'cause you got the shit shot out of you about two
minutes ago!" King suggested. He hobbled over to Bickerstaff
and knelt down to look at the big man's back. "You missed
one of the bad guys back there, but he didn't miss you."
Carla came over to look and gasped. The back and side of
Bickerstaff's suit had a row of ripped spots where the ceramic
slugs had ripped into it. King fingered each spot. The Kevlar
fabric had stopped the slugs, as Bickerstaff knew it would
when he put it on. As he felt each ripped spot, King put his
finger through two holes in the suit, bringing back blood on
his fingers.

"Looks like a couple of 'em got through, big guy," he told
Bickerstaff, who twisted around to look at the two holes under
his arm.

He ran his hand down his side and winced as it passed over the two penetrations. "I hate it when this happens," he said irritably.

"I know," King answered, sitting down beside Bickerstaff and sticking his wounded leg out in front of him. "Me, too."

41

The scene at the end of the sub dock was worse than he imagined. Knickerbocker slowed to a walk, then stopped, looking at the dead sailors all around him. His crew, the men he worked with, joked with, chewed out and encouraged every day, lay sprawled like bundles of dropped laundry on the dock. One, whose face he thankfully could not see, lay stretched out on the side of the *Houston*, shot as he tried to gain the safety of the ship.

Knickerbocker felt sick to his stomach. He was about to vomit when Hamilton called to him from the sail.

"Skipper!" Hamilton yelled. "We thought you were dead, too."

"Close," Knickerbocker answered as he stepped onto the sub and through the metal door into the sail. "Terry, how many have we lost?"

The exec turned to him, his face lit from below by the light coming up out of the hatch. His face was a mask. "I don't know, sir," Hamilton answered, his voice a monotone. "I haven't had a chance to count. A lot."

"Come on," Knickerbocker said, scrambling down the ladder, "we've still got the ship."

When the captain stepped down the ladder, a ragged cheer went up from the remaining crew. "What have we got, Terry?" Knickerbocker asked.

"We can't fight, but we can run," Hamilton replied. "We got the water pumped out of the machinery rooms and we got a lot of it pumped out of the weapons room. Forward ballast has been pumped dry. We're floating under our own power again. I don't know how fast we can go and I know we can't do

231

anything fancy, but we can get the hell out of Dodge, sir."

"Good work, Terry," Knickerbocker congratulated his exec. "Let's do just that. I don't know what's out there, but I don't want to fight it tied to the dock. How long will it take to get us under way?"

"We're good to go now."

"Then let's do it," Knickerbocker answered. "Cut us loose from the dock and take her straight out."

"Aye, aye, Skipper," Hamilton answered.

There was an audible gasp from the crew as the dock floats pulled away and dropped the *Houston* away from the dock. The attack sub nosed down briefly, then came back up to trim as Hamilton played with the air in the ballast tanks. When he was satisfied that the *Houston* was not going to roll over, Hamilton spoke to the helmsman.

"Ahead, dead slow."

The *Houston* shuddered as it moved forward, then settled down.

"Terry, have we got any sonar or phones left?" Knickerbocker asked.

"Yes, sir," Hamilton replied. "We've got the BQQ-5 sonar back on line. Still no conformal. We've got forward and aft hydrophones. The midships phones were damaged by the attack."

"Any weapons left?"

"Not yet, sir," Hamilton went on, "we just got back into that room. Maybe in a few minutes. We can control 'em okay if we can get them to fire."

"Get cracking on that, we may need them," Knickerbocker stressed. "How about communications?"

"We lost all the dockside antennas when they hit the support ship. When we get out from under DeepCore, we can deploy the XSTAT."

"Do that as soon as we're clear!" Knickerbocker ordered. "We need help here, not that it could get here soon enough."

Two minutes later *Houston* slipped clear of the DeepCore dock, headed for the open sea. Hamilton ordered the XSTAT communications buoy launched. The buoy rose quickly to the surface, trailing a pair of wires less than one one-hundredth of an inch thick. On the buoy were radio antennas. The buoy would provide the *Houston* with at least an hour of communications, long enough to raise the TACAMO plane circling somewhere over the Pacific.

"Comrade Captain, the American submarine is moving!"

"How?" Bondarchuk asked, incredulous.

"I do not know that, Comrade Captain," the sonarman answered, "but it is moving."

"What heading?" Bondarchuk demanded.

"015, away from the facility."

"We'll lower the communications buoy first," Salvador explained to the civilian. "If we can communicate with it, we'll be in business. If not, we'll try the sonar."

Beecher nodded and went forward again. In the cockpit, the search radar still glowed blankly. Bowman was using the forward-looking infrared scope, sweeping it from side to side. The infrared screen was black. Any warm object, like an engine exhaust or a human being, would appear white on the screen. The screen was monotonously black.

"Nothing so far," the pilot said. Beecher looked again at the navigation display. Their position was within half a mile of where the *UnderSea Pacific* should be tethered. Beecher had to catch himself as the pilot throttled back and pulled the tilt control, rotating the huge propellors up. The SV-22 slowed to a crawl just above the waves. A mechanical noise aft caught Beecher's attention. He looked over his shoulder to see Salvador operating the winch that dropped the communications buoy into the water. After a minute he stopped the winch and turned to the communications console in front of him.

Bowman handed Beecher an earphone set so he could listen in. Salvador began with a series of three-letter code groups to identify them, then switched to voice communication.

"*Houston*, this is Tango Delta Three Two, over," Salvador broadcast. Five hundred feet below the hovering SV-22, the communications buoy transmitted the message.

"*Houston*, this is Tango Delta Three Two, please respond, over." The faint hiss of static was the only reply. Salvador continued to broadcast for several minutes, then spoke to the pilot.

"Negative, sir," he reported. "I'm getting zip from them."

"Pull it up, Sal," the pilot replied, "we'll make a pass, then come back with the sonar." Beecher felt the SV-22 rise. When the buoy cleared the water, the pilot turned the propellors forward again and circled, coming in again over the spot where DeepCore should be.

This time, Parker, the sonarman, was ready. He lowered his dunking sonar transducer in the same manner that Salvador had deployed the communications buoy. When the sonar buoy was several hundred feet underwater, he began to sweep the ocean floor with electronic pulses.

Immediately, Parker was back on the intercom. "Multiple contacts!" he said. "One huge contact at DeepCore position. Second contact is unknown, on the bottom one thousand meters out, stationary. Another unknown contact just beyond the shelf; it's moving. Classifying."

Parker was punching the data into his computer, trying to identify the contact types. The computer had information about the sonar signature of most of the world's submarines. If it could match the readings coming back from their two unknowns, it would display the information on the screen.

"Contact three is still moving," Parker went on, waiting for the computer match. "Wait, here it comes. Damn! Unable to classify contact three. Contact two still unidentified, also."

"*Undersea Pacific*," Beecher said solemnly. "Number two is the *Undersea Pacific*."

Pierce turned to him and nodded. "Probably."

"Michaels," the pilot called to the sonobuoy operator in the back, "prepare to lay a pattern around contact three."

"Ready," Michaels replied. Parker was reeling in his sonar buoy with its electronic winch. When it popped up out of the water, Parker called, "Sonar up!"

The pilot shifted the SV-22's position and Michaels dropped a line of sonobuoys between the third contact and DeepCore. The sonobuoys were listening devices that would pick up engine noise from the sub and any other sounds from DeepCore. Michaels had dozens of the slim canisters in racks beside his console. While the first pattern sunk to their assigned depth, Michaels and Salvador hurriedly reloaded the ejection tubes on the SV-22's rear ramp.

By the time Michaels returned to his seat, the sonobuoys were transmitting. "Cavitation," he reported to the pilot. "He's maneuvering." Michaels fed the data into Parker's computer to aid in the classification. "Still maneuvering. Wait . . . Sir, I'm getting machinery noise. Sounds like torpedo tubes flooding."

"Contact identified!" Parker broke into the report. "Computer identifies contact three as probable India-class Soviet sub."

"All right, damn it!" Pierce barked. "What's it going to be? India-class subs are unarmed rescue boats, it can't be an India and have torpedo tubes!"

"All I know, sir, is that he just opened his outer doors," Michaels answered.

Pierce turned to the copilot. "Send this to base: No response from *Houston. UnderSea Pacific* presumed sunk. Possible Soviet sub contact. Request weapons release." Bowman switched his transceivers and sent the message.

"Sir, I'm getting something else," Michaels said. "Machinery noise. From DeepCore area." The sonarman's face lit up. "I think it's the *Houston*, sir." Michaels keyed the information into the computer. A second later the screen read: U.S. nuclear submarine, unable to classify.

"It's her, it's *Houston*," Michaels whooped. "She's making weird noises, though. Moving dead slow. I think she's been hit already, sir. I think the bastard is fixing to finish her off!"

"Bowman, send this message," Pierce snapped. "Believe U.S.S. *Houston* is under attack by unknown submarine. Request permission to fire." Bowman nodded. "Salvador, Parker, ready the weapons!"

While the two men armed the two MK50 torpedoes, Pierce put the SV-22 into a flat turn to bring it directly over the unknown contact.

"Weapons ready," Parker reported. "Ready to arm."

"Sonar down," Pierce ordered. "Keep tracking him." Parker dunked the sonar buoy again, pounding the contact with sonar pings.

"He's got to know we're up here," Bowman said to Pierce. "He can't think he'll get away."

"Who knows what he thinks?" Pierce answered. "We don't even know for sure who he is." The minutes dragged by as Parker tracked the contact.

"Sir," Michaels suddenly injected, "I've got something else. Propellor noise, funny sound. Getting louder. It seems to be heading for the Ivan."

42

Sgt. Kron hunched over Popov, watching as their submersible broke loose from DeepCore and started back to the *Odessa*. It felt bad, very bad, to leave the major, but there had been no choice. The mission came first. Drachev was smart, though. He had kept the hostages there. If he had sent the hostages along with the electronics gear, there would be no real need to recover him and the wounded. Captain Bondarchuk could destroy DeepCore and leave with his mission accomplished. Drachev would just be another Soviet soldier who died for the Rodina.

It could have been worse, Kron reflected, he could have ordered me to stay instead of him. Still, the Americans would hardly launch a frontal assault for fear of killing the hostages. If they could unload the minisub quickly enough, he could still go back for the major.

As they cleared the edge of the huge complex, Kron craned his head around to look at the submarine dock. The American submarine was still there. It was hard to believe the American was still afloat.

"Popov," Kron snapped at the pilot of the minisub, "are you sure you placed all the charges?"

The pilot looked up, his eyes wide with fear and anger at the accusation. "Of course, Comrade Sergeant," he shot back, "all of them were placed exactly as we practiced!"

"Then why is the American still afloat?" Kron shouted.

"I do not know!" Popov yelled back. He stared out the vision port. "Perhaps we did not use large enough charges."

That was true enough, Kron thought, an SPM limpet mine contained less than a kilo of TNT. That was enough to pierce the hull of a submarine, but maybe not enough to kill it. Even the smallest torpedo carried a fifty-kilo warhead.

Even clusters of limpets such as the ones Popov had placed were mere firecrackers by comparison. He glanced down at Popov. The man was sweating.

He is frightened that he will be blamed for the failure to sink the submarine, Kron realized, and well he might be if *Odessa* did not sink it.

Ahead, the thin dark shape of *Odessa* loomed, partly hidden by the rocky ridge. Popov steered up and over the mother sub, then settled slowly into the docking well. Moments later the hatch ring spun and Koslov's face appeared in the hatch. He smiled at the loot packed into the submersible, but his face fell when he saw the wounded men jammed in among the electrical parts.

"Where is Major Drachev?" Koslov asked.

"Not coming," Kron answered. "He ordered me to evacuate the wounded and return to *Odessa*."

"You will return for him?"

"Of course!" Kron answered as he and Popov began handing down the wounded men to the crewmen waiting below. When the wounded were on their way to *Odessa*'s sickbay, the captured electronics gear came next. They were nearly finished when Bondarchuk appeared below the hatch.

"Where is Drachev?"

"On DeepCore, with the hostages, Comrade Captain," Kron answered. "I am returning now to pick them all up."

Bondarchuk looked nervous. He stared at Kron for a second, then asked, "Who are these hostages?"

"The scientists in charge of the electronics project and the captain of the American submarine!" Kron replied. Bondarchuk looked both impressed and distressed.

"Hurry, then," he barked at Kron, "we are being tracked by an American helicopter! We cannot remain here long!"

"I understand, Comrade Captain," Kron snapped, "I am leaving now." Kron dropped the hatch in Bondarchuk's face, cutting short the irrelevant conversation. As he went forward in the minisub, he felt the thud of *Odessa*'s hatch closing.

It would be hard for Bondarchuk to leave now that he knew what prizes were still to be had. He would be unhappy, but he would wait.

Kron slipped into the pilot's seat and checked the minisub's batteries. They were partially discharged, but had more than enough power for this trip. As he disengaged from the mother sub, Kron felt a shudder. He checked the instruments and the controls again. There seemed to be nothing wrong. Still curious, he turned the minisub toward DeepCore. With his vision port turned away from the mother sub, Kron could not see the two torpedoes that streaked out from the *Odessa*. As the distant lights of the underwater complex appeared at the edge of the vision port, the little sub jerked and the world disappeared.

As Bondarchuk stepped onto the bridge, the hydrophone operator screamed, "The American submarine is moving, Comrade Captain!"

Bondarchuk shot a glance at Koslov. "How is that possible?" Koslov asked.

"Obviously, our special designation troops failed to incapacitate it as planned," Bondarchuk replied. "We will have to do so ourselves."

He turned to the weapons station. "Lock Torpedo One on the American submarine. Prepare to fire."

"Target acquired," the weapons officer replied.

"Fire one," Bondarchuk ordered. "Stand by to fire Number Two at the complex." The *Odessa* shook slightly as the torpedo sped from the tube. "Torpedo away," the weapons officer reported, "homing on target."

"Comrade Captain," Koslov whispered, "Major Drachev is still on board. Sgt. Kron is en route there now!"

Bondarchuk jerked his head around to his executive officer. "I am aware of that!" he hissed, leaning closer to Koslov. "Mission or no, I will not lose this ship just to save some Spetsnaz *churkas*!"

Koslov nodded and said nothing. "Lock Torpedo Two on the complex!" Bondarchuk barked.

"Acquired."

"Fire!" Bondarchuk ordered, looking at Koslov, who had wiped all expression from his face and stood now awaiting orders.

"Now, Koslov we will . . ."

"Comrade Captain!" the hydrophone operator interrupted. "High-speed screws! Closing! It's right above . . ."

The explosion knocked Bondarchuk to his knees. Koslov grabbed for the periscope to catch himself. The lights flickered for a moment, then went out, plunging the bridge into darkness. A second later the red emergency light winked to life.

"Damage report!" Bondarchuk shouted. "Weapons, reload both tubes!"

The voice on the radio broke into Parker's report. "Tango Delta, permission granted for weapons release. Establish contact with U.S.S. *Houston*. Aerial tanker en route with fuel. Good luck."

As Bowman acknowledged the message, Michaels broke in.

"Torpedoes!"

"Arm weapons!" Pierce shouted. "Sonar up!" Parker pulled the emergency extract handle on the dunking sonar reel. The metal cable whined as it flew back onto the reel. In seconds the sonar was on its way up out of the water. As it sped back up into the tiltrotor, Parker reported, "Weapons armed."

"Mayday! This is U.S.S. *Houston*, Mayday. Mayday. Mayday," the loud voice boomed in Bowman's headphones. "This is *Houston*. We are under attack!"

"It's *Houston*," Bowman blurted. "Look!" On the infrared screen, a thin white strip bobbed on the dark surface of the water.

"Release Weapon One!" Pierce shouted.

"One away," Parker answered. The SV-22 jumped slightly as the eight-hundred-pound torpedo dropped away. A second later it splashed into the water.

"Bowman, get *Houston* on the horn!" The pilot turned to look at the white smear on the water.

"How long to impact?" Pierce asked the sonar men.

"Forty seconds, sir," Parker replied.

"Damn," Pierce swore, keying his mike. "*Houston*, brace yourself for enemy torpedo impact. Repeat, brace for impact of enemy torpedo . . ." A blast illuminated the water below. A second later another blazed in the deep.

"Holy shit!" Pierce yelled. He keyed the mike again. "*Houston*, are you there? *Houston*, come in, over!"

Silence was the only response. "Parker," Pierce barked. "How long on our torpedo?"

"Ten seconds, sir. Still homing."

"Get 'em!" Pierce encouraged the MK50 that was boring in on the enemy below. "Rip 'em apart!"

"Impact . . . now!" Another blast, much smaller than the previous two, erupted below.

"*Houston*, this is Tango Delta. Do you read? Over," Bowman said, going back on the radio.

Knickerbocker had just begun to broadcast his Mayday when the radio speaker crackled to life.

"*Houston*, this is Tango Delta! Prepare for torpedo impact!"

"Who the fuck is Tango Delta?" Hamilton blurted. The sonarman on the hydrophones interrupted his query.

"High-speed props! Torpedo, portside, astern!"

"Hard right rudder!" Knickerbocker shouted. "Launch decoys!"

As the helmsman twisted his airplane-style yoke to the right, the *Houston* leaned over to starboard, lumbering into the turn. Amidships, the decoy streaked away, filling the water with sonar reflective slivers, trying to draw the torpedo away from its target.

"Time to impact?" Knickerbocker shouted at the operator.

"It's close!" the frightened sailor answered. "Seconds . . . it's . . ." The sonarman jerked his headphones off.

The *Houston* shook like it was being hit with a hundred telephone poles. The lights flickered, but stayed on.

"Damage report," Hamilton called for the hundredth time.

A few seconds passed before Thomlin, the engineering officer, answered. "Sir, it looks like we got lucky for a change," the engineer reported. "The aft hydrophone is gone portside. Looks like the fish hit it. We got some leaks in engineering and the turbine is damaged, but the reactor is still okay."

"Can we maneuver?" Hamilton asked.

"Negative, sir," Thomlin answered, "not for a while."

"Helm, what's the distance to the bottom?"

"One hundred feet," the helmsman replied, watching a readout on his console. "Coming up slowly."

Knickerbocker turned to Hamilton. "If we can't get her back up, we'll set 'er down on the bottom here. It's flat and . . ."

"*Houston*, this is Navy Tango Delta. Do you read? Over," the radio speaker crackled again.

Knickerbocker smiled. "Looks like the cavalry may be here already!"

"Parker, get the sonar down again," Pierce shouted. "I want another fix on that bastard. Michaels, what's happening on the phones?"

"They're dead, sir," Michaels answered, "we need to drop another line."

"Hold the sonar, Parker," Pierce ordered. He banked the SV-22 around again and swept slowly over the spot where phosphorescent bubbles marked where their torpedo had entered the water. Michaels dropped half a dozen new sonobuoys in a line. This done, Pierce hovered again as Parker dipped the sonar back into the dark water.

"Sir, I've got noises from that Red sub."

"Is it breaking up?" Pierce asked.

"No, sir," Michaels answered, disappointment in his voice. "It's still maneuvering. I think I hear tubes flooding again."

"God damn it!" the pilot cursed. "Parker, forget the sonar. We know where the bastard is. Drop on him again!"

"Weapon Two away!" Parker called as the second MK50 dropped into the sea beneath them. Pierce rotated the engines forward a bit and circled the spot, waiting for his second shot to hit.

"Bowman," the pilot said, jabbing a finger at his copilot for emphasis, "the next time someone tries to give me four weapons and I only want two, you just slap the shit out of me, okay?"

"Roger that," Bowman promised. The SV-22 was now unarmed. Tango Delta was out of the fight.

The radio crackled to life again. "Tango Delta, this is *Houston*, can you feed us sonar information?"

"On the way, *Houston*," Pierce replied. "Boomer, dunk the sonar and send it to 'em!"

As he pulled the handle to drop the sonar buoy again, Parker looked up at Beecher who sat belted tightly into his seat. His eyes were wide as saucers.

"Now we know what happened to your ship!" Parker yelled. Beecher nodded miserably. Michaels turned to them.

"Mr. Beecher, I'm afraid that second torpedo hit your place down there." Beecher's face knotted up.

"Oh, dear God!" he moaned. "Dear God above!"

43

They had been in a corridor on the way to DeepCore's sick-bay when the torpedo hit the industrial area. The collision alarm was redundant after the shock knocked everyone off their feet. Water sprayed from dozens of fittings and cracked valves.

"What the hell!" Moore moaned. "What now?" He struggled to his feet and slid down the wall to the intercom panel, using his hand to deflect a thin stream of water that was running down from a fitting above the panel while he punched Jackson's number.

"Tom!" Moore shouted over the screech of the alarm. "What's going on?"

"That Russian bastard hit us with something, probably a torpedo," Jackson answered. "Nancy has gone to the command center. Where are you?"

"On the way to sickbay, we've got some wounded."

Jackson's heart leaped up into his throat.

Please not Carla, Jackson prayed. "Who?" he asked, afraid of the answer.

"King and Bickerstaff," Moore said to Jackson's mixed relief. "We'll be in sickbay until we get them straightened out."

"Roger that, thank God everyone is still alive."

"Thank Elgin"—Moore laughed—"he did most of the work!"

"Jackson!" Nancy Collins's voice broke in over the intercom. "Get your butt down here! I need help!"

"On the way!" Jackson snapped as he reached for the door.

"What's our status, Thomlin?" Hamilton asked. The *Houston* had settled onto the bottom, but it had not been gentle.

"Good news and bad news, sir," the engineer reported. "We may have damaged the prop when we hit. That's the bad news. The good news is that we got some more air pumped out of the weapons room and got back in there. Sir, there's a warload in Tube One."

"What kind?" Knickerbocker asked, unable to remember what he had ordered a few days and a thousand years ago.

"MK48 ADCAP, sir," Thomlin answered. "I think we can fire it, too."

"We'll find out right now, Mr. Thomlin," Knickerbocker proposed. "Weapons control, take the data from Tango Delta and plot me a solution ASAP!"

A few seconds later the weapons operator, Paulson, answered, "Solution locked in, sir."

"Flood tube," Knickerbocker ordered, anxiously looking over at Hamilton, who crossed his fingers.

"Tube flooded."

"Open outer door!" Hamilton held up crossed fingers on both hands.

"Outer door open! Green light on Number One outer door!"

Knickerbocker held up his open palm and gestured to Hamilton. "Go ahead, Terry, you've been fighting them all day."

"Fire!" Hamilton shouted.

The *Houston* shuddered slightly as the 3400-pound torpedo shot from the tube and angled away from the submarine, guided by the two hairlike wires that linked it to the *Houston*'s MK117 fire-control system. It circled back up over the *Houston*, climbing to look for its prey.

The seconds dragged by. On the hydrophones, Michaels waited, listening for the sounds of more Soviet torpedoes on their way to kill the *Houston*. Their own MK50 was homing in now, the high-pitched sound of its propellors moving away as it tracked the Soviet target.

"Ten seconds!" Michaels called as the second fish neared its mark. "Five seconds . . . Impact . . . Now!" Another flash lit the water below.

"Get another batch of sonobuoys ready," Pierce snapped. "I want to hear him die!"

"High-speed screws!" Michaels shouted. "Two torpedoes! Correction, one torpedo! It sounds just like a '48!" Michaels gestured to Salvador, who ran to the back and dropped another pair of sonobuoys, reloading the tubes from others in the rack.

"Its definitely a MK48!" Michaels called. "It's homing!"

The explosion above had terrified everyone on the *Odessa*. It took a second to realize that they had not been hit. The loud clangs the minisub made when it fell against *Odessa* told the whole story. Damage reports from all departments were negative.

"It appears that Sgt. Kron has saved our lives," Bondarchuk remarked casually. He did not mention Major Drachev, trapped on DeepCore. There was no need to speak of that at all now.

"High-speed propellor, Comrade Captain!" the hydrophone operator yelled. "From above!"

"Launch decoy. Left rudder, flank speed. Take the boat down." He turned to Koslov. "The cats are upon us, eh, Koslov?"

The executive officer nodded. The captain's expression unnerved him. Bondarchuk seemed to be enjoying this fight.

"Time to impact?" Bondarchuk asked.

"Twenty seconds, Comrade Captain," the sonarman answered.

"If we can get below the ridge, we may trick this one!" Bondarchuk observed. Koslov nodded, estimating the chance to be slim.

"Five seconds. Four. Three." The sonarman pulled off his headset and looked up, as if watching the torpedo homing on his ship. Koslov grabbed the support rail and held on for dear life.

The *Odessa* lurched as a noise louder than any he had heard before boomed through the ship. The boom was followed by screams and alarm bells ringing. The lights failed again, replaced by the macabre glow of the red emergency lights.

Bondarchuk, knocked to his knees by the blast, stood and called for damage reports. The seconds dragged by like days as they waited for the first report.

"Comrade Captain"—the voice was Dubovik's—"the torpedo seems to have struck the submersible deck between the two wells. We have leaks and a sprung hatch, but no serious damage. I have sealed off the chamber below the hatch and pumped air into it. Injuries are minimal, two deaths from impact injuries."

"Thank you, Dubovik," Bondarchuk answered. "Koslov, come back up to a firing position. We will finish the American submarine and the DeepCore complex, then we will run for Petropavlovsk."

Their berth at the huge submarine base near the tip of Kamchatka seemed like a dream, an unlikely dream.

"High-speed propellor!" the hydrophone operator yelled again. "Starboard bow, searching." All eyes on the bridge turned to the man, who sat with his eyes closed, his hands cupped over his headphones. "Still searching. Homing! Torpedo homing!"

"Time to impact?"

"Forty seconds!"

"Crash dive!" Bondarchuk shouted. Koslov stepped in front of him.

"Comrade Captain, we are at the bottom of our operational limit already," Koslov reminded his captain.

Bondarchuk smiled. "Then we are caught, as they say, between the devil and the deep blue sea." Koslov stepped back. He had nothing to add to that.

As the *Odessa* slipped below the ridge and dove into the Challenger Deep, the sonarman continued to track the torpedo.

"Thirty seconds . . . Twenty seconds." The man looked back at Bondarchuk. "It sounds like one of their MK48s, Comrade Captain. Ten seconds . . ." The sonarman took off his phones and held tightly to his console. The air in *Odessa* was suddenly thick with the acrid smell of sweat and fear.

In an instant, the devil and the deep blue sea teamed up to demolish the *Odessa*. The MK48 torpedo slammed into the hatch in the forward submersible well. The 650 pounds of explosive ripped through the *Odessa*, nearly splitting the sub in two. Already diving, the *Odessa* continued on its way to the bottom of the Challenger Deep, thirty-five thousand feet below.

• • •

The MK48 torpedo's own sonar locked onto the invader and the torpedo went from search to attack mode. Running at fifty-five knots, it sped after its diving target.

The target fired a decoy, but the MK117 computer on the *Houston* ignored it. The MK48 caught the fleeing sub and slammed into it like an arrow.

"Impact!" the weapons operator reported redundantly. The dull thud of the explosion had rung through the hull like a distant gong.

"Yeah!" Hamilton shouted, jabbing the air with his clenched fist.

Knickerbocker was on the radio. "Tango Delta, what have you got?"

Below them, a bright flash erupted. Seconds later, a huge spout of water broke the surface to mark the spot where the Soviet boat was dying a thousand feet below. Parker was ready this time. As the water tumbled back in a white shower, the SV-22 flew across the splash, dropping four more buoys in a line. In seconds, they began to pick up sounds.

Knickerbocker's voice blared from the radio. "Tango Delta, what have you got?"

"I hear him, sir!" Michaels cheered. "He's breaking up. Sliding down the rocks! Here, sir, listen to this!" Michaels switched the sonobuoy over to the radio and the intercom.

In the cockpit, Pierce cupped one hand over his left earphone, struggling to hear. At first he couldn't hear anything, then a sound erupted through the phones. It sounded like a garbage can being dragged over concrete.

"He's going down, sir," Michaels yelled at the *Houston*'s captain. "You got him!"

The other crewmen's voices broke in over the intercom, hooting and congratulating each other.

"Shut up!" Pierce bawled. "I want to listen to this!" The others sat in silence, listening on their own phones as the Soviet sub broke up on the rock wall of the Challenger Deep.

As Bowman listened, the sub captain's voice broke in over his radio again.

"Tango Delta, this is Captain Knickerbocker on the *Houston*. Can you patch me through to ComSubPac?"

"Yes, sir, Captain," Bowman replied. "Wait one. Good shot on that Ivan, sir!"

A moment later Knickerbocker's coded transmission went out over the air to receivers all over the Pacific. The message was simple.

"We have engaged hostile forces in underwater combat. We have suffered heavy casualties, but have destroyed the enemy. We require immediate assistance. Knickerbocker out."

"Sir," Salvador asked Pierce, "are we goin' to paint half a sub on the side of Three Two?"

"Fuckin'-A!" the pilot replied.

44

In the command center, Nancy Collins was working like a dervish to keep DeepCore watertight. She glanced over as Jackson ran skidding to a stop. Her face was flushed with anger and frustration.

"Great!" she snapped. "Take the computer console!" Jackson slid into the chair and quickly scanned the screen. The color-coded schematic of DeepCore was totally red over the industrial area and had dozens of red flecks throughout the rest of the complex.

"This place is leaking like a sieve!" she shouted. "Get me more pressure in the industrial area!"

Jackson punched up the pressure system and opened the valves to the torpedoed sub dock. The pressure gauges barely flickered.

"It's not working !"

"I know, the bastards blew the door off!" she answered. "I'm just trying to keep the water out of the rest of the complex."

The monitors overhead showed dark seawater surging through the corridor leading to the industrial area. That was bad enough, but the water was also filled with dead bodies from both sides.

"I've got both ends of the corridor blocked," she explained. "If I can keep the water in there, we've got a chance."

"And if not?" he asked quietly. She turned and looked at him.

"Then this place'll flush out like a commode."

She flipped more switches and watched as the watertight doors, left open by the invaders, slowly closed. All down the corridor, indicator lights from sealed doors blinked green on the console. The final one, at the end of the corridor, stayed an angry red.

"Damn," she swore, switching in a backup circuit. The indicator was still red.

"What is it?" Jackson asked.

"One of the pressure doors is still open," she explained. "It's either jammed or the controls are cut." She looked over at him. "I need someone to go check it out. Will you go?"

"Sure," he answered. "Where is it?"

She motioned him over to the panel display. "Here"—she pointed to the glowing red diode—"past the sickbay."

"On the way." Jackson stepped to the intercom and punched up the sickbay. "This is Jackson. Anybody home?"

"Fuentes here."

"Carla, I need some help pronto. Got a door stuck open down the hall from you."

"We know," she replied. "It's nearly knee deep in here now."

"Right, I'm on my way."

"Hey!" Collins shouted as he stepped to the door. "Be careful, Tom."

Jackson smiled and winked, then turned and ran off down the hall.

The closer he got to the sickbay, the deeper the water was. Some of the electrical boxes near the floor were sparking, throwing golden fireworks across the corridor. Jackson prayed that the circuit breakers would pop before he got electrocuted.

In the sickbay, King, Ramos, and Bickerstaff were sitting up on the examination tables. Carla was wrapping Bickerstaff's chest with gauze. When Jackson sloshed into the room, they greeted him with surprisingly good cheer.

"What's up, Bro?" King asked.

"What do you mean, what's up?" Jackson asked incredulously. He scooped up a handful of water. "If this place wasn't already on the bottom, it would be sinking!"

"Lucky for us it is, then," Bickerstaff injected. "Not as far to go!" Jackson stepped over to look at Bickerstaff's wounds. On his right side, two angry holes bubbled and foamed as Carla probed them with a swab soaked in hydrogen peroxide.

She looked up as Jackson stared at the wounds, a quiet "Shit!" whispered under his breath.

"Not as bad as they look," she assured Jackson. "The Kevlar slowed 'em down. They barely penetrated the skin."

"Where they were stopped by my rock-hard chest muscles!" Bickerstaff added. He flexed his arms, but stopped, wincing in pain.

"The only rock-hard thing you have is your head," Jackson observed.

"And my dick!" Bickerstaff hooted. Carla looked up at her patient through skeptical brows. Bickerstaff merely rolled his eyes and mugged.

"Is he on something?" Jackson asked the other wounded.

"Only his own excitement," Bob Moore chuckled.

"That's right," Bickerstaff went on, undaunted, as Carla wrapped his chest with a long gauze bandage. "The cult of the thrill killers!"

"That's right," King agreed. "He's killed hundreds of thrills!"

"With my dick!" Bickerstaff exclaimed as Carla tied off the bandages, giving them a final tug. "OWW!" Bickerstaff complained.

"Come on, Carla," Jackson urged. "I need to get a door shut or these guys will be surfing on those tables in a minute." He looked at the wounded men. "If you guys can walk, I recommend it. If we can't close that door, it'll get deep in here."

As he and Carla stepped through the door, Bickerstaff called to them. "We got all the faith in the world in you, Tom."

"I hate it when he says that," Jackson confided as they slogged through the knee-deep water toward the stuck door.

"What?" she asked.

"I hate it when he says he's got all the faith in the world in me," Jackson explained. "I always think he's teasing me or just lying."

"He is," she assured him, laughing as he casually shot her the finger. "So, where's this door?"

Jackson scooped up a handful of water and threw it at her. "At the headwaters of the Nile here!"

They followed the current in the corridor until they reached the jammed pressure door. Water was pouring through a foot-wide gap between the door and frame. They worked their way down the wall using the pipes and conduits to pull themselves through the cold rushing flood.

"Hold on to me!" Jackson said. Carla got a grip on Jackson's belt and held on as he fished around under the surface, looking for whatever was keeping the door from closing.

"Got it!" he shouted, getting a mouthful of water in the process and choking. He pulled up a black-clad hand and arm from the water.

Behind him, Carla gasped, "Oh, yuck!"

"Here," Jackson said, pushing the cold arm toward her, "I'll pull the door back, you pull him out!"

Carla took the arm like she was handling a poisonous snake. Jackson moved back behind her and hooked his fingers around the edge of the door. Carla, pulled by the current, hung on to the arm for support, seeking a footing on the wet floor.

"Ready?" Jackson asked. She nodded and he leaned back on the door, pushing with his foot on the doorjamb. The door slid back a few inches and Carla fell backward into the swirling water as the dead man came loose and the current pushed him through the door.

Jackson jerked his fingers out of the door as it slowly shut, sealing off the corridor. He reached up and turned the metal wheel above the door that put more air pressure into the corridor.

"AAAUUGGHH!" Carla screamed from behind. "Get it off! Get it off me!"

The surging water had pushed both Carla and the corpse several feet down the corridor. Both now lay tangled in a necrophiliac embrace against a support beam. Carla was thrashing, unable to escape the dead Russian.

Jackson slogged through the now calf-deep water and pulled the dead man off her. She scuttled backward like a crab and got to her feet, her eyes never leaving the corpse.

Jackson turned the dead man over and dropped the body against the wall. The man's face, white and wrinkled from immersion, had three prominent holes in the face.

"Oh, gross!" Carla spat. "Between him and Freddy Kreuger back there, I'm going to be sick."

"Freddy who?" Jackson asked.

"A Russian back by the escape hatch," she explained, "he

was all burned." She wiped her face with the back of her hand. "He looked like a pizza."

"Spets-aroni," Jackson quipped, "my favorite!" Carla made a face. "Cossack flambé with Tatar sauce?" he asked. Carla looked stricken and turned away.

"Sorry, babe," Jackson apologized. He put his arm around her shoulders and they splashed off down the corridor back to the sickbay, leaving the human doorstop against the wall.

"You have heard nothing from *Odessa*?" Petrochenko asked.

"No, Comrade Colonel," Lavrov replied, struggling to keep the tension out of his voice.

Petrochenko stood looking out the tall windows at the stand of trees next to the Kremlin wall. He seemed to be oblivious, but Lavrov knew that the intelligence officer was anything but that. Finally, Petrochenko spoke.

"A satellite receiver picked up radio transmissions from that area. The transmitter was airborne. It was speaking to both its base and to another transmitter, possibly on the surface." Petrochenko continued to stare out the windows. "The satellite also picked up a Mayday signal from the American submarine *Houston*. A rescue force is now steaming toward the area, accompanied by an antisubmarine squadron." He paused. Behind him Lavrov stood silent, his heart in his throat. When Petrochenko did not speak, Lavrov offered a hope.

"Perhaps the information is old, Comrade Colonel," he suggested. "By now, the *Odessa* may be steaming toward home and maintaining radio silence to avoid detection."

"Perhaps"—Petrochenko nodded—"and perhaps our former allies in the Warsaw Pact will come to us on their knees, begging to be our friends again." He looked back at Lavrov. "But I doubt it very much." Petrochenko took a cigarette from a thin case and lit it, taking a long drag. "It is time now for massive denials, Lavrov," the colonel observed. "Hopefully, no Soviet soldier or sailor will surface to tell the tale." A horrible vision of Drachev or one of the others being grilled on television by an American prosecutor flashed through Lavrov's mind. No, not Drachev. He would not permit himself to be taken alive.

"Prepare a series of 'training accident' reports to explain the deaths of the *raydoviki*," Petrochenko said, interrupting

Lavrov's thoughts. "In case we need to notify their families." Lavrov nodded.

Petrochenko finished the cigarette, put on his hat, and gathered up his coat. "Date the letters over the next four months." Petrochenko stopped at the door and looked back at his nervous subordinate. "We face the danger, too, do we not, Lavrov?" Petrochenko asked. "We risk as much as those who carry the guns." With that, the colonel disappeared, leaving Lavrov alone in the tall room.

First the letters, Lavrov mused, then time to pack. With luck, I may be allowed to remain in the service as a latrine orderly on the Mongolian border.

Back in the command center, Nancy Collins was swearing, coaxing, and urging some system to life, fighting to keep DeepCore intact. As the wounded security team staggered in from the sickbay, she focused her frustration, anger, and fear on them.

"You fuckers!" she shouted. "Look what you've done! Leaks everywhere, the sub dock gone, half the crew dead! Bastards!"

"Well, excuuuse meee!" Bickerstaff began, stepping toward the engineer.

Bob Moore cut him off. "Not now, Bick," Moore cautioned, holding the big man back with his arm. Jackson stepped through the others. "We got that door closed," he told her, "anything else we can do?"

"Yeah," she shot back, "make this a bad dream I'm goin' to wake up from!"

Moore motioned for his team to leave. As they turned to go, Collins called to them. "There is something you can do!" she barked. "The rest of the crew are still holed up in their quarters. Tell 'em to get back to work! I can't do this alone!"

"Will do," Moore assured her as they left the command center. They were in the corridor when she yelled after them.

"Hey!" she shouted. They turned their heads back to hear her parting shot. "Thanks," she said, the anger gone from her voice, "I guess you guys saved our lives."

"That's our job!" Bickerstaff sang. She smiled and went back to her damage control.

Halfway to the crew quarters, they rounded the corner and ran right into Colin and a handful of the crew. Colin had a wrench drawn back, about to smack them when he recognized his rescuers.

"Hullo, China!" Colin boomed. "I thought you were goners!" He looked back at other crewmen who were armed with knives, clubs, and a lone spear gun.

"My mates and I were on a punitive expedition," he explained.

Moore laughed and nodded. "We could've used the help, but it's over now."

"You mean they're gone?" one of Colin's troops asked.

"Yeah, gone," Bickerstaff shouted, "real gone."

Relief washed over their faces. Several of the men slumped against the wall, their makeshift weapons at their sides. The spear gunner pulled the rubbers from the notches on his spear.

"The chief engineer needs all the help she can get," Moore told them. "She's in the command center."

The crew set off down the corridor, laughing and chattering, burning off the lingering tension.

45

"Come in, Marc!" McLaughlin called. LeFlore stepped into the spacious office and stood meekly by the door. There was no need to rush to destruction.

The Old Man was sitting at his desk, his chair turned away, reading a newspaper whose headline blared. UNDERWATER ATTACK!

LeFlore's heart sank. The news from DeepCore was depressing. Fifteen crew deaths, a dozen wounded or hurt trying to save the complex. The U.S.S. *Houston* was still on the bottom although the surviving crew had been evacuated by divers from DeepCore.

Most of the material from the Positrack project was gone, but at least Dr. Brittan and his assistant were still alive. The Positrack project was on hold, though, until the industrial area could be rebuilt. The explosion had blown one wall in and flooded the area. The engineer, Collins, had a plan to seal the wall and blow the place dry, but it would be weeks, even months, before it was usable again.

"Come here, Marc!" McLaughlin called. "I want you to read this!"

LeFlore's heart rose into his throat as he walked toward the Old Man's desk. That damned newspaper was his death warrant.

"What is it, sir," he asked quietly.

McLaughlin turned in his huge red leather chair and read from the newspaper account. "The attack was thwarted by the heroic efforts of UnderSea Corporation's elite security team. Led by Robert Moore, a former Navy SEAL, the security team freed the hostages and prevented the kidnapping of a group of American scientists. Most of the security personnel were wounded in the fighting, but defeated the determined attackers in hand-to-hand combat."

McLaughlin put down the paper and stood. "You realize what this means, of course?" he asked. LeFlore's guts were turning to jelly.

"No, sir," LeFlore asked, bracing for the ax.

"It means that you were exactly correct in sending Security to DeepCore!" McLaughlin beamed. "If they hadn't been there, the facility would be lost with all hands, not to mention that nuclear sub. Your clear vision on this has saved our hash in a big way, Marc!" McLaughlin stuck his hand out, his polished fingernails a contrast to the rough, scarred skin on his hands. LeFlore shook it, impressed by the Old Man's viselike grip. Relief swept over him like a hot flash. He had come up here expecting a pink slip and now it looked like he was a hero instead.

"I'm glad it worked out that way," LeFlore answered, careful to keep it humble, "I'm just sorry so many people had to die."

McLaughlin scowled and LeFlore was instantly sorry he had reminded the Old Man of the body count. McLaughlin looked out the window and rubbed his face with his hands. "Yes, well, I guess we need to rejoice that so many were saved."

"Any idea who did it, yet," LeFlore asked, trying to change the subject.

McLaughlin looked at him over the tops of his reading glasses. "No official identification," he replied, "but Bob Moore says they were Russians. Of course, the Russians deny any knowledge and claim that it was some third-world power seeking to steal the nuclear weapons on the *Houston*."

"The *Houston* had nuclear weapons?" LeFlore blurted.

"Of course not!" McLaughlin shook his head. "*Houston* is an attack boat, not a missile sub. The bastards were after Positrack, not the sub." McLaughlin ran his finger up through his silver hair. "Damn near got it, too." McLaughlin looked back up at LeFlore and pulled off his reading glasses. "Except for you and Bob Moore, Marc!" McLaughlin sat back down in the red leather chair and spun it around to look out the windows at the city below. "I'll need biographical sketches of all the security team this afternoon," McLaughlin said. "The press'll want to know more about them. And you, too, of course. Get to work on them and give them to Petri in Corporate Communications."

"Yes, sir," LeFlore answered, recognizing his cue to leave. As he walked back to the door, McLaughlin called to him. "Marc." LeFlore turned. "You did good!"

LeFlore beamed. "Thank you, Mr. McLaughlin!" With those words of praise ringing in his ear, LeFlore returned to his office to unload the cardboard box he had been packing.

Constantine Petrochenko tried to project an air of satisfaction, but it seemed to escape the man behind the desk. General Pavlovskiy was staring a hole through him, puffing on a thick Havana cigar.

"The Positrack project has been set back at least half a year," Petrochenko assured the general, "and the DeepCore facility heavily damaged. The goals of the operation have, therefore, been largely met."

"But not completely!" Pavlovskiy growled. The general dropped the cigar into a heavy crystal ashtray and picked up a sheaf of papers from his desk. "These are inquiries from the Supreme Soviet, asking for details of the operation!"

"What have you replied," Petrochenko inquired, "if you do not mind my asking?"

"I have told them that no Soviet personnel were involved," Pavlovskiy replied. "Hopefully, there will be no proof to the contrary!"

"It would appear that the submarine sank in twelve thousand meters of water, Comrade General," Petrochenko assured him. "No one will ever find the *Odessa*."

The general stood and turned to look at a print depicting the Soviet crossing of the Dnieper River during the Great Patriotic War. "And the *raydoviki*?" Pavlovskiy asked, pulling another cigar from his pocket and lighting it, oblivious to the one already burning in the ashtray.

"Major Drachev's family has been notified that he was assassinated by Moslem extremists in Tbilisi," Petrochenko replied. "The others are listed as killed in training accidents, car crashes, and illness."

Pavlovskiy did not answer, but sat back down, puffing on the new cigar as the old one smoldered in the crystal bowl.

After a long pause, he jabbed the cigar at Petrochenko.

"The Americans know who was responsible for this failure," he asserted. "If they ever find a way to identify the bodies or to examine the *Odessa*, they will tell the world. Until then, we can ignore their protests." The general slumped back in his chair. "I cannot believe that a handful of American security guards defeated a section of Naval Spetsnaz!"

"If I may intrude with an observation," Petrochenko said softly, "the American security detail was made up of Navy SEALS. They were aided by the submarine crew. There was no way to foresee their intervention."

Pavlovskiy did not answer, but continued to puff on his cigar. After a moment he snubbed out the cigar in the ashtray, frowning as he found the first cigar still burning. He crushed it out as well.

Petrochenko sought to defuse the general's anger. "We destroyed the means to implement Positrack during our own research and development stage," he pointed out again. "The Americans have lost a valuable facility for at least half a year and have been shown to be vulnerable in their underwater lair. Surely that is a victory!"

"Possibly," Pavlovskiy replied. "Let us hope it will be enough to keep our testicles out of some politician's garlic press." He waved Petrochenko away.

That unpleasant image of his gonads in a smelly garlic press haunted Petrochenko all the way back to his office.

46

"Finally!" Ty King exclaimed as they stepped out of the decompression tank onto the deck of the guided missile frigate that had been their home for nearly two weeks.

He, Bickerstaff, Ramos, and Bob Moore had come up from DeepCore to return to the States. All but Moore were headed for a hospital; Moore was off to the company's home office. Carla Fuentes and Tom Jackson were still below in DeepCore, helping with the reconstruction of the facility. The two weeks in decompression had mostly been an endless debriefing by spooks of all sorts, the National Transportation Safety Board, and even a bunch from OSHA. After the long confinement in the tiny decompression chamber, they were ecstatic about going home.

On the fantail, the Navy SH-60 helicopter was waiting to ferry them over to the aircraft carrier *Enterprise* where the company's V-22 was waiting for them to take them back to Guam. Commander Greerson, captain of the frigate, was waiting by the helicopter to say good-bye. As the four civilians put on their life jackets, Greerson shook each of their hands and wished them well.

"It was a ton of fun," Bickerstaff told the commander, a statement that pretty well summed it up for all of them.

The next twenty-four hours were a blur of air travel. The Navy provided transportation from Guam to Hawaii. UnderSea took over from there. Alex Throckmorton was waiting with his Gulfstream. It was stocked with alcohol of every sort and a petite stewardess named Bambi hired just for the occasion. Bambi's job was easy, since Moore and the others fell asleep after one glass of champagne.

A delegation from UnderSea Corp. met them with a reception in the airport's VIP lounge. Reporters put them through the same grilling they had endured on the frigate.

The Old Man wasn't there, of course. He was off talking to some folks about underwater oil drilling in the Red Sea. The only two unexpected occurrences were Alice's reaction to Moore's return and Marc LeFlore's glaring absence. Alice seemed unusually distant, but begged Moore to see her after the reception. In an empty departure gate next to the VIP lounge, she broke down and sobbed out her story.

"I'm so glad you're back," she began, "I was about ready to quit."

"Why?" Moore asked, a bit afraid of the answer.

"It's Marc LeFlore!" she blurted. "He's—he's such a bastard!"

"Okay," Moore sympathized, "tell me about it." She wiped her eyes and took a deep breath.

"Ever since you left, he's been moving the Security Department out. He has me stuck in a broom closet down in the basement with just a telephone and a file cabinet!" She took a tissue from her purse and blew her nose loudly. "Plus," she went on, "he has been hinting that if I want to keep my pitiful job, I might want to get friendly with him."

"How friendly?" Moore asked, his old animosity toward LeFlore surging to the surface.

"Very friendly," she answered miserably, "biblically friendly." She looked in Moore's eyes. "I know I'm not that attractive, Bob," she stated flatly. "He doesn't want to have sex with me. He wants to humiliate me. He said if I don't like it, I can quit. Sheila treats me like white trash."

Moore stared out the plate-glass wall, watching a 727 pull up to the gate. He sat silent for a few minutes as she sniffled.

"Don't worry," Moore reassured her, "I'll take care of Mr. LeFlore." She hugged his neck and disappeared into the ladies' room to salvage her makeup. The rest of the reception was a red-tinged blur.

Moore was officially on vacation for a week, but the next day he was outside LeFlore's office as the clock struck twelve.

Moore waited until Sheila walked out the door, purse in hand, headed for lunch.

"LeFlore in there?" he asked.

"Uh-huh," she answered flatly. "Welcome home." She shouldered her way past him, cutting off any further conversation. Moore stepped into LeFlore's outer office and shut the door. He slipped the big Beretta automatic out of his belt and screwed the short Hushpuppy silencer onto the threaded barrel. This done, he took a deep breath and opened LeFlore's door. As usual, LeFlore was on the phone. When he looked up and saw Moore, his eyebrows shot up.

"Listen, babe, I gotta go, someone just came in. Yeah, you, too. Bye."

"Now, Bob," LeFlore began as he hung up the receiver, "I know . . ."

Moore pulled the gun from behind him and pressed the muzzle against the side of the telephone. When he pulled the trigger, the gun coughed and the telephone flew off the desk, scattering bits of plastic and wire as it flew, abruptly jerking to a stop as it hit the end of its cord.

LeFlore's eyes, big as saucers, snapped over to the wrecked phone, then back to Moore. Moore poked the big snout of the silencer between LeFlore's eyebrows, pushing his head back.

"Now that we're sure not to be interrupted," Moore began, "I want to have a talk with you."

"Now, Bob," LeFlore stammered, repeating himself in a voice tight with fear, "take it easy."

"I am," Moore said quickly. "If I weren't, you'd be over there with the phone."

LeFlore tried to push his chair back and stand up. Moore cut him off with the muzzle. "Sit down, I'll tell you when to stand."

LeFlore dropped back into his chair.

"I know what you have been pulling with Alice," Moore began, "and it's going to stop today, understand?"

"I don't think . . ." LeFlore interrupted.

"That's right," Moore barked, "you don't think. But now you don't have to. All you have to do is keep away from her and never talk to her,'cause if you do, I'll blow your nuts off. Understand?"

LeFlore was silent.

"I know you're thinking about what you're going to do to me for talking to you like this and you need to forget it. If the folks in Human Resources find out what you've been doing to Alice, they'll have you terminated on the spot. If you keep it up, I'll terminate you myself." Moore straightened up a little.

"Later on, you may even think about having something bad happen to me. Remember this. I have a life insurance policy payable to Elgin Bickerstaff. If anything ugly happens to me, he'll pay you a visit and he will be the last person you ever see."

LeFlore was stiff, sweat beading up on his upper lip. Moore knew that the armpits of the little wimp's shirt were soaked by now, too.

"So, that's it. I'm glad we had this opportunity to chat. I know that you are a reasonable person, and you know now that I am not." Moore stepped back to the door and tucked the pistol into his belt.

"You have a thoughtful and reflective day," he said, then stared at the terrified LeFlore for a long second. LeFlore was still silent, stiff in his chair. Moore slipped through the door and was gone.

LeFlore leaped to his feet and started for the phone on Sheila's desk. He only made it a few feet before his nervous system kicked in. "Oh, shit!" was all LeFlore had time to utter before his comment became a reality that filled his jockey shorts.

In the hallway, Moore passed Johnny Wilson from the mailroom.

"Hi, Mr. Moore!" the mail clerk gushed. "I heard what you guys did on DeepCore! You really kicked ass!" Johnny reached in the grocery cart in which he carried the mail. "Here's a letter for you," he said, "all the way from Greece!"

Moore took the letter, shook Johnny's hand, and started for the tiny security office in the basement. He opened the letter in the elevator.

"Dear Mr. Moore," the letter began, "I am writing you with regard to an investigation we are conducting concerning the disappearance of two of our local police officers . . ."

Moore flipped the envelope over. The return address was Balbos, Greece.

"Bend over," Moore said as the elevator doors opened, "here it comes again."

EPILOGUE

Tom Jackson pressed himself against the metal wall and slowly, silently inched toward the corner. He peeked slowly around the edge.

Watanabe had maintained a very low profile since the attack. Now he was standing on a pipe, reaching up into the ceiling grid for something. He smiled when he found it and stepped down from the pipe. Jackson could make out the green color of the circuit board as Watanabe slipped it into his coveralls. He waited for the technician to zip up the garment, then stepped around the corner and called, "Hello, Kinji."

Watanabe felt his skin crawl at the sound of Jackson's voice. He turned for the corridor leading to the Positrack lab. Jackson was on him in a second. "What's in your little suit?" Jackson asked, stepping in front of Watanabe and pressing his hand over the square bulge beneath the cotton coveralls.

"Nothing!" Watanabe replied, trying to go around the irritating security man. Jackson got him by the arm and held on tight.

"I think maybe something." He reached for the zipper on Watanabe's coveralls.

"No, there is nothing there." The obnoxious security guard was reaching into his coveralls for the board. Watanabe fished in his pocket for the little hyper-velocity gun. His fingers closed around it and Watanabe tilted the short barrel up to fire through his pocket into the round-eye barbarian who was pawing inside his clothing for the stolen circuit board.

Before he could fire, claws ripped into his arm, sending a sharp burning pain up into his armpit. Watanabe's eyes jerked down to his side. The four dark red fingernails were sunk deeply into his wrist, turning it outward. His finger jerked on the trigger. The heavy needle shot out, ringing as it bounced off the pipes and beams around them. Jackson was flinching, his face turned away, but the other, the fingernails' owner, had him by the hair and wrist.

"Make one more move," Carla Fuentes's voice hissed in his ear, "and I'll tear your head right off!" Watanabe went limp as Jackson removed the Positrack logic circuit from his coveralls.

"Well," Jackson crooned, "what have we here?" He looked over Watanabe's shoulder at the Amazon who held him captive. "Did we get this on tape?" Jackson asked.

"Everything," she replied, pressing her face so close to him that he could smell the perfume dabbed at her temples. "Kinji here is going to be a star!" She yanked his hand out of his pocket and the little gun clattered to the floor. The metal handcuffs were cold and bit into his wrist. She reached around and took his other hand, cuffing it, too.

"Want to tell us about it, Kinji?" Jackson asked. Watanabe shook his head no.

"It's okay," Jackson assured him, "we have all the time in the world."

IN A WORLD ENSLAVED,
THEY'RE FIGHTING BACK!

Freedom is dead in the year 2030—megacorporations rule with a silicon fist, and the once-proud people of the United States are now little more than citizen-slaves. Only one group of men and women can restore freedom and give America back to the people:

THE NIGHT WHISTLERS

The second American Revolution
is about to begin.

THE NIGHT WHISTLERS #1: by Dan Trevor
Available October 1991 from Jove Books!

Here is an exclusive preview . . .

PROLOGUE

Los Angeles, 2030: Seen from afar, the skyline is not all that
different from the way it was in earlier decades. True, the
Wilshire corridor is stacked with tall buildings, and there are
new forms in the downtown complex: the Mitsubishi Towers,
a monstrous obelisk in black obsidian; the Bank of Hamburg
Center, suggesting a vaguely gothic monolith; the Nippon
Plaza with its "Oriental Only" dining room slowly revolving
beneath hanging gardens; and, peaking above them all like a
needle in the sky, the Trans Global Towers, housing the LAPD
and their masters, Trans Global Security Systems, a publicly
held corporation.

The most noticeable difference in this city is a silver ser-
pentine arch snaking from downtown to Dodger Stadium and
into the valley, and in other directions—to Santa Monica, to
San Bernardino, and to cities in the south. Yes, at long last,
the monorail was constructed. The original underground Metro
was abandoned soon after completion, the hierarchy claiming
it earthquake prone, the historians claiming the power elite did
not want an underground system of tunnels where people could
not be seen, particularly since the subways in New York and
other Eastern cities became hotbeds of resistance for a short
period.

But to fully grasp the quality of life in this era, to really
understand what it is like to live under the Corporate shadow, one ultimately has to step down from the towers and
other heights. One has to go to the streets and join the rank
and file.

Those not lucky enough to inherit executive positions usually live in company housing complexes—which are little more

than tenements, depending upon the area. The quality of these establishments vary, generally determined by one's position on the Corporate ladder. All in all, however, they are grim—pitifully small, with thin walls and cheap appliances and furnishings. There are invariably, however, built-in televisions, most of them featuring seventy-two-inch screens and "Sensound." It is mandatory to view them during certain hours.

When not spouting propaganda, television is filled with mindless entertainment programming and endless streams of commercials exhorting the populace to "Buy! Buy! Buy!" For above all, this is a nation of consumers. Almost all products, poorly made and disposable, have built-in obsolescence. New lines are frequently introduced as "better" and "improved," even though the changes are generally useless and cosmetic. Waste disposal has therefore become one of the major problems and industries of this society. A certain amount of one's Corporate wages is expected to be spent on consumer goods. This is monitored by the Internal Revenue Service and used somewhat as a test of loyalty, an indicator of an individual's willingness to contribute to society.

The Corporations take care of their own on other levels as well. Employees are, of course, offered incentive bonuses, although these are eaten quickly by increased taxes. They are also supplied with recreational facilities, health care, and a host of psychiatric programs, including Corporate-sponsored mood drugs. In truth, however, the psychiatric programs are more feared than welcomed, for psychiatry has long given up the twentieth century pretence that it possessed any kind of workable technology to enlighten individuals. Instead, it baldly admits its purpose to bring about "adjustment"—the control and subjugation of individuals "who don't fit in."

Because this is essentially a postindustrial age, and most of the heavy industry has long been shifted abroad to what was once called the Third World, the majority of jobs are basically clerical. There are entire armies of pale-faced word processors, battalions of managers, and legions of attorneys. Entire city blocks are dedicated to data entry facilities, and on any given night, literally thousands of soft-white monitors can be seen glowing through the glass.

There are also, of course, still a few smaller concerns: tawdry bars, gambling dens, cheap hotels, independent though licensed brothels, and the odd shop filled with all the dusty junk that only the poor will buy. And, naturally, there has always been menial labor. Finally there are the elderly and the unemployed, all of whom live in little more than slums.

Although ostensibly anyone may rise through the ranks to an executive position, it is not that simple. As set up, the system invites corruption. Even those who manage to pass the extremely stringent entrance exams and psychiatric tests find it virtually impossible to move up without a final qualifying factor: a sponsor. Unless one is fortunate enough to have friends or relatives in high places, one night as well not even try. If there ever was a classed society, this is it.

In a sense then, the world of 2030 is almost medieval. The Consortium chief executive officers in all the major once-industrial nations rule their regions with as much authority as any feudal lord, and the hordes of clerks are as tied to their keyboards as any serf was ever tied to the land. What were once mounted knights are now Corporate security officers. What was once the omnipotent church is now the psychiatric establishment.

But lest anyone say there is no hope of salvation from this drudgery and entrapment, there are the national lotteries.

Corporately licensed and managed, the Great American Lottery is virtually a national passion. The multitude of ever-changing games are played with all the intensity and fervor of a life-and-death struggle, drawing more than one hundred million participants twice a week. There are systems of play that are as complex and arcane as any cabalistic theorem, and the selection of numbers has been elevated to a religious experience. Not that anyone ever seems to win. At least, not anyone that anyone knows. But at least there is still the dream of complete financial independence and relative freedom.

But if it is an impossible dream that keeps the populace alive, it is a nightmare that keeps them in line. Ever since the Great Upheaval, the Los Angeles Corporate Authority, and its enforcement arm, the LAPD (a Corporate division) have kept this city in an iron grip. And although the LAPD motto is still "To Protect and Serve," its master has changed and its methods are as brutal as those of any secret police. It is much the same in all cities, with all enforcement agencies around the world under the authority of Trans Global.

What with little or no legal restraint, suspects are routinely executed on the streets, or taken to the interrogation centers and tortured to or past the brink of insanity. Corporate spies are everywhere. Dissent is not tolerated.

And yet, in spite of the apparently feudal structure, it must be remembered that this is a high-tech world, one of laser-enhanced surveillance vehicles, sensitive listening devices, spectral imaging weapon systems, ultrasonic crowd control instruments, and voice-activated firing mechanisms.

Thus, even if one were inclined to create a little havoc with, for instance, a late-twentieth-century assault rifle, the disparity is simply too great. Yes, the Uzi may once have been a formidable weapon, but it is nothing compared to a Panasonic mini-missile rounding the corner to hone in on your pounding heartbeat.

Still, despite the suppression, despite the enormous disparity of firepower, despite of the odds, there are still a few—literally a handful—who are compelled to resist. This savage world of financial totalitarianism has not subdued them. Rather, if it has taught them anything at all, it is that freedom can only be bought with will and courage and blood.

This is the lesson they are trying to bring to the American people, this and an ancient dream that has always stirred the hearts of men.

The dream of freedom.

ONE

The city was still sleeping when the whistling began. The streets were still deserted, and the night winds still rattled through strewn garbage. Now and again, from deep within the tenement bowels came reverberations of harsh shouts, the slamming of a loosely hinged door. But otherwise there was nothing beyond the echo of that solitary whistler.

For a full thirty seconds Phillip Wimple stood stock-still and listened, the collar of his sad and shapeless raincoat turned up against the foul wind. He looked out at the city with calm brown eyes, his slightly lined face expressionless. He stood as detectives the world over stand, with all the weight on his heels, hands jammed into the pockets of his trousers, his cropped, gray head slightly cocked to the left.

Although not a particularly reflective man, those high nocturnal melodies had always left Wimple vaguely pensive. As to the fragment of some half-remembered tune that continually tugs at one's memory, he had always felt compelled to listen—to turn his tired eyes to the grimy Los Angeles skyline and allow the sounds to enter him.

A patrolman approached, a sleek doberman of a man in Hitachi body armor and a Remco mini-gun harness. Below, on a stretch of filthy pavement that skirted the weed-grown hill, stood four more uniformed patrolmen. Gillette M-90s rested on their hips. The darkened visors of crash helmets concealed their eyes. Turbo-charged Marauders idled softly beside them in the blackness.

"With all due respect, sir, the Chief Inspector wants to know what's holding us up."

Wimple turned again, shifting his gaze to the distant outline of an angular face behind a smoked Marauder windshield. "Well, tell her that if she would be so kind as to join me on this vantage point, I would be more than happy to explain the delay."

"Sir?"

"Ask Miss Strom to come up here."

Wimple returned his gaze to the skyline. Although the whistling had grown fainter, scattered by the predawn breeze, the melody was still audible: high and cold above the city's haze; dark and threatening in the pit of his stomach.

The woman entered his field of vision, an undeniably grim figure in black spandex and vinyl boots—a full-figured woman, about an inch taller than his five-ten. Her shimmering windbreaker was emblazoned with the Corporate logo: twin lightning bolts enclosed in a fist. When Wimple had first laid on eyes on her, he took her as a welcome change from the usual Corporate overlord. Not only was she smart, but she was beautiful . . . in a carnivorous way. He had also liked her fire, her determination, and her willingness to fight for a budget. But that was three days ago. Now, watching her stiffly approach through the smog-choked weeds and yellowed litter, he realized that Miss Erica Strom was no different from any of the boardroom commandants sent down to ensure that the Los Angeles Police Department toed the Corporate line.

"You want to tell me what's going on?" Miss Strom planted herself beside him.

Wimple shrugged, studying her profile: the chiseled features, the red-slashed lips, the hair like a black lacquered helmet. "Ever heard a rattler's hiss?" he asked.

Strom narrowed her sea-green eyes at him. "What are you talking about?"

Wimple extended his finger to the sky to indicate the echo of the unseen whistlers. "That," he said. "That sound."

Withdrawing a smokeless cigarette, one of the Surgeon General–sanctioned brands that tasted like wet hay, Wimple said, "Think of it like this. We're the cavalry. They're the Indians. Maybe they can't touch us up here, but down there it's a whole different story."

"So what are you trying to tell me? That you want to call this patrol off? You want to turn around and go to bed, because some Devo starts whistling in the dark?" Her deep voice had a masculine edge, a hardness.

Wimple shook his head with a tired smirk. Devo: Corporate catchword for any socially deviate individual, generally from the menial work force. "No, Miss Strom," he said, "I'm not trying to tell you that I want to call the patrol off. I'm just saying that if we go down there now, we could find ourselves in one hell of a shit storm."

Strom returned the detective's smirk. "Is that so?"

"Yes, ma'am."

"Well, in that case, Detective, move your men on down. I can hardly wait."

Long favored by patrolmen throughout the Greater Los Angeles sprawl, the Nissan-Pontiac Marauder was a formidable machine. With a nine-liter, methane-charged power plant, the vehicle was capable of running down virtually anything on the road, and was virtually unstoppable by anything less than an armor-piercing shell. Long and low, it was not, however, built for comfort, and the off-road shocks always wreaked havoc on Wimple's spine.

He rode shotgun beside Miss Strom: shoulders hard against the polymer seats, feet braced on the floorboards, right hand firm on the sissy bar. Earlier, when Strom had given the order to move out, there had been several whispered complaints from the patrolmen. Now, however, as the three-vehicle convoy descended into the black heart of the city, the radios were silent.

"Why don't you tell me about them?" Miss Strom said, easing the Marauder onto the wastes of First Street.

Wimple shrugged, his eyes scanning the tenement windows above. "There's not really much to tell," he replied. "About eighteen months ago, we start getting reports of a little Devo action from the outlying precincts. Vandalism mostly. Petty stuff. Then comes July and one of the IRS stations goes up in smoke. After that, we start finding it spray-painted all over the walls: Night Whistlers."

"Any idea who's behind it?"

"Yeah, we've got some ideas."

Strom's thin lips hardened. "So what's been the problem? Why haven't you cleaned them out yet?"

Wimple lifted his gaze to the long blocks of tenements ahead—to the smashed windows and rotting doorways, the grimy, crumbling brickwork and trashed streets. "Well, let's just say that the Whistlers turned out to be a little more organized than we thought." His voice was dull, noncommittal. She gave him a quick look then went back to scanning the street.

They had entered the lower reaches of Ninth Street, and another long canyon of smog-browned tenements. For the most part, the residents here were members of the semiskilled labor force, popularly known as the Menials, officially referred to in ethnological surveys as the Lower Middle Class. Included among their ranks were whole armies of word processors, retail clerks, delivery boys, receptionists, and secretaries. By and large, their lives were measured out in pitiful production bonuses, worthless stock options, and department store clearance sales. They also, of course, spent a lot time pouring over their lottery tickets, even more in front of their television screens, watching tedious Corporate-controlled programming. Still, no matter how blatant the propaganda, it was more entertaining than their dull existences.

The radio came alive with a harsh metallic burst from the last Marauder in the line: "Possible six-twenty on Hill."

Six-twenty meant curfew violation—which invariably meant Devo action.

Strom dropped her left hand from the steering wheel and activated the dispatch button on the dashboard. "Let's show them a response now, gentlemen." Then bringing the Marauder into a tight turn, she activated the spectral-imaging screen and switched the infrared cameras to the scan mode.

Wimple, however, preferred to use his eyes. He initially saw only a half-glimpsed vision among the heaps of uncollected refuse: a thin, brown figure in a drab-green duffle coat. For a moment, a single perverse moment, he actually considered saying nothing. He actually considered returning his gaze to the bleak stretch of road ahead, casually withdrawing another smokeless cigarette and keeping his mouth firmly shut. But even as this thought passed through his mind, the image of the fleeing figure appeared on the screen.

The radio crackled to life again with a voice from the second Marauder. "I've got clean visual."

There was a quick glimpse of a sprinting form beneath a

sagging balcony, the sudden clamor of a trash can on the pavement.

Strom powered her vehicle into another hard turn, screeching full-throttle into the adjoining alley. Then, as she deftly lowered her thumb to activate the spotlight, he was suddenly there: a wiry Hispanic huddled beneath an ancient fire escape.

Strom activated the megaphone, and her voice boomed out in harsh, clipped syllables: "Remain where you are! Any attempt to flee will be met with force!"

The figure stumbled back to the alley wall, glaring around like a blinded bull. He was younger than Wimple had first imagined, no more than ten or twelve. His duffle coat was army surplus. His blue jeans were Levi knockoffs. He also wore a pair of black market running shoes—the badge of the Devos.

Strom eased the Marauder to a stop alongside the number two and three vehicles. Then, reaching for the stun gun beneath the dash, she slipped free of her harness and turned to Wimple. "Come on, Detective, let me show you what law and order is all about."

Strom and Wimple approached the suspect slowly. To their left and right, scanning the rooftops with Nikon-Dow Night Vision Systems atop their M-90s, were the four helmeted patrolmen from the backup Marauders. Given the word, they would have been able to pour out some six hundred fragmentation flechettes in less than a fifty-second burst—more than enough to shred the kneeling suspect to a bloody pulp.

Wimple looked at the boy's scared eyes. They kept returning to the stun-gun that dangled from Strom's gloved hand.

Manufactured for Trans Global by Krause-Nova Electronics in Orange County, the XR50 Stun gun had become the last word on hand-held crowd control. It was capable of dispersing a scatter charge of nearly fifty-thousand volts, instantly immobilizing a two-hundred-pound man. At closer range, and against bare skin, the pain was beyond description.

The boy could not keep himself from shivering when Strom laid the cold tip of the stun gun against his cheek, could not keep himself from mouthing a silent plea. In response, however, Strom merely smiled, and turned to Wimple again.

"Why don't you see what he's carrying, Detective? Hmm?

See what our little lost lamb has in his pockets."

Wimple pressed the boy facedown to the pavement, consciously avoiding the terrified eyes. He then lowered himself to a knee and mechanically began the search. On the first pass, he withdrew only a greasy deck of playing cards, a half-eaten chocolate bar, and a stainless steel identity tag made out to one Julio Cadiz. Then, almost regretfully, he slowly peeled a six-inch steak knife from the boy's left ankle.

"Well, well, well." Strom smiled. "What have we here?"

Wimple rose to his feet, turning the steak knife over in his fingers. "These things don't necessarily mean much."

Strom let her smile sag into another smirk. "Is that so, Detective?"

"It's just kind of a status symbol with these kids. They don't ever really use them. They just like to carry them around to showoff to their buddies."

But by this point, Strom had already withdrawn a pair of keyless handcuffs . . . had already released the safety on the stun-gun.

She secured the boy's wrists behind his back, then yanked up his coat and T-shirt to expose the base of the spine. Although once or twice the boy emitted a pleading whimper, he still hadn't actually spoken.

"Tell your men to secure the area," Strom said as she hunkered down on the pavement beside the handcuffed boy. Then again when Wimple failed to respond: "Secure the area, Detective. Tell your men."

Wimple glanced over his shoulder to the blank faces of the patrolmen. Before he actually gave the order, however, he turned to the woman again. "Look, I'm not trying to tell you how to do your job, Miss Strom, but this is not going to get us anywhere. You understand what I'm saying? And this is not a safe place for us to be wasting our time."

Strom ran a contemplative hand along the gleaming shaft of the stun-gun, then dropped her gaze to the shivering boy. Not looking at Wimple, she finally said, "Detective, I think you should get your men to secure the area before this little brat starts screaming and brings out the whole neighborhood."

She waited until the patrolmen posted on the corner fixed their night vision systems on the balconies and rooftops and chambered clips of flechettes into their weapons. Then very gently, very slowly, she pressed the cold tip of the stun gun to the boy's naked spine.

"Look—," Wimple began.

"Shut up, Detective," she said, her eyes cold, then lowered her gaze back to the boy.

"Well, now, young man. You and I are going to have a little heart to heart. You understand? A frank exchange of views, with you starting first."

An involuntary shudder crossed the thin, feral face of the boy. "Look, lady, I don't know—"

She clamped her hand to his mouth. "No, no, no. That's not how this game is played, my little friend. In this game, you don't speak until I ask a question. Got it?"

The boy may have tried to nod, but Strom had taken hold of his hair. Then, yanking back his head so that his ear was only inches from her lips, she whispered, "Whistlers, my little man. How about telling me what you know about the Whistlers?"

The boy responded with another frenzied shiver, then possibly attempted to mouth some sort of response. But by this time Strom had released his head, activated the stun gun, and pressed the tip home.

The boy seemed to react in definite stages to the voltage, first arching up like a quivering fish, then growing wide-eyed and ridged as the scream tore out of his body. And even when it stopped, he still seemed to have difficulty breathing, while the left leg continued to tremble.

"Now, let's try it again, shall we?" Strom cooed. "Who . . . are . . . the Whistlers?"

The boy shook his head before answering in spluttering gasps. "Look, lady, I don't know what you're talking about. I swear to God. The Whistlers, that's just something that they write on the walls."

"Who writes it on the walls?"

"I don't know. Just some of the Devos around here. I don't know who they are."

"Just some of the Devos, huh? Well, I'm sorry, young man, but that's just not good enough." And lifting up his T-shirt again to expose the base of his spine, she laid down another fifty-thousand volts.

There was something horrifying about the way the boy's eyes grew impossibly wide as he thrashed on the pavement with another trailing scream. There was also something chilling about the way Strom's lips twisted up in a smile as she watched.

Wimple turned his head away, stared for a moment into some distant blackness. Finally, unable to stand the sobs any longer, he approached again.

"Look, don't you think that's enough, Miss Strom? *Miss Strom!*"

She slowly turned on her haunches to face him, her left hand still toying with the boy's sweat-drenched hair. "You got a problem, Detective?"

Wimple met her gaze for a full three seconds before answering, a full three seconds to taste the woman's hatred. "Yeah," he finally nodded. "I got a problem. Quite apart from my personal objection to this activity, I'd like to point out that you are seriously endangering my men. If you think that this neighborhood is asleep right now, you are sadly mistaken. The people up in those buildings know exactly what's going on down here. They know exactly what you're doing, and I can assure you that they don't like it."

She withdrew her fingers from the boy's hair, and his head lolled back to the vomit-smeared pavement. "Well, now, that's very interesting, Detective. Because, you see, I *want* them to know what's going on here. I *want* them to hear every decibel of this little bastard's scream and, remember it—"

"Shut up!"

"How dare you tell me to—"

"Shut up and listen!" Wimple said, as the first cold notes of the solitary whistler wafted down from the blackened rooftops.